First Published in Great Britain 2017
By Mills & Boon, an imprint of HarperCollins*Publishers*
1 London Bridge Street, London, SE1 9GF

"A horse isn't … They show you … you. Just like a man does."

Riley's voice had softened to a whisper. His gaze was intense, hypnotic. The need inside Dani swelled until she was dizzy.

He pulled her into his arms and lowered his face until their lips touched. In that moment every inkling of control vanished, melted in the heat of his kiss.

Dizzy with desire, Dani swayed against Riley. Her pulsing need vibrated through every erogenous cell in her body. She parted her lips and his tongue slipped inside her mouth. Thrusting. Probing. Ravenous. As if he couldn't get enough of her...

QUICK-DRAW COWBOY

BY
JOANNA WAYNE

Joanna Wayne began her professional writing career in 1994. Now, more than fifty published books later, Joanna has gained a worldwide following with her cutting-edge romantic suspense and Texas family series, such as Sons of Troy Ledger and Big "D" Dads. Joanna currently resides in a small community north of Houston, Texas, with her husband. You may write Joanna at PO Box 852, Montgomery, TX 77356, USA, or connect with her at www.joannawayne.com.

Thanks to all my friends and neighbors who've taught me so much about living in Texas. Now that I'm settled into my own small-town Texas lifestyle, I can't imagine living anywhere else. And, as always, thanks to my hubby for constantly being willing to rearrange our life to make time for my writing and research.

Chapter One

Dani Boatman piped the last exquisite rose onto the top layer of the tiered wedding cake. She stood back and examined her handiwork. Magnificent, she decided— *almost* too pretty to cut and eat.

But it would definitely be eaten. According to the bride, the guest list kept growing. Weddings were apparently a big deal in the small town of Winding Creek, Texas—a chance to dress up, visit with friends and neighbors and dance to a live band. And, of course, to celebrate the new couple.

The exciting part was that this time, she was not only invited to the festivities, but was also actually going to be involved. Maid of honor in the wedding of Grace Addison and Pierce Lawrence.

She'd be the only attendant, except for Pierce's five-year-old daughter, Jaci, who'd be the flower girl.

Grace had helped Dani pick out her dress, which was made of an emerald-green satin that brought out Dani's eyes and went well with her mass of unruly coppery curls.

The style worked, too. The dress was fitted at the waist with cap sleeves and a slightly flared skirt that fell to her ankles—easily long enough to cover her chunky calves.

The rounded, no-frills neckline revealed only a minimum of cleavage and fully covered her size 38 D puppies. A plump lady's version of chic.

Grace had been her first and only close friend since moving here. Not that the people weren't nice, but Dani's spare time amounted to pretty much zero.

Dani put the finishing touches on the cake, the last rose with petals so thin they were practically translucent. She'd entwined the roses with deep green vines to represent the way Grace and Pierce's lives had joined together forever.

Dani was a sucker for anything romantic. Not that she had any romance in her life. She'd dated, but never anything serious. Never met a guy who'd blown her away with just a smile, the way it happened in books.

Hadn't been with a guy who'd made her heart go tripping or left her breathless the way Grace claimed Pierce affected her.

But Dani was only twenty-six. One day her prince would come charging in on a white horse. Of course, with her luck, he'd probably be dropping by to order a wedding cake for his marriage to some hot chick with a drop-dead gorgeous body.

So, who needs a prince?

Dani had her very own bakery and she had her adorable, drama-queen niece, Constance, who'd dropped into her life totally unexpectedly. Between her job and her niece, she was kept busy enough that she hit the bed exhausted every night.

And Dani was just about there now. She rubbed the tired muscles in her neck and glanced at the wall clock next to the cooling racks. Eighteen minutes after nine.

Not late by most people's standards for a Friday

night, but she'd be up and baking before sunrise to-morrow morning. Fortunately all she had to do was descend the stairs from her second-floor living quarters and she was on the job.

She started cleaning the mess she'd made while icing the cake. The old building that housed her bakery was never totally quiet. It creaked and groaned at will, as if yesterday's ghosts still haunted the place that had originally been a bordello more than a century ago.

If only walls could talk.

Dani was startled from her mind's imaginative drifting at the sound of someone hammering a fist against the front door of the shop. The sign on the door clearly indicated they were closed and the lights in the serving section were out.

No one could be this desperate for a late-night sugar high.

She removed the chef's hat that kept her wild hair under control while she worked, and walked briskly to the front door of the shop. She arrived as the knocking started again. She flicked on the outdoor light to see who was so rudely persistent.

The man who stared back at her looked harmless enough. He was dressed in a pair of jeans and a blue plaid, long-sleeved sport shirt, open at the neck. Needed a haircut, but was clean-shaven. He looked a tad familiar, but she couldn't place him.

She motioned to the closed sign. The man didn't take the hint but kept standing there and waiting for her to let him in.

It was Friday night, so there were still a few people out and about in Winding Creek's downtown area. A couple were leaving the pharmacy across the street. A family of four with ice-cream cones were checking out the display window of a candle shop next to the pharmacy. A group of twentysomethings spilled out of a double cab pickup truck and into the middle of Main Street, no doubt headed to Caffe's Bar and Grill around the corner.

The man at her door looked no more of a threat than the rest of them. Besides which, the town of Winding Creek was practically crime-free. She pulled the key ring from her pocket, unlocked the door and opened it a crack.

"We're closed," she said. "Open again at seven tomorrow morning."

"Sorry to bother you, but I think I left my windbreaker here earlier today."

The pieces suddenly fell together. He was obviously the man who'd left the jacket she'd found on the floor beneath one of the tables.

"Was it blue?"

"Yep. Navy blue."

"I'll get it for you."

He put a foot in the door, basically inviting himself inside. His pushiness irritated her and made her a bit nervous.

She checked to make sure her cell phone was still attached to the waistband of her flour-splattered slacks. A call to 911 would have a deputy at her door in seconds. There would always be at least one in the downtown area on Friday evenings.

"Nice place you have here," he said. "Dani's Delights, catchy name, too."

"Thank you. I'll be right back with your jacket."

She retreated to her office off the kitchen, picked

up the jacket and took her cell phone in her right hand. When she turned around, the man was standing a few feet from her, blocking the door.

"Here's your jacket," she said. "You can go now."

"After we talk."

His attitude alarmed her. "We have nothing to talk about."

"Yes, we do." He took a step toward her, almost backing her against her desk.

Every muscle tensed. "If it's conversation you want, I'll yell and my husband will rush down the stairs to join the chat. I should warn you, he's an excellent shot and will be toting a forty-five."

"You don't have a husband, but you do have *my* daughter. So now that we have the essentials out of the way, why don't we sit down and discuss this quietly like two rational adults?"

"I don't know who you think you're talking to, but you've obviously mistaken me for someone else."

"No. I know exactly who you are, and that you were granted custody of my daughter, Constance Boatman. That's where the mistakes comes in. I'm her father, which makes me next of kin—not you."

"You're lying." The words had flown to her mouth. Only she couldn't be sure of their accuracy. She had no idea who Constance's father was. She had her niece's birth certificate filed away in her upstairs living quarters, where Constance was sleeping right now. No father was listed. She was certain of that.

The social workers who'd testified in the custody hearing had insisted there was no record of the father's identity. That had been eight months ago, weeks after her sister, Amber's, tragic death. If he was the father, where had he been all this time?

"Who are you?" she demanded.

"You know my name. James Haggard. It's on the birth certificate. Your sister, Amber, and I were very much in love back then. Your niece is a love child, if that matters to you. That was before your sister let the addiction turn her into a slut."

"My sister is dead and I will not tolerate you talking about her that way. Get out now or I will call the police."

"Not a good idea. Once the law gets involved, things get really sticky. I prove I'm Constance's birth father, I get custody. Case closed. Trust me, I'd make a lousy father. She's better off with you."

That she believed, but she refused to accept he had any claim on Constance. But what if he did? Someone contributed the sperm that led to her birth. That person might well be an obnoxious jerk like James Haggard.

From the time Amber turned sixteen and moved out, she had slept with any man who'd supply her with drugs. And her sister had ignored both their mother's tears and Dani's constant pleading for Amber to go into rehab. Their mother had never fully recovered from the heartbreak.

Dani's precious niece was all she had left of the sister who had meant the world to her. She wouldn't turn her over to this irresponsible jerk even if he was her biological father.

Dani's stomach retched. She had to deal with this. "What is it you want?"

"My share of the insurance settlement from the car manufacturer. The faulty air bag that led to my dear, sweet daughter losing her mother earned you a hefty payout."

"I should have known it was greed that brought you here."

"Don't be so pious, Dani. This little business setup you have here didn't come cheap. You didn't pay for it with pocket change."

"No, which is why I'm up to my eyeballs in debt." Not that it was any of his business.

"Don't try to pull one on over me. I've had all of that I'm putting up with. I know how much the payoff was. By my estimates, even after you paid for the bakery and the lawyers took their share, I figure you have at least a couple of million dollars left. I deserve all of that, but to show you what a nice man I am, I'll settle for a mere million. In cash. In one week."

"You…" Dani bit back the words she wanted to hurl at him. They wouldn't phase a lowlife like him. Yet she could easily believe he would have gotten Amber pregnant and then abandoned her and the baby.

Amber had been a stunning beauty before her addiction took its toll, just as James Haggard said. She'd had long auburn hair that fell in loose curls about her shoulders, gorgeous amber-colored eyes, lush eyelashes and a dynamite body.

Amber had always been the pretty sister. Everyone had said it. The comments had cut Dani to the quick when they were growing up. That hadn't changed the fact that she worshipped her older sister.

Now it was Constance who mattered more than anything.

"Even if you are Constance's father—which I seriously doubt—you're wrong about the insurance money. It's all in a trust fund for Constance and can't be touched until she turns twenty-one."

"Yet you found a way to get your greedy little hands on it," the man snarled. "And you can cut the pretense. We both know you have at least a copy of the birth certificate that lists me as the father."

She shook her head. She'd had enough. "You're wrong. Now get out. And stay away from here. If you show up again, I'll call the sheriff and press harassment charges."

He glared at her, his eyes dark and penetrating, and it was almost as if she could feel a bizarre mix of evil and madness fighting for his soul.

Chills ran up her spine, but she stood her ground. She pointed to the door. "Out. Now."

"I'm leaving, but I'll be back next week for the stacks. If you don't have all the big ones, I'll not only file for paternal custody, but have you prosecuted for stealing my daughter's money. Is that what you want?"

"You won't have a prayer of getting custody without proof of paternity. Bluffing won't help you. DNA won't lie for you."

"DNA won't have to lie. In the meantime, take care of my beloved daughter." He smiled at his own sarcastic quip, turned and walked away.

Anger and dread left Dani shaking. This was blackmail, plain and simple. A scam. A bluff. James Haggard's name was not on the birth certificate.

But what if a paternity test proved he was Constance's father? Was there a judge alive who'd actually take a child who'd been through what Constance had suffered and rip her from this safe, secure life, where she was loved?

Would any judge grant custody to a man who'd abandoned his child and her addicted mother years before? Wouldn't a judge realize that Haggard was in this strictly to find a way to get at Constance's trust fund?

But then, crazier things happened in the court system every day.

"I've told you the insurance is in an untouchable trust and there's no way I can come up with the amount of money you're talking about."

"Then I guess I'll just have to do that myself—once I have custody of Constance." He started to the door, then turned and pointed at her as if he was pulling a trigger. "Next Friday. Before noon."

She waited until she heard the front door slam behind Haggard before she walked over and locked the door behind him.

She looked out the huge front window and stared at the dance of light and shadows beneath the antique streetlights. Winding Creek was the ideal, small Texas town. Friendly. Safe.

A place where Constance could heal from the ordeals she'd endured living with Amber and her addictions. A home where she felt protected and loved after years of neglect and frequent abandonment by her own mother. That had been the deciding factor in Dani's going into debt to open her own bakery here.

James Haggard had shattered that illusion.

Dani went back to the kitchen to finish cleaning up. The cake she'd worked hours on meant nothing to her as Haggard's vicious threats echoed through her mind.

She was not convinced he was Constance's father, but she was certain he'd told the truth about at least one thing.

He would be back.

Chapter Two

Ten o'clock on Saturday in downtown Winding Creek, Texas. Not just any Saturday. This was the date Riley Lawrence's older brother, Pierce, was giving marriage a second chance. Sounded downright crazy to Riley. He'd never had the guts to tie the knot even once and didn't plan to remedy that any time soon.

Riley figured it was too early for a beer even though he'd been driving since five that morning after a few hours of restless sleep. The motel bed had left a lot to be desired in the way of comfort.

Not that comfort mattered all that much to him. He'd slept under the stars many a night with no more than a rolled-up jacket for a pillow.

He turned onto Main Street. He'd expected at least a fleeting sensation that he was home again. Didn't happen. The town looked almost exactly the same as when he'd lived here until just before his fifteenth birthday. It also looked completely different.

Perspective changed everything.

When he'd lived here, Winding Creek was all he really knew. Now he'd seen most of the country, at least the parts of it he was interested in seeing. Any place he hung his Stetson was home.

He should probably just keep driving and head straight to the Double K Ranch, but as eager as he was to see his brothers, he wasn't quite ready to dive into wedding chaos. He definitely wasn't eager to start hiding his doubts about Pierce's decision to jump into the fire again.

He pulled his old black pickup truck into a parking spot, got out and stretched. The antique streetlights were familiar. So were the buildings. Even a few old hitching posts were still scattered along the curb.

The storefronts were a different story. The old Texaco station was now a sandwich shop. The barbershop where he'd gotten his hair cut as a kid was now a candle shop. Who'd have guessed you needed a separate shop to buy candles?

He glanced at the signs. An ice-cream parlor. A Christmas store. A toy shop. Even a jewelry store. Practically a shopping mecca compared to where he'd been living in Montana.

He caught a whiff of coffee and followed the scent to a bakery. Dani's Delights. The cookies, scones and cupcakes displayed in the window looked incredible, but it was the aroma of the day's grind that lured him in.

The dozen or so tables in the place were all taken. The line to order was at least ten people deep. He wasn't sure any cup of coffee was worth that kind of wait.

Easy to see the problem. There was only one person to take orders, collect money and mix the fancy coffee drinks. The woman behind the counter looked a bit harried and her smile was clearly forced.

He continued to study her as he stepped into the line. A full head shorter than his six foot two. Heart-shaped face. Cute upturned nose. A mass of wild cinnamon-colored curls that hugged her cheeks.

Maybe her coffee was worth waiting in line for after all. Marriage and commitment might scare him half to death, but that didn't mean he couldn't enjoy the company of a vivacious woman every now and then.

Women were in short supply on the ranch where he'd been living in Montana. Available women were nonexistent.

Riley inched up when the line moved and glanced around the small shop. He recognized Dan Dupree, who was sitting in the back with who were probably his grandkids. Dan and his wife had been friends of Riley's parents before their fatal car accident.

Mrs. Maclean, Riley's ninth-grade English teacher, was at another table with two women he didn't recognize. Neither Dan nor Mrs. Maclean showed any sign of recognizing him.

Fortunately, he'd changed from the skinny, awkward, pimpled teenager he'd been last time he lived in Winding Creek. He'd added a few inches in height and muscled up a bit.

The door opened and four more people squeezed in and joined the line.

A freckle-faced kid with braided red hair, eyeglasses and cut-off jeans ran noisily down some back stairs that led into the bakery. She maneuvered around the sign at the foot of the stairs that read Private. Do Not Enter. Prancing like a showy filly, she made her way across the shop.

The youngster propped her elbows on the far end of the counter. "I'm bored," she announced loud enough for everyone in the shop to hear.

"Did you finish your homework?" the busy woman asked without looking up from the display case, where she was gathering raspberry scones for her customer.

"Yes, except for the math. I hate word problems. They don't even make sense."

"They make sense, Constance, but I'll help you with your homework later. I'm really busy right now. Why don't you watch TV upstairs until Sally and her mother pick you up for the movie?"

"I'm tired of being upstairs by myself. I wanna stay down here, Aunt Dani."

Ah, aunt. Not the kid's mother. Made sense. She didn't look old enough for that. He checked out the busy redhead's ring finger. No golden band. Looking better all the time.

"Can I have a cookie?" the girl asked.

"Not before lunch. You know the rules," the aunt answered as she added whipped cream to a coffee drink.

The kid's hands flew to her hips. "Everybody else in here has a cookie, or a muffin, or something."

"We'll talk about this later, Constance."

Constance rolled her eyes. Quite a performer and with an attitude. Call him crazy, but Riley liked that about her.

The woman in line behind Riley began to complain. "I just came in here to pick up a birthday cake I ordered a week ago for my daughter. At this rate, the party will be over before I get the cake."

"Guess there's a run on coffee and scones this morning," Riley said. "But the woman's working as fast as she can."

"Dani needs to hire more help for her shop on Saturdays. Then she wouldn't have to do everything herself."

So the woman behind the counter was also the owner of Dani's Delights. Interesting.

The next person to approach the counter gave a to-go order for four cups of plain coffee, two-flavored lattes and a mixture of pastries.

Dani was still smiling, but she had to be overwhelmed. At least the little girl was helping now, keeping the customers in line entertained with a series of funny faces.

Riley stepped out of line and walked up to the counter. "You look like you could use some help."

"You think? I had two teenage workers not show up this morning without bothering to call in and let me know."

"Big night in town last night?"

"Not that I know of. Anyway, sorry for the delay, but I'm moving as fast as I can."

"I wasn't complaining. In fact, I have a proposition that's too good to refuse."

"I don't know," she said, without looking up. "I'm extremely good at saying no."

She bagged the pastries for the current order and started on the lattes. "What's your offer?"

"Behind-the-counter help. I can handle pouring coffee, but I could never concoct those fancy drinks you're making. By the way, my name's Riley Lawrence."

Dani looked up, a slightly surprised expression parting her full lips. "You must be Pierce's brother."

"Yep, but don't hold that against me."

"Never. Pierce is terrific and marrying my best friend. I'm sure he's thrilled you made it here for the wedding," she said as she went back to boxing pastries. "He was afraid you'd back out at the last minute."

"I was a bit afraid of that myself. Actually, I haven't made it to the Double K yet."

"Then what in the world are you doing here?"

"Saving your beautiful ass—pardon my French. That is if you want my help."

"You're serious?"

"Serious as a bull on steroids."

"I have no idea what that means, but you've got yourself a job."

"How about we start two lines?" Riley suggested. "One for the people who want specialty coffees and-or want to pay with credit cards. Another line of the people who just want plain coffee or to pick up some bakery items and pay with cash."

"You'll handle the cash line?"

"Yep. I've had very limited experience with cash registers, but that one doesn't look too complicated."

She sighed. "It would be a tremendous help, but I can't let you do that."

"Afraid I'll sneak too many cookies?"

"No. Afraid Esther will kill me for delaying your arrival at the ranch."

The door opened again. This time a family of four came in, stretching the line around the corner.

"If the line grows any longer, you may have a mutiny on your hands."

"Okay, but remember you asked for this. Prices are marked on the items on display," Dani explained. "Pre-ordered items are boxed and in the kitchen right behind us. Name of the customer and price are on the ticket taped to the top of the box. If you have any questions, just ask."

Dani raised her voice to get everyone's attention and

explained the new lineup procedures. Someone clapped and several more joined in. They moved into the two lines with amazing order and good manners.

That was the Winding Creek he remembered.

"By the way, my name's Dani Boatman," she offered.

"Glad to meet you, boss."

His first customer spoke up. "I'm picking up a dozen cupcakes for Jamie Sandler. She ordered them yesterday."

"Coming right up."

And with that Riley was officially on the job. He'd never sold anything in his life, except horses or cattle at an auction and admission tickets once at a local rodeo in Wyoming. His cash-register experience was limited to gate ticket sales.

Turned out this was much easier. Almost everybody was friendly and happier now that the line was moving a little faster.

The guys gave him a howdy, several introducing themselves. It was the Texas way. Young women—and some of the older ones—flirted with him. A little boost for the ego.

None of the females were as tempting as Dani Boatman. He might just be staying around Winding Creek a little longer than originally planned.

Two HOURS LATER, the Saturday morning rush had come and gone. Only three tables were occupied and there was no one in line. Constance was off to the movie with her friend.

And Dani Boatman was totally infatuated with the witty, personable, hunky cowboy who'd saved the day. But then he'd charmed almost every woman who'd walked into the bakery. Some men had a knack for winning hearts with just a smile. Riley had it in spades.

"Whew…" Riley said. "Are Saturday mornings always this busy?"

"Unfortunately, no. They're my busiest day of the week, but not usually this kind of crazy. The sunny day and the wildflowers in full bloom brought out the tourists."

"I get that. I'm not much of a flower man, but even I noticed the sea of bluebonnets driving in this morning. Damned impressive."

"You'd be amazed how many people visit the Texas Hill Country every spring just for the scenery."

"Scenery in here looks pretty good to me."

"Thanks. I try to make the pastries too tempting to resist."

He smiled seductively. "I wasn't talking about the pastries."

A flush of heat crept up her face. She turned away quickly, hoping he hadn't noticed the blush. He'd think she was either incredibly naive, or had never had a man casually flirt with her.

Tough to admit, but neither was that far-fetched.

"Did you bake all this?" he asked, motioning to the display cases full of her cookies, cupcakes, scones and other pastries, as well as loaves of bread.

"Yes."

"And you babysit your niece. When do you have time for a life?"

"This is my life. And I don't babysit Constance. My sister died this past year. Constance lives with me."

"So it's just you and Constance?"

"That's it."

"Instant motherhood. That must have thrown your life into a tailspin."

"It's been an adjustment, but I'm loving it. We live above the shop so I can be with her as much as possible."

The door opened again and Sandy O'Malley rushed in, her short skirt swinging around her thighs, her long blond hair pulled back in a ponytail. "I'm so sorry, Miss Boatman. My alarm didn't go off this morning. I mean I know I set it, but it didn't go off and Mom had gone into work early and I guess I got to bed late and…"

"Take a breath, Sandy," Dani said, stopping the on-slaught of excuses. "We'll talk later. For now, you can start clearing the tables."

"Yes, ma'am. I'll get right to it."

"Guess I'm officially replaced," Riley said.

"Yes, but you saved me from total chaos this morn-ing. If there's anything I can do to thank you for jump-ing into the madness…"

"Let me give it some thought. I'm sure we can think of a way. Will I see you at the wedding tonight?"

"Can't miss me. I'm the maid of honor."

"How 'bout that? I'm one of the two best men. Pierce had to give his brothers equal billing. I've yet to meet the bride, but according to Pierce, she hung the moon and outshines most of the stars."

"And she's just as crazy about him. They're a per-fect couple."

"More than a couple," Riley said. "They have Pierce's five-year-old daughter, Jaci, at least part-time. They'll be an instant family with all the complications that can bring. Glad it's him and not me."

Which was in perfect agreement with how Pierce had described his brother. Riley was a rambler, never stayed in one place long enough to get serious about any woman. The love-'em-and-leave-'em type.

"I'll see you tonight," Riley said. "Save me a two-stepper. I hear there's going to be a country-and-western band."

"Sure." As if he'd notice a short, plump pastry chef once he was besieged by every other woman there.

"Thanks again for helping out," she said. "If you ever need a steady job with long hours, low pay and lots of work, give me a call."

"I appreciate that generous offer, but unfortunately I start to rust if I spend more than a couple of hours indoors. See you tonight."

She watched Riley walk away. That was when she saw James Haggard staring at her through the window. She braced herself to deal with him, but he made no move to enter the shop. He just continued to stare, every muscle in his face stretched taut.

There was no doubt that he meant to intimidate her, to make her shudder in fear and realize that he'd meant what he said.

She'd lain awake for hours last night, considering his threats, trying to decide what her next move should be. She'd told the truth about the money being in a trust fund—it had been at Dani's insistence. That didn't mean that as Constance's father, Haggard couldn't challenge her decision.

If he was her biological father.

All she needed was a sample of his DNA to prove him wrong. Or prove him right.

If she could somehow get a sample of his DNA, she could have the testing done without his cooperation. But then why wouldn't he cooperate? He didn't want

Constance. He wanted to basically sell her for a million dollars.

If he wasn't her biological father, Dani would report him and his rotten scam to the sheriff. If he was… She couldn't bring herself to go there now.

She was closing at three today, an hour earlier that her usual time to make the sundown wedding without too much of a rush. She'd search paternity testing labs in San Antonio before she left for the Double K Ranch, to get the facts about how to go about the testing.

And then she'd insist Haggard provide a DNA sample. If he refused, that was as good as an admission that he was lying.

No matter what the results, she had to keep Constance out of the hands of James Haggard. If it came down to it, she'd protect her niece from scum like him with her life.

Chapter Three

Riley propped a booted foot on a bag of feed. It was the first time he'd managed a few minutes alone with Pierce and their younger brother, Tucker. They'd taken a walk out to the barn to get some privacy.

"So you're serious about staying on here at the Double K?" Riley asked. "As a hired hand?"

"Not exactly. Esther and I have been talking. She's willing to sell me the ranch as long as she can keep her house, her gardens and her chickens. I'd never dream of taking those from her anyway. As you know, Grace, Jaci and me are living with her now and it's working out fine."

"I just never figured she'd sell the Double K."

"Frankly, she doesn't have the resources to keep it going, and to be honest, I've never been as happy as I've been these past few months. I have some money saved and this seems like the perfect investment."

"Last time we were together, you said you'd never been happier than being a Navy SEAL," Riley said.

"That was the truth then and exactly what I needed at that time in my life. But this life is the kind of satisfaction that seeps bone-deep. Not just the ranch, though

I sure feel I belong here, but it's Grace and Jaci and, I don't know, man. It just feels so right."

"Don't you just have temporary custody of your daughter until her mother and new stepfather get back to the States?" Tucker asked.

"Yes, but we're working on more permanent arrangements. It seems Leslie's new husband will be working on the project in Cuba longer than expected. We're talking about joint custody, but with Jaci spending summers and most holidays with her mother and the rest of the time with me and Grace."

"How does Jaci feel about that?"

"She loves the ranch. Well, mostly she loves horses, but she's handling the divorce like a trouper. We're family. She even calls Esther 'Grandmother' and Grace 'Mommy.'"

"And Esther seems to love that," Tucker said.

"So getting married so soon after meeting Grace doesn't frighten you at all?" Riley asked.

"Not in the least."

"You've definitely been roped and tied," Tucker said.

"Except I was the one doing the roping. I was hooked from practically the moment I met Grace. When I thought I was going to lose her to a madman, I knew for certain my life would never be complete without her."

"I guess that explains the rush to the altar," Riley said.

"I was ready to marry her the day after she said yes. She was the one who encouraged me to wait until you two could actually coordinate your schedules enough to show up for the ceremony. She's big on family ties."

"It all sounds great," Riley agreed, "but you were madly in love before and look how that worked out."

"I failed in that marriage," Pierce admitted. "Leslie and I were like two horses pulling in different directions. There was no way we were going to arrive at the same destination."

"But you got Jaci out of that marriage," Tucker said. "She's a terrific kid, so it wasn't a total loss."

"Exactly," Pierce confirmed.

And Riley should probably leave it at that, but what kind of brother would he be if he didn't say what he was thinking?

"You haven't known Grace very long. What happens if you and Grace start pulling in opposite directions? Another divorce? More emotional trauma for Jaci?"

"I get your concerns," Pierce said. "But I have no doubts about Grace or my love for her. It's about love, but it's also about shared experiences and trust and knowing that the other person will always be there for you. Grace and I have that."

"Then I guess you're ready for the marriage game."

"It's not a game," Pierce argued.

"Right. It's your life. If you're happy, then I couldn't be happier for you."

Riley meant that. It was just that settling down to one woman, one ranch, one set of options seemed a lot like sticking a horse in one pasture and never letting it taste the grass on the other side of the fence.

"To change the subject, do you guys remember our first day on the Double K Ranch?" Tucker asked.

"All too well," Pierce said. "I was scared to open my mouth, afraid Esther and Charlie would kick us out if we did anything to annoy them."

"Same here," Riley said. "And if we got rejected by the Kavanaughs, that scary old hag of a social worker would take over and place us in three different foster homes."

"I cried the day the social worker said that," Tucker said, "but I hid so you two couldn't see me. At twelve, I figured I was way too old to cry."

The truth was they'd all had trouble dealing with the grief. One morning they'd had loving parents, a home, security. A few hours later a policeman showed up at the door and told them their parents had died in a car crash.

They'd spent the next ten months with Charlie and Esther before a great-uncle they'd never met showed up and took them to live in Kansas with him until they turned eighteen.

But Riley had never truly gotten over that feeling that he was one second away from a catastrophe. Maybe none of them had. Could be that was why Tucker risked his life almost daily riding two-thousand-pound bulls that would just as soon crack his skull with a hoof as not.

Maybe that was why Pierce had become a Navy SEAL and had been so good at it. And the reason Riley could never commit to anything. There was no certainty of anything in life.

Or maybe they were all just three brothers out there trying to find where they fit.

"I had a few minutes alone with Esther this morning," Tucker said. "She still seems to think Charlie was murdered."

"I know," Pierce said. "I've looked in to it some, but there's just no evidence to support that."

"Yet hard to believe he committed suicide," Riley said. "Were there health issues?"

"Not that Esther's mentioned," Pierce said. "But like

I said, there are lots of money issues. The ranch is mortgaged to the hilt and Charlie was behind in his payments. His bank account is down to a few thousand dollars and he'd been steadily selling off his livestock since the drought two years ago."

Riley leaned against a bale of hay. "Looks like your offer to buy in came just in time to save the ranch."

"It's working out that way," Pierce agreed. "It's great for Esther, too. She gets to stay in her home she shared with Charlie for so many years and still tend to her beloved chickens and her vegetable garden. Charlie's ranch doesn't fall into the hands of the bank. It's a win-win all the way around."

"Except that you're buying a ranch that you admit has fallen into a state of serious disrepair."

"I like a challenge. Besides, I had some money saved, thinking I might buy a ranch. Even after I pay off the debts, I'll have enough left to hopefully make the Double K a profitable operation again."

"You've got your work cut out for you," Riley said.

"Yep, and I'm hoping my brother the rambler might settle down for a few months and help me out."

"Why did I not see this coming?" Strangely, Riley wasn't put off by the idea. He had to be somewhere; might as well be here helping out his brother and Esther—for a while.

"Just don't get any ideas that I'm going to settle down in Winding Creek forever, big brother."

"That possibility never entered my mind."

So now the cute, little redheaded pastry chef with the sparkling eyes and the heart-melting smile wasn't his only excuse for hanging around Winding Creek.

"You think we have time to saddle a few horses and

race out to the swimming hole like old times?" Tucker asked.

"I don't see why not," Pierce said. "I'm banned from seeing my bride until the wedding and it's not going to take me long to shower and struggle into the monkey suit."

"Now you're talking," Riley said.

The three Lawrence brothers racing on horseback once again. This was as good as it got.

Chapter Four

Riley stood with Pierce and Tucker a couple of yards to the left of the flowered arbor, where the minister was patiently waiting.

Guests had been arriving for the past half hour or more, filling up the rows of folding chairs.

Riley recognized very few of them. "You must be giving away a new tractor to draw this many people."

"And to think this started out as a small family wedding," Pierce said."

"You've only been back here on a permanent basis since Christmas. Do you even know half these people?" Tucker asked.

"Not many, but Esther knows them all. Once she got involved in the plans, the size of the wedding at least quadrupled. We didn't have the heart to reel her in. The busier she is, the better she does with handling the grief over Charlie's death."

"This must have cost a fortune," Riley said. "Did you win the lottery and forget to tell me?"

"Nope. But this is Texas. You have a shindig, everyone chips in to help. The only food we had to furnish were the briskets that I smoked myself. And the booze, of course, though not even all of that. Some old friend of Charlie's I've never even seen before dropped off a few cases of beer today."

"They've been bringing in food for a good hour," Tucker said. "I guess we'll find out who the best cooks in the area are."

"None better than Esther," Pierce assured them, "though I doubt you'll find a bad dish in the bunch."

"Then I guess I'll have to try them all," Tucker said. "You lucked out with the weather, but what were you going to do if it rained? If I remember correctly, this area turns into a giant mud puddle with every shower."

"We had the option of moving the affair to the new community center next to the high school. The folding chairs and tables belong to the center anyway. The portable dance floor, too, though I had to rent it. Cost me a whopping twenty-five dollars."

"And all the lights you've got strung through branches and around poles?"

"Those I bought and Esther's part-time wrangler, Buck, and some of his buddies set them up."

"I didn't buy a wedding present," Tucker said. "Figured if there was something you needed, you already had it. Why don't I throw in some money to cover the cost of the reception tent?"

"Appreciated, but not necessary. One of Charlie's good friends, Harvey Mullins, has a son in San Antonio who rents party supplies."

Harvey had insisted on providing the tent with no charge for it, or for putting it up and taking it down. He said Charlie had helped him rebuild his barn last year when lightning had hit and he was glad to do something to repay the favor.

"Sounds like this is a community affair, so who do I see about filing a formal complaint?" Riley quipped.

"File thirteen is behind the woodshed. What are you complaining about?"

"This straitjacket I'm buttoned into. Shirt's so stiff I can barely move."

"I couldn't get Grace to budge on that, but she did agree to our wearing our cowboy boots as long as we had then cleaned and shined."

"What a woman," Riley said. "All heart."

"The real question is, does she have a friend for Riley?" Tucker said.

Thankfully they didn't get to finish the conversation. The music started and they were motioned into place by the minister.

Riley watched as someone he didn't recognize escorted Esther to her seat. He wasn't sure if Esther was acting as mother of the bride or mother of the groom, but she was smiling and dabbing at her eyes at the same time.

He knew what having the Kavanaughs take them in for ten months after their parents died meant to him and his brothers. He guessed he never fully realized what it had meant to Esther and, no doubt, to Charlie. From now on, he'd see that he kept in closer touch.

He flashed Esther a smile and looked over to see if Pierce was starting to panic yet. Nope. The man had ice water in his veins. Must be all that SEAL training.

When Riley looked up again, Dani was walking down the makeshift aisle between the rows of folding chairs. The wow factor sent his head spinning. She'd been cute and witty in the bakery. She was absolutely stunning in a brilliant green dress that set off her gorgeous eyes.

Damn, he even liked the way she walked. She didn't glide or prance like some haughty mare. She just walked, like a gal who knew who she was and what she was about.

Would be right interesting to check her out a little further, find out if she was as authentic as she seemed. If he hung around awhile, they could have some good times before he hit the road again.

Horseback riding up to the gorge at Lonesome Branch. Do some fishing for bream or catfish. Maybe even take a dip in the swimming hole if the weather cooperated.

Desire revved inside him at the thought of her in—or out of—a bikini.

When she reached the arbor, her gaze met his. She smiled and suddenly all he could think about was getting the wedding over with and getting his arms around her on the dance floor.

The rest of the wedding procession barely registered with him until it was time for him to hand Pierce the ring. He watched as Pierce slid it onto Grace's finger. He saw the way they looked at each other and he had to admit it did look like love.

But then this was the easy part of a marriage—when everything about the relationship was new and exciting. Before the ties didn't bind. Before hard times and resentments started pulling a couple apart.

Riley didn't see himself ever vowing to love anyone or anything for forever. Yet, when the happy couple were pronounced man and wife and Pierce kissed his bride, Riley hoped with all his heart that marriage worked this time for Pierce and Grace. And mostly for his five-year-old niece, Jaci.

Riley had dreaded coming to this wedding, but now that it was nearly over, he had to admit he'd never seen his brother happier. Even more of a shocker, Riley was looking forward to the rest of the evening. He was downright excited about getting to know Dani better.

For all the roving around from ranch to ranch and from state to state that he did, could it be that he was the one in a rut?

No. He was a born wanderer and he liked it that way.

But if he was ready to settle down, he'd be looking for a woman who had it all together. He'd be looking for a woman like Dani.

"THAT'S GOOD. LET'S get one more shot before we lose that sunset. Just the women this time. Esther, Grace, Dani and our little flower girl."

Not the words Dani had hoped to hear. The air was cooling off as the sun made its final descent, but the Texas humidity had not let up. She could feel herself starting to wilt like a rosebush in a heat wave.

The wedding had been beautiful and touching and perfect in every way, but the photographer was getting a bit carried away with his after-ceremony wedding-party shots. Dani was not the only one growing restless. Jaci kept sneaking away from the group only to be tugged back by one of the adults.

"If we move a few yards to the left, we can—"

"Whoa there," Pierce interrupted. "Feels like Miller time to me. I'm sure that's enough pictures of this group."

"Are you sure?" Tucker queried. "I thought we were going for Prince William and Kate's record."

"Okay, okay," the photographer said, relenting. "Just trying to give you your money's worth."

Jaci tugged on Pierce's hand. "Can I go play now, Daddy?"

"I think we're all ready to go and play," Grace said. "But before you all scatter, I want to say thank you one more time for being part of our wedding. You've made the happiest day of my life even more special by sharing it with us."

Pierce put an arm around her. "That goes for me, too. And, bros, I'll be sure and be there when you tie the knot."

"Find me a winner like Grace and I'm in," Tucker said.

DANI REACHED FOR a glass of bubbly from the tray of full flutes someone had been nice enough to bring them. Scanning the area, she quickly spotted Constance with her good friend Sally and a couple of other school friends. They were ceremoniously sliding across the portable dance floor in their socks while the band set up their instruments.

Happy. Surrounded by friends. Watched over by Sally's mother, Crystal. Safe.

But for how long? Dani shuddered. She'd done a good job of keeping James Haggard out of her mind during the ceremony, but now he was back and tormenting her thoughts.

She'd found several labs in San Antonio that promised quick results with paternity testing.

She ordered a DNA collection kit online from

Corinthian Court Labs and paid extra for overnight delivery. With luck, she'd have it in her hands by Monday morning.

The next time Haggard dropped by, she'd insist he cooperate. She seriously doubted she'd have to wait until Friday to see him again.

Having a plan helped but didn't alleviate her apprehension.

"Are you okay, dear? You look like you've checked out of this hoopla."

Esther's words of concern jolted Dani back to the present. "I'm fine, but I'd best get back to the reception area and help control Constance."

"I'll walk with you. Jaci, why don't you come with us and we'll check out the party?"

Jaci clapped her hands and skipped over to join them.

As the photographer folded his tripod, several guests rushed up to congratulate the groom and hug the beaming bride. Riley and Tucker were quickly accosted, as well, by two very attractive young women. Dani had seen both of them in the bakery a few times, but didn't actually know them. In their early twenties, she'd guess. Both thin as a blade of grass.

Not that Dani cared. She'd never expected any more from Riley than a dance and she wasn't putting much faith in that. He certainly didn't owe her anything.

Dani picked up her pace, determined not to be annoyed by the sound of Riley's laughter, probably at something one of the flaunting flirts had whispered in his ear.

By the time she reached Constance, the little manipulator and Sally were swiping maraschino cherries from a tray on the portable bar in back of the tent.

"That's enough," Crystal said. "You'll get a stomachache and no one else will get any cherries in their drinks."

Dani tiptoed up and surprised Constance with a quick hug. "How about a glass of orange juice instead?"

"Or a couple of Shirley Temples," the cute young cowboy behind the bar suggested.

Constance's mouth flew open and she covered it with her hand, her eyes wide as she looked up at Dani and then back to the bartender. "My aunt would kill me if I drank that."

Dani laughed. "You can have a Shirley Temple if you like."

"I can?"

"Sure. It's not alcohol."

"What is it?"

"It's sort of like a Sprite with a cherry."

"Oh. Then I'll just have a Sprite with a cherry in it."

"Me, too," Sally said.

Crystal stepped around the girls. "And I'll have a white wine."

"Coming right up." The bartender took his time with them with little concern for a couple of guys waiting on service.

"My feet are killing me," Crystal said, reaching down to make an adjustment on the strap. "And these shoes felt so good when I tried them on in the shop."

"Have you guys eaten yet?" Dani asked.

"We have," Crystal said. "Food is great, especially the brisket sliders and Esther's fabulous creamed-corn casserole, but I controlled myself. Have to save room for wedding cake."

"Your cake is beautiful," Sally said. "When I get

married, I want you to bake my cake and make it as tall as me."

"Why don't I just practice on a few birthday cakes shorter than you first?" Dani responded.

"I second that," Crystal said. "We're a long way from talking weddings."

The bartender handed them their drinks.

"I'll carry your drink," Crystal said, reaching for Dani's flute of champagne. "You can grab a plate of food while the girls and I snag seats—away from the band, so we can talk about how beautiful the wedding was and how smashing you look."

"Thanks. I like smashing." She had felt rather smashing until she'd compared herself to the two model-thin ladies hitting on Riley and Tucker. That had put things back into perspective pretty quickly.

Dani wasn't hungry, but champagne on an empty stomach would make her giddy.

Several guests stopped to say hello and talk for a minute as she made her way to the food line. The band broke into their first number. Pierce and Grace stepped onto the dance floor that had been sprinkled with sawdust.

They looked incredibly happy. So perfect together that Dani's eyes grew moist.

She blinked and then spotted Riley and Tucker standing near the dance floor surrounded by a different cluster of fawning women. No surprise there. It would be difficult to find three more hunky cowboys than the Lawrence brothers.

When she'd first spotted Riley in his tux, he literally took her breath away. Her pulse had gone into orbit as she walked the aisle. He looked even better now that he'd shed the stiff bow tie and donned his black Stetson.

She felt a touch to her arm and turned around. Millie Miles was standing at her elbow. Dani had met the woman while visiting Grace at the Double K Ranch a couple of months back and had run in to her in town and at the bakery several times since then.

The woman was always friendly, but there was no missing the sadness in her eyes. She'd recently lost her grandson, and her husband was in prison for manslaughter related to the tragic accident that had also claimed the toddler's life.

It was the kind of story you expected to see on TV, but never in a town like Winding Creek.

"I just wanted to say what a beautiful maid of honor you were," Millie said. "I love the dress. You should always wear that shade of green."

"Thanks. I'll certainly give that some consideration. Not sure how it would look with food-coloring stains, though," Dani joked. Compliments always tended to make her uncomfortable—unless they were in reference to her pastries.

"This is probably not the best time for this, but may I ask a favor of you?"

"Sure," Dani said.

"It's my daughter, Angela. She's the blonde in the red dress talking to Riley Lawrence."

"Yes, I've seen Angela in the shop with you."

Angela always dressed provocatively, but perhaps never looked as dynamite as she did tonight in the skin-tight dress with the revealing cutouts.

"What about Angela?"

"I don't know how much you know about our situation, but Angela's two-year-old son died in a freak accident last year. I won't go in to all the tragic details, but it has been extremely hard on Angela, as you might guess."

"I'm sure this is difficult for all of you."

Dani had no idea where this was going, but it didn't seem the time or place to discuss this.

"I'm increasingly worried about Angela," Millie said. "She seems to be in a state of denial, as if she refuses to believe any of the past actually happened."

Definitely not the time or place for this conversation. Dani had to agree that she didn't look like a grieving mother of a dead child, but… "I'm not the one you need to talk to about this."

"I know. I tend to go on once I get started. I was just hoping you could give her a job at the bakery."

"Does she want a job?" From what Dani had heard, the Mileses were wealthy enough that Angela wouldn't need the small salary Dani could pay her.

"She needs something to help settle her. A job that's not too complex but would force her to stay on a schedule and demonstrate a level of responsibility."

That didn't answer Dani's question. Or maybe it did. Millie was looking for an intervention for her daughter whether Angela wanted it or not.

"I don't think Dani's Delights fits her needs. It's very hectic at times. People expect good service and a smile."

Dani needed dependable help, but she wasn't a psychologist and had no experience dealing with serious emotional issues.

"If you'd just give her a chance."

Millie was pleading. Dani was still convinced it would be a mistake, but she didn't have the heart to say no with Millie looking as if she might start weeping at any second.

Dani let her gaze go back to Angela. The woman was animated, laughing, her hands now all over Tucker. Riley had disappeared, probably hijacked by some other hottie.

"I can't promise you anything," Dani said, "but have Angela come by and talk to me tomorrow afternoon around four. We close at three on Sunday, but I'll be around. Just tell her to ring the bell."

"Thank you. You won't be sorry."

Dani had a disturbing premonition that would not be the case, especially now, when her patience was being stretched to the limits by James Haggard.

Deep in thought as Millie walked away, she was caught off guard when Riley came up behind her and put both hands on her shoulders. A traitorous tingle of awareness rushed her veins.

"You're not trying to avoid me, are you?" he asked.

"No, but you looked to be well cared for the last time I noticed."

"Tucker's fan club was spilling over. He puts out that virile, macho vibe that all bull riders do." Riley hooked an arm around her waist. "I think you owe me a dance."

"Then I guess we should get that over with," she teased in an effort to hide her pleasure that he'd remembered.

"You have a cruel side, you know that?"

"You can't expect every woman here to fall all over you."

He leaned close and whispered in her ear, "I'll settle for one."

In spite of her vows to be sensible, her insides melted

as he led her onto the floor. He fit his arms around her and pulled her closer. Desire swelled to the point she could barely breathe, much less dance.

She was so lost in the moment that she didn't realize at first that Tucker was cutting in when he appeared over Riley's shoulder.

"You have to share this beauty, bro. *All* the best men get to dance with the maid of honor."

"Okay, but one time only," Riley said.

Dani tried to make conversation with Tucker, but she was in such an emotional state, it was hard to pull off a simple sentence. She watched Riley leave the dance floor and return a minute later with not one but two adorable partners—Constance and Jaci.

He held both their hands and twirled them like some of the other couples were doing. They giggled and spun as if they were dancing queens.

That did it. The most she'd ever get out of Riley was a few heart-stopping moments, but she was ten tons of crazy about that man.

She had no plans to let him know that.

The rest of the evening was like a dream. Not that she danced every dance with Riley, but he was never gone from her side for long.

They were over three hours into the reception and many of the guests had left before she finally found herself totally alone with Riley near the back of the reception tent.

The band was playing a slow ballad and a lot of the remaining couples, along with Pierce and Grace, were dancing.

Constance and Jaci had finally run out of energy and

had settled down with their iPads. Esther was sitting next to them, nodding and yawning.

"Looks like it's time for me to get Constance home," Dani said. "I'm sure Esther is ready to put Jaci and herself to bed even if the newlyweds party on."

Riley slipped an arm around her waist. "I was hoping we could escape and take a walk beneath the stars before you left."

Conflicting emotions sent her heart to her throat. His touch set her on fire, but what did he want from her. A kiss? A short fling before he moved on again? Or was this just the routine with a love-'em-and-leave-'em cowboy?

Not that she was actually looking for more. Getting the bakery on its feet and helping Constance adjust to her new life took practically every waking second.

And now there was James Haggard to add to the mix. There was no time for even a temporary romantic escapade in her life.

"I'll have to take a rain check on the walk. I really should take Constance home. This is well past her bedtime."

Riley slid his hand from around Dani's waist and took one of her hands in his. "You're not afraid of being alone with me, are you?"

"Should I be?"

"I'll never do anything you don't want me to do."

That wasn't a lot of reassurance. All she had to do was look into his eyes and her willpower would melt like butter on a hot cinnamon bun.

"I'm making you uncomfortable," he said. "That's not at all what I intended."

"It's not that," she lied. "But I do need to get home. I have a busy day tomorrow."

"You have to work on Sunday?"

"My boss is a slave driver."

"What time do you close the bakery?"

"Three on Sundays. Four every other day. Except Monday. Then we're closed all day, but this week I may have business in San Antonio." If by a stroke of luck she could get a sample of James's DNA.

"Are you always this tough on a guy trying to get to know you better?"

"I have been accused of that before." More than once.

"I'm not giving up," Riley said. "What about dinner Monday night, or better yet, why don't you and Constance come back out to the ranch after you close tomorrow? We can explore the ranch on horseback or in my pickup truck. I need to reintroduce myself to the Double K."

She wanted to say yes, but her overly cautious nature held her back. Riley Lawrence was a heartache waiting to happen.

"I'll see. If not, perhaps one afternoon next week if that works for you. Constance doesn't have school Monday through Wednesday. Teacher workshops."

"How about both Sunday and a couple of afternoons next week? Every kid needs some time on a ranch."

"No promises, but I will try."

"And I'll keep thinking of you back in that kitchen creating all those delicious pastries. Spreading the creamy fillings. Dripping the caramel sauce. Licking the bowl."

A traitorous craving rippled through her body, a need

so intense she had to fight the urge to wrap herself in his arms the way she had on the dance floor.

A walk with him in the moonlight would most definitely do her in.

"I really have to go now," she said, suddenly terrified by the strength of her feelings for a man she barely knew.

"Then let me drive you home," Riley persisted.

"I have my car here."

"But it's late. No reason for you and your niece to be out alone on these old country roads this time of night."

"It's Winding Creek," she reminded him. "I don't think there's any reason to worry."

"You drive a hard bargain, Dani Boatman."

She loved hearing her name on his lips. The name she'd had since birth, but it had never sounded erotic before.

"Dani."

She turned at Grace's frantic voice. An armed deputy with a dead serious expression on his face was walking at her side.

"What's wrong?" Riley asked.

The deputy looked past him and spoke directly to Dani. "There's been a break-in at your bakery."

She swallowed hard past a lump in her throat. "Are you sure? Sometimes the wind can set off the alarm system."

"There has definitely been a break-in and some damage. Deputies are on the scene. I can drive you there if you want."

"I'll drive her," Riley said.

Her first impulse was irritation that he took control, as if she couldn't handle this. But in truth she had no idea what she'd find when she got to the bakery and she didn't want to face it alone.

"Is there a problem?" Esther asked, joining them.

"My bakery has been broken into."

"Oh, mercy me. What is this world coming to? Did you catch the no-account bloke who did it?"

"Not yet," the deputy said, "but we will."

"Well, you can't do it soon enough to suit me. Terrible when a hardworking person can't even operate a business without someone stealing from her."

"Right about that," the deputy agreed.

"Why don't you just leave Constance here with me for the night?" Esther offered. "No use to drag her into that mess."

"I can't ask you to do that. You must be exhausted after all you've done today."

"You didn't ask. I offered. Besides, Constance isn't a bit of trouble. I figure she and Jaci will be so tired they'll fall asleep the second their heads hit the pillows. I'm sure I can find a cotton T-shirt she can sleep in."

"She should definitely stay," Grace said. "Pierce and I aren't leaving for San Antonio until tomorrow morning. I can help with the girls tonight."

"You're on your honeymoon."

"I've been on a honeymoon since the day I met Pierce. Helping get the girls to bed won't change that."

"It's settled," Esther said.

This time Dani didn't argue. "Thanks. I appreciate this more than you know. Constance bought her backpack with her, so she has her favorite doll and some books. She changed into her wedding finery after we got here, so she can put on the jeans and shirt she was wearing earlier when she gets up in the morning."

Grace put her arm around Dani's waist. "Don't worry about her.

"Riley, you take care of Dani," Esther ordered.

"I plan to."

He took her arm protectively as they followed the deputy back toward the house where he'd parked his squad car. Dread clawed at the lining of Dani's stomach as they made the drive into town.

The bakery wasn't just a shop. It was her livelihood. Her home. Constance's home, the place where Dani always wanted her to feel safe.

The first thing she saw when they turned onto Main Street was a squad car and the sheriff's vehicle in front of her shop, blue lights flashing. A cluster of strangers stood on the opposite side of the street observing the action.

The second the car stopped, she jumped out and rushed to the open door of the shop. Anger erupted at the havoc she faced. The feeling was so fierce, her insides seemed to explode.

She didn't have to wonder what had happened here. No one ever broke into the shops in this area. James Haggard had returned, just as he'd promised he would. Only he hadn't waited a week. He'd barely backed off for twenty-four hours.

If it was hardball he wanted, he'd get it.

Chapter Five

The intense odor of coffee sent Dani into an immediate coughing fit. A black film covered every surface and hung thick in the air. Two giant-sized canisters of coffee she had ground for the morning rush lay empty on the floor in front of the counter.

She braced herself against the display case as she scanned the rest of the destruction. It looked as if a tornado had blown through the shop and literally picked up everything and sent it crashing back to the tile floor.

Tables and chairs were overturned. Pastry cookbooks and coffee-themed gift items normally shelved along the side walls had been knocked to the floor, many cracked or shattered. Both cash-register drawers were open.

She had a crazy urge to pick up one of the chairs and hurl it as hard as she could against the wall, or to start screaming and pull out her hair. Fortunately, since she wasn't two years old, she refrained from doing what came naturally. She took a deep breath and managed a small measure of composure.

A deputy rushed in from the kitchen area. "This is a crime scene. No trespassing."

"I'm Dani Boatman. I own Dani's Delights, at least what's left of it. And this is my friend Riley Lawrence."

"Sorry, but I'll need to see some ID."

Sheriff Cavazos joined them from the back of the shop. "She doesn't need any ID. I'll vouch for her and her friend." He put out a hand to Riley. "I'm Sheriff Cavazos. We haven't met, but I know your brother Pierce and have known Esther Kavanaugh for years."

They exchanged handshakes.

"Sorry we're meeting under such down-and-dirty circumstances," Cavazos said. "Glad you're here to offer Dani some moral support. Always tough seeing your business trashed like this."

Dani picked up and righted an overturned chair that blocked her path. "I'm not sure I can stomach looking at the rest of the place."

"Fortunately, this is the worst of it," Sheriff Cavazos said. "There's no sign of damage in your fancy kitchen. Not even a scratch on those giant ovens. All your cinnamon-roll fans will be thankful for that. Me included."

"What about the upstairs living area?" Riley asked.

Dani held her breath, her stomach churning as she waited for his response. If Haggard had been in Constance's room—if he'd handled any of her things...

"Untouched as far as we can tell," Cavazos said. "And believe me, we gave it a thorough check. Had to make sure the culprit wasn't hiding up there."

Dani shuddered. She hadn't even thought of that. She scanned the area again. "How did he get in?"

"Through the back door that opens to the alley. He broke the lock."

"So you think this was all done by one person?" Riley asked.

"I checked the area myself and only saw one set of fresh footprints in the patch of dirt between the door and the alleyway. Big feet. Definitely an adult male. Not wearing Western boots like so many around here do. Prints indicated he was wearing sneakers, no doubt looking for a fast getaway."

"So no eyewitness?" Riley asked.

"Nope." Cavazos raked his fingers through his thinning hair. "But we couldn't have missed the scoundrel by much. He busted the hell out of the system keypad next to the back door, but not before the call went through to the security company.

"When the company couldn't reach you, Dani, they called us."

"I was at the Double K for the wedding reception. Evidently I couldn't hear the phone over the band."

"Wouldn't have changed the results if you had. The first two deputies were on the scene in under five minutes. Your burglar wasted no time wrecking the place."

"Any suspects?" Riley asked. "Is this a pattern of similar vandalism and break-ins in Winding Creek?"

Cavazos shook his head and scratched his whiskered chin. "Last downtown business break-in we had was dang near three years ago. Then it was a couple of teenagers camping out down at the park on Winding Creek. They got high and hit Caffe's Bar looking for booze. Didn't make a mess like this, though."

"Your registers were emptied of all the bills," one of the deputies said. "That was probably the intruder's first order of business."

"That didn't gain him much. There was very little money in them. I emptied them when I closed shop for the day, except for enough bills and change to start business in the morning. Not that I'll be opening to customers tomorrow now."

"What about the cash you took in this morning?" Riley asked. "Where's that money?"

"I made a deposit at the drive-through lane before the bank closed. The rest is in a hidden safe upstairs."

"That might be your motivation for the vandalism," Cavazos said. "Jackass went for the cash and when there wasn't enough to satisfy him, he got pissed and did as much damage as he could before he heard the approaching sirens."

"Guess I'm lucky you got here so fast," she said.

But she felt certain that wasn't the motivation for the vandalism. The culprit was that rotten James Haggard. He was devoid of any decency. A scoundrel who was determined to steal the trust fund of a motherless girl he claimed was his own flesh and blood.

Riley took off the jacket to his tux and wrapped it about her shoulders. That was when she realized she was trembling.

"I know you've got a major clean-up job here," he said. "The good news is there's very little costly damage. The best news is neither you nor Constance was home at the time of the break-in."

"I agree," she said. She wasn't sure if Haggard had only come by to threaten her again and then decided to break in when she wasn't here, or if vandalism had been his goal.

"I wouldn't advise you to try and stay here tonight," Cavazos said. "The lock on the back door is busted. Fact is, the whole door is busted up. It will have to be replaced, and it will likely be Monday before you can get someone out to take care of that for you."

"I'll secure it until the door's replaced," Riley said.

"And I'll replace all the locks once the door is in, just to be on the safe side."

"Good idea," Cavazos said. "Now if you two will excuse me, I need to return a phone call. The deputies will be finishing up here in a few minutes. After that, the place is yours, but if you think of anything I should know about, give me a call on my private line."

He handed them each a business card. He spoke briefly to his deputies and then left through the front door.

Dani's mind was reeling. Cleanup seemed all but insurmountable and she wasn't sure she had the strength or willpower to even start on it tonight.

And then there was Riley. She'd known him one day, yet he'd taken over tonight as if they were lifelong friends—or more. He was protective, and far more clearheaded than she was at the moment.

He was both of those things now, but he could be gone tomorrow. She couldn't start depending on him.

"You don't have to stay tonight, Riley. Really, you've done so much already. I'm starting to feel guilty about taking up all your time when you're in Winding Creek to visit your brothers and Esther."

He looked puzzled. "Do you have a problem with my being here?"

"Of course not, but—"

"Then drop the guilt talk. No cowboy worth his boots would ever walk away from a woman in distress. Especially one who can bake the way you do," he added teasingly.

He smiled and suddenly she was unable to tear her gaze from him. He was still in his tux but seemingly as relaxed as if he was wearing his favorite jeans.

He was undoubtedly the most intriguing and seductive man she'd ever met. Not pretty-boy handsome, but rugged and masculine, with eyes the color of dark chocolate, thick locks of deep brown hair that fell devilishly onto his forehead and a smile that could melt glacial ice.

"I love you in that dress," he said, "but I'm not sure it will ever come clean if it keeps collecting coffee grinds. And I'm damn sure that staying in this monkey suit for much longer will stop the blood flow to my brain—and other parts."

Her lustful thoughts cooled as she looked down at her once beautiful dress. It looked as she'd been caught in a whirlwind of black sand.

"So much for ever wearing this again," she said. "I'm going upstairs and change. I'm afraid I don't have anything in your size to offer you."

"No problem. I look terrible in feminine attire anyway. Do you want me to go upstairs with you, give the area another look around?"

"No, but if I run in to any unpleasant surprises, I'll yell."

"And I'll come running."

That might be the first time a man had ever said that to her. Fortunately there were no surprises waiting at the top of the stairs. The living area looked exactly as she'd left it.

She peeked into Constance's room. Also untouched. She breathed easier. The thought of Haggard handling any of Constance's possessions would have made her physically ill.

She headed straight for the shower, peeling off her clothes as she walked. Hot water and soap couldn't wash away the feeling she'd been sprayed with Haggard's special brand of poison, but at least she'd be more comfortable.

All of this would be far more traumatic if she was facing it alone. She wished she dared tell Riley about James Haggard, but she couldn't lay this on him.

Haggard was her responsibility and she couldn't afford a mistake. If there was one, Constance, in all her innocence, would be the one to pay.

RILEY WENT TO check out the back door while the deputies finished with their investigation of the crime scene. One was taking snapshots. The other was collecting fingerprints from the cash register.

True to the sheriff's report, the solid wooden door was a disaster. It hung from one hinge, open enough that a man could squeeze past it to get in and out of the shop. The top half of the door had a huge hole in it, as if someone very strong had slammed his fist through it. The bottom half was splintered.

Riley squeezed through the opening. There were no lights in the area, but the moon was bright enough that he could get a fair take on his surroundings.

The door opened onto a covering of dirt that bordered the alley. Three huge trash cans sat just to the right of the door. There was a fenced-in area about four feet deep that ran nearly the length of the building on the left. The gate to it had a latch but not a lock.

He walked over and peeked inside. Two air-conditioner units were housed there. A couple of empty clay flowerpots sat next to them beside a half-empty sack of pottery soil.

He stepped into the alley and scanned the rest of the

area. Except for a couple of cats, Riley was the only sign of life.

It made sense a man would come in the back way if he was sneaking around. Chances were slim that he'd be noticed after dark—unless he set off an alarm system.

Riley suspected all stores had alarm systems these days, even in Winding Creek. The burglar should have expected that.

So why risk getting caught or possibly shot to break in to a bakery? It wasn't like there was anything that could be sold at the pawnshop for ready cash. So was it desperation, stupidity or a personal grudge against Dani?

She didn't seem the type to make enemies, but she was relatively new in town. Perhaps it was her past that was coming back to haunt her.

He reached for his phone and punched in Tucker's number.

"About time you called," Tucker said. "If I didn't hear from you by the time I finished loading these chairs on the back of the truck, I was planning to drive into town and see for myself what's going on."

"Loading chairs? Does that mean the guests have all left?"

"For the most part. The bride and groom have already been showered with birdseed and good wishes and escaped to their bedroom in the big house. And the band finished its last set about ten minutes ago. So what's up with the bakery?"

Riley filled him in as succinctly as possible.

"Poor Dani. She must be freaking out."

"All in all, she's handling it pretty well."

"What can I do to help?"

"Bring me some lumber—a few sheets of plywood and some two-by-fours if Esther has some lying around the ranch."

"You need all of that tonight?"

"Yep. I need to board up the back door until she can get it replaced. Can't even close it now, much less secure it."

"What about tools?"

"I've probably got all I need in my truck. But I need some jeans and a shirt. Got to get out of this tux before it strangles me."

"I get that. I've already changed back into jeans myself. Does this mean you're going to start cleaning tonight?"

"Not if I can help it. Tomorrow's soon enough for me, but I figure I'll spend the night here and help Dani get an early start on tackling the rubble remains tomorrow."

"Spend the night? Really? Am I missing something here?"

"Just living by the code, bro. Gotta protect the women."

"And, of course, it doesn't hurt if they're cute. Lumber and a change of clothes. Anything else?"

"That should do it."

"I'll be there as soon as I can break free here. That shouldn't take long."

"Appreciate it."

"No problem," Tucker said. "Who knew Winding Creek would be this exciting?"

Certainly not Riley. And to think he'd been wasting his time with a bunch of cows.

Chapter Six

James Haggard stood on the bank of Winding Creek
beneath the shadowed branches of an ancient oak tree.
The moon was so bright he could see three deer at
the edge of the woods on the opposite bank. An owl
hooted and somewhere in the distance he heard the
howl of coyotes.

In another situation, he might have appreciated the
setting. Tonight he felt nothing but the desperation roaring through his veins like a runaway freight train.

He'd seen his daughter for the first time yesterday.
It hadn't been planned. He'd been sitting in the back
of Dani's Delights, sipping a coffee and sizing up Dani
Boatman as an adversary.

It was after three when the door opened and a
freckle-faced girl, her hair in braids, swung through
the door, a huge smile on her face. She was friendly and
full of life the way her mother had been in the old days.

Memories of Amber had flooded his mind. She'd
been so beautiful and loving. When they made love,
he had felt he was the luckiest man in the world. He'd
have done anything she'd asked him to do.

He had even almost gotten shot once while robbing a

liquor store to keep her in the fancy rehab center while she was pregnant with Constance.

His woman and his child. He hadn't wanted to steal, but he couldn't let them down.

The rehab had never taken root. After Constance was born, Amber had hit the drugs harder than ever. Eventually, she'd kicked James out of her life.

But she'd loved him. He knew she had. It was the drugs and other men who'd torn her away from him.

He'd half expected to feel some instinctive connection with Constance when he saw her. Nothing clicked. All he could think of was Amber and the way she'd used him when all he'd wanted to do was take care of her.

But this wasn't about Constance. This was what was owed him. He was Constance's father. By rights the insurance settlement should have been his. All he wanted was his rightful share.

Tonight had been a near catastrophe. He'd lost his cool, let the situation lead to uncontrolled rage. He'd always had a problem with that, more so lately than ever before.

But tonight's episode had gained him nothing. He'd been barely inside, trying to decide where to start searching for Constance's birth certificate, when he heard the approaching sirens.

The birth certificate would prove he was the father. He knew it and Dani knew it, no matter what she claimed.

Frustrated, he'd given in to rage, wrecking what he could before escaping out the back door as men with guns raced inside through the front.

At least Dani would know he meant business now.

Red drops of blood plopped onto his shoe.

Damn. His hand had begun to bleed again. He turned and headed back inside the cheap rental cabin for another makeshift bandage and a glass of whiskey to dull the pain.

This had been a damn rotten night.

Chapter Seven

Dani turned on the vacuum cleaner but then just stood staring at the mess that faced her. She'd been so proud of her shop, thrilled that the future in Winding Creek had felt so promising for her and Constance.

The senseless destruction created an empty feeling inside her, as if it was a harbinger of things to come. It was exasperating how much pain one greedy, vengeful man could spawn, just for the sake of proving to her that he had no boundaries when it came to getting what he wanted.

But he would soon find out she had no boundaries when it came to keeping Constance safe.

She vacuumed and then mopped a swath down the middle of the shop to at least provide a clean walkway. It was only a start but all she felt like tackling tonight.

Tucker and Riley were probably just as fatigued as she was after the long day, but she could hear the hum of the saws and the pounding of the hammers as the men boarded up the back door.

She stopped at the pile of broken items around the nearly empty shelves. She picked up a delicate teapot, one of her favorite purchases from her last trip to market. The handle was missing and there was a chip at the spout. It would have to be trashed. Still, she carefully placed what was left on it back on the shelf for now.

That was when she noticed the smeared crimson dots along the edge of one of the shelves. She visually followed the trail of stain to a mound of broken glass. Drops of blood, not quite dry, glistened on what had once been an etched trifle bowl.

The glass was mostly shards except for one larger curved piece of the bowl. At least a tablespoon of blood had pooled in the curved remains.

Her heart jumped to her throat. That had to be James Haggard's blood. His DNA. Right at her fingertips.

Excitement trilled through her. Luck might just have taken a swift turn in her direction. Unfortunately, she didn't have the sterile container the kit would provide.

She considered her options. A plastic ziplock bag would have to do.

She hurried to the kitchen for the bag and a pair of protective gloves. Afraid of spilling even a drop, she gingerly tipped the piece of glass so that the blood flowed into the bag.

She wrapped the bag in the same white paper she used to line boxes of pastry and then slid it to the seldom-used top shelf in her bakeware pantry.

Now it was just a matter of waiting. According to information at the website, results would be ready in three to five days by phone after the DNA was in their hands and the written document would arrive by mail a workday or two later.

Dani would see that the samples were at the Corinthian Court Lab by Monday afternoon.

A happy ending for everyone except Haggard—as

long as the DNA proved his threats were nothing but a scam. Right now she had to think positively about that.

DEAD TIRED BUT with the back door to the bakery secured, Riley adjusted the spray so that it was as hot as he could stand it. He liked his showers *caliente*, his salsa *picantes* and his life uncomplicated. He hadn't even been in Winding Creek twenty-four hours yet and his life was as complicated as it had ever been.

He was feeling a bit like he'd blown into town on a hurricane and dropped into a stampede of wild horses. Only wild horses might not have been nearly as disruptive to his life as Dani Boatman.

Sure, she was cute, smart and witty, but that didn't fully explain the instantaneous attraction to her from the moment he'd walked into Dani's Delights. Kind of like a bite of one of her famous cinnamon rolls that, if he could believe all the comments he'd heard this morning, left everyone wanting more.

Riley was yet to taste one of those rolls, but he'd known immediately he wanted to get to know her better. He'd never expected to be standing naked in her shower tonight—albeit alone.

Not that he could chalk up that development to his irresistible charm. He owed his being here tonight to the jerk who'd wrecked her bakery. Crazy timing for sure, for a town that seldom saw this type of senseless crime.

A random attack or was the bakery targeted? If it was the latter, what would have happened if the alarm hadn't gone off or if Dani had been in the shop's kitchen when the son of a bitch busted through the door?

What if he came back when she and Constance were here alone?

Those troubling thoughts kicked around in Riley's mind as he soaped his body and shampooed his hair.

The back door to the shop was boarded over for now, but Riley planned to replace it with one reinforced with iron bars that would be a lot more difficult to break through. He'd checked the front door. It needed better and more secure locks, as well.

But no matter how secure the doors were, the huge display window would always be an easy point of entry. The best he could do with that was encourage her to make sure her replacement alarm system was top-of-the-line.

He had the next few days' work cut out for him—as long as she let him keep hanging around.

He stepped out of the shower and grabbed a thick, sky-blue towel from the rack. The towel was slightly damp and smelled of the same intoxicating scent that clung to Dani. He'd never taken much notice of fragrances before, but tonight even that was a turn-on.

A competing odor grabbed his attention—a whiff of bacon made his mouth water and his stomach grumble. It occurred to him as he yanked on his jeans that he'd had nothing to eat tonight except a couple of bites of stuffed quail appetizers.

He'd skipped the other reception food, partly because he was more interested in enjoying Dani's company. Admittedly, also because of the fabulous noon meal Esther had on the table when he'd finally arrived at the Double K Ranch after leaving the bakery.

He and his brothers had chastised her for cooking for them when she was so busy with wedding preparations. She'd claimed cooking was her balm when things got hectic.

Maybe that was true of Dani, too. Perhaps she was in her commercial kitchen, pounding and shaping dough or measuring ingredients for her next creation.

But he wasn't familiar with any pastries that smelled like bacon. He headed downstairs without bothering with shoes or a shirt.

Dani was cutting dough into triangles, so absorbed in what she was doing she didn't even notice when he joined her. He stared appreciatively.

She was in faded jeans, the interesting kind with authentic rips in suggestive, though not indecent, places.

Nice hips. Even nicer ass. No red-blooded cowboy under ninety could fail to appreciate that. He struggled to resist walking over and fitting his hands around the tempting buttocks.

"What are you making?" he asked.

She spun around.

"Didn't mean to startle you."

"Not your fault. My nerves are still a bit on edge. I'm making stuffed breakfast croissants. Hope you're hungry. They'll be ready in about twenty minutes."

"I'm starved. Can I help?"

"Sure. You're in charge of the bacon. When it's nice and crispy, lay the strips on the paper towels I spread out on the counter. Once they cool enough to handle, crumble them in bite-size pieces."

"Got it." Her hands seemed to fly as she poured heavy cream into a bowl and added a generous sprinkle of powdered sugar. Using a hand-held electric mixer, she whipped the cream into mounds of fluff.

"What are we going to do with the whipped cream?"

"You'll see," Dani promised. She dipped one finger into the bowl and then held it to his lips.

He sucked and swallowed the gooey sweetness while his imagination went on a wild ride. His appetite switched gears. Now it was Dani he was hungry for.

She went right back to the task at hand, cracking large brown eggs into another bowl. This time she used a fork to beat them until they were the color of lemons and smooth as silk.

He was so mesmerized by her graceful, competent movements that he almost let the bacon burn. He forked it quickly onto the paper towels and turned off the gas.

His ravenous desire for her was as sizzling as the bacon had been. He wasn't exactly getting those same vibes from her, but he couldn't help visualizing what those long, mesmerizing fingers of hers could do to him.

Unless… "Is there a significant other in your life?" he asked as she scrambled the eggs.

"You mean besides Constance, who pretty much rules the roost?"

"Yeah. Some guy you're crazy about who's got you all wrapped up and off the market."

She laughed softly and shook her head. "I'm not sure I was ever really *on the market*, as you put it."

"Why not?"

"I'm a born workaholic. I haven't had a date since Constance came to live with me eight months ago. Tonight's the first time I've danced since the last wedding I attended, and that was over a year ago."

"We'll have to remedy that."

"That would be fun, except that my time for a social life is extremely limited these days."

"I'm starting to think you have something against cowboys."

"Absolutely not. If I did, you'd be getting stale muffins tonight instead of my croissant specialty."

She folded the eggs into the whipped cream while he crumbled the bacon. Next, she spooned the egg mixture across the widest part of the doughy triangles and then sprinkled it with the bacon and grated cheese.

She reached down and grabbed a scoop of flour from somewhere and sprinkled it on the work surface.

"Are you also a magician? It looked like you just pulled that flour from thin air."

"No, but I indulged big for my super-convenient flour-canister drawers. Close the drawer and a built-in cover keeps the flour dry and clean. Open the drawer with a foot control and the canister is open, the flour ready to scoop or measure without my touching sticky or floured hands on clean surfaces."

"Who knew being a pastry chef required so many expensive gadgets?"

"The salespeople who make a living convincing us we need them."

He watched her roll the first one and then joined in, rolling one in the same time it took her to finish the other four. In minutes she'd slid six filled croissants into a hot oven.

"This is guaranteed to be the fanciest midnight snack I ever had," he said. "Of course, you're only competing with a glass of milk and store-bought cookies."

"Store-bought cookies. Wash your mouth out with soap."

"Hate the taste of soap. Do you have any wine?"

"No, but there are a few beers in the larger refrigerator that I keep for when Grace and Pierce come to dinner."

"That's even better."

He retrieved two beers, opened both of them and slid one across the worktable next to where Dani was arranging raspberries and strawberries on two white plates she'd decorated with swirls of chocolate sauce. He felt like he'd crashed a TV cooking show.

As Riley sipped his beer, his mind tripped back to his earlier concerns that she was a target. "I know you said that you had no idea who broke in to the shop."

"I don't," she answered quickly.

"I just thought that since you've had time to think of it, a suspect might have come to mind. Perhaps some jerk who wants to get back at you for some real or perceived injustice?"

She visibly tensed. "No. I've made no enemies since moving here."

"What about before you moved to Winding Creek? A disgruntled employer? A vicious neighbor? Some guy you dumped and broke his heart?"

"No. No one. Look, I don't want to talk about this anymore tonight. I don't even want to think about it."

The conversation had definitely upset her. Her hands shook as she yanked the pan of croissants from the oven and set them down hard on a cooling rack.

All convincing signs she was lying. He had a strong hunch that she knew who'd broken in and was afraid to say. But why? To protect the intruder? Or to protect herself or Constance?

She pushed his filled plate across the counter to him. "You know, now that the back door is secured, there's really no reason for you to stay overnight. You should go home after we eat and get some rest. You're here to see your family and Esther, not to babysit the chef."

"Let me worry about that." He reached across the work surface and covered her hands with his. "If you're having problems, you can trust me, Dani. I'm one of the good guys. Texas roots. Cowboy code. All that and a plate of tacos."

"I am leveling with you."

"Doesn't feel that way."

She pulled her hands away. "It's just been a long day—for both of us. You surely need a break from rescue duties."

She'd tried to lighten her tone, but it wasn't quite working. Riley trailed a finger from her shoulder to her chin and tilted it so that she had to meet his gaze. "Do you want me to go, Dani?"

She sighed and took a deep breath, as if trying to come to grips with her own feelings.

"I'd like you to stay," she murmured. "Just no more talk tonight of the break-in."

"You got it."

"Now let's eat," she said, "before your most-elegant-ever midnight snack gets cold."

He wouldn't push anymore right now, but he wasn't letting this go, either. Not just because she'd crawled under his skin and stirred desire on every level. She might need his help, even if she was too stubborn to admit it.

A few seconds later he bit into the golden, flaky croissant. The warm creamy eggs and crispy bacon filling flooded his mouth and created a heaven for his taste buds.

"What do you think?" Dani asked once he'd swallowed and licked his lips.

"Wow. Will you marry me?" he said, not sure at that exact moment that he was teasing.

"Depends on what kind of job you do on the back door," she teased.

The tension had passed, at least on the surface. But the issue of her safety was far from over. Somehow he had to win her trust.

Which translated to the fact that he'd best control his manly urges. No trying to jump her bones tonight.

DANI WOKE WITH a start, jerking to a sitting position, her mind wedged between nightmare and reality. She shivered, slowly realizing that her cotton nightshirt was soaked in cold sweat.

Even as the dregs of sleep faded, the nightmare continued to stalk the edge of her consciousness. She'd been reaching for Constance, trying to save her before she backed off a craggy ledge. But no matter how close Dani got, Constance remained just out of reach.

Dani hugged her knees to her chest as her eyes adjusted to the dim moonlight squeezing through the blinds and striping the shadowed walls. The terrifying sense of helplessness wouldn't let go.

She was in Constance's room, having insisted Riley, with his much larger frame, sleep in her king-size bed. His being here seemed right on so many levels but wrong on just as many others. He'd come to her rescue without hesitation, taken control, flirted just enough to make her feel feminine and desirable. Mostly he'd made her feel safe tonight.

The nightmare had been a horrifying reminder that locks and reinforced doors couldn't keep her and Constance safe from James Haggard. If he was Constance's biological father, there was a heartbreaking chance that he could gain custody of her.

Amber, how could you have created such a marvelous daughter with a heartless monster like Haggard?

Dani kicked away the covers, crawled from between the sheets and padded to the window. Gathering the hem of her nightshirt between her fingers, she pulled the damp shirt over her head and dropped it to the floor. The pulsing fear of the nightmare settled into an uneasy drumming of her nerves.

She'd feel better if she could hear Constance's voice and know that she was safe. She glanced at the clock—3:00 a.m. She'd only upset everyone in Esther's household if she called now.

But unless she was wrong about Haggard's being the one who broke in to her shop, she'd soon know if he was Constance's biological father, as he claimed.

If it turned out that he was…

She couldn't even go there. All she knew was that as long as she had enough breath to fight, he would never get custody of Constance.

Dawn crept back through the windows before she fell asleep again.

DANI MEASURED THE square of poster board, making marks to ensure that her sign was symmetrical and at least semiprofessional-looking. She wanted it on the door before she tackled the clean-up job.

"Want a refill?" Riley asked as he picked up his empty mug.

"Not until I finish this. I don't want to risk dripping coffee on my work of art. But could you bring me my phone off the counter? I called Esther about thirty minutes ago to check on Constance, and she hasn't called me back."

"They're probably all involved with seeing off Grace and Pierce. Two days is a lousy honeymoon, but I can see why they're putting off their trip to Italy until July. Spring on any ranch is a hectic time."

"So I've heard. Before moving here, I'd never been on a ranch."

"But you do ride horses?"

"I have ridden a few times, mostly since I started spending a little time with Grace at the Double K. I wouldn't say I ride."

"Honey, we have a lot of work to do in a short time. What about Constance? Does she know how to ride?"

A short time. At least he wasn't pretending he was interested in long-term commitment.

"Pierce has been giving Constance riding lessons every Wednesday afternoon. She loves it."

"You can't let her show you up." Riley looked over her shoulder as she started printing. "You know you could just leave the sign that's already on the door turned to closed instead of wasting so much time constructing a new one."

"Not in a town the size of Winding Creek. The regulars know I'm supposed to open at ten on Sundays. If I don't provide at least a minimal explanation, they'll be banging on the locked door trying to make sure I'm okay."

"Checking up on their favorite pastry chef." He refilled his mug and grabbed another warm morning glory muffin from the basket next to the coffeepot. "So, what explanation are you giving them?"

"Closed today for personal emergency."

"Oh, yeah, like that won't get the gossip mills grinding."

"I know, but everyone in town will know about the break-in before the day is over. I just don't want them bothering me while I'm cleaning, especially since I won't be dressed for company."

"When do you plan to reopen?"

"Tuesday morning at my usual time of seven."

"Why not take the whole week off? It's a shame to spend all this beautiful spring inside."

"I can't take off. This is a business. I already have orders for two birthday cakes, petits fours for a bridal shower and filled croissants for a ladies auxiliary committee meeting on Friday night. I can't just toss my responsibilities aside."

"Right." He put up a hand to stop her arguments. "The workaholic's creed."

"That's not it."

Oh, who was she kidding? She hadn't had a real vacation in over a year. Constance was out of school until Thursday. A couple of days off would give them time to have fun together.

Dani couldn't take a week off, but her business wouldn't fall apart if she was closed a couple of extra days.

"Maybe I will take Tuesday and Wednesday off," she said.

"What about your birthday cakes and petit fours?"

"Actually only one of the cakes is due before I'd reopen on Thursday—a birthday cake for Myrtle Higgins's ninety-year-old mother. I'll give Myrtle a call and assure her I'll have it ready whenever she wants to pick it up."

"I like this spontaneous you."

"Now I just have to decide how Constance and I will spend our unexpected mini-vacation."

"I know the perfect place. Close by. Free room and board in a homey ranch house. Wide-open spaces. Fishing. Horseback riding. Picnics by a creek. Roasting hot dogs over a campfire under the stars—with a personal guitar strummer if that's your fancy.

"Best food in nine counties—besides yours, of course. And a personal entertainment guide, guaranteed to please."

"Sounds like an offer too good to refuse."

"Then my job is done. I'll call Esther and tell her to expect two more guests. She'll be thrilled. The more people she can feed, the happier she is."

"Only for Tuesday and Wednesday," Dani said, "if that's actually okay with Esther."

"It's a deal."

It would be a perfect vacation for Constance, who could never get enough of the ranch—Esther was always inviting her out for a few days. And it would mean she could likely avoid James Haggard until after she had the paternity testing results.

There was only one drawback with Riley's plan. He would be the guide guaranteed to please. Love-'em-and-leave-'em Riley Lawrence.

She hated to even think of the hearts he'd left broken in his wake. If she wasn't very careful, she'd be the latest.

"I have just one question," she said.

"Ask away."

"Why do you want me at the Double K Ranch? You have your brothers, Esther and an adorable niece of your own to get to know. Why are you bothering with a headache and a half like me?"

He smiled, the boyish grin that rocked her heart. "I wish I knew, Dani Boatman. I wish to hell I knew. But I'm just a cowboy. Long as I've got a good horse and a decent saddle, I don't question fate."

Chapter Eight

The relief Dani felt after talking to Esther and Constance gave her just the energy jolt she needed to get to down to the serious work of cleaning up.

She ripped through her closet, looking for something old and worn enough she wouldn't mind if it bit the dust during the cleaning process. She pulled out a plastic storage container of clothes that she'd worn for working in her postage-stamp-size yard before moving to Winding Creek.

Rummaging through the oldies, she pulled out a pair of faded jean cutoffs. If she could squeeze into them, they'd be perfect for scrubbing floors. She checked the size label as she stepped into them. Size ten.

She snapped and zipped them easily. If anything they were too loose. Nothing sexy about loose denim, but she was thrilled to be losing a little weight.

Besides, if Riley was looking for sexy model types, he'd have to go find one of the hotties who had been hanging on to him at the reception.

Dani couldn't compete with them and wouldn't try.

Grabbing a gray, slightly-stained T-shirt, she pulled it on, yanking it down to fit around her hips. She slipped her bright-blue polished toes into a pair of flip-flops and checked her appearance in the closet mirror.

Gross.

She ran a brush through the mass of tight curls that hugged her neck and cheeks, a move that did little to tame them. A quick brush of lipstick and she'd have to do.

The front doorbell was ringing as she headed down the stairs, followed by what sounded like a fist pounding on the wood. Adrenaline flooded her veins.

Surely Haggard had better sense than to show up here before the vandalism he'd caused was even cleaned up.

She heard the door open.

"Help has arrived. Let the fun begin!"

It was Tucker, in running shorts and an Oklahoma State T-shirt. "Good morning, gorgeous," he said, giving her a peck on the cheek.

Nice-looking guy. Friendly and funny. So why didn't her heart skip beats when he touched her?

"You're out and about early," she said.

"I figured you could use an extra pair of hands this morning."

"Yes, we can."

"Before I forget, Esther said to tell you that she was taking the girls to Sunday school and church and then to the spring festival and students' rodeo at the high school. She said if that's a problem, let her know. Otherwise, they'll see you later today."

"Not a problem. She mentioned that they might do that when she returned my call earlier this morning. I'd like to have this place back to near-normal before Constance sees it. I can't keep the break-in from her.

There are no secrets in Winding Creek, but I don't want to frighten her."

"Hopefully this will be over and done before she has time to give it much thought. The sheriff will likely have the jerk in jail before the day is over," Tucker said. "Chances are he's already got a good idea who's responsible."

Dani doubted that.

"Did you go shopping?" Riley asked, joining them from upstairs and spying the two large brown bags Tucker had brought in with him.

"No. I raided Esther's supply closet. Figured we might need these." He pulled out a half-gallon bottle of bleach, two large bottles of household cleansers and a half-dozen sponges.

"There's more where these come from. I never realized Esther was such a hoarder, but she has enough assorted household gadgets, jars and cleansers in that closet off the laundry room to supply half the town."

"Hopefully we won't need all this," Dani said, "but then again we might."

Riley looked in the other bag and lifted out two six packs of beer. "Now we're getting down to the real necessities."

"Brewskies before noon?" Dani asked teasingly.

"It's five o'clock somewhere," Riley quipped.

"I also went through your things and discovered a pair of jeans that looked as if you might have worn them to a fight with a wildcat," Tucker said. "Figured if you accidentally splashed bleach on them, it would be an improvement.

Riley held up the jeans. "These are my favorite. You have no appreciation for style."

Tucker folded the emptied brown bags. "So, where do we start, boss lady?"

She loved his attitude.

"If we're not careful, we'll be getting in each other's way all day," she said.

"Agreed," Riley said. "I say Tucker and I tackle the jobs that only require elbow grease and leave the ones that require expertise to you."

Dani went to the counter and grabbed a pad and pen. "We need to clean the floor first. Then all the counters and display cases should be cleaned." She looked around the room. "Even the light fixtures and fans are black."

"What about all the stuff that was on the shelves?" Riley asked. "Some of that will have to be trashed, but some is hopefully salvageable."

"Yes," Dani agreed. "And everything that's trashed will have to be listed and reported to the insurance company." She quickly scribbled down the tasks. "Pick your poison, gentlemen."

"I'll tackle the floors with the vacuum to start with," Tucker offered.

"I'll follow him with a mop," Riley said. "And if you don't mind taking a suggestion from a mere mop maid, you should work on the gift items, Dani."

And they were off. It took her a few minutes to get organized. Just as she started actually sorting the items, Riley returned from changing clothes. He was shirtless and barefoot. The well-worn jeans were snapped just below the waist.

A scattering of dark hairs sprinkled his chest, some curling around his nipples. The hair narrowed into a triangle that disappeared inside the zipper of the faded denim.

Lean. Muscular. Mouthwatering.

She looked like a homeless woman. He looked like a Greek god. No. He looked like a cowboy. A hunky, gorgeous, authentic cowboy.

She struggled to tear her gaze from him before she gave in to the ravenous temptation to trail her fingers down his bare abdomen.

She counted to ten silently and hoped the sensible, controlled workaholic that never melted into unadulterated lust would reappear. It didn't work.

Riley turned on the radio and found a country music station. He and Tucker joined in on half the songs as they worked, Riley actually in key.

When the floors were done, Tucker popped the top on some beers and handed her one. She stood and stretched, then massaged her neck with her fingers.

Riley walked over, stopped behind her and took over the neck-rub duties. His thumbs put pressure in all the right spots to ease the muscle fatigue. His fingers were gentle on her skin, brushing her earlobes, then tangling in the wild, curly locks of her hair.

Her pulse soared until she was giddy with emotions that she could neither understand nor control.

A new song started on the radio, an old classic... slow, mellow. Riley tugged her around to face him and pulled her into his arms. He started to sway, not so much a dance as what felt like a prelude to making love.

She melted against him and then grew tense when she felt his own desire stir and harden. She pulled away quickly.

"What do you think?" he asked.

What she thought was that she was in big trouble. Her expression must have given her away.

"What do you think about the floor?" he added quickly to clarify.

"It's spotless. I'm not sure it's ever been that clean before."

"Well, you've never had me before," Riley teased. "Now that you have, you'll want me back."

"I'm sure I can't afford you."

"I'm always willing to cut a deal."

And that she definitely couldn't afford. She finished her beer and got back to work while Riley went to find a ladder to get started on the ceiling fixtures and Tucker started setting up and cleaning the overturned tables and chairs.

Two hours later, Tucker slipped out to go pick up some tacos for lunch. Dani packed away the last unsalvageable gift item, some cup towels decorated with cupcakes. They were one of her best sellers, but she had another dozen or two in the storeroom.

Most of her money was made from bakery items, but the extras added to her bottom line.

The front doorbell rang again. Dani's muscles tensed. She wasn't afraid of Haggard with Riley and Tucker around, but if they got involved, the complications would increase.

She reached the door a step before Riley did. She took a deep breath and unlatched and opened the door. This time it was Angela Miles.

"I know I'm not supposed to come by for the interview until around four, but I heard about the burglary. I thought maybe there was something I could do to help you get the place cleaned up."

"How did you hear?"

"I was out at Hank's, you know, the country bar down the highway near the gravel pit."

"I know it." She'd never been there, but she'd heard of it.

"They have live music on Saturday and Sunday nights. Anyway, we dropped by there after the wedding. We were just having a beer and dancing when a couple of the deputies came in and started questioning some of the guys at the bar. Word gets around."

Apparently all the way out to Hank's.

"Did they arrest anyone yet?" Angela asked.

"Not that I've heard."

Since Angela was making no move to leave, Dani opened the door for her to come in.

"Oh, hi, Riley," Angela said. "I didn't know you were here."

"I forgot to post it on the town bulletin board," he said.

She laughed, a tinkling, flirtatious sound that didn't resemble anything that had ever come from Dani's mouth.

"I'm here to join the volunteers," Angela said. "Just tell me what to do, and I'll get busy. Maybe I can help you, Riley."

"I'm got my tasks covered. Dani gives the orders around here."

Dani considered Angela's offer, wondering what she was capable of doing, especially dressed the way she was. The red shorts came up to just below her navel and barely covered her rear. Her white blouse was tied above the waist, revealing a band of toned and tanned flesh. Her makeup was heavy, the mascara exceptionally thick for midday on Sunday.

"The display cabinet needs to be cleaned inside and out," Dani said. "Do you think you could handle that?"

"Do you have gloves? I just had my nails done."

"No gloves," she lied, wishing Angela would leave.

"Well, I'll just be careful," Angela said. "I can always get Eve at the Nail Spa to give me a touch-up."

Of course she could. Dani would guess Angela's hands had never been dirty and a broken nail would cause her extreme suffering.

Not only would hiring her be a big mistake, but just letting her in the door was also probably a big mistake.

But Angela had lost her son. Sometimes grief took a bizarre path to healing. Who was Dani to judge? Since Angela was here, Dani could at least give her a chance.

"Start with the outside of the display cases," Dani said.

"I don't want to get the front of my shirt wet. I'll just help Tucker," Angela said.

"No help needed," Tucker said.

She never started on the display cabinets, but merely flirted with the guys for a half hour and then had the nerve to ask about a job.

Dani reluctantly told her to show up at seven on Thursday and they'd see how things worked out.

If it went like today, she'd have no choice but to fire her before the busy weekend.

RILEY STOOD NEAR the front door, where he had a good look at the entire main room of the bakery. "Hard to believe this is the same place I walked into last night."

"And only a few dozen aching muscles later," Tucker added. "Did anyone take a 'before' picture? The transformation is amazing."

"I'd as soon never see that sight again, not even in a photograph," Dani said.

Riley stretched and straddled a chair. "Just too bad the guy who did the vandalizing wasn't the one to do the cleanup."

"With me standing over him with a whip," Tucker added.

"I'd have paid to watch that," Dani said.

"I bet it's one of your regulars," Tucker said, "or maybe one of your delivery people, like the FedEx guy, angry that you never offer him a warm cinnamon roll or a chocolate chip muffin."

Dani waved off the idea. "It's only the FedEx guy in extremely bad fiction, Sherlock. Besides, I always feed my deliverymen. The postman likes the raspberry scones and straight black coffee."

Tucker grinned. "I could go for one of those scones right now myself. But seriously, don't you have some idea who had motive to trash the place? Unjustified motive, but motive."

"No. And I'm sick of thinking about all this. Let it go."

There it was again, Riley thought. She was too quick to deny she suspected the identity of the culprit. Too determined not to discuss the possibilities.

She knew who'd wrecked her place, or at least had a strong suspicion. But why not say—unless she was afraid of him?

He had to get to the bottom of this. To do that, he needed to get her alone—the sooner, the better.

Dani turned her back on both of them and walked toward the kitchen. "I'm going to wash my hands, start a pot of coffee and then go shower and change while the brew perks. I don't have any fresh raspberry scones, but I do have some of my special-recipe cowboy cookies to go with the coffee."

"And exactly what goes into those?" Riley asked.

"Chocolate chips, oatmeal, peanut butter, pecans and a secret ingredient."

"How secret?" Tucker asked.

"If I told you I'd have to ban you from my cookie jar forever."

He crossed his heart. "I swear I'll never ask again."

Riley leaned back, stretched his long legs out in front of him and cradled the back of his head in his hands. He studied Dani's movements, the way she held herself—she was natural, nothing fake or flaunting about her. Her hands were graceful as she attacked everything she did with easy precision.

He wondered how long it would take to reach the point where just the sight of her didn't stir a sensual desire.

"Infatuation becomes you," Tucker said, once Dani had gone upstairs.

"Am I that obvious?"

"Yep."

"It would be hard not to be turned on by Dani," Riley admitted. "She's like a sexy robot, never still, always focused on the task at hand. But then she's got this softness about her, too. She'd make a black bear want to cuddle."

"You do have a poetic side. Who knew?"

"Better than the X-rated limericks we used to make up as teenagers."

"I know. Some of those crazy things still come to mind from time to time. But back to Dani."

"Let's not. What I said probably doesn't make sense to you. I was never great at putting my feelings into words."

"No, I get what you mean about Dani. It's just I'm not sure she's being totally truthful with you or with any of us for that matter."

"Care to clarify?"

"She clammed up awful fast when I asked her about someone having motive to trash the bakery. It was clear she considered the subject off-limits."

"She did the same last night," Riley admitted. "I'm worried that someone may have it in for her. Hopefully, she'll trust me enough to level with me soon."

Tucker nodded. "Also, I have to wonder what she was thinking when she offered Angela Miles a job. That woman's a catastrophe waiting to happen. The way she was hanging on me a couple of times, I figured she should pay for us to get a room."

"Same here. Hell-bent on slutty, and I don't like saying that about any woman. I haven't had a chance to talk to Dani about her, but I figure she's sympathetic to the tragic and bizarre situation involving her father and the death of her son."

"Gotta say, that whole tragedy has the ring of a soap opera."

"I agree," Riley said. "Angela was a year behind me in school until we moved to Kansas to live with Uncle Raymond. She was always a spoiled brat. A form of affluenza, though we didn't have a name for it back then."

"And now her behavior is just weird. I know that Charlie thought the world of Dudley Miles, but now I have to think the whole Miles family is living on the edge of reason."

"I'm considering paying a visit to Dudley Miles."

"In prison?" Tucker asked.

"Why not? He's in a state facility not more than a couple of hours from here."

"I know he was charged with manslaughter, but how did that come about?" Tucker asked.

"The way Esther described it, he was supposed to be watching his toddler grandson, had a drink or two too many and the kid fell off the kitchen counter and died from a head injury.

"I won't bring up the reasons he's behind bars," Riley continued. "I'd just like to get his take on whether or not Charlie committed suicide."

"Good idea. Pierce may want to go with you. I know he's still wrestling with that in his mind. I'd go, too, but I can't stay but a few more days and I think I'll do more good by helping out around the Double K."

"Yeah. I'll stick around until next week's roundup myself—maybe longer."

Maybe a lot longer, though if he was smart he'd run like crazy soon.

He knew himself. Too long in one place and the urge to roam would take over and he'd just wake up one day and hit the open road.

To the next ranch. The next adventure. Alone and uncomplicated.

It was his way.

RILEY LOWERED THE windows in his truck, letting the bracing air flow through Dani's hair and across her face. She was convinced that there was no more invigorating and beautiful time and place than April in the Texas Hill Country.

Trees and rolling pastures turned greener by the day and a million wildflowers burst into bloom with each new sunrise. The late afternoon sky was a background of royal blue, iced with layer upon layer of fluffy white clouds that looked as frothy as the whipped cream she doled out so generously in her shop.

Dani shifted in her seat so that she was facing Riley. He'd showered in her bathroom again before they left for the ranch. She had no doubt that for months to come she'd imagine him naked and glistening with suds every time she stepped into that same shower.

He smelled of soap and musk and a walk in the woods on a spring morning. He reeked of virility. And if she didn't stop thinking like this, she'd wind up in his arms again with or without any pretense of dancing.

She turned her gaze back to the road that stretched in front of them. The road Riley had come in on just yesterday on his way to the Double K Ranch.

The road he'd leave on any day now.

Riley reached over and flicked on the radio, keeping it low so that they could still talk if they had something to say. So far they'd ridden most of the way to the ranch in silence.

"Is the wind too much for you with the windows down?" he asked.

"No, it feels good. Clears the stench of bleach and cleansers out of my sinuses."

"I always ride with the windows down unless the heat and humidity are like an oven—which definitely happens when summer arrives full blast in Texas. Most women complain that it messes up their hair."

"Mine is always a mussed tangle of curls, so that's not a problem for me."

"I like your mussed look," he said. "It suits you."

"Mussed suits me? That doesn't sound exactly like a compliment."

"Ah, but it was. Makes me want to wind those curls around my fingertips. Makes you so touchable."

"Best not to while you're driving," she teased. "My curls are dangerous. Your fingers might become so entangled in the thick mass we'd end up in a wreck."

"Not if we pulled off onto the shoulder first or turned onto a dirt road."

She wasn't sure if he was serious or joking, but her insides quivered at the thought.

Her phone rang. Saved by the bell. She answered quickly, her voice tinged with the unfamiliar sensations rushing her senses. "Hello."

"Hi. It's Crystal. I just heard about the break-in. Are you and Constance okay?"

"We're fine." She explained the situation, providing only the details necessary for clarity.

"I hadn't heard about the vandalism. Is there anything I can do to help? Bring you dinner? Scrub floors? Come pick up Constance?"

"No. Constance spent last night at the Double K Ranch. I'm on my way to pick her up as we speak. The bakery is clean and ready to go."

"So you'll open again on Tuesday?"

"Believe it or not, I'm actually taking a few days off. I want to keep Constance having so much fun she can't worry about our being burglarized."

"I'm impressed and I think that's a great idea. I'm closed on Monday. Why don't we take the girls hiking at the state park? The drive there is beautiful this time of the year and we'll get some fresh air and exercise."

"I'd love to, but I have some business in San Antonio I have to take care of tomorrow."

"Then let Constance spend the day with us. The girls always have fun together."

That would be the perfect solution—provided the DNA kit actually arrived in the morning. Otherwise she'd have to take Constance into the city with her to be certain she collected the sample correctly.

"Constance would love a hiking outing, but can I get back to you in the morning? I want to get a feel for how Constance is handling all this first."

"Sure thing. And do let me know if I can do anything to help around the shop or if you just need a place to crash for a few days."

"I will, but right now everything's under control."

More specifically, as much under control as it could be under the circumstances.

By the time she'd broken the connection, Dani couldn't wait to see Constance. And once again she wondered what kind of perverted bastard James Haggard was that he basically wanted to sell his own daughter.

But then her sister had sold herself for far less than a million dollars, so this might be exactly the kind of man she'd have a child with.

Dani jumped from the truck the second Riley stopped in front of the sprawling ranch house. Constance met her at the door, all smiles and showing no sign of distress.

Dani pulled her into her arms and held so tight Constance pushed her away.

"You're hurting my ribs."

"Sorry, sweetheart. I missed you so much."

And she'd fight the devil himself to keep her safe. The scary part was, it might come down to exactly that.

Chapter Nine

"Jaci couldn't ride the big Ferris wheel because she's too young, but I rode it with Carolyn Sawyer. Her little brother was too young to ride it, too."

Jaci put her hands on her hips. "I can ride it when I'm six."

"We both rode the carousel," Constance said, "and Esther rode it, too."

Esther put her right hand to her heart. "About the only kind of horse I can ride these days. That was enough excitement for me."

"I got prizes," Jaci said. "Want to see them?"

"Prizes? Wow," Dani said encouragingly. "Of course I want to see them."

"All I got was a whistle and some bubble-blowing liquid," Constance said, "but the bubble-blowing stuff is all gone. I shared with Jaci."

"That was nice."

For the past half hour or more, the girls had talked nonstop about their adventure at the spring carnival. Clearly, Constance hadn't let any concern about the break-in interfere with her fun. It was nice to be eight.

Jaci returned with her prizes, all five of them together probably worth less than a dollar. But she'd won them and that was all that mattered.

"You girls had positively too much fun," Riley said. "And yes, I'm talking about you, too, Esther."

Jaci and Constance giggled at the thought of Esther being a girl.

"I'm sorry I missed it," Dani said. "I can't thank you enough, Esther, for taking Constance with you."

"No trouble at all," Esther insisted.

"Keeping up with these two wound-up bundles of energy has to be exhausting. Constance and I will get out of here now and let you get some rest."

"You can't run off before supper," Esther said. "I'm making macaroni and cheese for the girls."

"That's far too much trouble."

"No, it isn't, Aunt Dani. Ple-e-ease. I love macaroni and cheese, and Tucker is fixing the rope on that broken tire swing so that Jaci and I can play on it."

"You've already put Tucker to work for you, too?"

"He'd promised Jaci yesterday that he'd get to it today," Esther said. "All my Lawrence boys are as good as their word. They got that from Charlie."

"We're not exactly boys anymore," Riley said, "but Charlie taught us a lot about good living and being a man of your word. That's no lie."

"C'mon, Jaci," Constance said. "Let's go see if the swing is fixed."

Dani gave up on the idea of leaving before supper. That wasn't a sacrifice on her part. Everything Esther cooked was delicious. Even better, the girls hadn't gotten tired and cranky and started fussing with each other yet.

In spite of the three years between them, they got

along well most of the time. That was one of the reasons she and Grace had become such good friends so quickly. They were both new to town. They were both still learning to be caretakers of energetic, precocious little girls.

Grace's role as new stepmother was somewhat different than Dani's, but both Grace and Dani loved every part of their new lives, including the responsibility. Neither of them wanted to make a single mistake, though they knew that was impossible.

"Did you hear from Pierce or Grace today?" Dani asked.

"Heard from both of them," Esther said. "They were sipping margaritas on the River Walk and having a wonderful time."

"Sounds romantic," Riley said.

"Yes, but they're cutting the short honeymoon even shorter."

"Why?" Riley asked. "Is anything wrong?"

"Plenty." She reached over and patted Riley on the shoulder. "You and Tucker are here and Pierce is not. It's like we're having a family reunion without him."

"How does his new bride feel about that?"

"Land sakes. That wife of his is sweeter than stolen honey, and Grace understands Pierce. She's the one who made the decision that it was silly to be in San Antonio now when they can go there anytime."

"He's probably just worried Tucker and I aren't following all his orders," Riley joked.

"That, too," Esther agreed. "He told me to remind you to feed and water the horses tonight and Tucker to put out feed for the rest of the livestock and check on the pregnant cows."

"With all that to do around here, now I really feel terrible that I dragged you and Tucker off to help me," Dani said.

"Exactly," Riley agreed. "Now it's payback time. You get to help me take care of the horses."

"I'm not sure how much help I'll be. I know ridiculously little about horses."

"Not a problem. What you don't know, I'll teach you."

The humor in his tone and the mischievous glint in his eyes insinuated he wasn't only talking about horses. Fiery flashes of desire heated her senses.

They weren't strangers anymore. They'd spent most of the last two days together. In chaos, fun, frustration and cleansers.

It was inevitable that the sexual tension that tinged each touch, each moment they spent together, would eventually erupt into a roaring fire. That eruption might very well come tonight.

THIS WASN'T DANI'S first time in the Double K's horse barn, but it seemed entirely different this evening.

It seemed smaller, as if Riley sucked all the oxygen from the area and left her struggling for air. Every nerve in her body seemed to vibrate with anticipation, though she wasn't exactly sure what she was anticipating.

Wooden signs with the horses' names hung over each stall, but Dani was familiar enough with a few of them that she could recognize them even when they were in the pasture.

Some, like Dreamer and Beauty, she felt fairly comfortable around. The bigger stallions, like Rocket and Torpedo, she shied away from.

A few of the horses neighed as Riley walked past them on his way back to the feed storage area. Dreamer pawed and stuck her head over the top of her stall to be sure she was noticed. Beauty, the black quarter horse that Constance usually rode, pretended she didn't notice him.

Dani walked over to Beauty's stall and stood still for a few moments so as not to startle her. Then she put her hand out below the horse's nose, palms up, fingers pressed together, just as Pierce had shown her. Beauty lowered her head and stepped closer.

"Hello, Beauty. I don't usually get to visit you this late. Are you glad to see me?" She reached over the top of the stall and scratched the horse's neck and withers.

"I see you're not a total novice around horses," Riley said.

"Pierce, Grace and Esther have taken me under their wing."

"Have you fed the horses before?"

"Carrots, apple chunks or an occasional peppermint."

"Want to try ladling their grain mix into their feed pails? Unless you'd rather fill their water pails. The feed is easier."

He was serious about her helping. She felt foolish for thinking he had an ulterior motive for asking her to come with him. It was her own infatuation that was getting out of hand. "I'll feed them the grain if you show me how much and where to put it."

He gave her basic instructions and she measured the mixture and ladled it into the feed buckets as Riley took the pails to the outdoor hose and rinsed and refilled them.

He talked to the horses in a voice that calmed them and resulted in nuzzling and head movements that seemed to indicate they understood him. These were horses that had never seen him before yesterday.

He stopped at Huckleberry's stall. "What's the matter, boy? You've got a limp there. Want me to take a look at it?"

He opened the stall, squatted and picked up the right front hoof. "Looks like you have a stone wedged in there. Doesn't feel too good, does it? I'll take care of that. Won't even hurt."

Dani watched as he retrieved a hoof pick and loosened and removed the stone from the horse's hoof. Then he brushed the hoof thoroughly, removing smaller pieces of debris.

"We got it, boy. All done."

Huckleberry made a low nicking sound and nuzzled Riley's shoulder as if he was saying thank you. Dani stood silently and watched the show of affection, too moved to speak.

Finally she walked over to where Riley was putting away the brush. "Are you a horse whisperer?"

He laughed. "Never been called that before."

"But you're so good with the horses. It's like you're speaking the same language."

"Horses aren't that big a mystery if you pay attention to their actions. They show you what they need from you. Just like a man does. If you don't need the same, you have to let him know."

His voice had softened to a whisper. His gaze was intense, hypnotic, and she knew they were no longer talking about horses.

The need inside her swelled until she was dizzy.

Riley pulled her into his arms and lowered his face until their lips touched. In that moment every ounce of control vanished, melted in the heat of his kiss.

Chapter Ten

Dizzy with desire, Dani swayed against Riley as the kiss deepened. The pulsing need swelled, vibrating through every erogenous cell in her body. She parted her lips, and his tongue slipped inside her mouth. Thrusting. Probing. Ravenous. As if he couldn't get enough of her.

He pulled her closer still and she arched toward him until his erection pressed hard against her trembling body. He lifted her and let her slide down the hard length of his need.

A soft moan escaped her lips and he slipped his right hand beneath her shirt, his fingers like fire on her skin as he traced a path to her breast. The first two snaps on her paisley Western shirt burst open.

He cupped her breasts and her nipples tingled and grew hard as he massaged and tweaked them. He sucked her bottom lip and then kissed his way down the smooth column of her neck until his face was buried in the swell of her breasts.

She couldn't think, couldn't deal with anything except the pleasure that possessed her. Right or wrong, she was lost in the ecstasy with no will to fight it.

Her phone rang. She was so riveted to the carnal hunger that gripped her that she didn't even hear it until

Riley pulled away. She checked the caller ID. "It's Cavazos."

"Damn bad timing that man has. But you should probably see what he wants."

She took a deep breath and exhaled slowly, hoping to regain enough composure that Cavazos didn't detect her passion overload over the phone. "Hello, Sheriff."

"Glad I caught you, Dani. I have good news. I think we've arrested your burglar. No proof yet, but my hunch is he's a credible suspect."

She hadn't expected that. "Who is it?"

"Young feller named Cory Boxer. He and a group of his fraternity brothers are using one of the fishing cabins a few miles up the river from here. Doing more partying than fishing from what I could tell."

His suspect was not James Haggard. There must be some mistake.

"Did Cory Boxer admit to the vandalism?"

"He's denying it, but one of my best deputies caught the guy red-handed, breaking in to the trunk of Joe Clark's car in broad daylight."

Joe Clark. She recognized the name. He and Jill owned the gift and card shop on Second Street, about two blocks from her bakery.

"Where was the car parked?" she asked.

"In the alleyway behind their shop. Joe carried in some boxes of merchandise he was helping Jill shelve. Wasn't in the shop more than a few minutes when he came out and saw Boxer standing over his open trunk and peering inside."

"Did Joe confront him?"

"He hollered at him. The guy took off running. Joe took off after him since he wasn't sure if he'd taken anything. One of my deputies spotted them and he stepped in and made the arrest."

"But he denied breaking in to my shop?"

"Yes, but he also argued he wasn't up to no good when Joe saw him with his head stuck in the trunk."

"Was anything missing from the trunk?"

"Nope. Luckily, Joe spotted him before he made off with his laptop which was right there in plain sight. Darn shame when a man has to lock his car downtown in broad daylight."

Still, checking out an unlocked truck in a deserted alley wasn't quite the same as breaking into and vandalizing a bakery.

"We'll get a fingerprint check to make sure we have the right guy, but just wanted you to know you can rest easier tonight. I've got a prime suspect in central lockup for twenty-four hours."

"I appreciate your calling."

A stranger with no motive to wreck her business. If the sheriff was right, the DNA she'd collected was worthless to her. She was back to square one again. Except… "Did Cory Boxer have any wounds?"

"Matter of fact, he had some ugly scratches on one arm. Said a cat got hold of him. Why do you ask?"

"I found some blood. I think my vandal must have hurt himself in the process."

"Makes more sense than getting scratched by a cat. I reckon you've seen the last of this kind of trouble, hopefully for a good long while."

"Yes, hopefully," she agreed. But even if Cory Boxer had broken into her shop, this was not the last of James Haggard.

When the call was finished, she shared the news with Riley.

"You don't sound very relieved," he said.

Surprisingly, she wanted to spill the full truth to him. The anxiety had burgeoned with the sheriff's arrest of a suspect other than Haggard. Or maybe she just wanted some reassurance that she was making the right decisions.

It was too chancy to drag him into this while she was still reeling from his kisses.

He'd go his way in a few days. If it turned out Haggard was Constance's biological father, her battles would be just beginning.

THE GLOW OF twilight painted the sky with wide brushes of burnished gold. It was the time of day on a ranch when the magic came together—the time Riley felt like the luckiest man on earth, living the dream.

A lot of cowboys he knew were poets. He'd always wished words came that easy to him, but mostly he just responded with a peaceful feeling, at home with himself and the whole beautiful country to roam.

Tonight held a different kind of magic that had nothing to do with the pastoral splendor. It had everything to do with Dani Boatman.

He couldn't explain it, no more than he could explain the lure of the open range. He couldn't deny it, either. He felt things differently with Dani.

It wasn't just the way she'd turned him on back in the horse barn. He'd felt that way even before they'd kissed. He couldn't imagine ever getting enough of her. This was not how his visit to Texas was supposed to go.

He'd figured he'd visit with his brothers and Esther,

get acquainted with his niece and new sister-in-law, do some fishing and then head out to West Texas before all that togetherness started to make him feel fenced in.

No reflection on his brothers or Esther, but it was Dani he wanted to be with. Mostly it was just enjoying her company, but the need to protect her was high on the list, too. And that was where he found himself now.

The facts didn't add up. Dani should have been relieved that the sheriff had arrested a suspect. Instead, she'd seemed annoyed or worried. Also, she'd never mentioned finding bloodstains to him, though he must have been nearby when she discovered them.

There was more going on than she was admitting. Somehow he had to find a way to get her to open up to him.

The front door opened and Dani and Constance stepped out, joining him on the porch. Constance was dragging her backpack, the head of a freckled doll in braids that looked a lot like her peeking out of the half-zipped bag.

Dani had her handbag over her shoulder and a reusable green bag no doubt filled with eggs or something from Esther's garden.

"I was wondering where you'd gotten off to," Dani said. "I was looking for you to tell you goodbye."

"It's early. With all the talk and laughter surrounding that board game you were playing, I didn't expect you to be leaving for hours."

"I wasn't ready to go," Constance assured him. "Aunt Dani said we have to."

"I'm the baddie," Dani joked. "If only we didn't need sleep."

"Oh, wait," Constance called, forgetting her argument. "I left my whistle." She went rushing back into the house.

Dani laughed. "I should have tossed that squeaky toy while I had the chance."

She started down the steps. Riley walked beside her, hesitant to see her leave without him.

He couldn't get past the uneasiness she'd exhibited when taking to the sheriff. Nor could he brush off the impression she'd given last night and again today that she knew or at least strongly suspected the identity of the intruder.

"I think you should invite me home with you for a slumber party," he said, trying for a nonchalance he didn't feel.

"Sounds tempting, I admit, but I'm not ready to go there with Constance in the house."

"I'll sleep on the sofa and I promise I won't make a move on you tonight, even if you beg," he teased.

"Such a gentleman. I don't think you'd even fit on my sofa." She stopped by her car and looked up at him. "What's this really about, Riley?"

"I think you might be uneasy staying alone so soon after the break-in."

"I'll be fine. Seriously. You secured the back door. You can't be my full-time caretaker."

"Just until you get the alarm system fixed."

"I'll call them first thing in the morning. The sheriff indicated I have nothing to worry about."

But he wasn't sure she believed Cavazos, and if she didn't, how could he?

"If you don't share your sofa, I'll camp out on the street in front of the bakery," he said. "Imagine the gossip that will cause."

"Do you ever take no for an answer, Riley Lawrence?"

"All depends on the question."

She rolled her eyes. "Okay, but follow me back in your truck. I'll need my car in the morning."

"Give me a minute to grab a few necessities like a razor and a toothbrush."

She'd given in too easily, which meant she was somewhat nervous about her and Constance being alone tonight even if she wasn't admitting that to him. She might not even be admitting it to herself.

The next challenge was finding a way to make her trust him enough to tell him the truth about what was going on. Which meant he'd have to keep his word not to come on to her tonight.

And that might take all the control he could muster.

JAMES HAGGARD HEARD the blaring sounds of a mediocre country band when he stepped out of his pickup truck in Hank's parking lot. He wouldn't stay long. Two beers at the most. It was when he was drunk or high that he made foolish mistakes.

Like breaking in to Dani's Delights.

His brother, Lenny, had warned him to stay in the cabin and make sure he wasn't seen around town until he went back to pick up his money on Friday.

Lenny was always right. He took care of James. Always had. He was the only who'd never lied to James, or cheated him. The only one who didn't take advantage of him every chance he got. The only one James trusted.

But Lenny wasn't the one stuck inside that cheap, ratty cabin that stank like dead fish. He had to get out for a little while or he'd go crazy. He walked through the double doors into the stench of stale smoke and the tantalizing smell of whiskey. He went straight to the bar and dropped onto a tall stool.

"A shot of Jack. Make that a double," he added, already backing down from his vow of sticking to two beers. He gulped down the whiskey in one swallow and swiveled so that he could see the band.

The female singer reminded him of Amber back in the day, except that the singer wasn't nearly the looker Amber had been. In his mind, he always remembered her as she'd looked the night they'd met. Short white shorts, a halter top, no bra and those bright red stiletto heels.

Her auburn hair cascaded down her back in loose curls. And those lips, those full, heart-shaped lips that could drive any man crazy.

But she'd changed. She'd treated him like dirt. Walked all over him. He motioned to the bartender. "Another double."

The singer might not be as pretty as Amber, but he'd bet she was the same two-timing, double-crossing, bitch Amber had become. And after all he'd done for her.

He was Constance's father. Half of that damn insurance money rightly belonged to him. Dani had better believe he meant business.

A blonde strutted over and took the stool next to him. "Want to buy a girl a drink?"

"Sure." He looked her over. Firecracker-hot. A red dress that hugged every curve. A little drunk, but he might be there himself in a few minutes. "You got a name?"

"Angela." She leaned in close, giving him a good

look at the breasts pushing out of a scrap of lacy black bra. "I haven't seen you around here before."

"Just passing through."

"Too bad. We might have gotten to know each other."

He put a hand on her thigh. She didn't move it away.

"We can still get to know each other," he ventured. "We just have to work faster."

She laughed, a tinkling sound that crawled right under his skin.

The night might not be such a drag after all.

RILEY QUICKLY CAUGHT up with Dani's car. He followed it to the downtown area but pulled away at the head of Main Street. Driving slowly, he took the alley that ran behind her shop.

The area was quiet without even a cat to be seen tonight. The bakery's back door was still boarded over just as he and Tucker had left it last night. He stopped, crawled from beneath the wheel and took the few steps to the fenced area.

All clear, so he turned at the corner and drove back to Main Street. Ten before nine on a Sunday night and the locals were settled in for the night. The quiet isolation, the hitching posts, the century-old wooden buildings and the soft glow from the antique streetlights gave the eerie impression that he'd stepped into the Old West.

He pulled into the diagonal parking spot next to Dani's car. She was standing at the open back door. He didn't see Constance until he was standing next to Dani.

"She's sound asleep," Dani whispered. "Has been almost ever since we left the ranch. Little stinker would never have admitted that she was tired."

Dani tugged on Constance's arm. "Wake up, baby. We're home."

Constance mumbled in her sleep and curled even tighter into the fetal position.

"We're home, sweetheart. You have to get out of the car so we can go inside."

Constance opened her eyes and rubbed them with her fists. Dani helped her to a sitting position and managed to get her to the edge of the seat.

"Let her sleep," Riley said. "I'll tote her upstairs. What's the use of having your own cowboy bodyguard if you can't get a few perks?"

Riley reached down and picked her up, carrying her as if she was an oversize doll. "You get the door," he said. "I'll carry her up to her bed."

Constance's arms tightened around his neck and she rested her head on his shoulder. His throat grew dry, making it difficult to swallow. He wasn't sure he'd ever carried a kid before. The most he'd done was help one in or out of a saddle. This felt too...

He wasn't sure what it felt. Too much like a family? Too involved? Too fatherly.

He experienced a sudden suffocating sensation. What the hell was a man like him doing in a situation like this? His breathing came hard as he pushed back the impulse to get back in his truck and drive away.

Instead he started walking calmly toward the bakery as the frightening truth hit full force. He was already where he really wanted to be.

DANI GULPED IN a deep breath as she stepped into her bakery and let the familiarity seep into her bones. The lingering odors of spices and baking bread. The empty display cases calling out to be filled. The chairs and tables awaiting customers.

For a man like Riley, who never settled in one place long enough to put down roots, this life probably felt like fatal boredom. To her, it was a dream come true.

Their lives would never mesh. They were a few days in a lifetime, a thrill that would live in her memories, a mountain high before the next valley. As long as she didn't expect more than that, she'd be fine.

She set Constance's backpack on the floor and went back to the car for the two dozen fresh eggs Esther had insisted she bring home with her. She checked to make sure Riley's car was locked and then opened the passenger-side door of her car to retrieve the eggs.

She sniffed and caught the stench of cigarette smoke and alcohol. Footfalls approached from the street behind her. She jumped back from the car as panic rocked her ragged nerves.

"Luch who sh-h-owed up."

Dani's heart flew to her throat. Even with the drunken slur, there was no mistaking James Haggard's voice.

Chapter Eleven

Haggard staggered forward and fell against Dani's front bumper.

"You're drunk," she said.

"Damn r-r-right." He stumbled nearer.

She scanned the area. Only two cars other than hers were parked on this block. Both of them belonged to shop owners with upstairs living quarters. "How did you get here?"

Haggard waved his arm as if dismissing her question. His hand was bandaged. She stared at it, breathing hard. It was his blood she'd collected. *His* DNA. Her instincts screamed that was true, but she needed proof.

"Why did you break in to my shop last night?" she demanded. "What were you looking for?"

His response was a string of profanity and words so slurred she couldn't make sense of them.

"You were here last night," she persisted. "Admit it."

He mumbled a curse and then used the cuff of his shirt to wipe spittle from his lips and chin.

"I'm not afraid of you, James Haggard. Wrecking my shop won't help you get what you want."

"Wre-e-ecked it. Next time. Burn it down."

The slurred pronouncements were followed by another assault of foul language.

But he had said next time, which had to mean he'd been here last night. The blood she'd collected was his. That was all she needed to know.

Dani tried to push past him. Haggard grabbed her right arm. He lost his balance and fell against her, clutching her shirt with both hands in an effort not to slam to the pavement.

Miraculously, she managed to hold both of them up. "What the devil…"

Dani looked up as Riley flew out the door and stormed across the walk. Reaching down, he grabbed Haggard by his shirt collar and yanked him away from Dani.

She grabbed Riley's right arm as he was about to punch Haggard. "Don't. He's just drunk. I know him."

Haggard tried to shove Riley away. Riley easily pinned him against the car.

"Your friend needs to learn some manners," Riley said.

"I said I know him. I didn't say he was a friend."

Haggard started cursing again, spraying the air with saliva. Riley let go of him and Haggard slid slowly down the fender, landing on his butt, his shoulder pressed against the tire.

"Call 911," Riley said. "He can sleep it off in jail."

And then the law would be involved and things might spin out of control just as Haggard had warned. A custody suit. Constance used as a pawn.

"I'd rather not bring the law into this."

"I seem to be missing something here. Exactly how well do you know this man?" Riley asked.

"Not well," she admitted.

"If you know where he lives, I'll drive him home."

"I don't."

"What about the name of someone in his family we can call to come get him?"

She shook her head. "I don't know anything about him. He's just a customer."

"Then what's your problem with letting law enforcement handle this, especially considering someone broke into and vandalized your bakery last night?"

She hated lying to Riley and knew it was unlikely that he was buying her story. No one would. But if she gave Riley any part of the truth, he'd manage to get the whole story out of her.

He'd jump into the middle of the situation.

Subconsciously, she might even want that, but it wouldn't be fair to Riley on any level and she might completely lose control of everything.

Dani watched as Riley helped Haggard to a standing position and then half dragged the intoxicated man to the metal bench across the street from the bakery. Haggard's feet stretched out in front of him. He slumped forward. His eyes closed.

Riley walked back to Dani and took her hands in his. "Here's the deal. We're going inside and you're going to tell me the truth. The actual truth and not some doctored version of the facts. Once I know what the hell is going on, we'll decide what to do with your vulgar-mouthed, drunk acquaintance."

"You'd be wiser to get in your truck and drive away."

"Probably, but I've got a mighty strong hunch that you're in a heap of trouble, Dani Boatman, and like it or not, you need my help."

He was right, of course. Things had gone too far, become incredibly complicated. Continuing the lies wouldn't be fair to him.

Once they were back inside, she searched for a truthful way of presenting the details that didn't scream for his help. Riley listened to Dani's bizarre explanation and to his credit he didn't interrupt or comment until she'd finished.

He stared incredulously. "What kind of fool would expect you to just turn over a million dollars without any proof to back up his claims of paternity?"

"The kind of fool you just helped to the bench. Only he talked as if I already knew he was the father and deliberately cut him out of money that was rightfully his."

"How were you supposed to have gotten that information?"

"From Constance's original birth certificate."

"Where is her birth certificate?"

"Upstairs in my safe. No father is listed. I told him that, but I don't think he believed me."

"Sounds like he's a practiced rip-off artist to me," Riley said. "He may not even know your sister or Constance. He might have heard or read about the insurance settlement and is trying to con you out of the cash."

"I wouldn't put that past him," she agreed. "But I can't know that for sure without seeing DNA test results."

"If he is Constance's biological father and thought he had a chance in hell of getting custody, he wouldn't bother with you," Riley said. "He'd file for custody and try to cash in on the entire settlement."

"He admitted he doesn't want custody. He wants cash—by Friday at noon."

"I'm sure he does. You surely aren't planning to give it to him."

"I couldn't even if I wanted to. The money is in a trust fund for Constance and can't be touched until she's twenty-one. The one exception is that she can draw out an allowance to pay for college and living expenses if she is a full-time student at the accredited university of her choice."

"Did you tell Haggard that?"

"All except the college stipulation. He didn't believe me or else he thinks there is some way around that. He wants his money within the week or he files for custody."

"Nothing but trash talk from a con man and that's the best I can say about him. I should have punched the drunken thug when I had the chance."

Physical violence was the last thing she needed.

"Call the sheriff, Dani. Tell him exactly what you just told me. He won't even have to go looking for Haggard to arrest him."

"It's not that simple."

"It is the way I see it. Get a restraining order to keep the lunatic away from you and Constance. If Haggard still gives you trouble, the Lawrence brothers will pay him a visit. We can be very persuasive."

"I'm sure you can, but I can't take chances with Constance's future. I have to do this my way."

"What is your way?"

Dani explained the blood sample she'd collected and the paternity-test kit that should arrive in the morning. "With luck, I'll have the test results back by Thursday or Friday. If they show Haggard is not Constance's father, I'll call the sheriff and press charges immediately."

"And if he is?"

"I'll do whatever it takes to make sure he never gets custody."

"In that case I'm going with you to San Antonio in the morning."

She threw her hands up in exasperation. "I can handle this. They need you at the ranch."

"Tucker will be there and Pierce is heading back in the morning."

"He's cutting his honeymoon short so that he can spend time with you and Tucker."

"My brothers would do the same in these circumstances. Besides, I will be spending time with them and so will you and Constance. There's no reason your ranch vacation can't start tomorrow night."

"I can't believe you'd still want me there."

"I've always been a sucker for a woman who looks good in jeans and can bake croissants. I do have one question, though."

"I was afraid you might."

"You collected the blood last night. You must have strongly suspected then that Haggard was behind the break-in. Why didn't you admit that to me?"

"I didn't want to drag you into my problems."

He walked over, caught her wrist and pulled her into his arms. "Is that the only reason?"

"No. I didn't trust you to understand. I barely knew you, Riley. We had no basis of trust."

He nudged her chin with his thumb until she met his gaze. "Do you trust me now?"

"I'm trying, Riley. It's just so hard to let go. I've never had anyone to depend on but myself."

"Now you do. I can't explain what's going on between us, Dani. I do know that if you don't let me protect you I'll go crazy. How's that for my scientific analysis?"

He kissed her on the tip of her nose and then let his lips brush hers. The need swelled inside her, but he pulled away.

"Go upstairs and get some rest," he whispered. "Just toss a sheet and a pillow on the sofa. I'll be up later."

"I should check on Haggard first—see if he's sober enough to say where he's staying. I may need that information for future reference."

"I'll check on the swindler."

"Okay." She turned and started toward the stairs. She stopped on the bottom step. "Riley."

"What is it?"

"You really shouldn't be here, but thanks. See you at breakfast."

Breakfast with Dani. Crazy how much he liked the sound of that.

RILEY WAITED UNTIL Dani reached the top of the stairs and then walked into her gleaming kitchen. There wasn't much in there he dared to touch, but he had watched her make coffee in the small French press that morning and he felt good about tackling that.

Probably easier than brewing a pot over an open campfire, though it wouldn't give the same level of satisfaction—especially since he was making this pot for Haggard. He couldn't care less if the jerk slept on the bench all night or curled up under it.

His concern was getting the point across to Haggard that the man's underhanded, thieving gig was up. Keep messing with Dani and he'd answer to Riley. Riley never started a fight without good cause, but he never backed down from one that needed to be won.

He filled a tall white mug with the brew and took it outside to try to rouse Haggard. A brisk breeze carried the fragrance of honeysuckle and jasmine from a hanging pot across the street.

All was quiet. Too quiet. No guttural snoring. No ragged breathing.

The bench was empty.

Either someone had picked Haggard up, or that was the fastest damn sobering up Riley had ever seen. He flicked on his phone's flashlight app and checked the space between their parked vehicles to make sure he hadn't staggered there. No luck.

He walked back and shot beams of light around and beneath the bench to see if Haggard had dropped anything that might give a clue to where he was staying. There was nothing.

A deputy or town constable patrolling the area could have picked him up, but if so, it was odd Riley hadn't noticed any flashing blue lights through the bakery's large window.

Which meant there was a good chance Haggard was not in this alone. So, was it his blood Dani had collected or that of an accomplice? Would the test she was putting so much faith in prove nothing at all?

BREAKFAST IN THE small kitchen of the cozy second-floor living space was mistake one of the new day. An emotional wreck from the chaotic weekend and her unexpected infatuation with Riley, Dani needed a break from the nonstop sensual overload.

She wasn't getting it. Riley had insisted on "fixin'

up" an authentic Texas, trail-ride breakfast even though it meant a quick trip to the local market for fresh tortillas and ingredients for fresh-made *pico de gallo*.

He wanted to prove he wasn't completely without skills in the kitchen, he'd said.

She hadn't needed that proof. She'd experienced his kitchen skills Friday night and was still recovering. Sleeping a room away from him last night hadn't helped the recuperative process.

And now this.

The food was not the mistake. The problem was the three of them gathered around the comfy dining nook talking, laughing and passing around the *pico de gallo* and extra grated cheese as if they were a family.

Not the kind of family setting Dani had ever known and probably not Constance, either. She wasn't sure about Riley's family life, except that his parents were killed when he was fourteen and he and his brothers had come to live with Charlie and Esther Kavanaugh.

She did know he was a rambler, which made their relationship and this easy familiarity all the more confusing. He was determined to protect her, but what did he really want in return?

And the most puzzling aspect of all—why Dani? If he was looking for a fast and easy fling, why not go for a thin, sexy, fun-and-games hottie like Angela Miles instead of a plump pastry chef whose life was a boiling pot of trouble?

She took a bite of her fried egg and sausage taco. The combination of flavors exploded in her mouth.

"And the verdict?" Riley asked.

"Great, but with a kick."

He leaned over—close—as if he was about to kiss

her. At the last second, he dabbed the corner of her mouth with a napkin. "You may have overdone it with the salsa."

Her pulse slowed to near normal, but the air was thick with sensual tension.

"I like tortillas, but not as much as I like Aunt Dani's cinnamon rolls," Constance said, breaking the tension without even knowing it existed.

"Yes, but could she make cinnamon rolls out on the trail over a campfire?"

"No, I can't, cowboy, and I have no intention to try it."

"Is this really what cowboys eat on the trail?" Constance asked.

"It is if you're in Texas and lots of other places. The vaqueros have been a major influence in the ranching world."

"What's a vaquero?"

"That's Spanish for cowboy."

"Have you ever been on a cattle drive?"

"Yep. Many times. I don't usually do the cooking, though."

"What do you do?"

"Keep the cattle moving in the right direction."

"Or they might get lost?"

"A good cowboy will never let that happen."

"I wish I could go on a cattle drive."

"You'd have to miss too much school for that, but maybe we should start getting in shape for that tomorrow with a sunrise trail ride out at the Double K Ranch. I hear you're a good rider."

"I am. Jaci's daddy taught me. Can I go, Aunt Dani?

Puh-leeeze." She put her hands together in prayer for-
mation.

Dani realized she'd been had. Riley had just made it
practically impossible now to back out of spending at
least one day at the ranch. Not that she wanted to back
out, but who knew what complication James Haggard
would hurl her way next?

"Please, Aunt Dani?" Constance begged again.
"There's no school and I finished my homework, even
the word problems."

"Reneging is a coward's way out," Riley said.

Dani gave up. Saying no to Constance's pleadings
and Riley's insistence would amount to cruel and unusual punishment—mostly to Dani.

"A trail ride sounds fun," she said, relenting. "As
long as I can come along."

"The more the merrier," Riley said.

Riley reached for a second soft breakfast taco.

Constance took a second bite of her first one.

The shop's doorbell rang.

"I'll get it," Riley said.

"No, let me," Dani insisted. She dashed to the landing and then down the stairs, aware that Riley was right
behind her.

*Please let it be the overnight delivery of the DNA kit
and not James Haggard coming back to finish what he'd
started before he vanished in the night.*

Chapter Twelve

A FedEx truck stopped in the middle of the street, blocking Lenny Haggard's view of the front door of Dani's Delights. Package in hand, the deliveryman got out, walked between a pickup truck and Dani Boatman's car and approached the bakery's front door.

Lenny Haggard folded the newspaper he'd been pretending to read, got up from the bench where he'd found his irresponsible, screw-up of a brother last night and crossed the street for a better view.

The printed sign on the shop's front door read Closed until Thursday, but he knew Dani was on the premises. He'd spotted movement upstairs through the open windows. That didn't mean she wasn't about to take Constance and go on the run rather than hand over money that she knew wasn't rightfully hers.

The door to the bakery opened and Dani stepped outside. She looked as if she was dressed to travel. Nice slacks, a white blouse with a bright green cardigan. A minimum of makeup, but she looked damn good.

Not a stunner like Amber had been at her peak, but then he'd met only a handful of women in his life who could measure up to Amber's beauty and sparkle when she'd first dropped into his life.

DANI SIGNED FOR DELIVERY. The package was about the size of a shoe box, so not the right shape for legal documents that might indicate she was moving money around—for good or bad.

When the deliveryman turned to leave, Lenny rushed toward Dani. His ignorant brother had done nothing but mess things up. Lenny would handle this from here on out, the way he should have all along.

A few steps before he reached the opposite curb, a tall, muscled guy appeared at the door and joined Dani. Lenny turned away and kept walking. His plan would work much better if he caught her alone.

She was getting a reprieve this morning, but this was far from over. All he had to do was convince Dani Boatman that he wasn't playing around. He had to have that money. He had to have it fast or all he had to look forward to was three holes in the back of his brain.

He wouldn't go down alone.

IT WAS EXACTLY 1:16 p.m. when Dani and Riley stepped out of the Corinthian Court Lab and into bright sunshine and a cool spring breeze. She felt lighter than she had at any time since James Haggard appeared in her life like a venomous snake, spewing his poison into every corner of her existence.

"We're just a few blocks from the River Walk," Riley said. "How about we head there and find a restaurant along the waterway?"

"A great idea. All of a sudden I'm starved."

"You should be, since you only ate a few bites of my mouthwatering breakfast."

"Sorry. I promise it wasn't your cooking. It's just that my stomach was in knots."

"And now it's not?"

"Surprisingly, no. Temporarily, at least. It helps that I've finally done something proactive instead of just waiting for Haggard to hit with his next attack."

"I still think we should tell Cavazos and hand the case over to him," Riley said.

"I know, but I'd really like to know if James is Constance's biological father first. You've almost convinced me of one thing, though. I've thought a lot about something you said last night."

"I'm thrilled to get an honorable mention. What gem of my wisdom weighed in?"

"That if James Haggard was certain he could prove he was Constance's father, he'd have gone directly to the courts with that information and tried to weasel his way into getting all the money."

"That's definitely how I see it," Riley agreed. "Whereas if his name is on the birth certificate, all he has to do is convince you the information is accurate in hopes you'll be so worried about losing Constance or the money you'll play right into his hands."

"Which means he believes his name is on the certificate, but he's not sure she's his child. It hurts to say this, but knowing my sister the way I do, I think there's a good chance she didn't even know whose sperm impregnated her."

"So unless the paternity test comes out positive for Haggard, you still won't know the identity of Constance's father."

"So an endless chain of men could show up claiming to be her father. Thank you, Riley Lawrence, for returning the knots to my stomach."

"A good prickly pear margarita will fix that."

"It may take two."

Riley took her arm as they crossed the street and continued to the concrete steps that descended to the network of beautiful arched bridges and walkways that ran along both sides of the San Antonio River.

The streets were lined with shops, restaurants and colorful umbrellas and decorations that celebrated the Mexican heritage so closely connected with San Antonio. A brightly decorated barge filled with people cruised the shallow waterway.

Dani raced down the remaining few steps and then crossed the first bridge she came to, stopping at the top of the arch for a better view of the lively waterway. "It's beautiful. Are you sure we're still in the same country?"

"Don't tell me this is your first visit to San Antonio?"

"No. I drove to the city several times when I was getting the bakery up and running, but all the supply shops were on the outskirts of town. There was never any time to spare, since I had to hurry back before Constance got home from school."

"You and Constance have got to get out more."

"We are. We're about to visit what I hear is a very exciting ranch."

"It will be, once you arrive."

"Problems and all?"

"You just left those behind at a highly rated lab. The next few days are fun, relaxation and getting to know each other better. Much better."

He reached for her hand and squeezed it, leaving no doubt what he meant. Hot pangs of anticipation stirred a new wave of desire. She wanted to taste his lips, wanted to explore the passion he ignited with his touch.

Wanted to escape her own inhibitions and go where temptation led her.

But could she do that knowing this had nowhere to go, knowing she'd be just another charm to add to his collection?

"We'll have to come back during the Christmas season," Riley said, "when the entire River Walk glistens from the illumination of millions of tiny lights. Then it really does look magical."

"And which Christmas are you likely to make it back to Texas for, Riley Lawrence?"

He hesitated, then shrugged. "Guess I'd have to figure that one out."

In other words, don't count on him. No surprise. She'd known that from the beginning. But he was here today and she needed this fairyland break from reality. "Where do we go for those margaritas you were touting?"

"We're almost there."

RILEY SIPPED HIS MARGARITA, his gaze fastened on Dani as she dipped her chip into a bowl of guacamole. When she parted her lips and slipped the chip into her mouth, desire bucked deep inside him. Nothing about this crazy attraction made sense. He'd been with lots of women. Some prettier than Dani. Some younger. Some older. Some with kids—some without.

None had ever intrigued him the way Dani did. He liked her verve, her spark and determination, the way she took on life. He'd seen it that first morning when she just kept pouring coffee, serving pastries and smiling as the line snaked around the room. She'd been flustered but still congenial, and greeted every customer in a way that made them forgive her for the wait.

He was impressed by her business savvy, her cooking skills and her relationship with Constance.

A lot of young, single women would have resented having to take over the care of a motherless niece. Dani acted like it was a gift from the gods. James Haggard might not know it yet, but even without Riley's intervention, he had met his match.

Not that Riley was going anywhere until Haggard was gone for good.

Dani picked up the lunch menu and studied it. "It all looks wonderful. Any suggestions?"

"I've had their chicken enchiladas verdes before. They're great. If you like lobster, the lobster empanada is excellent. All their tostados are good. Or we could share fajitas if you're up for that. You might want to bear in mind that while suppers at the ranch are usually light, Esther can't resist an overflowing table when she has a full house."

"Are you certain you checked this ranch vacation out with Esther and that she's good with it?"

"How well do you know Esther?" he teased.

Dani laughed. "You're right. You could invite half the town over and she'd just start smiling and frying chicken. She's ecstatic over having her three *boys* home, as she refers to you and your brothers."

"If she's still around when we go on Medicare, we'll still be her boys."

"And here I am, stealing you away again."

"And you had to work so hard at it."

The waitress came by to take their order.

"If you need a few more minutes, that's fine," she assured them.

"I think we're ready." Dani turned back to him. "Are you still in for sharing fajitas?"

"I'm in. The combo fajitas for two, with extra jalapenos."

"Will there be anything else?" the waitress asked.

"Not for me," Dani said.

"That'll do it," he agreed.

Dani commented on the sightseeing barges on the waterway and the pedestrians strolling by a few steps from their table. Bringing her here was a great idea. She needed this taste of normalcy in her life.

Keeping her mind off James Haggard until she heard the results would be a challenge.

She turned back to face him. "You're a hard man to figure, Cowboy Riley."

"Only if you're looking for something hidden beneath the surface. I am what you see. No surprises or great depths to be discovered."

"I don't believe that. What was your life like growing up in Winding Creek?"

"That's going back a long way."

"Not that long. You're, like, what? Twenty-five?"

"Twenty-eight. You?"

"Twenty-six. That gets the basics out of the way. So back to your life growing up as the middle brother."

"The typical life. We lived in town. Went to local schools. Never worried about much except getting in trouble for not doing our homework or for breaking something while wrestling inside the house."

Odd, but he didn't think about that life much anymore. It was like his pre-life, before the tragedy that had reshaped the rest of his life.

"A good life," Dani said. "The kind I hope to give Constance from here on out."

He nodded. "A good life. Safe. I guess if I had to describe those years in one word, it would be safe."

He'd never thought of it that way before, and he seldom dwelled on that part of his past, but it was true.

"And then my parents left one morning and never came back. They were there and then they were gone. Killed in a five-vehicle pileup on the way to San Antonio."

"How traumatic to lose both your parents at once. How old were you then?"

"Fourteen. I was angry with them at first." He'd never told anyone that before, wasn't sure he'd ever admitted that to himself. The truth had always had a way of hiding inside him, tamped down so tightly it couldn't escape.

Dani had somehow loosened the cap, releasing even the darkest of memories.

"I remember one day standing on the edge of the gorge at Lonesome Branch. I came within inches of ending my life that day. Instead, I stood there and screamed curses at my parents for leaving me until I finally broke into sobs."

"Anger is a natural step in dealing with grief."

"I wasn't reasoning all that out at the time."

"I'm sure. A trauma like that would knock you off-kilter at any age."

"Yep. Thankfully Charlie Kavanaugh taught me the value of climbing back into the saddle even when you think you don't have the courage to try."

"And he obviously got you hooked on the cowboy lifestyle."

"I owe him big for that." Owed him enough he should be digging a lot deeper into whether or not Charlie's death was actually a suicide.

"It may seem odd, but in the days that followed, the gorge became my special place to go when something good or bad happened in my life. The spot where I went to celebrate or just to get my head on straight."

"Everyone needs a place like that."

"Where is yours?"

"I guess I'd have to say it's in my kitchen making dough."

"I get that. I hate to change the subject, but would you mind if we make a quick stop at the prison on our way back to Winding Creek? It's only a few miles out of the way."

"For you to see Dudley Miles?"

"Yeah. How did you guess?"

"I've heard Esther talk about what great friends Charlie and Dudley were."

"And had been for years. Good men. Strong willed, but fair and honest. Both had ranching in their blood. Seems unreal that their lives would take such bizarre and disastrous twists within months of each other."

"I know. That's why I gave in to Angela's mother's pleas that I give Angela a job. To lose a child and have your father go to prison for manslaughter and then hide the evidence by trying to get rid of the body must be taking its toll on her."

"Your decision, but don't be surprised if it doesn't work out with Angela. My guess is she's got more problems than a job can fix."

"I'm afraid I agree, and, of course, I don't mind stopping off at the prison. Why don't you give them a call while I take a restroom break and see what you can arrange?"

Riley watched her walk away. Damn, did she look good leaving! Almost as good as she did coming. And that was with her clothes on. His body sprang to life just imagining what she'd look like with them off.

He motioned to their waitress. "One more margarita for the lady."

"And for yourself?"

"Designated driver. I'll take a sweet iced tea."

He looked up the phone number for the prison and made the call. After a few runarounds to different departments and several on-holds, the visit was arranged.

He wasn't sure how to approach Dudley or what he expected to get out of him that might help. He just felt like he owed this to Charlie.

DANI STROLLED THE aisles of dozens of open-air stalls that dotted Greenhorn Fairgrounds. Spring Fest days in the rural community proved to be the perfect spot for her to while away an hour on her own.

It was only one mile off the exit for the prison and a world away from James Haggard. Not that she hadn't thought Winding Creek was a world away from scum like him until he showed up there.

She pulled her phone from her handbag and checked for messages she might have missed. There were none. Hopefully that meant no more destruction of her bakery. She made a quick call to Crystal to satisfy herself all was well on that front, too. She spoke to Constance, as well.

The conversation lasted about two minutes, which was all the time Constance could spare from the day's adventure. Hiking was done. Next up was hamburgers and chocolate shakes.

Feeling mellower and more relaxed than she had in days, Dani stopped at a pottery display, immediately captivated by the brilliant colors of the glaze. She picked up a gorgeous pitcher in shades that ranged from sand to a dazzling turquoise.

"That's one of my favorite pieces," the lady standing inside the open stall said. "The glaze is lead-free and safe for all types of food and beverages."

"It's exquisite. Did you make it yourself?"

"I made everything that's on display, all one-of-a-kind."

Dani's thoughts jumped circuits, quickly switching to business. Several of the pieces on display now would not only add a touch of real class to the bakery's decor, but also likely be moneymakers for her and the artist.

"My name's Dani Boatman and I own Dani's Delights in Winding Creek."

"Really? I've heard of your shop from some of my customers. Best chocolate croissants and cinnamon buns in Texas."

"Maybe I should have that painted on my window."

"I'm Judy Kates. I also paint signs and windows."

In minutes, they'd made an appointment to discuss a business arrangement and Dani had purchased the pitcher for a thank-you gift for Esther after their ranch stay. The pitcher was so heavy she left it with Judy to be picked up when Riley called and said he was waiting for her at the exit.

As she walked away, she was surprised to realize that

despite James Haggard's threats, despite the fact that she had no guarantee how the paternity testing would come out, she was still making plans for her and Constance to have a life in Winding Creek.

Riley's confidence had to be playing a role in that. His masculinity and virility screamed self-assurance. His protectiveness gave her the freedom to have faith in herself. His…

His rambling ways meant that he wasn't a forever type of guy.

He was who he was. Here and now. That would have to do.

She picked up a few more items—beautifully illustrated books about horses for Constance and Jaci, a jar of jalapeno jelly for Riley and a teal Western shirt with pearl snaps for herself.

Her phone rang as she paid for the shirt. She wasn't expecting Riley to be back for at least another half hour. She checked the caller ID. Unavailable.

Her throat tightened, and her hello sounded ragged even to her ears.

There was a moment of silence. She started to break the connection.

"I'm sure your cowboy lover will like you in that shirt."

The voice was unfamiliar. Anxiety ran roughshod through her veins.

She looked around, expecting to see James Haggard. When she didn't, she suddenly felt as if every man around was staring her. "Who is this?"

"It doesn't matter. I know where you went today. A waste of your time. I could have told you how the test results will come out. Get the money ready for James or start planning your life without any contact with your niece. That's not a threat, it's a promise."

Chapter Thirteen

Riley looked through the rectangular piece of glass that separated him from Dudley. The man in prison orange was barely recognizable as the man Riley remembered from a short visit to the Double K Ranch about four summers ago. The man was likely around seventy. He could easily pass for eighty.

Riley had gone fishing with Charlie and Dudley in a stocked pond on Dudley's sprawling ranch. They'd caught a few bream and trout, but mostly the two old friends had guzzled beer and swapped stories from the old days.

Both men were ranchers, and there the similarities had ended.

Dudley Miles was probably the wealthiest guy in the county, his riches coming from his success in ranching and his wife's enormously large inheritance from her father's oil business. Millie loved their extravagant lifestyle. Dudley liked his cattle.

To look at the gaunt angles of Dudley's face and the loose bags of pale skin below his eyes and chin now, you'd assume Dudley hadn't enjoyed anything in decades.

The guard walked away. Dudley stared questioningly

until the light of recognition reached his pale blue eyes. "Quick Draw." His lips twitched but didn't quite form a smile. "Wasn't expecting to see you here."

It had been years since anyone called Riley by the nickname Dudley had given him the first time he and Charlie took the brothers shooting.

"I'm in town for Pierce's wedding. Just thought I'd drop by and say hi."

"I appreciate that. Not many do, but I don't blame them. No good reason for it. Nothing changes in here. Nothing to talk about."

Dudley reached up and ran his wrinkled fingers through his thinning gray hair. "I heard about the wedding."

"I suppose Angela told you."

He shook his head. "No reason for her to come here. Wouldn't be good for either for us. Millie says Angela is dealing with the grief in her own way."

Riley doubted if Millie had told him that meant falling all over every guy who gave her a second look and some who didn't.

Looking at Dudley now, it was hard to imagine he could have a daughter close to Riley's age. But according to Charlie, Dudley had married late and it had taken Millie years to carry a baby full-term. Supposedly that explained why Angela had been known at school as a spoiled, stuck-up snot.

None of that was what had brought Riley to the prison today. Might as well cut to the unpleasant chase. "I have to admit I'm not just here to say hello."

"Didn't figure you were. I reckon you have questions about Charlie. Pierce did, too, when he drove down here to see me a couple of months back. Maybe more than a couple of months. Time doesn't seem to matter much around here."

And Dudley had a good chance of being here for the rest of his life.

"If I knew what got into Charlie, I'd tell you," Dudley said. "He never let on to me he was thinking about taking his life. If he had I would have found a way to stop him."

"Did he mention to you that he was having financial problems?"

"He admitted times were hard. They were for most ranchers after the big drought. I offered him money. A loan. A gift. Hell, I would have given him the shirt off my back. You know that."

"He turned you down?"

"I reckon he did. To tell you the truth, I don't remember much about what was going on back then. Had my own problems. My grandson…" Dudley's voice broke and he looked away.

"Want to talk about that?"

"No." He drew his lips together as if he was forcing the words to stay inside them.

He was hurting bad. Even Riley could see that. He could buy that Dudley had a couple of drinks and then fell asleep on the couch when he should have been caring for a toddler. What he couldn't bring himself to accept was that Dudley took that boy's dead body and tossed it into a woody area to rot.

"What really happened that day your grandson went missing, Dudley? We both know you'd never dump his body and then say he was kidnapped."

Dudley covered his face with trembling hands. He stayed that way for what must have been a full minute. Finally, he lowered his hands and spread them out, palms down, on the small table where he'd been resting his elbows.

He stared at them, avoiding eye contact. "It happened like I said. Now get out of here, Riley, and don't come back. Not you or your brothers. Life is over for both me and Charlie. Get out there and find your own life."

Dudley stood and strode away as if he was in a big hurry to get somewhere.

He'd been lying. Definitely about himself. Maybe about Charlie, as well. Riley likely wouldn't be around long enough to get to the bottom of this, but someone should.

Get out there and find your own life.

The essence of Dudley's order echoed through Riley's mind as he walked the long tiled corridor to the exit.

He'd thought that was what he'd been doing for years. Traveling the world. Taking risks. Never settling. Finding his own life.

Yet here he was, back in Winding Creek, and all he wanted to do was get back to Dani.

RILEY PULLED INTO the pickup lane near the gate to the fairgrounds. He spotted Dani almost immediately, her arms full of packages, her coppery curls catching the afternoon sun rays.

He got out of the car and waved. It wasn't until she'd started in his direction that he noticed how upset she looked. No smile. No rhythmic sway to her shapely hips.

He helped her load the packages into the backseat and then held the door for her.

He waited until he was seated at the wheel before questioning her. "What's wrong?"

"Am I that easy to read?"

"No, I'm that talented a reader. Judging from those packages, including the one you're still cradling like a precious treasure, you enjoyed the shopping. And yet you're still not smiling."

He eased into traffic as the car in front of him pulled forward.

She looked around, turning so she could see out the back window. "I'm being followed."

"You mean someone followed you around the booths?"

"I mean someone has apparently been following us ever since we left Winding Creek this morning."

He grew madder by the second as she shared the details of the alarming phone call.

"Are you certain the caller wasn't Haggard disguising his voice?"

"If it was, he did an excellent job of it."

"He may have hired a private detective to take over his dirty work for him. Not that he gained much from following us around all day."

"He knows we visited a lab."

"That shouldn't come as any surprise except that Haggard may not have realized you have a sample of his DNA."

"I still don't like the ideas of being stalked."

"I agree. I think it's time we do a little snooping of our own—find out everything we can about James Haggard. His past might prove him so unfit to be a parent that no judge would ever grant him custody of Constance."

"After some of the bizarre rulings I've read about, it's still risky trusting judges. But I'm game," Dani admitted. "I don't suppose you know any private detectives."

"Better. Pierce has a close friend with the FBI. Andy Malone, an old SEAL buddy. I know he helped out when Grace was in danger. He might be able to run a check and find something on Haggard, especially if has a criminal record. I'll talk to Pierce tonight and run the possibility by him."

"I'd like that, but about my staying at the ranch—"

"I already don't like where this is going."

"I'm being followed, Riley. I can't take this kind of trouble to the Double K Ranch."

"Are you going to sit there and tell me that you don't think Pierce, Tucker and I can handle the worst of what James Haggard can dish out?"

"I didn't mean it like that."

"You did. I'll forgive you this once. Don't let it happen again or we'll have to titillate you with thrilling recaps of Pierce's Navy SEAL exploits and videos of Tucker's mastery over a ton of bucking bull. If that doesn't do it, I'll demonstrate my legendary quick-draw skills."

"This isn't a joking matter, Riley."

"I'm not joking. It's all set. You and Constance need this vacation. Either you go with me willingly or I'll have to hog-tie and drag you there. Your call."

"Do you really want us there in spite of everything?"

"I've never wanted anything more." And that scared him a thousand times more than threats from James Haggard ever could.

IF DANI HAD any remaining doubts concerning the Double K vacation, they disappeared the second she saw the excitement in Constance's eyes as Jaci, Esther and Grace came running out to the car to welcome them.

"We're staying two days and two nights," Constance announced ceremoniously as she reached back into the truck for her backpack.

"Everybody's here," Jaci said, clapping her hands. "It's a giant slumber party all over our house."

"It's a vacation for us," Constance amended. "We're going on a trail ride."

"I know," Jaci said. "Mommy told me. I'm riding Dreamer. And guess what?"

"I can't guess what I don't know. You have to tell me."

"You can sleep in my room just like after the wedding."

"Except this time there better be more sleeping than giggling or you'll be too tired for an early morning trail ride," Esther warned.

The girls ran ahead.

"I swear to goodness," Esther exclaimed. "Those girls are quicker than jackrabbits and have more energy, too. Grace, why don't you show Dani to the bedroom with the private patio? I'll show Riley to the sleeping alcove off the back porch."

"What, no patio for me?" Riley asked.

"In town three days and you've yet to put your head on one of my pillows. You're lucky to get a bed, young man. If you'd been doing anything besides helping out Dani, you'd have gotten a pile of hay in the barn."

Riley put an arm around Esther's shoulders. "Aw, c'mon, admit it. You know I'm your favorite."

"I don't have any favorites among my boys, but come

around more often and you might work up to a room with a view of the woodshed."

"You have no heart."

Dani followed Grace to the end of the west hall. Grace opened the door and they stepped inside.

"Wow," Dani said. "I wasn't expecting this. A Queen Anne four-poster bed that looks so inviting I think I could melt in it. An antique dresser. The beautiful brass lamp. Fresh bluebonnets in a milky white vase. I had no idea Esther collected antiques."

"The furniture was all handed down from her maternal grandmother. She likes the part of her house where she says the living goes on to be simple. She keeps her treasures, as she calls her heirlooms, in the seldom-used guest rooms."

"I'm impressed."

"Be sure and let her know. She'll be delighted." Grace dropped to the edge of the bed. "What's the latest with your problems with James Haggard?"

"How much do you know?"

"Only what Riley has had time to tell Pierce."

"I feel terrible that my problems cut into your honeymoon," Dani said.

"Don't give it a second thought. I know it sounds a bit pretentious, but every day with Pierce is a honeymoon. I love him so much. I seriously can't put how happy he makes me into mere words."

"That's a powerful endorsement of commitment."

"So, back to the subject. Did you get the DNA to the lab today?"

"I did."

"I'm glad you came to the ranch with Riley."

"To be honest, I tried to back out, but Riley insisted."

"I'm glad you caved in. This much I know—the Lawrence brothers stick together and James Haggard will not get the best of them. Remember that Pierce's bravery and fast thinking are the reasons I'm alive today."

"I think Riley must have those same protective genes."

"He's a great guy, but Pierce says he's a rambler. Definitely a man you can depend on in a jam, but perhaps not a man to hitch your star to."

"So I've heard."

"I know. You heard it from me, but I don't want you to get hurt. You don't deserve a broken heart."

"I'm not going to fall for him."

True, she already had done so. That didn't mean she expected a miracle, or that she'd let Riley or anyone else make the final decision about how to best keep Constance safe.

Dani walked Constance back to bed for the third time in the last hour.

"I know how excited you are about all the fun activities you and Jaci have planned for the next two days, but if you don't get some sleep you'll be too tired to get up for the trail ride in the morning."

"I know, but I was too thirsty to sleep."

She was extremely creative when it came to excuses for prolonging bedtime. First her thumb had itched. Then her sheet was too twisted.

Constance stopped at the bedroom door. "I wish we had a ranch with horses and chickens and four-wheelers to ride through the mud."

"Who would I sell my pastries to?"

"We could still have the bakery. Some people have

two houses. Bridget's family has a beach condo. They're there this week."

"But they don't have a bakery. I'll make a deal with you, though. It stays light a lot longer in summer. We'll try to come out to the Double K Ranch more often to ride horses."

"And feed the chickens?"

"And feed the chickens," Dani agreed. "Right now you need to get some sleep. And we have to be very quiet not to wake Jaci."

Constance nodded and put a shushing finger to her lips as she eased open the door. She tiptoed across the wood floors in her bare feet, then climbed into bed and crawled between the sheets.

Dani straightened the comfy coverlet and tucked it beneath Constance's chin. "I love you, sweetie," she whispered.

"Love you, too."

Dani kissed her good-night and Constance closed her eyes, hopefully this time to fall into a deep sleep colored with sweet dreams.

Her niece's life had never been easy before she came to live with Dani. Without the intervention of Health and Human Services on more than one occasion, she might not even be alive.

Dani had never been given the chance to make a difference then. Now she had. Biological father or not, James Haggard would not rob Constance of happiness—not as long as Dani was alive to stop him.

The house was whisper-quiet when Dani left the girls' bedroom. Esther might have retired for the night, but the others were more likely outside catching up on each other's lives. It was practically the first time

Riley had managed any bonding time with his boisterous brothers.

She definitely wouldn't barge in on that. A shower and early to bed actually sounded good. She might have needed this time away as much as Constance.

She stopped off in the kitchen for a glass of water for herself. The back door swung open, letting in a cool breeze and a grinning cowboy who sent her senses whirling.

"We were starting to wonder what happened to you."

"Constance was resisting bedtime."

Riley reached into the fridge for some beers. "Maybe I should go back for my guitar and play her a little George Strait."

"Like that wouldn't have Jaci and Constance both up and ready to dance. Actually I think they're both sleeping now, so let's leave it that way."

"Does that mean you're ready to join the party that's going on outside?"

"I was thinking I'd take a shower and hit the bed."

"I like your idea better. Your shower or mine?"

"Nice try, but I don't think that's in keeping with the rules of the house." Not that the offer wasn't titillating.

"I don't do rules. Did I not mention that?"

"You've given a few indications."

"What'll you have? Beer? Wine? Margarita on the rocks?"

"As a chaser for the margaritas I had earlier?"

"That was hours and one of Esther's five-thousand-calorie meals ago."

"I hate to crash a family gathering especially after stealing you from your brothers for days."

"They'll probably thank you for that. Besides, it's not

like we're shaking old family skeletons around. We're mostly jamming out a little and laughing a lot."

"In that case, make mine a light beer."

"Got it." He pulled another bottle from the fridge.

"Let me grab a wrap and I'll help you carry those."

"Forget the wrap. The temperature's dropped several degrees, but we've got a campfire roaring. If that's not enough, my denim jacket's out there somewhere. And don't worry about the girls. Esther will hear them if they wake up and call for anyone."

She fell in step with Riley as they left through the back door and closed it behind them. The smell of smoke and the sound of laughter led them to the impromptu party.

Pierce and Grace shared an oversize lawn recliner and were entwined like the lovebirds they were. Grace had kicked off her shoes and tossed a red sweatshirt over her feet.

Tucker was in a folding lawn chair next to them, his booted feet stretched toward the fire, a banjo around his neck. There were two more chairs in the circle, one holding a guitar, one empty. She might not be wanted, but she'd evidently been expected.

She exchanged greetings and took the empty chair. Riley passed around the beers, then picked up his guitar and dropped into the chair next to hers.

"What did I miss?" Riley asked.

"Truth or lie," Tucker said.

"Ugh, I came back too soon."

"But you lie so well," Pierce said.

"I'll sit this one out a round or two until I get the hang of it," Dani offered. She wasn't a legitimate part of the family and she was a terrible liar, a virtue that sounded as if it would work against her in this game.

"Your turn, Tucker," Pierce said. "What's the least amount of time you stayed on a bull during a rodeo event?"

"Six seconds."

"Lie," they all shouted at once.

"You're right. It was seven."

"Lie."

"You gotta make music." Grace threw out a song title. "'Won't You Come Home, Bill Bailey.'"

Tucker jumped into the song on his banjo. Riley strummed a few hot chords on his guitar. Pierce pulled out a harmonica and joined in.

To Dani's surprise, they were all good. Really good. Even more impressive, they were all having fun. Surprisingly, so was she.

"Okay, Quick Draw," Grace said. "What's the longest time you ever stayed in one town?"

"That's easy. Winding Creek. Home, sweet home. I was here for almost fifteen years."

"I mean one town after you left college, rambling man," Grace clarified.

Dani couldn't help worrying if that question was for her benefit. She knew Grace meant well, but love didn't always come wrapped in neat packages. It had for Grace. Dani had no expectations that it would for her.

"Let's see," Riley said. "That would probably be Kentucky. I fell in love with a golden-haired beauty and couldn't bear to leave. Fastest two-year-old I ever worked with. I trained her so well I had hopes she might end up winning the roses."

"What happened?" Tucker asked.

"Boss's daughter didn't like being rejected when she threw herself at me. Lied and accused me of coming on to her. I got fired. Horse lost the race."

"How long were you there?" Grace asked.

"Eight months, give or take a week or two."

"I'll buy that as true," Grace said.

Riley grinned and played a run on the guitar. "Sucker. I've never lived in Kentucky and never trained a racehorse. I've thought about it, though."

"Never believe a thing old Quick Draw says," Pierce said.

They went around a few more times. More lies than truth from all of them.

Tucker kicked at a log, stirring up a few more flames before their fire died. "You haven't asked a question yet, Dani."

"I have one for Quick Draw."

"Sorry. Out of time," Riley teased.

"Where did you get the name Quick Draw?"

"So happens I got that name by using my considerable skills with a very large gun to save my brother's life."

Tucker groaned. "Here we go again."

"Dudley Miles and Charlie were giving Tucker, Pierce and me a shooting and gun-safety lesson. I won't go into all the details, but as usual, I was catching on faster than my brothers."

Pierce and Tucker booed on cue.

"We'd put the guns on safety. Tucker and Pierce returned their guns to our instructors. I slid mine into the holster I had buckled above my hips and took a few steps away from the group."

"The next thing we heard was his gun firing in rapid succession," Tucker said.

"Followed by Charlie yelling at me. All I'd done was aim my pistol at a humongous rattlesnake lying dead less than a foot from where Tucker was standing. The viper had been ready to strike when I spotted him. If I'd yelled, Tucker would have jumped and the snake would have nailed him. So my quick draw and even quicker thinking saved Tucker's life."

Riley stood and took a bow.

"Lie," Dani said, sure she'd been taken.

"Tsk-tsk. How can you look into these honest eyes and doubt me?"

"It was the truth," Tucker said. "I could never forget that day, especially since Riley misses no opportunity to remind me."

They all laughed. For brothers who spent so little time together, they seemed exceptionally close.

Perhaps it was the shared tragedy of losing their parents. But Dani suspected it was also the experiences and love they'd shared with each other and Esther and Charlie Kavanaugh right here on the Double K Ranch.

"If I'm going to make a sunrise trail ride, I'd better head to bed," Grace said.

"Same here," Tucker said. "You guys may be used to ranching hours, but we bull riders sleep in till noon and tend our bruised and aching bodies."

"And draw the big paychecks," Pierce said.

"Only when we win."

Dani stood with the rest of them. Riley reached up, took her hand and tugged her back down beside him. "We'll stick around and see that the fire is fully out."

Truth or lie.

The question was, did she dare stay?

Her heart answered that one for her as she snuggled by his side to watch the fading glow of dying embers.

She might never have forever, but she had now.

Chapter Fourteen

Winding Creek, Texas. The Double K Ranch. Home again. Nothing like what Riley was expecting when he'd made the long drive down from Montana.

It was always great getting together with his brothers, except that it brought back the heartbreaking moments along with the good. And with this visit was the added sadness of Charlie's death.

Riley knew without Esther saying it that she was walking around with a huge hole in her heart, one that could never be filled. He saw it in her eyes when Charlie's name came up in the conversation, heard it in her voice when she spoke of him.

It was life. No matter how much you loved someone, you could lose them forever in a heartbeat. That message was set as firmly in his mind as if it was engraved in stone.

And yet staring into the fire with Dani's hand in his, Riley felt a whirlwind of emotions roaring inside him, and not one of them had him wanting to back off.

If that weren't bad enough, his protective urges equaled the ones his libido was fueling.

He stood, took the guitar from around his neck and

set it in his chair. "Let's move to Pierce and Grace's spot," he suggested. "More room to get comfortable."

He sat down first, scooted to the back of the wide lounger and spread his legs so that she could sit between them. He wrapped his arms around her waist and pulled her close so that her back rested against his chest.

He nuzzled her neck, intoxicated by the flowery fragrance of her perfume. "I've been dying to hold you ever since you walked out here." He nibbled and sucked her earlobe. "You take my breath away."

"You're too easy to impress."

"Not true. But whatever it takes to turn me on, you rock it, baby."

"You must have a fetish for plump chicks."

"What?"

"A fetish for plump chicks or chubby thighs."

He laughed out loud. He couldn't help it. The comment was so far off true it would have blown the motor out of a lie detector test. "Where did you ever get the idea you are plump? Do you never look in a mirror?"

"All I have to do is look around me at the size zeros, twos and fours, the sexy young women who look as if their skinny jeans were painted on them and they haven't had a chocolate croissant in their lives. They don't even take cream or sugar in their coffee."

"Pity the men who have to eat their cooking. You're not skinny, Dani. I'll give you that. You've got curves in all the right places.

"Like here." He cupped her breasts with his hands and felt himself grow hard as her nipples pebbled and arched at his touch.

"And here." He slid his hands to her hips. "And for the record, you have got the best-looking butt in at least seven counties, and that's without having your jeans painted on. Though I'll be glad to supply the paint and brushes if you want to try that."

"I'll keep that in mind, Picasso."

He readjusted her in his arms so that his lips could find hers. Once he started, he couldn't stop. He ravaged her mouth as his hands slid along her abdomen and his fingers worked their way between her thighs. Even through the denim, he felt the heat and imagined her getting slick and ready for him the way he was burning hot for her.

He covered her hands with his and led them to the aching swell of his erection. She massaged the length of his hardness through the rough denim of his jeans. His blood pulsed fast and hard. His breathing was clipped, his voice husky when he moaned her name.

She pushed away quickly. "Not here," she murmured. "Not yet. Not like this."

He struggled for breath and relief from the frenzied hunger that had taken over his brain. "I'm sorry. I didn't mean to come at you like a wild man."

"Please, don't apologize. It wasn't what you did— what we did. It's just that so many people are around. Someone could walk out that door any minute. I think the wisest move for me right now is to go inside and go to bed—alone."

"This is a huge ranch. We can find a place to be alone."

"Not tonight. Not here. Not yet."

"Then at least let me walk you to your room."

"Not a good idea. Just stay out here and put out the fire."

"You just did that for me."

"I have no doubt you can get it roaring again when the time is right."

He watched her walk away. Fat? Hardly. Every inch of her looked fantastic. Every inch of her cried out to be made love to.

What was the longest he'd ever been in one place? Truthfully, he didn't know. He'd just always known when it was time to move on.

It definitely wasn't now.

IT WAS EIGHT in the morning when they stopped for breakfast in a grove of pecan trees. They'd traveled slowly on a short, easy path that was safe enough for Jaci and Constance to ride single.

Pierce helped Jaci from the saddle and tethered her mount. Riley did the same for Constance, who was as excited as Riley had ever seen her. Both girls went running to meet Esther, who'd driven up in the truck with the food and cooking utensils.

Jaci wasn't quite six, but she already looked like a natural in the saddle, especially riding Dreamer, the calmest horse in the stalls. Constance was older but not as experienced, since she didn't get the chance to ride nearly as often. She'd improve quickly with a little more time in the saddle.

Pierce walked over to the truck, where the other two guys were hauling out a camp stove.

"Thanks to Esther there's not a lot of preparation left to do," Pierce said. "The sausage is scrambled. Potatoes are diced and fried. All we have to do is scramble the eggs in with the sausage and potatoes and heat the tortillas while chugging down a mug of coffee and making it appear like we're working hard."

"I'll pour the coffee," Tucker said. "Shall I serve the ladies?"

"Sure. Nothing bur five-star service on the Double K Ranch. Thermos is in the back of the truck."

Pierce started cracking eggs. "We didn't get much chance to talk privately yesterday. Any new developments with James Haggard?"

"Not directly." Riley told him about the stalker call.

"Strange," Pierce said. "Was she sure it wasn't Haggard disguising his voice?"

"I asked the same thing. She assured me she was as certain as she can be from a phone connection."

"He may have hired a private eye, but I don't see the point of that. In fact, none of his actions make much sense. If he's the father, prove it. He can't expect to make a million-dollar deal with Dani without proof. Even if his name was on the birth certificate, that wouldn't prove anything."

"Which makes me question if there's a reason he doesn't want his DNA information revealed," Riley said.

"Like a criminal record?"

"Exactly." Riley started heating the tortillas in an iron skillet while Pierce stirred the eggs into the sausage and potatoes that had been warming as they talked.

"You may be on to something," Pierce agreed. "At the very least there may be an event in Haggard's past that would prevent any judge from granting him custody or even a token amount of the insurance settlement. That would leave threatening Dani into just handing over the cash his only chance of financial gain."

"I hate to ask," Riley said, "but are you still in touch with your old SEAL buddy who's with the FBI?"

"Andy Malone. He's working out of Florida, but he

came through for me big-time when Grace was in danger. I'll give him a call right after we get back to the house. He may not get back to me immediately, but I'll let you know as soon as he checks out Haggard."

"I appreciate that, more than you know."

"Seems like you're getting into it pretty deep with Dani."

"Is that a problem?"

"Not for me. Grace is a little worried you'll break her heart."

"Isn't anyone worried about my heart?"

"Nope. I just hope you have enough sense to know when it's time to lay it all on the line. Take it from me, love done right is as good as it gets."

"I'll keep that in mind."

THEY WERE GETTING ready to mount the horses again for the last half of the trail ride when Dani's cell phone rang. She hesitated to even check the caller ID. It would be unbearable to discover that yesterday's stalker had followed her here.

"Aren't you going to answer that?" Grace asked. "It could be important."

"I just hate to take a chance on a call spoiling our perfect morning."

"Don't worry. We'll have lots more. You needed this and Constance is definitely getting horse fever. You won't be able to keep her away."

The phone stopped ringing. Dani breathed a sigh of relief until it started again. This time she checked the caller ID. Her alarm company. She was bordering on severe paranoia.

She took the call and made arrangements to meet the repair tech at the bakery at eleven o'clock.

Riley walked over the second he noticed her on the phone. "Is everything all right?"

"Yes, except that I have to tell Constance there's a kink in our vacation plans."

"What kind of kink?"

She explained the situation and Grace didn't hesitate a second before coming to the rescue.

"I'll keep the girls busy. You get your alarm fixed and you'll be back at the ranch by early afternoon."

Dani groaned. "I am so taking advantage of all of you."

"It's Winding Creek. We take care of our neighbors. You have to love that about this place."

"We'll stop at the lumberyard up on the highway and pick up a new back door," Riley said. "If we leave as soon as we get the horses settled, I can install it and be out of their way before they arrive."

"I don't suppose it would do any good to say you don't have to do that," Dani said.

"You heard Grace. It's Winding Creek. I'd lose my native status if I failed to be a good neighbor."

"We can't have that."

Which meant she'd be alone at the bakery with Riley after the security technician left.

She'd lain awake half the night fantasizing about making love to Riley. This time if he wanted her, she wouldn't pull away.

JAMES HAGGARD LEANED back in the front passenger seat of the red sports car and smiled. "Really? Your dad's in prison. I like you better by the minute. What did he do?"

"Does it matter?"

"It might. Did he kill someone?"

"No. He'd never have the guts to do that."

"He's your dad. Where's your respect?"

"He's all right. He was always on my case. I got tired of the lectures. But he's fine. The other prisoners probably love him."

James whistled as Angela pulled up to a huge metal double gate supported by tall brick columns. The house he could barely see in the distance reminded him of a Southern plantation house he'd seen in Louisiana years ago. "Does all of this belong to your family?"

"Sure. It's the biggest ranch in the county or something like that."

"How rich are you?"

"I don't know. No one ever talks to me about things like that. I'm their precious Angel. It works."

"I thought your name was Angela."

"It is. Mom and Dad are the only ones who call me Angel."

"The dad who's in prison?"

"Well, yeah. Back when I was growing up."

"Is your mother home now?"

"I don't know. Don't worry. You won't have to meet her. She goes ape if I bring friends home to get high. Gotta keep up appearances like there's anyone in this Podunk town to impress."

He wasn't sure what he was getting into, but he figured it was going to be a hell of a ride and he had nothing better to do.

The ranch road they were on veered off to the left. A narrow dirt and gravel road jutted off to the right. She kept going left.

"Let's go back and take the other road," Haggard said. "Better chance of not meeting up with any nosy wranglers."

"No. No one goes down that road. Not anymore."

"What's wrong? You're not afraid I'll turn into a big bad wolf if we get lost in the woods, are you?"

"Just shut up about that road. There's nothing down there but a ramshackle, rotting fishing camp."

"On a lake or a river?"

"Might have been a river once. Just a mostly dried-up creek bed now."

"Sounds like the perfect place to light up."

Angela hit the brakes and skidded to a stop. "Get out. I mean it. You go where I take you or get out and walk back to town."

"Hot damn! You sure look good when you're mad." And was probably as mean as a bobcat. He'd be sure to keep that in mind.

She finally stopped the car near a sparkling clear pond. Parked right out in the open, where any cowboy riding by could see them. She might be a little nuts.

Angela got out, popped the trunk and pulled out a quilt. She spread it beneath a tall swamp willow and motioned him over.

The second he settled on the quilt, she dropped down beside him and started ripping his shirt open. Buttons popped and flew in all directions.

"Whoa there, baby. We haven't even shared a joint yet."

"Are you here to party or not?" she demanded.

"I didn't know we were racing to the finish line. I thought we'd talk first."

"About what?"

"Your job at the bakery. When do you go back to work?"

"Thursday, I guess, if I bother to show."

"I need you to show and do a big favor for me."

"I'm not stealing from the register."

"It's nothing like that. All I need is for you to do some snooping around. Keep your eyes open for an official-looking document to arrive from Corinthian Court Lab in San Antonio. While you're watching for that, look for anything official with Constance's name on it—like a birth certificate."

"Why would Dani leave something like that lying around?"

"She won't. You'll have to sneak around. Go upstairs. Open a drawer or two. Check the file cabinet."

"What's in it for me?"

"I'll do your shopping for you, take all the risks like I did today."

"Whatever I want?"

"As long as you got the cash to pay for it," he assured her."

"You're not planning to do anything to hurt Constance, are you? You wouldn't try to kidnap her."

"I don't have to kidnap her. I'm her dad and that's a fact. Get me that birth certificate and I'll just have to grab her and go."

EVERY MUSCLE IN Dani's body tensed as Riley turned onto Main Street. She hadn't heard from yesterday's stalker again, yet all of a sudden she was sure he was near.

Watching. Waiting to…

She couldn't finish the thought. She had no idea what

he was planning, but the same creeping fear she'd felt when she heard his voice yesterday skulked inside her now.

Whatever he wanted, it had to do with James Haggard, and that meant it had to do with Constance.

"You're awfully quiet," Riley said. "Is anything wrong?"

"I'm just thinking maybe you're the one who has it right. Don't put down any roots and then it won't hurt so much if your world goes up in smoke."

Her phone rang. She checked the caller ID. Unavailable. Her stalker had no doubt called to welcome her home.

"Who is it?" Riley asked as she hesitated to take the call.

"Unavailable."

"Ignore the ring. Don't give the pervert the satisfaction of knowing he's making you uneasy."

She scanned the area. "He's out there somewhere, likely planning his next sinister move."

"If he shows up at Dani's Delights looking for trouble, he'll get more than he can handle."

"You're not carrying a weapon, are you?"

"Yes, but I know my way around a pistol."

"I don't want a gunfight, Riley. I don't want you shot."

"Nor do I. Being ready for trouble is not the same thing as looking for it or even expecting it. At this point there's no reason to suspect Haggard's more than a cowardly, money-grubbing bully attempting to frighten you into giving in to his demands."

She knew many of the ranchers and wranglers kept a gun on them when they working. It was usually a rattlesnake they were looking to kill. She couldn't push the thought of deadly violence out of her mind. "Have you ever killed anyone?"

"Does a two-hundred-and-fifty-pound grizzly in attack mode count?"

She shuddered. "You came face-to-face with a grizzly?"

"Yes, ma'am. My friend Jack and I were fly fishing in a glacial stream in Alaska. Jack and I had seen bears before in that area, but when they'd show up, we'd just back away and let them have their fishing spot.

"That time we didn't see the bear until it came charging at my buddy. Fortunately, I was able to take the grizzly down seconds before he attacked. Admittedly I was shooting a lot more firepower than I have with me today."

Leave it to Riley to take her mind off her own problems if only for a few seconds. "Truth or lie?" she queried, though it didn't matter. Either way the story had served its purpose.

"Truth. Alaska is a magnificent state, almost like traveling to another world."

He passed Dani's Delights and kept going.

She tensed. "Why didn't you stop? Is something wrong?"

He reached across the console and pressed his hand against her thigh. "Everything's fine. I'm just going to unload the new door in the back."

She'd forgotten all about the extra-strength metal replacement door he'd bought and loaded into the bed of his truck at the lumberyard a half hour ago.

She was so anxious about the stupid stalker she

couldn't keep her thoughts straight. Time to pull herself together the best way she knew how.

It was time to bake.

WITHIN MINUTES OF getting down to business in her immaculate, commercial-grade kitchen, Dani felt her nerves beginning to settle. It had been that way since she made her first batch of chocolate chip cookies as a little girl. In her mind, there was something magical about measuring, creaming, blending and folding in myriad ingredients to create something as beautiful to look at as it was to taste.

To lose her bakery would be like losing a piece of herself.

Normally she worked to the sounds of Mozart, Wagner, Bublé or Sinatra. Today she was working to the beat of hammers and the whir of drills. The sounds weren't the only things that were magnified with Riley around.

He added a new spice, a robust flavor that she'd never experienced before.

"Hate to interrupt the genius at work, but do you know if there's any leftover paint around here to match the door facing?"

She looked up to find Riley at the kitchen door in his worn jeans and sneakers, shirt off, thick, dark hair mussed and falling over his brow.

The carpenter's belt hung below his waist, the tools dangling past his hips. His bare chest was as bronzed as his face and the rest of his hunky, tanned body.

Her insides quivered. Her legs grew weak. Her mind was muddled. She held on to the edge of the counter as the full effect of his virility left her dizzy.

"What did you say?" she asked.

"I said, 'Wow, do you look good punching that dough!' Do you need help?"

"Sorry, sir, but I don't believe those tools you're sporting could sufficiently coddle my red velvet cupcakes."

"You might be surprised what kind of satisfying work my tools are capable of."

And once again it wasn't the time or place to find out. "The repair tech will be here any minute. He's already ten minutes late."

"Well, okay, if you'd rather wait for him, but I predict he'll be a big disappointment."

"Paint," she said, knowing she'd best cool the flirting before she lost all control. "You were asking about paint."

"Right. The woodwork and trim around your back door needs a touch-up. Did your painters leave any extra when they finished your bakery remodeling?"

"They left a few partial cans of paint. I'm not sure which colors. They're on the top shelf of the storage cupboard between the men's and ladies' restrooms. The key is in the drawer under the first register."

"Good. I'll check it out."

He turned and was gone. It was uncanny how James Haggard's threats and calls from a taunting stalker could have her totally on edge and still she was falling this hard for Riley.

Temporary or not as this relationship might be, she no longer could be ruled by caution. When the security alarm was up and running and she and Riley had the house to themselves, she'd let him know she was ready to finish what they'd started last night.

No promises or love or forever expected.

She had just slipped her croissants into the oven and was about to start on chocolate cupcakes for the girls when her front doorbell rang.

She rushed to usher in the alarm tech. The sooner he got started, the sooner he'd be out of here. She swung open the door.

"I realize your shop is closed, but it's urgent that we talk," the man standing there said.

"You're not from the alarm company?"

"No, I'm Elton Sheldon, James Haggard's attorney, and I think you know why I'm here."

Chapter Fifteen

He was wrong. Dani had no idea why he was here. The rules seemed to change with James Haggard every day. First she'd had a week to pull a million dollars from a hat. The next night he'd vandalized the bakery, apparently just to let her know he shouldn't be taken lightly.

Next a hired stalker. Now he'd sent his attorney to add more pressure.

"Your client doesn't seem to know what he wants, so how could I possibly know what you want?"

"Let me make it clear, then. James is Constance's father. You could start by acknowledging that his name is listed that way on the original birth certificate. A birth certificate that should have been given to him along with custody of his daughter. He is the legal next of kin and you know it."

"His name is not on the birth certificate, which explains why he doesn't have a copy of it."

"We also know that you delivered a fake sample of James's DNA to a lab in San Antonio to deliberately infringe on his rights."

"You are the one who was following me yesterday. Is stalking women part of your attorney duties?"

"Only when working with dishonest women who'll do anything to hold on to an innocent child's money."

"Go to hell." She was practically screaming, but she'd had enough.

"What's the problem?" Riley asked, appearing with his usual perfect timing.

Sheldon took a step backward, putting him closer to the door. Clearly he'd expected to find her alone so he could bully her into complying with James's demands before she received the lab report.

"This man claims to be James Haggard's attorney and he's basically calling me a liar and a sleaze."

"Is that a fact?" Riley asked as he took off his tool belt.

"He's also my stalker and he seems to be quite concerned that we made a visit to a lab."

"I've said what I have to say," Sheldon said. "Your fake DNA testing will prove nothing. Cooperate or lose Constance. Time is running out."

"Actually it just ran out," Riley said. "James Haggard isn't fit to father a rat. The two of you tried to pull off a million-dollar scam. You picked a victim way out of your league. I hope you enjoy prison life."

"Why, you…"

The attorney doubled his fists and came at Riley, landing a punch to his jaw. Riley got in the second blow. Blood shot from Sheldon's nose and splattered his face and the front of his shirt. He staggered back, but managed to keep his balance.

Sheldon lunged for the tool belt Riley had shed, wrapping his fingers around the handle of a hammer and struggling to wrench it free.

Riley grabbed him from behind, ramming his knee

into Sheldon's crotch. The lawyer turned white, looked as if he might faint and then twisted around and came at Riley again.

This time Riley delivered a solid blow to his right jaw. Sheldon stumbled for a few seconds, spitting out streams of blood, before he finally went down.

Dani opened the door, and Riley literally tossed Elton Sheldon to the street.

"You'll pay for this," the lawyer muttered through the blood dripping from his split bottom lip.

"Bring it on."

A crowd quickly gathered around Sheldon. He muttered a string of vile curses as he got to his feet and staggered away.

A few seconds later, Dani heard the scream of sirens. The police. An ambulance. Or both.

"I'm sorry I dragged you into this. I never expected things to go this far so quickly. I definitely didn't think an attorney would take things to blows."

Riley wrapped her in his arms and swayed gently, rocking her to him. She felt his warm breath on her neck as he whispered in her ear, "There you go, apologizing again for something you couldn't control. I doubt he's an attorney, but he came here looking for a fight. Only the cowardly skunk was expecting it to be with you—not me."

"Do you think he was arrested or taken to a hospital?"

"Either way, he won't stay long. He's not going to admit he got beat up while working a con."

"I guess we won't know for sure it's a total con until we get the DNA test results back," she said. "But if Haggard really believes the tests will come back positive, why not wait until I have the proof? Wait. That's it. Haggard knows the tests will come back negative. He's desperate because it's now or never for him."

Her spirits lifted. "The second I get those negative test results, I'm calling Cavazos. I hope Haggard's tried and sentenced. Prison life will be exactly what he deserves.

"Now you're talking." Riley sniffed. "Do I smell something burning?

"My croissants." She dashed for the kitchen. Too late. Burned to a smoky black.

Even that couldn't bring her spirits down now. The alarm repairman would come and go, and then she'd be alone with Riley. The time couldn't pass quick enough.

THE SECOND BATCH of croissants came out perfect. As many as Dani had made in her career, they should. She rinsed her pans and skidded them into her oversize specialty dishwasher.

The dishwasher, like her bakeware, had been a real splurge, but well worth it. She'd invested with the thought that she'd be here until Constance graduated from college and perhaps beyond.

Over the past few days, she'd feared that dream might be lost. Now she had more reason than ever to believe James Haggard was just a nightmarish glitch in her life's plans.

She picked up her phone and called Grace to check on Constance. No answer. In spite of her newfound hope, she felt a shudder of apprehension. She tried Esther's number. Finally, a cheerful hello.

"Hi, it's Dani."

"I thought you might be calling soon. How are the repairs coming along?"

"The back door is hung and looks great and very sturdy. The repairman is putting the alarm system through its final tests."

"Then I guess I'll see you and Riley soon."

"We might be delayed a little while, a few small tasks to finish."

"You take all the time you need, dear."

"I tried to call Grace but didn't get an answer. Do you know where she and the girls are?"

"Sure do. They went to the new movie theater up by the consolidated high school. The one with six theaters, though I can't see why a living soul would need that many to choose from. I don't know what they went to see, but they were mighty excited."

"I'll owe Grace several free child-care days after this."

By the time she said good-bye and broke the connection, the alarm tech was tapping on her open kitchen door.

"It's all set up, including a few advanced tasks you didn't have before. Have you got a few minutes for me to show you how all the settings work?"

"Sure." A few minutes of talk and then time alone with Riley. She could almost taste the salty thrill of his kisses.

Assured she knew how to operate the new and improved security system, she saw the nice young technician to the door and went in search of Riley.

She heard him before she saw him. He was on the back staircase talking to someone on the phone. She stopped and turned around, not wanting to eavesdrop on his conversation.

She didn't get away fast enough.

"I am so ready to get out of here. I'll be there as soon as I can make it. Time to start chilling the wine."

She rushed back to the kitchen, her stomach churning, suffocating fingers clutching her heart. She had been mooning over Riley like a foolish schoolgirl all day. He couldn't wait to get out of here.

Tears burned at the back of her eyes. She blinked repeatedly, forcing the tears not to fall. Why was she surprised? Grace had tried to warn her.

She couldn't even blame Riley. He'd been embroiled in her problems from the first minutes he arrived in Winding Creek. He'd had hardly a minute with his brothers or any of his old girlfriends from his high-school days.

He went with his instincts, knew when life got overly complicated it was time to move on. Apparently, where she was concerned, that time was now.

Riley joined her in the kitchen. "I think we've taken care of everything, including Elton Sheldon. Are you ready to roll?"

"You go ahead. The girls are at a movie with Grace, so there's no reason for me to rush. I'll take my car this time and be out in a while."

"That's a terrible idea."

"Why?"

"Because I promised Esther we'd be back early afternoon and I'm not leaving you here alone."

"Okay. But I'll drive my own car. I may need it tomorrow."

"I doubt it. I fear Esther and Grace are conniving

to give you the full ranch experience tomorrow and to make sure you have at least one day of actual vacation."

"I love your family."

"They obviously feel the same about you and Constance. Only they think you are family. I'll load my tools in the truck and leave by the back door. You set the alarm and I'll follow you to the Double K."

And then he'd hurry off to see someone who was chilling the wine.

SETTING UP A seduction scene was new to Riley. He'd never been accused of being a romantic, though he wasn't a jerk about it. He just tended to go with the flow. When the moment was right and the woman was willing, he let the details work out for themselves.

This time was different. Dani was different. He knew he'd never forget their first time making love, and he wanted it to be just as memorable for her.

He'd already saddled two horses and filled his saddlebag with the necessities. Now he just needed to persuade Dani to go riding with him.

That might not be as easy as he'd expected. She'd been a tad standoffish since they made it back to the ranch—she had shrugged off his attempt to kiss her when he left to go ready their mounts.

He was counting on that having more to do with the visit from Haggard's dubious attorney than with something Riley had said or done. Not that he'd ever pretended to understand women.

It was a good fifteen minute walk back to the house from the horse barn. Riley made it in ten. Dani was on the front porch with Esther, who was talking a mile a minute. Dani was bent over a potted plant, pinching off dead blooms.

That sight alone was enough to get his juices pumping. It was hard to figure how some guy hadn't roped and tied her years ago. He figured it wasn't for lack of trying. Tough on a man's ego to come in second to a pile of dough or a bowl of batter. He was finding that out for himself.

"Afternoon, ladies." He tipped his hat as he climbed the steps to the porch and lolled against a support post.

"What are you still doing around here?" Esther asked. "Gorgeous spring day like this, a cowboy should be out on his horse." Her eyes twinkled. She loved playing conspirator, especially if she sensed a little romance was involved. She'd packed the snacks and chilled the wine.

"I'm looking for a riding partner," he said. "How about you, Dani?"

She looked surprised and maybe a tad suspicious. "I think I'll pass this time and stay here with Esther."

"Lordy mercy, don't let me hold you back," Esther urged. "I've been up since before sunup and I feel a nap calling me."

"The horses need to be ridden," Riley said. "Have two saddled and waiting. Be a help to me if you come along." If subtlety didn't work, he'd raise the stakes. She wasn't getting out of this one.

"I'm not an experienced rider."

"The horse is experienced enough for both of you. Besides, I saw you ride this morning. You were in full control."

"That was a short, easy ride."

"We're not exactly going to be galloping down a mountain this afternoon. You'll be fine."

"If you're sure."

"Wouldn't be standing here cajoling if I wasn't."

"Then give me a minute to kick out of these sandals and change into my boots."

"Don't forget your hat and you might want sunglasses, as well. We'll be short on shade."

"Isn't our Dani something special?" Esther said once Dani was out of earshot.

"She is that."

"You don't think she's in any real danger of losing custody of Constance, do you?"

"How did you hear about that?"

"I'm not as deaf as you guys think."

"Ah. Selective hearing. How much do you know?"

"That some lying creep is pretending to be Constance's biological father and is trying to blackmail Dani into giving him half of Constance's trust fund."

"That's it in a nutshell. But whether the creep is lying or not, I can't believe any judge would rule in favor of that jerk. I don't see Constance going anywhere."

"What about you, Riley Lawrence? Where are you running off to next?"

"Is that what you think I do, run off?"

"It is. First ill wind slaps you in the face and off you go, running to find what you don't even know you're looking for."

"Sounds like you've got it all figured out." Which was a lot more than he did.

"I think it's time you quit running. It won't protect you from bad moments in life. Nothing will. It might keep you from finding true happiness, though.

"All I wanted to do that day I found Charlie's body was run and never stop. Ran myself into a heart attack that I prayed I wouldn't live through."

"I'm glad you did," he said.

"So am I now. I still miss my Charlie every second of every day, but that don't keep me from knowing how blessed I am to have Pierce and Grace in my life. It don't keep me from lovin' and laughin' and getting downright soggy-eyed when Jaci gives me a hug and calls me Grandma. Don't keep me from loving it when you Lawrence boys are all at my kitchen table like the old days."

"I'll come back and visit more often. That's a promise."

"I'd like that, but I'm still saying that maybe if you stopped running around the country long enough and just looked around you, you might find that the best thing for your soul is right here."

He couldn't argue with that.

But what if he tried and everything went wrong? What if he made promises he couldn't keep?

Was that what he was setting himself up for now? If so, Dani deserved better than that.

Dani swung through the screen door that went on every spring to let the breeze in and keep the mosquitoes out. His brain screamed that he should run for the hills for both their sakes.

His brain was fighting a losing battle.

IT WAS A slow but steady climb up the sloping incline. Riley and his stately, chestnut-colored quarter horse led the way.

Dani loved riding behind Riley. She liked the tilt of

his head and the sway of his body, seemingly in perfect harmony with his horse.

He looked like a man who owned the world and yet she knew he owned nothing except what fit in his truck when the need to roam hit him again.

They were opposites in so many ways. She felt most at home in her bakery. Rising before the sun to light her ovens and start rolling out her first batch of cinnamon rolls was balm for her soul.

That was not a portable life.

But she couldn't knock Riley's choices, either. Reveling in the view of rolling pastures, meandering creeks and myriad wildlife was more exhilarating than she'd ever imagined. If she lived to be a hundred, she doubted she'd ever tire of sharing moments like this with Riley.

Not that she'd ever get the chance to find out.

Riley reined in his horse as they left a cluster of cedar trees and entered a clearing. She followed his lead.

"This is a good place to give the horses a rest and let them drink their fill of water."

She looked around as he dismounted, her breath catching at the magnificent view. Off to the east were rolling pastures as far as she could see.

To the west was a slow-flowing stream. Riley led his horse there and tethered him to a low branch of a mulberry tree.

"The gorge at Lonesome Branch," Riley said as he helped Dani from the saddle. "Best view on the Double K Ranch."

The gorge. His special place. He'd bought her here to his special place. Emotion welled until she felt her heart was caving into her chest.

He tethered Dani's horse and then reached for her hand. "You haven't seen the best part yet."

"No, but I can hear the waterfall."

They walked together to the edge of the cliff. The water from the stream cascaded over layers of huge boulders and made a steep drop to the bottom of the gorge.

She stared at the drop-off, her mind painting the vivid image of Riley as a boy of fourteen poised on the edge of the precipice, struggling to come to grips with his fears and grief.

He was no longer that boy. He was every inch a man. Strong. Virile. Tough enough to face a grizzly. But somewhere inside that hulk of masculinity, a remnant of that frightened boy must still exist.

"I always compare this place to life," Riley said. "There's always a cliff waiting just around the corner. One false step and you plunge over the edge. That's why I go for the gusto. Do it all before you fall."

"I guess that worldview is okay if it works for you."

"What's yours? Maybe I'll adopt it."

She gave the question serious thought. "I suppose it's find the place that's home to your heart and then live life to the fullest, without regrets, every day."

"And that place for you is Dani's Delights in Winding Creek, Texas?"

"It definitely feels that way now."

He walked back to where the horses had waded into the cool stream. For a second, she thought he was upset with her and ready to saddle up and ride back to the house.

Instead of untying his horse, he reined it back to the bank and began unloading his saddlebag. By the time she joined him, he was spreading a lightweight blanket in a grassy area a few yards from the bank.

She grabbed one corner and helped him straighten it. He went back for two small tote bags. He set them on the blanket, hunched down and started unloading small containers of deviled eggs, veggie sticks, purple grapes, cheese and crackers.

"You come prepared."

"With a little help from Esther." He pulled out a bottle of white wine, uncorked it and filled two plastic glasses.

Dani's heart beat faster, her pulse climbing.

This was the chilled wine he'd ordered. He'd been talking to Esther. The wine was meant for Riley to share with Dani at the gorge at Lonesome Brach.

She was such a dope. Falling back into her old ways. Never really expecting guys to become serious about her. But she'd never felt about any other man the way she did about Riley.

She sipped her wine and then lay back on the blanket, her hands cradling the back of her head. Riley stretched out beside her and pulled her into his arms. When their lips met, she closed her eyes and melted into the thrill of him. This time there would be no pulling back.

Riley wasn't a forever guy, but the glow from their lovemaking would warm her soul for the rest of her life.

Chapter Sixteen

Dani raised herself up on her elbow and laced her fingers through the fine hairs on Riley's sun-bronzed chest. His eyes were closed, his hat lying beside him. His naked body was dappled by late afternoon sun rays that penetrated the leafy branches that had been shading them for the last two hours.

They'd made love twice. The first time had been a delirious rampage of passion. He'd kissed, nibbled and sucked every inch of her body until she was so hot and slick with desire that she was begging to feel his erection inside her.

He'd swept her into an orgasm so intense that she'd felt as if her chest might explode. She'd lain in his arms for long minutes after that, totally spent, basking in the afterglow and thinking she'd never recover. A few grapes and another glass of wine were all it had taken to have her hungering for more of Riley's sweet kisses on her lips.

And on her neck. And on her breasts and her abdomen and the hot, slick pool at the triangle of her desire. The lovemaking had gone more slowly that time. He'd teased and tasted, brought her to the edge of ecstasy only to slow his rhythm again and again until she could take the sensual titillation no longer.

They'd exploded together in a frenzied eruption that rivaled the first time. And then sweet, honeyed contentment had flowed through her like warm cream.

There had been no soft whispers or throaty moans of love. She hadn't expected it. Riley was who he was. She'd been warned before they even met.

She was who she was, too. And she was a woman in love. How could she not be in love with Riley Lawrence?

THE WOMEN HAD cooked the evening meal. The men drew KP duty. It wasn't the way it had been when the Lawrence brothers lived here as teenagers. But even on the ranch, times had changed. No one complained.

Riley loaded the last of the dishes in the dishwasher as Tucker swept up and Pierce wiped down the counter.

"Anyone for a beer?" Tucker asked.

"Wouldn't turn one down," Pierce said.

Riley took three beers from the fridge and passed them around. The brothers settled back around the scarred kitchen table.

"Now that the women aren't listening, are you gonna tell us the fight that is making your jaw a new shade of purple?" Tucker asked. "And then explain why we didn't get invited to the brawl?"

"To be honest, I didn't see it coming until I saw my obnoxious opponent's fist flying at me."

Riley explained the situation, assuring them he gave better than he got.

"I don't get the worry over a birth certificate," Tucker

said. "DNA would take precedence over that in any court of law."

"As close as I figure, either Haggard knows the paternity test will come back negative or he fears it will," Riley said. "In which case he'll have as much chance at getting his hands on Constance's trust fund as he does at winning a spot on the Dallas Cowboys' roster."

Tucker rocked his half-empty beer bottle back and forth on the table. "So you see this as a desperation dance?"

"Most likely."

"Guess it was a gamble," Pierce said. "If it had worked and Dani had been so frightened by his threat that she'd paid off, he'd have been up a million."

"And that possibility was not as far-fetched as it sounds," Riley said. "If Haggard's name had been on the birth certificate and Dani could have gotten her hands on the money, she might have caved. That's how frightened she is at the thought of that conniving bastard gaining custody of Constance."

"And then she'd been opening herself to more blackmail," Pierce said.

"Nothing will be completely settled until you get the lab results," Tucker said. "And not even then if the results come back positive or maybe if it doesn't."

"Any word from your buddy with the FBI?" Riley asked.

"He called back to say he got the message and he'll see what he can find."

"That's all I can ask. I've been thinking more about my prison visit with Dudley Miles."

"Can't even imagine what came over that man unless he got into his daughter's stash."

Riley downed the last of his beer. "There's something fishy going on there. I can't figure it out yet, but I'm not giving up."

Tucker stood and gathered the empty beer bottles. "Unfortunately, I have to give up on all of you. I'll be out of here Friday morning and doing my damnedest to stay personal with an ugly bull for eight seconds on Friday night."

"You're heading out quicker than I expected," Riley said.

"And you're sticking around longer than I expected. Not that I blame you. Just saying. But I've got a proposition for both of you before I leave."

"Let's hear it," Pierce said.

"I'm challenging you to a brother-against-brothers chili cook off tomorrow afternoon. You don't have a chance of winning, but the challenge will do you good."

"Count me in," Pierce said. "Ten dollars to the winner. I love taking you guys' money."

"I'll be here unless something develops with the continuing Haggard saga," Riley said. "See you then if I don't catch up with you before that."

"Where are you off to in such a hurry now?" Tucker asked. "Oh, never mind. Sorry I asked."

Riley grinned.

It was great hanging with his brothers, but it was Dani he wanted to be with now.

JAMES HAGGARD WOKE up on the side of a country road behind the wheel of his old pickup truck. He groaned and grabbed his head, pressing hard against his hammering temples. He had no idea where he was or how he'd gotten here.

His truck smelled like vomit and sweat. He poked his head out the window and gulped in the clean air.

Revived a little, he worried the handle until he got the door open. He stepped outside, then grabbed on to the door as his head went spinning. It wasn't daylight, but it wasn't the pitch-black of night, either.

His right leg started to cramp. There was no way of knowing how long he'd been crunched up beneath the wheel.

Using the truck for support, he worked his way to the passenger side and then staggered into the woods to relieve himself.

Something scurried over his foot. He jumped and then fell backward, landing on his rump. Whatever he'd inhaled, injected or drunk with crazy Angela, he never wanted to touch again.

He sat there in the underbrush with mosquitoes buzzing about his face, and his stomach and head taking turns with the torture.

Slowly, disjointed bits and pieces of information popped into his consciousness. Something about a toddler buried in the woods. Crying that wouldn't stop. A kidnapper. None of it made any sense.

The night grew darker. Finally James staggered back to his truck and passed out.

The next thing he knew, some frigging idiot was slapping him over and over in the face.

He opened his eyes as much as he could, which was only a slit. His brother was staring down at him.

"Stop hitting me," James bellowed.

"Where the hell have you been? You smell like a latrine."

James tried to focus on Lenny's black eyes and mis-shapen face. "Somebody beat the crap out of you."

"Because I was out trying to get you the million dollars that tramp in the bakery stole from you. It's just like always, I try to take care of you and you just get drunk or high. I'm through saving you. You're not worth it."

"No. Don't be mad at me, Lenny. I'll do whatever you say. Anything. You're too good to me." His head kept pounding. He was going to be sick. Lenny would hit him again if he threw up.

"This is the thanks I get," Lenny said. "You can't even get your hands on the birth certificate for the kid you claim is your daughter."

"She's my daughter. Amber was crazy in love with me back then, same as I was about her. She would never have cheated. Not then. I'm sure of it."

That made one of them.

RILEY WOKE TO the smell of coffee and Dani's cinnamon rolls. He kicked off the sheets and reveled in the tender ache in his crotch and upper thighs.

In the hope of tamping down speculation, Dani had kicked him out of her bed and back to his bed before daylight this morning, but not before they'd made love for the fourth time in less than twenty-four hours.

Keep up that pace and he'd never be able to ride a horse again. Whatever kind of spell she'd cast on him, he hoped it lasted forever.

Forever?

He hadn't known that word was even in his internal vocabulary. He threw his legs over the side of the bed and headed for the shower.

It was the last day of her impromptu vacation. He

wanted it to be special and free of visits or calls from Haggard or his crooked attorney.

Riley would love to hear from Andy Malone but only if it was good news, whatever that might be.

He ran the water in the shower until it was as hot as he could stand it before stepping under the spray. He wasn't too keen on washing Dani's scent and love juices off his body, but that just meant he'd have to acquire them again.

DANI SLID HER second pan of hot cinnamon rolls from the oven. The original six had disappeared with the first pot of coffee. These should go slower, since Esther had just placed a platter of bacon on the table and Grace was busy frying fresh eggs.

Riley was the last to join them. His brothers immediately started ribbing him.

"About time you made it up, Quick Draw."

"Were you up all night researching losing chili recipes?"

"Are you kidding? I can beat you guys with chili made with my right hand behind my back."

"Ten bucks says you can't."

Riley poured himself a cup of coffee. "You guys will bet on anything."

"What are we going to do on my last day as a cowgirl?" Constance asked. "I hope it's ride the horses."

"I'm sure we can fit that in," Grace said.

"How about me taking the females to a high school female barrel-racing event?" Tucker suggested.

"What's barrel racing?" Constance asked.

"A rodeo competition. Both of you young ladies

could be barrel-racing champions in practically no time if you worked at it."

"Yes," Constance squealed. "I want to be in a rodeo. I used to want to be a pastry chef like Aunt Dani, but now I want to be a cowgirl so I can live on a ranch and ride horses every day."

"What time's the competition?" Pierce asked.

"One o'clock," Tucker said. "We can stay awhile and easily be home in time for me to embarrass you two in the chili cook-off."

"I'm fixing to take a drive over to the Wallaces' spread and look at some Angus breeding stock he's looking to sell," Pierce said. "If either of you guys has the time to come along, I'd appreciate your input."

"How much stock is he selling?" Riley asked.

"All he owns, but I'm not interested in anything but the Angus. He's planning to sell off a few thousand acres of his ranch come fall if he can get a decent price for it."

"I don't remember the Wallace spread," Tucker said. "How would you rate it?"

"Excellent water sources and great grazing land. You and Riley should take a look at it. Consider going in together and buying it. You have to settle down somewhere one day."

"I might consider that," Tucker said. "Bull riding is not a job you can grow old in."

Not surprisingly, Riley didn't comment.

Dani was passing the bacon to Pierce when she saw him reach for his phone. He checked the screen, nodded to Riley and silently mouthed the name Andy.

Pierce left the room with Riley at his heels. She stood and hurried to follow them to the family den. This was her fight and she wasn't sitting it out.

Chapter Seventeen

"Riley and Dani Boatman are here with me."

"Then put your phone on speaker. Nothing I have to tell you is classified."

"Ready on this end," Pierce said.

Dani scooted closer to the phone, not wanting to miss anything the FBI agent had to say.

"James Haggard has an arrest record that is miles long, though he's never served much time and hasn't been arrested in over five years. His crimes range from online scamming to unarmed robberies."

"Seems he's picked up his old habits," Riley said. "What's the possibility he could escalate to more violent crimes?"

"Not great, but you can never rule that out with a man like Haggard, especially with this amount of money involved. He's been a petty thief for the most part."

"It may sound like a lot of money," Dani reminded him. "But it's not as if someone can just write a check for it. It's in a trust fund."

"If you're a legal parent, there are always ways around that if you try hard enough," Andy offered. "The real danger is that the trust-fund money might lure

James's older brother into the mix if it hasn't already. I wouldn't be surprised if he's behind Haggard's scam."

"What do you know about him?" Pierce asked.

"Have you ever heard of Cecil Molina?"

"Sounds familiar," Riley said.

"He runs the most profitable smuggling operation the Western Hemisphere has ever seen. Guns. Illegal drugs. Humans. An underage sex ring. He's active across South and Central America and on our southern border."

"Sounds like he spreads himself thin," Riley said.

"Which is why he's still at large. If he gets close to being caught in one area, he moves somewhere else."

"I'm not following this train of thought," Dani said. "What does Cecil Molina have to do with James Haggard or his brother?"

"Sorry," Andy said. "We FBI agents tend to get caught up in the big picture. Lenny Haggard *was* Molina's top hit man. Lenny is wanted for murder in Texas, Arizona and California. His last hit was a judge's family of five in south Texas."

"Sounds like he's probably pulling down his share of money on his own," Pierce said.

"He was, but we hear through very reliable sources that he crossed Molina and now Lenny is on Molina's hit list. He may have split the country by now, but there's a chance he's looking for funds to get him far away from Molina's large base of operations."

"Which would explain the desperation and the rush to settle with cash," Riley said. "And up the likelihood for violence."

"Let's just say Lenny has killed for a lot less," Andy said.

"Do you have a picture of Lenny?" Riley asked.

"On my computer, which is right here."

"Start the transfer anytime." In a matter of seconds, the pictures started popping up on the phone's screen.

"Son of a bitch," Riley muttered.

"Does that mean you recognize him?" Andy asked.

"Let's just say that if there's a price on his head, I'm ready to collect."

Riley explained the fact that Lenny was in Winding Creek and posing as James's attorney. "Do you want me to call the local sheriff?"

"Not unless you feel you're in immediate danger. Winding Creek will be crawling with FBI agents by the end of the day. Someone will call you back within the next half hour to find out everything you know. In the meantime, be careful and don't go near Dani's house until I give you the all-clear."

"I own a bakery," Dani protested. "I open for business at seven tomorrow morning and I have to be there at least three hours before that to start baking."

"If all goes well, that won't be a problem. We hope to have both James and Lenny in custody by then. If not, we'll get back with you on how to handle the situation with the bakery."

"You guys are damn serious," Pierce said.

"You got that right, especially when the suspects may lead us to Cecil Molina."

"Just think," Pierce said when they'd finished the call. "You beat up a real badass today, Riley. This may even replace your grizzly story for an attention grabber."

"And to think I could have held him until the FBI got there and really earned hero status."

Dani knew that they weren't taking this lightly, that it

was just the way men handled things when they couldn't admit fear. She was afraid and didn't mind admitting it.

"No rodeo for Constance this afternoon," she said.

"Not a problem," Riley said. "There will be no rodeo for the others, either. We'll all stay here where you've got three bodyguards until the FBI makes an arrest. I don't expect that to take long."

Dani whispered a prayer as she went back to the kitchen, where she could be close to her precious niece.

Please don't ever let either of the Haggards touch Constance's life. And please keep everyone safe.

DANI WAS STRETCHED out in a yard chair next to Grace and Esther, a few yards away from where the girls were playing on the tire swing and a bit farther away from where the men were drinking beer and tending their pots of chili simmering over outdoor propane cookers.

The ringing of her cell phone startled her and a wave of anxiety coursed through her. She checked the ID. Sheriff Cavazos. As far as she knew, the FBI hadn't contacted him, so she was surprised at his call.

"Hello."

"Don't have the best of news for you, but hope I didn't catch you at a bad time."

"Just trying to relax. What's the news?"

"Cory Boxer is no longer a suspect in the vandalism of your shop."

No surprise there, at least not for her.

"He has an airtight alibi for the time of the break-in," the sheriff continued. "Turns out he didn't even actually break into Joe Clark's trunk."

That was a surprise. "I thought he was caught in the act."

"Caught in the act of snooping but apparently nothing worse. The lock on the truck wasn't broken and Joe Clark finally admitted that he might have accidentally left it open since he was planning on coming right back. Cory said he only ran off because Joe started yelling curses at him. At any rate, he's not your suspect."

She didn't tell him that she felt certain her vandal would be officially identified soon.

Another call came in only seconds after she broke the connection with the sheriff. This time it was the FBI with instructions as to how they wanted her to handle her end of the situation.

The shop and that entire block of Main Street would be under tight scrutiny tomorrow and they requested she open the bakery as usual. They didn't want the Haggards to suspect a thing if they approached Dani's Delights.

They assured her that neither Lenny nor James would be allowed to enter the bakery and that her customers would not be put in danger. She had no choice but to take them at their word.

"Good news, I hope," Grace said when Dani slipped her phone back into her pocket.

"As good as can be expected until I hear they've arrested both of the Haggards. I can open my bakery as usual tomorrow with the assurance the FBI has everything under control."

"Too bad we didn't think to call them sooner," Esther said.

"Even if we had, we wouldn't have gotten this kind of response before Lenny entered the picture, and that was only yesterday. I guess I should go and give Riley the latest news, though I hate to interrupt all that stir-

ring and boisterous bragging he's doing over his big
iron chili pot."

"I admit Riley's surprised me," Grace said. "I kept
hearing about his rambling ways and I mistakenly in-
terpreted that to be an unwillingness to grow up and
take on responsibility. But he's really come through for
you and Constance."

"All my boys have good hearts," Esther said. "I never
want to see a one of them ride off in the sunset, as Charlie used to say. He also used to vow that the Double K
Ranch was never more alive than when the three of
them were here."

She reached up and wiped an unexpected tear from
her eye.

"You must still miss your husband very much," Dani
said.

"Too much. Don't ever waste a minute of the time
you can share with the man you love. Once he's gone,
you can never get him back. All you have left to cher-
ish is the memories."

Dani agreed. She walked over to the cooking area
and gave Riley a hug around the waist, burying her face
beneath his broad shoulders.

"Guess the odor of my chili is making you crave
my body."

"No. I just have a thing for men with big iron pots."

"You okay?" he asked.

"Yeah. I'm okay. Who can worry with you and the
FBI in charge?"

When she got her next call she was taking a walk
alone, trying to come to terms with all that happened
over the last few days. This time it was the lab.

Chapter Eighteen

"I'm calling for Dani Boatman."

"Speaking."

"This is Courtney Graves with Corinthian Court Laboratories. I talked to you when you were in Monday morning."

"I remember. Is there a problem?"

"No. We're open late on Wednesday evenings and I was just handed your finished report. You signed the permission form that you wanted to be notified by phone as soon as the report was finished."

"I remember."

"Are you ready for the results?"

"Yes. I didn't expect to hear before tomorrow, but I'm ready."

"The test came back negative for paternity."

The breath she'd been holding came out in a gush. "That was so what I wanted to hear."

"There's more."

"Like what?"

"The results are negative for paternity but positive for a familial relationship."

"What are you saying exactly?"

"The man whose blood was sampled is the uncle of the child."

"That can't be."

"I'm sorry the results are not what you were hoping for, but all we can do is give you the findings. You'll receive a written copy of this via FedEx possibly in the morning, but Friday morning by the latest."

So it was likely Lenny Haggard was Constance's biological father. The thought made her sick. But Constance was no more like Lenny than Dani was like what her sister, Amber, had been.

The news she had to hold on to was that this would all be over soon. She had the FBI's word on that. If she couldn't trust the FBI, who could she trust?

Dani hurried back to join Riley and the men. Perplexed and sick at heart, she just needed to be near him.

"TRY THIS," RILEY SAID, pushing a spoon of chili at Dani. She parted her lips for the tiniest taste.

Her mouth exploded in peppery fire.

"Water," she called, fanning her open mouth with her hand. "Water to put out the fire."

"She likes it hot," Riley announced loudly. "One vote for me."

She'd break the news about the test results after they had their chili. She'd already stolen too much of the brief time Riley could have spent with his brothers. She'd give him this reprieve and then they'd contact the FBI with the news that Lenny Haggard was Constance's biological father.

THE BAKERY OPENED as usual on Thursday morning.

"Such a shame about the break-in. I head they had

to let that Boxer fellow go. Have they arrested anyone else?"

"Not that I've heard," Dani answered as she handed Mrs. Dupree her change.

"I hope they do soon. We can't stand for this kind of senseless crime in Winding Creek. We're all neighbors and we stick together."

"I agree. I'm sure the sheriff will arrest a credible suspect soon."

Her next customer, Jenny, another of her regulars, stepped up to the counter. "One of your delicious cinnamon rolls and a caramel latte."

"For here?"

"Yes. I'm meeting Sara Pendleton, but she's always late. If I order for her, it's never what she wants."

"Sara does like variety," Dani agreed.

"I can't tell you how disgusted I was when I heard about your break-in. The whole town is. I'm probably not supposed to mention this, but Sara's Bible study group is collecting money to help you recover your losses."

"That's extremely thoughtful, but really, I'm fine."

"It's the principle of the thing. We stand together just like we always have in this town. Let the criminals move in and first thing you know, the shops start moving out and Main Street becomes a ghost town."

"I'm not going anywhere," Dani assured Jenny as she topped off the latte with one dollop of whipped cream, just the way she liked it.

It had been like this ever since she opened the door at seven. A steady stream of customers. A steady stream of empathetic comments.

Everyone in town seemed to know about the vandalism. So far no one seemed privy to the fact that an infamous criminal was hanging out in their area or that the FBI had invaded Winding Creek.

Dani was almost certain the two men drinking their second cups of coffee at one of the back tables were agents. And there would be others observing the shop from locations on Main Street and the alley behind her shop.

Riley had spent the night. He'd been as shocked as she was by the news that Lenny was Constance's biological father. But even knowing that, he'd felt enough confidence in the FBI's protection that he'd left a few minutes ago to drop off Constance at school. Then he was making a quick stop at one of Dani's local suppliers to pick the freshest carrots for the carrot-cake muffins she'd be making later.

The bell above the door rang. This time it was Angela who strode in, wearing a clingy knit pullover, denim shorts that barely covered her behind and a pair of red Western boots.

She yawned and came over to the counter. "Sorry I'm late. My alarm didn't go off."

Improper attire. Not punctual. Zero motivation. Dani would have to fire her, but the last thing she needed this morning was a scene with Angela.

"You can start by clearing and cleaning the vacated tables," Dani said as she poured an espresso. "Make sure you don't leave them sticky and get all the crumbs from under the table or chairs."

"What do I wipe the tables with?"

"Clean white bar towels are on the wire shelves just inside the kitchen. The lobby sweeper for the floors is behind the far end of the counter."

Angela looked as if Dani had just asked her to scrub the floor with a toothbrush, but she did start clearing the tables. Dani went back to waiting on her customers.

The first break in business came just after Riley returned. That was also when she noticed that half of the tables in the shop still needed to be cleared. She looked around. Angela was nowhere to be seen.

Dani poked her head into the kitchen, where Riley was pulling bunches of carrots from reusable bags. "Can you watch the shop for a second?"

"No problem."

Dani marched to the back door, assuming Angela was taking a cigarette break. She opened the door and scanned the area. No Angela. No cigarette odor. No sign of FBI agents, but that didn't mean they weren't watching from somewhere.

As she stepped back inside, she heard what sounded like a door banging upstairs. She walked halfway up to the second floor. "Angela."

"Yeah. Up here."

Where she had no business being. Patience stretched to just past its limit, Dani took the rest of the stairs two at a time.

She heard the commode flush and found Angela at the open bathroom door. This time the smell of smoke was stifling. "This area is private and off-limits at all times."

"The bathroom downstairs was in use and I had to go bad. I didn't think you'd get all bent out of shape about that."

Maybe Dani was overreacting. Her nerves were ragged and strained.

Angela walked toward the staircase. Dani had started

to follow when she noticed the door to her bedroom was open. She hadn't left it that way. She glanced inside and saw that half the drawers in her tall chest were open.

Her temper exploded. She raced down the stairs and grabbed Angela's right wrist. "I suppose you also have a reason for rummaging through my private belongings."

"I don't know what you're talking about."

"I'm talking about invasion of privacy. I want you out of Dani's Delights and I never want to see you in here again. Never."

"You can't fire me over nothing."

"Get out, Angela. Now."

"Bitch."

Dani was seeing red, so mad she was shaking as she followed Angela into the bakery to make sure she left without breaking anything.

A customer was at the counter, but Dani didn't see Riley. She went back to the kitchen to check on him. He was calmly boxing cookies that she'd never had time to get to the display case.

"What's the problem?" he asked. "You look like you're ready to horsewhip someone."

"I just found Angela Miles going through the drawers in my bedroom."

"Did she take anything?"

"Probably not. My clothes would swallow her skinny body. I was so perturbed I fired her on the spot."

"You had to see that coming."

Riley tied a length of decorative string around the filled box, then leaned over and gave her a peck on the cheek as he passed to deliver the cookies to the waiting customer.

Dani dropped to a chrome work stool and took a deep

breath. There couldn't be another man in the world like Riley. Dani's Delights would never be the same without him. Neither would she, but she had known that going in.

ANGELA WAS FURIOUS. If Dani Boatman thought she was going to get away with treating her like that, she was dead wrong. Angela always found a way of getting back at people who mistreated her.

She shoved open the front door of the bakery. A man with a package in his hand blocked her path.

"That was quick," he said. "I didn't even ring the bell."

He scooted away from the door to allow a couple entrance to the shop. She started to shove him out of the way, but the company logo on the brown envelope caught her attention.

Corinthian Court Lab. This was the envelope James Haggard was looking for.

"Are you Dani Boatman?"

"Yes," she lied.

The man who was obviously new on this route handed her the electronic signature gadget. "Just sign here."

She signed Dani's name and took the package. She might give it to James. She might just toss it in the street. She walked to her car before opening the package. The enclosed document looked official.

"'Results of paternity testing,'" she read aloud.

She kept reading. She'd definitely call James. He'd owe her big-time for this.

THUNDER REVERBERATED THROUGH James Haggard's head as he read the lab report, growing louder and louder until he felt like a 747 was roaring through his skull.

The only woman he'd ever loved had been a slut. Not just in the later years when the addiction had turned her into a monster he didn't recognize, but in the beginning.

Amber slept in his bed, told him how much she loved him, made him feel like a king.

He'd done everything but kill for her, and he would have done that to keep her with him. And all the while she'd played him for a fool.

Lenny had told James from the first that he couldn't trust Amber, but it was his own brother he couldn't trust.

James read the last few lines of the test results and then threw the document to the floor of his beat-up pickup truck.

"I don't know why I'm shocked. Lenny treated me like I was stupid all my life. A stupid jerk who couldn't do anything right without him interfering, so why would he have any qualms about sleeping with my woman?"

"Who are you so angry with?" Angela asked. "Constance's mother or your brother?"

"Both, but Amber's no longer alive to taunt me. It's Lenny who's still cheating and double-crossing me."

"How?"

"He pushed and coerced me to go for the insurance settlement. Even when I wanted to drop it, he kept pushing."

Angela leaned over and picked up the forms. "I don't see how that's so bad. Why not go after the money? He must have thought you were the father."

"Lenny's a taker, not a giver. If there was any money to be gotten, it would have ended up in his pocket."

"I guess it will for sure now."

"No. It damn sure won't."

"How can you stop him? He's the father."

"He's also a wanted criminal who'd never be granted custody. That's why he pushed me to do it. That's why he kept harping about the birth certificate. He knew all along the DNA might show him as the father."

A plan began to coalesce in James's mind. "I'm going to need your help."

"Not if you're going to do something illegal."

"You left me passed out in my pickup truck on a deserted road the other night. You were lucky I didn't come back at you for that."

"That was Mother's doing. Remember? I told you. She goes ape when people get me high."

"You got yourself high. And you will help in whatever way I tell you to, or I'll leak those deep, dark secrets you told me. A dead child. The cover-up."

"Stop." She put her hands over her ears. "Stop saying those lies."

"If they were lies, they wouldn't be driving you crazy. Now, here's what I want from you or your murderous secrets will climb out of their graves and drag you into the pits of hell with them."

AT LEAST HALF the tables in the bakery were taken and there were several people in line when the group of three nicely dressed young men walked in. They walked over to the counter but did not get in line.

"May I help you?" Dani asked.

"Actually, we're here to help you." One of the men flashed his FBI ID. Brad Grogan. "I'm looking for Riley Lawrence or Dani Boatman."

"I'm Dani. Give me a minute." She handed the bag of assorted muffins to her customer, then went and summoned her young assistant, Sandy, from the kitchen with instructions to take over for a few minutes.

"Could we talk somewhere private?" Brad asked.

"In my office, just off my kitchen. Riley is upstairs. I'll call him. He'll definitely want to hear what you have to say firsthand."

She called Riley while she led the men back to her office.

Riley bounded into the office a few minutes later. "Good news, I hope."

"Not for Lenny Haggard, but we're writing it up as a highly successful day for the FBI."

They introduced themselves and the one already identified as Brad took the lead.

"At twenty-two past twelve this afternoon, the body of Lenny Haggard was found in one of the rental cabins at Bosley's Bait and Tackle. He died from three gunshots at close range to the back of his head."

"He's really dead?" Dani asked. "You're sure that was him?"

"No doubt about it."

"I can't believe I'm saying this about a murder, but that is the best news I've had in months, if not forever."

"His death will be a relief to a lot of innocent and not-so-innocent people," Brad agreed.

"That was quick," Riley said. "Less than twenty-four hours after we called with information that he was in Winding Creek, he's dead."

"It works that way more than you'd guess," Brad said. "We search for months, get a hot tip and then wham. We have our man."

"You said you found him dead. Does that mean it wasn't one of your guys who shot him?"

"That's what it means. Three shots to the back of the head is a trademark of Cecil Molina. Looks like one of his hatchet men got to Lenny before we could."

"That doesn't come as a real surprise, either," one of the other agents said. "He was so desperate to get his hands on your niece's trust fund he got careless. Stalking you. Showing his face around Winding Creek. Staying in a rental cabin that was registered in his brother's name. Careless errors. That's what desperation does."

"Do you have James Haggard in custody?" Riley asked.

"Not yet. We'll leave that to local law enforcement. Our agents have already talked to Sheriff Cavazos and he'll be talking to you about charging James with vandalism, harassment and an attempted scam to steal money."

"I doubt you'll see him again," the third agent said, "especially if he witnessed Lenny's murder. He'll be on the run and scared to death."

"Then this is over," Dani said. "My niece's biological father is dead, so he can make no claims on her trust fund. James Haggard isn't the father, but he is Constance's uncle."

"With an extensive criminal record, so his claim would never override yours. You can go back to running your shop."

"I'm ready to have that life back," she said.

"One more thing," Brad said. "We've been hearing about your cinnamon rolls and chocolate-filled croissants all day from the lucky team hanging out inside the bakery."

"So those were the guys consuming everything in sight. Can I offer you anything from my display case?"

"Thought you'd never ask."

"Take a seat and I'll serve you at your table. My assistant will take your coffee order. It's all on the house."

Riley put his hand to the small of her back as they followed the team of agents into the serving area.

"What an ending to a wild ride," he whispered.

"It was that."

Only she wasn't ready for all the wildness to end.

I'LL BE THERE for Tucker's goodbye dinner by six, I promise. I just have to take the ham-and-cheese croissants out of the oven and drop them off at the ladies auxiliary planning meeting," Dani said.

"We'll wait on you." Riley offered.

"No, we can't," Constance pleaded. "I won't get there in time to ride horses with Jaci if we don't leave now."

"Didn't you get enough of horses over the three days?" Dani asked.

"No. I have to practice a lot if I'm going to be a rodeo champion. We really need to live on a ranch."

"Better forget the ranch idea and stick with becoming a champion barrel racer. You have a far better chance of success with that." Dani gave Constance and Riley a quick hug and pushed them out the door.

It was early Friday evening. The streets were crowded with locals out for dinner, or shopping or just to grab an ice-cream cone or indulge in happy hour.

She wasn't afraid and she wasn't going to become a prisoner in her own shop. Besides, Sheriff Cavazos had promised to have deputies in the area constantly until James Haggard was arrested or until they were sure he'd left town.

She walked into the kitchen and breathed in the quiet,

safe familiarity of her surroundings. She would have Constance and her bakery for years to come. No place had ever felt more like home.

As for Riley, she couldn't imagine life without him, but she would never demand or even plead with him to stay in Winding Creek.

He was who he was. All she could do was love him for as long as he let her. And then she'd find a way to live with great memories and a breaking heart.

WHERE WERE HER car keys? Dani could swear she'd left them on the counter next to her croissants when she went back upstairs for her purse. Obviously she was mistaken, since they weren't there now.

She turned around and then realized they were in her pocket. Oh, well, it had been an exciting day.

Someone banged on the door. Hopefully it was FedEx since she was yet to receive the promised official copy of the lab report. She started toward the door and stopped when she saw Angela—no doubt here to complain about being fired.

Angela had problems and needed help, but Dani had a bakery to run. She didn't have the time, energy or expertise to take Angela on.

Still, she couldn't very well ignore her. She walked over and opened the door. "You caught me at a really bad time, Angela. I'm already running late for a dinner engagement."

"I'm not here to listen to your problems, bitch."

So this was how it was going to be. "Get out of my shop this minute before I call 911."

Angela shoved her hard, thrusting Dani back into the shop. "You want to keep living, you do as you're told."

Dani reached for her phone. Before she could punch in even one number, a large hand closed around her wrist and knocked the phone from her hands.

James Haggard had followed Angela in. The pistol clutched in his right hand was proof enough that this was not a visit to express his regrets.

"I didn't kill your brother," she said.

"I know. I did it. I killed the lying scum like I should have done years ago. Before he screwed me out of everything that mattered to me."

He took a step closer and pointed the gun at her head. "I'm through with being cheated. By Lenny, by Amber. By you."

"I've never cheated you, James. I don't have anything that belongs to you. Constance isn't your daughter. I have paternity testing that proves that." Unfortunately, she didn't have the copy at hand.

"I saw your tests."

"How could you?"

"It doesn't matter now. The results don't matter anymore. I've settled that score. You stole Constance's money and used it to buy this bakery. Money that belonged to me just as much as it belonged to you.

"No," he continued, anger hardening his voice. "I'm even more deserving. I took care of Amber when she was pregnant. You never came around."

He knew about the test results. She had no idea how he knew, but clearly discovering that Lenny was the father of Amber's child must have pushed him over the edge.

"The money was never yours or mine, and was never Lenny's, either," she said. "I would never steal from

Constance. Never. The money is in a trust fund just like I said. I didn't lie to you. I'm not lying to you now."

"You're just like Lenny. All you do is run over people like me and Constance. I won't be run over again."

His face was twisted in rage. A cold, calculating rage. She'd never be able to talk sense into him. She needed a weapon or help from Angela. Only Angela had a blank look on her face, as if she was falling into a trance. No telling what she'd smoked, inhaled or shot into her veins.

There was no weapon in sight. Her only hope was to escape.

"I'm here to see that you finally get what you deserve, Dani Boatman."

"Please don't do this, James. If you kill me, you'll go to prison. Is that what you want?"

"Only the stupid ones go to prison. I'm not stupid. Get the knife and the tape, Angela. Bind her wrists and her ankles the way I instructed. There's no time to waste."

"Why are you with him, Angela? He's using you. You must see that."

"Shut up," Angela said, her voice suddenly shaky.

"Don't do it, Angela," Dani pleaded. "Don't let this monster ruin your life, too."

"She has no choice," James said. "No choice at all. She and her dirty little secrets belong to the devil and now to me."

Angela reached into her tote and pulled out a butcher knife and then two large rolls of duct tape, laying them all on one of the serving tables.

"Start with the wrists," James ordered.

"Don't do this," Dani pleaded. "If it's money you want, I'll find a way to get it for you."

"You had your chance. But you're just like Amber. You take and take and take. You never give."

"I'm nothing like Amber. I'll take good care of your niece. I love her with all my heart. Doesn't that matter to you?"

"The wrists. Now," James demanded. "I can't wait all night." He turned the gun toward Angela.

Dani's pulse raced. It was now or never.

She made a run for the kitchen. She tried to close the door behind her, but James was too fast. She careened onto the top of her solid worktable and slid the three feet across the surface on her stomach.

It took a few complicated moves to enable her to land on the floor feet first instead of head first.

She squatted down so that James couldn't see her, but now she could no longer see him. And there was nowhere else to run. If she went into her office, she'd be like a cornered rat.

She crawled on the floor behind the worktable, trying to find something she could use to defend herself. But there was nothing she could use to stop a bullet.

"Bring the tape," James bellowed. "Dani has to pay."

"I'm not going to prison for you. You're on your own," Angela shouted.

"You'll do as I say, you murdering bitch."

"Go to hell."

A shot sounded. The sound of Angela's scream reverberated sickeningly through the room.

"Why?" Dani screamed. "Why are you doing this?"

"Your slutty sister made a fool of me. So did Lenny.

You're not going to get that chance. With you dead, all of Constance's money goes to me."

The bell over the front door rang and Dani heard noises drifting in from outside as the door opened and quickly closed again.

"What the hell?"

The voice was Riley's. Panic hit Dani hard and fast. She stood up behind the counter.

"It's James," she screamed. "In the kitchen. He has a gun."

James pointed the gun at her, his finger on the trigger. The evil that darkened his eyes said it all. He was going to kill her now.

Instinctively, she grabbed the two overflowing flour canisters by their rims and swung them one by one in rapid succession, the contents covering him as if it was a blizzard of snow.

James clawed at his face as the flour coated his fury-flamed eyes.

He shot at her, but the bullet flew wild. He turned at the sound of Riley's footsteps and fired in his direction. Fear paralyzed Dani as the shot rang out.

One shot, but it was James who went down.

A second later, Riley was on her side of the work-table and she was in his arms.

She held on tight as tears filled her eyes, washing streams of flour down her face. "Where's Constance?" she asked suddenly, realizing she wasn't there.

"Riding horses. We ran into Tucker at the feed store. I had this not-so-crazy premonition that we were not quite through with James. I sent her on with him and I put the pedal to the metal to get back to you."

"Quick Draw, to the rescue," she said, holding him

even tighter. She'd almost lost him. She never wanted to be that afraid again.

Seconds later sirens screamed. Riley held her tight until the bakery filled with paramedics and deputies.

James and Angela were both taken to the hospital.

Sheriff Cavazos arrived, took one look at the flour-strewn kitchen and shook his head. "You Lawrence brothers and your women bring a heck load of trouble to my county. Lucky for you that Dani sure can bake."

"Lucky for me," Riley said, "she sure can handle her flour."

Only she was the lucky one. She was alive and safe in Riley's arms.

Epilogue

One month later

It was a beautiful Monday afternoon, a perfect day to enjoy the outdoors. But as much as Dani was enjoying her time with Grace while the girls were riding with Pierce, she was truly hoping to casually bump into Riley.

Up until a week ago, he'd been his usual self—attentive, sexy and always ready to make love or even to just hang out with her. For the past week he'd been mostly absent, claiming he was busy. When they were together, he seemed distracted.

She had a sinking feeling in her heart that he would soon be moving on. She'd promised herself she'd never ask for forever. Never ask him to give up the lifestyle he loved to become stuck in the town and the life she loved.

She never wanted him to feel trapped with her, but how was her heart going to survive without him?

Grace lifted her glass of lemonade and took a slow sip. "Pierce is delighted Dudley Miles is being released from prison today. He credits you and Riley for most of that."

"It is a bizarre twist to a convoluted and incredible

mystery," Dani agreed. Thankfully Angela survived the gunshot wound and decided to clear up much of the mystery."

"Still, I'm surprised Angela finally broke down and told the truth. I don't know her that well, but the few times I was around her, she showed no signs of grief or guilt."

"My guess is she just had the guilt and grief buried so deeply in her psyche she couldn't move past it. When James insisted she help him kill me, her psychological facade cracked."

"That's so sad and a very scary," Grace said.

"I'm just lucky and supremely grateful that never happened with Amber and Constance. Amber was my sister. Mother and I both loved her dearly and tried everything we could to keep help her kick the drugs. I wish now that I had tried even harder."

"You can't save everyone no matter how hard you try, but you have Constance now and she's a fantastic kid in spite of everything her mother put her through."

"You're right. I can't change the past anyway."

"How about a recap," Grace asked, "just to be sure I have all my facts straight?"

"I'll try. To start with, James is under arrest for attempted murder and for the murder of his brother, Lenny. In the meantime he's receiving psychological assessments to determine if he's mentally stable enough to stand trial."

"And Angela?"

"She's admitted to being the only adult at home the day her son died. She got high and passed out. He climbed onto the counter, apparently trying to get a cookie. He fell and died from traumatic brain energy to the back of his head.

"She panicked, knowing she might face charges of neglect or manslaughter in his death. She tossed his body into the woods and then went home and told her family he'd been kidnapped from the house. The body was found months later and the evidence in the case soon pointed to Angela."

"But why would Dudley admit to the crime when he wasn't guilty?"

"To save Angela from going to prison. He and his wife, Millie, couldn't bear to see their precious, spoiled daughter take responsibility for anything. She's in a mental and psychological facility in Houston now, awaiting testing, treatment and eventually a trial."

"I read once that family ties can be the sweetest ones on earth or they can be as deadly as a blood-sucking leech," Grace said. "Sounds like the Miles family ties were definitely closer to the latter."

"Hopefully, they can make something good from all this."

"At least it's good that Dudley can go home. By the way, what's up with Riley lately? He's always rushing off without saying where's he's going, and when he is here, he seems preoccupied."

"I haven't noticed," she lied, trying to keep the anxiety from her voice. She couldn't think about his leaving without getting literally ill.

Her cell phone dinged. She had a text from Riley.

Important that I see you and Constance. Can I take you two to dinner tonight at sixish?

He'd never asked her out by text before. More indication that this was the night the bomb would drop. No matter how upset she got, she wouldn't let him see her cry. There would be time enough for tears after he'd left.

RILEY SHOWED UP at ten after six and the three of them climbed into his pickup truck. Dani was a wreck, talking too much and too fast, nervously jumping from one subject to another.

It was a few minutes before she noticed he'd taken a back road that she was certain didn't lead to a restaurant. Still, she didn't ask questions. Maybe he just wanted a quiet place to talk and get this over with.

He turned in at a gate that said Wallace Ranch. They drove past acres and acres of fenced and cross-fenced pastures before stopping on a hill overlooking a small lake.

Constance bounded out of the backseat and then rushed off to chase a fluttering butterfly.

Riley opened the car door for Dani. They stood in silence for a few minutes, watching the sun set in the western sky.

"What do you think?" Riley asked.

"It's a beautiful area."

"I'm glad you think so. I put a down payment on this ranch today."

"You're buying this ranch?"

"It's not that incredible. I haven't bought anything before except pickup trucks, so I have the savings to be able to afford it."

"But what about your rambling ways and need to keep moving?"

"I think I was always just working my way to you. I

want to marry you, Dani. I want to take care of you and Constance. I want to love you for the rest of my life."

Constance came running over and tugged on Riley's shirtsleeve. "Does this ranch have horses?"

"It will when we move out here. Horses and cattle and I'm thinking a big yellow dog."

"We're gonna have a ranch?" Constance asked.

"If your aunt whom I love very much will marry me?"

Constance started to jump up and down. "Say yes, Aunt Dani. Please say yes. Riley loves us and we love him. We'll be a family. With a ranch. And horses. And a dog!"

From heartbreak at the prospect of losing him to a marriage proposal. This was coming so fast. Her head was spinning. "What about my bakery?"

"We'll be like the elites, have a place in town and one in the country," Riley said. "Only difference is ours will be only fifteen minutes apart."

He took both her hands in his. "I would never expect you to give up the bakery any more than I'd give up ranching. I'll work the ranch during the day. You'll work at the bakery. Nights we'll be together at one place or the other. We can work it out."

It sounded like heaven, but…

"Are you sure this is what you want to do, Riley? "Are you very, very sure?"

He dropped to one knee, pulled a brilliant diamond solitaire from his pocket and slipped it onto her finger. "I'm very sure that there is no place in the whole world I'd rather be than with you. I love you more than I ever dreamed I could love anyone. Will you marry me, Dani Boatman, and make me the luckiest guy on the planet?"

"Yes. Yes. Yes." Tears filled her eyes. No one had the right to be this happy.

He stood and took her in his arms. Constance joined in the family hug and then dashed off to the nearest stump, jumped on top of it and started yelling to no one except perhaps the hidden wildlife this was moving to this ranch.

"What shall we do next?" Riley asked. "Eat. Go share our good news with the folks at the Double K?"

"Later," Dani whispered.

"Don't tell me this is one of those baking moments?"

"No, I just want to savor this feeling. But you never know what might come up once I get you in my bakery kitchen."

"No doubt. Ever since I met you I've been dreaming of escapades involving your whipped cream."

"I'll see that a lot of those dreams come true."

Riley Lawrence. No longer a rambling man but every inch a cowboy. The man she'd love every day for the rest of her life.

Who said you can't have it all?

* * * * *

"You do not have to carry me upstairs."

Looking into Nicole's green eyes, Slade narrowed his gaze. "Because you don't want this?"

"Oh, I want whatever this is, but you don't have to lug me up the staircase to get it."

He chuckled. Yep, like no other high-maintenance society girl he'd ever met.

"No lugging required. You're as light as a feather."

"That may be, but I just survived a sniper's bullet and an attack on the train. I'm not going to risk tumbling down the stairs, even if I do end up on top of a hot navy SEAL."

"You don't have to take a fall down the stairs to wind up on top of this navy SEAL."

ALPHA BRAVO SEAL

BY
CAROL ERICSON

First Published in Great Britain 2017
By Mills & Boon, an imprint of HarperCollins*Publishers*
1 London Bridge Street, London, SE1 9GF

© 2017 Carol Ericson

ISBN: 978-0-263-92883-9

46-0517

Carol Ericson is a bestselling, award-winning author of more than forty books. She has an eerie fascination for true-crime stories, a love of film noir and a weakness for reality TV, all of which fuel her imagination to create her own tales of murder, mayhem and mystery. To find out more about Carol and her current projects, please visit her website at www.carolericson.com, "where romance flirts with danger."

To Joanne, my trusty treasurer

Prologue

Slade Gallagher sucked in a ssalty breath of air and got ready for the kill.

Oblivious to the sniper rifles pointed at their heads from the yacht bobbing on the water just over three hundred feet away from them, four Somali pirates held their hostages at gunpoint as they communicated their demands to the two men who'd boarded their rickety craft. The two were US Navy seamen, but the pirates didn't know that—didn't need to.

The relatively calm seas made tracking his target easy—and safe for the hostage.

Slade zeroed in on his target, his dark skin glistening in the sun, one skinny arm wrapped around the hostage's throat, gun nestled beneath her ear. Slade's focus shifted to the hostage, a young woman with light brown hair blowing across her face and a tall, thin body, taut and ready.

What the hell was a woman doing out here in the Gulf of Aden? The orders for this assignment had made clear that this rescue didn't involve a cargo ship. This time the Somali pirates had captured a documentary film crew. *Idiots.*

Not that Slade couldn't understand the thrill of risk taking, but he preferred risks that pitted him against a big wave or a cave on the ocean floor, not desperate men in desperate situations.

The negotiator waved his arm once and shifted his body to the right, giving the SEAL snipers their first signal and a clear view of all four pirates. Slade licked the salt from his lips and coiled his muscles. He adjusted the aim on his M107.

The snipers had to drop their targets at the same time—or risk the lives of the hostages. He tracked back to the pretty brunette, now scooping her hair into a ponytail with one hand and tilting her head away from her captor. *Good girl.*

Had the negotiators been able to hint to the hostages that a team of Navy SEAL snipers was on the boat drifting off their starboard and watching their every move? It didn't matter. The men on deck would make their best assessment and the snipers would take action.

It wouldn't be pretty. That tall drink of water would suffer some blood spatter—but at least it wouldn't be her own. He'd make sure of that.

The other negotiator held both hands out in supplication, the final signal, and Slade set his timer to five seconds. He murmured along for the count. "Five, four, three, two…"

He took the shot. All four pirates jerked at once in a macabre dance and fell to the deck.

Slade inched his scope to the woman he'd just saved. She hadn't fainted dead away, screamed or jumped up and down. She formed an X over her chest with her blood-spattered arms, looked down at the dead pirate and spit on his body.

Hauling back his sniper rifle, Slade shook his head. That was one crazy chick—just his type.

Chapter One

Eighteen months later

A sick feeling rose in Nicole's gut as she skimmed the online article. The rumor was true. She hunched forward, reading aloud. "'Freelance cameraman Lars Rasmussen was found dead of an apparent suicide in his parents' home in the Hellerup district of Copenhagen.'"

She stopped reading and slumped in her chair. "No way."

Lars, with his sunny smile and scruffy goatee, wasn't even acquainted with the word *depression*.

Nicole grabbed her cell phone and scrolled through her contacts. Lars had picked his brother, Ove, as his emergency contact, and she'd kept all of those numbers. Maybe she'd had a premonition.

She squinted at the time on her computer screen, hoping Ove was an early riser. She tapped his number, which already contained the international calling code for Denmark, and placed the call.

He picked up after two rings. *"Hej."*

"Hello. Is this Ove Rasmussen?"

"Yes. Who's this, please?" He'd switched to English seamlessly.

"This is Nicole Hastings. I worked with your brother, Lars, on a couple of projects."

"Of course, Nicole. My brother mentioned you often."

"I heard the news about his death, and I just wanted to tell you how sorry I am." *And to give you the third degree.*

"Yes, yes. Thank you. It was a shock."

"Was he? I mean, what…?" She closed her eyes and shoved a hand through her tangled hair. "What I mean to say is, I can't believe Lars would take his own life."

Ove drew in a sharp breath. "Yes, well, some girl trouble, a failed project."

Ove didn't know his brother very well if he thought a woman could send Lars over the edge, but she couldn't argue with a bereaved family member.

She loosened her death grip on the phone. "I'm so sorry. He was a good guy and a helluva cameraman."

"That's how I know he must've been depressed."

"How?" Her pulse ticked up a notch.

"When we…discovered his body, we couldn't find any of his cameras in the house. He'd been staying with our parents after his last project, the one after the debacle in Somalia. He had been working on a local story about the Syrian refugees in Denmark."

"His cameras? Why would he get rid of his cameras?"

Ove sighed across the miles. "I don't know, Nicole. He mentioned you, though, a few weeks before he died. You were with him when you all got kidnapped in Somalia, right?"

"Yes." Her pounding heart rattled her rib cage. "What did he say?"

"Just that he was sorry the film never got released, because he'd captured some amazing footage. He was thinking about contacting you about the project, reviving it, turning the film over to you."

"He never did." She tapped one fingernail on the edge of her laptop. "Did he happen to mention Giles Wentworth, too? He was another member of our film crew."

"Giles. English guy, right?"

"That's right." Nicole held her breath.

"Not lately. I don't think so. I don't remember."

"I was just wondering because… Giles passed away a few months ago."

Ove spewed out a Danish word that sounded like an expletive. "Not suicide?"

"A car accident in Scotland."

"That's a shame. It would seem that story you were trying to capture in Somalia was bad luck."

"It would seem so." She bit her lip, toying with the phrasing of her next question. "D-did Lars—was he worried about anything before his death?"

"Just that woman." He released a noisy breath. "I have to go to work now, Nicole. Thank you for calling."

"Of course. My condolences again on your loss."

"And, Nicole?"

"Yes?"

"It sounds like you need to be careful."

When she ended the call, she folded her arms over her stomach, gripping her elbows. Ove had been referring to the coincidence of two of the film crew dying within months of each other, but Nicole wasn't so sure it was a coincidence.

She pushed back from the desk and sauntered to

the window overlooking the street below. Even at 2:00 a.m., taxis zipped to and fro, and the occasional pedestrian ambled along the sidewalk, two blocks up from Central Park.

Nicole caught her breath when she spied a figure under the green awning of the brownstone across the street, his pale face tilted toward her window. Twitching the drape, she stepped back and peered from the edge of its heavy folds.

She'd dimmed the lights in the apartment earlier, only the glow of her computer screen illuminating her workspace. Someone ten floors down wouldn't be able to see her at the window.

Then why was her heart racing and her palms sweating? This was the first time she'd noticed a suspicious person outside her building, but not the first time in the past few months she'd felt watched, followed, spied upon.

Her fear had started, not just with news of Giles's accident, but with his death along with her inability to reach Dahir, the Somali translator who'd been a part of their film crew. She still hadn't located Dahir, and rumors swirling around Lars had sent her into a panic. Now that she'd confirmed Lars's passing, a strange calm had settled about her shoulders like a heavy cape.

Four people on that film crew, four people held hostage by Somali pirates, four people rescued by the Navy SEALs, two of those people dead eighteen months later, one missing and…her. Was this just some bizarre twist of fate, claiming the lives of people who should've died a year and a half ago? That sort of stuff only happened in horror movies.

The man across the street made a move, and she

peered into the darkness as he emerged from beneath the awning and loped down the sidewalk. Her eyes followed him until the night swallowed him whole at the end of the block.

She huffed out a breath and drew the drapes. She'd planned an extended stay in New York while her mother hit Europe for the fashion shows—starting with Paris in March and winding up with Rome in July. Maybe she should get a bodyguard.

Nicole turned and surveyed the office of the lavishly furnished Upper East Side apartment where her mother had lived for years. It wasn't like she couldn't afford a 24/7 bodyguard.

A bodyguard for what? Who could possibly have it in for a documentary film crew that hadn't even managed to release the movie about the underground feminist movement in Somalia? The women they'd met had reason to fear for their lives, but after the kidnapping their translator had gone into hiding and the rest of them had scattered, abandoning the project.

Nicole hadn't even seen the footage Lars had shot—and it must've been good if he'd mentioned it to his brother. As talented as he was, Lars wasn't one to puff out his chest.

She planted herself in front of her computer again, and her fingers flew across the keyboard in a desperate search for Dahir Musse. She'd lobbied to get Dahir out of Somalia after the kidnapping incident, but even her mother's political connections hadn't been able to get the job done.

If they had, would Dahir be alive today instead of missing in action? Or would he be just as dead as Giles and Lars? Just as dead as she might be?

THE NEXT MORNING, heavy eyed and yawning, Nicole sucked down the rest of her smoothie and tossed the cup in the trash can on her way back to the counter.

Skye raised her eyebrows. "Ready for another?"

"Just a shot of wheatgrass. If I hope to get in even two miles today, I need a little energy."

"You look tired. Late night at the clubs?"

"I wish." She swept up the little paper cup Skye had placed before her and downed the foul-tasting liquid in one gulp. Then she crushed the cup in her hand. "See ya."

Skye waved as Nicole pushed out the door of the shop. Leaning forward, she braced her foot on the side of the building to tie the loose laces of her running shoe. She caught a movement out of the corner of her eye—a man walking on the sidewalk across the street.

She bent over farther but slid her gaze sideways to watch the tall, lean guy lope down the block—*lope*. He had a distinctive rangy, loose-limbed gait, one she'd seen in the wee hours of the morning across the street from her building.

Narrowing her eyes, she watched his back, the sun gleaming off his blond hair. Now that she'd confirmed Lars's death, her paranoia was going into overdrive. The man hadn't looked at her once, and he certainly wasn't following her.

She straightened up and rolled back her shoulders. She needed that run more than ever, and the fresh greenery of the park beckoned. She launched forward with one last glance over her shoulder, then tripped to a stop.

He wasn't following her because he was heading for her apartment. To lie in wait? To break in?

She abandoned her run and made a U-turn in the street. She didn't want to confront the man, but two could play the stalking game. Veering to the left, she cut in one street ahead of her own. If she came into the building's lobby through the back way, she might catch him trying to get through the front door. Leo, the doorman, might have something to say about that.

Nicole tightened her ponytail and turned down the alley that led to the back of her building. She might be way off here, but something about that man had seemed familiar. If he wasn't hanging around trying to get into the building, she'd go for her run with a clear mind—at least as clear as it could be while worrying about the mysterious deaths of her colleagues.

When she got to the apartment, she pulled her key ring from the little pocket in the back of her running shirt and plucked out the building key.

She slid it into the lock and eased open the door. Flattening herself against the wall, she sidled along toward the mailboxes. If she peered around the corner of the hallway where the mailboxes stretched out in three rows, she'd have a clear view of the lobby and the front door.

She crept around the corner and jerked back, dropping her keys with a clatter.

The tall stranger, his gleaming hair covered with the hood of his sweatshirt, glanced up, the mail from her box clutched in his hands.

She should've turned and run away, but a whip of fury lashed her body and she lunged forward.

"What the hell are you doing going through my mail?"

Then her stalker did the most amazing thing.

A smile broke across his tanned face, and he lifted a pair of broad shoulders. "Guess you caught me red-handed, Nicole."

Chapter Two

The color drained from her face as fast as it had flared
red in her cheeks. "Do I know you? And even if I do,
I'm about two seconds from screaming bloody murder
for the doorman and getting the cops out here."

He believed her. A woman who would risk sailing
the dangerous Gulf of Aden just to get a story wouldn't
fear some creeper in New York City—not that he was
a creeper.

"Sorry about the mail." He fanned out some bills and
a few ads. "I'm not very good at this."

"Good at what?" She inched past him and the row of
mailboxes until she had one foot in the lobby.

"Skulking, I guess."

"Are you going to tell me what you're doing, or am
I going to call the NYPD?" She jabbed her cell phone
into the space between them.

"You see? I suck at this." He bundled her mail, which
he hadn't had a chance to look at, and held it out to her.
"I'm Slade Gallagher, the US Navy SEAL sniper who
saved your life eighteen months ago off the coast of
Somalia."

She blinked, licked her lips and edged closer to him.
"Is this some kind of trick?"

Trick? What kind of trick would that be? He stuffed his free hand into the pocket of his sweatshirt and withdrew his wallet. He flipped it open with one hand, his other still gripping the mail she'd refused to take from him.

"Take it and look at the card behind my driver's license. It's my military ID. Hell, look at my driver's license, too."

She reached forward to take the wallet from him between two fingers, as if stealing something from a snake ready to strike.

"And if my ID isn't good enough for you, I can tell you what you were wearing that day." He closed his eyes as if picturing the scene all over again through his scope. "You had on army-green cargo pants, a loose red shirt and a khaki jacket, with a red scarf wrapped around your neck."

His lids flew open, and Nicole was staring at him through wide green eyes. She might be surprised, but he'd pictured the woman on the boat—Nicole Hastings—many times over the past year and a half. Some nights he couldn't get the picture of her out of his head.

"We never knew your names. The Navy wouldn't tell us." She traced a finger over his driver's license picture behind the plastic, and his face tingled as if she'd brushed it. "But while we were in the infirmary getting checked out, we saw you walking toward the helicopter before you boarded it and left the boat. I do recognize you."

Her sculpted eyebrows collided over her nose. "But what are you doing here? Why have you been following me?"

"Following you?" A pulse hummed in his throat. "I just got here two days ago."

"Last night?"

"I was watching your building." He shook his head. "Damn, you noticed me out there?"

"Yes. Why are you watching me?"

"I hadn't planned on having this discussion with you so early, but it works out better for me if we do." He jerked his thumb at the ceiling. "Can we continue this conversation in your apartment?"

Her gaze shifted toward the lobby and back to his face.

"You can introduce me to the doorman and tell him we're going up to your place. In fact, that's the smart thing to do."

She snapped his wallet closed and thrust it at him, and then spun on her heel. He followed her, still clutching the mail.

The doorman leaped into action and swung the door open for her before she reached it. "I didn't see you come in, Nicole."

"Came in through the back door." She leveled a finger at Slade. "This is a…my friend. He's coming up to my place, Leo, in case you see him wandering around the building."

Leo tilted his head. "Okay. Nice to meet you. Any friend of the Hastings women has gotta be good people."

Slade swept the hood from his head and held out his free hand. "Slade Gallagher."

"Leo Veneto."

Slade glanced at the tattoo on Leo's forearm. "Marine?"

"Yes, sir. Tenth Marine regiment, artillery force. Served in the first Gulf War."

Slade pumped his hand. "Hoorah."

"Hoorah." Leo gave Slade the once-over. "Navy, right?"

"You got it—SEAL sniper."

"You boys saved our asses more than a few times."

Nicole broke up the handshake and the mutual admiration. "We're going to go up now."

Leo grinned. "I'll be right here."

Slade followed her to the elevator where she stabbed the call button and turned to him suddenly. "I never knew Leo was in the Marines."

"Has *Semper Fi* tattooed right on his arm."

She finally snatched the mail from his hands as the doors of the elevator whisked open. "See anything interesting in my mail?"

"You didn't give me a chance to go through all of it, but it looks like Harvard's hitting you up for a donation."

"They wouldn't dare. I'm not even an alumna, and my father already funded a library for them."

"So why'd you go to NYU instead of Harvard, where I'm sure they would've found a spot for you?"

"Film school." She narrowed her eyes. "It's not all family connections, you know."

"Doesn't hurt." He should know.

They rode up to the tenth floor in silence, but he could practically hear all the gears shifting in her head, forming questions. He didn't blame her. He just didn't know if he'd have any answers that would satisfy her—rather than scare the spit out of her.

The elevator jolted to a stop on the tenth floor, and

he held the door as she stepped out. "No penthouse suite, huh?"

"My mom didn't want to be too ostentatious." Her lips twisted. "And I'm being serious."

Still, there seemed to be just two apartments on this floor. The size and location of this place must've run her mother, Mimi Hastings, more than five mil.

Nicole swung open the door with a flourish and watched him out of the corner of her eye as she stepped aside.

His gaze swept from one side of the opulently furnished room to the other, taking in the gold brocade sofas, the marble tables, the blindingly white carpet, the curved staircase to another floor and the artwork he could guarantee was worth a fortune. "Impressive."

"This is my mother's place. I'm here watching the…"

Before she could finish the sentence, a ball of white fur shot out from somewhere in the back of the apartment and did a couple of somersaults before landing at Slade's feet, paws scrabbling for purchase against the legs of his jeans.

She rolled her eyes. "That's a dog, believe it or not, and I'm taking care of her for my mother."

Slade crouched and tickled the excited Shih Tzu beneath the chin. "Hey, little guy."

"It's a girl, and her name is Chanel."

"Let me guess." He straightened up. "She has a diamond collar."

"You pretty much have my mom all figured out."

"Where is she, your mother?"

"Are we discussing my mother or why a Navy SEAL is spying on me in Manhattan?" She crossed her arms and tapped the toe of her running shoe.

He waved his arm at a deep-cushioned chair. "Can I sit down first? Maybe something to drink? This spying is tough business."

Her lips formed a thin line, and for a minute he thought she was going to refuse. "All right."

"Water is fine, and I'll even get it myself if you show me the way."

She crooked her finger. "Follow me, but no more stalling."

Was that what he was doing? He had to admit, he didn't want to be the bearer of bad news—and he had bad news for Nicole Hastings.

The little dog jumped into the chair he was eyeing, so he followed Nicole's swaying hips, the Lycra of her leggings hugging every gentle line of her body. She was thin, but curved in and out in all the right places.

As she passed a granite island in the center of the kitchen, she kicked the leg of a stool tucked beneath the counter. "Have a seat."

She yanked open the door of the fridge. "I have water, sparkling water, iced tea, juice, soda, beer and a 2008 Didier Dagueneau sauvignon blanc—a very good year."

Was she trying to show off, or did that stuff just roll from her lips naturally? "Sparkling water, please."

She filled two glasses with ice and then set them down in the middle of the island. The bottle with a green and yellow label hissed as she twisted off its lid, and the liquid fizzed and bubbled when it hit the ice.

She shoved a glass toward him. "Now that the formalities are over, let's get to the main event."

"You don't mess around, do you?"

"I didn't think you'd be one to mess around, either,

the way you dropped that pirate who had me at gun-point."

"This is different." He took a sip of the water, the bubbles tickling his nose. "You know that Giles Wentworth died in a car accident last February?"

"Went off the road in Scotland."

"A few weeks ago, Lars Rasmussen committed sui-cide—took an overdose of pills."

"I know that." She hunched over the counter, drilling him with her green eyes. "What I want to know is the location and general health of Dahir Musse."

He took a bigger gulp of his drink than he'd intended, and it fizzed in his nose. He wiped his eyes with the heel of his hand. "You've already connected the dots."

"I don't know if I've connected any dots, but Giles has driven on some incredibly dangerous roads with-out getting one scratch on the car, and Lars was about the least depressed person I know. Girl trouble?" She snorted, her delicate nostrils flaring. "He had a woman in every port, literally."

Had she been one of those women?

The thought had come out of left field, and Slade took a careful sip of his water. "So, you already have a suspicion the deaths of your friends weren't coinci-dental."

"It's not just that." She caught a drip of condensation on the outside of her glass with the tip of her finger and dragged it back to the rim. "You said you've been here in New York just a few days?"

"Yeah."

"I've had a feeling of being watched and followed for about two weeks now, ever since I heard rumors about Lars."

"Anything concrete?"

"Until I caught you going through my mailbox? No."

Heat crawled up his face to the roots of his hair. He'd tried to tell the brass he'd be no good at spying.

"You still haven't told me what you're doing here and why you were going through my mail."

"Someone who monitors these things—our rescues, I mean—noticed the deaths. This guy raised a red flag because there was a hit stateside on another person our team had rescued—a doctor who'd helped us out in Pakistan. That proved to be related to terrorist activity in the region."

She'd folded her hands around the glass, her white knuckles the only sign of tension. "You're telling me that someone is after the four of us? Do you know where Dahir Musse is?"

"We don't know where he is, and I can't tell you for sure that someone is out to get your film crew, but I'm here to find out."

"A Navy SEAL operating in the US? Isn't that illegal or something?"

"Not exactly, but it is top secret. I'm not really here." He pressed a finger to his lips. "I am sorry about the loss of your friends."

"Thanks." Her chest rose and fell as the corner of her mouth twitched. "Giles's mother called to tell me about the accident. At the time, I figured it was just that—an accident. Then a few weeks ago, I started hearing rumors that Lars had killed himself. That's about the time I started feeling watched. I put it down to paranoia at first, but the feelings got stronger. Then I verified Lars's death last night with his brother and seriously freaked out, especially since I saw you lurking across the street at two in the morning."

"Sorry about that. What were you doing up at two o'clock?"

"Working."

"Did you ever release that documentary? I looked for it but never saw anything about the movie."

Her eyes widened. "We never finished the film. We were all shaken up after the kidnapping and moved on to other projects—with other people."

"The film was about Somali women, right?"

"About Somali women and the underground feminist movement there—dangerous stuff."

He scratched the stubble on his chin. "That might be enough to get you killed."

"Maybe, but why now? We never finished the film, never discussed finishing it. I never even got my hands on the footage." She swirled her glass, and the ice tinkled against the side. "Are you here to figure out what's going on?"

"I'm here to…make sure it doesn't happen again."

"To me."

"To you."

"I have no idea why someone would be after us now. Why weren't we killed in Somalia if someone wanted to stop the film?"

"Our team of snipers stopped that from happening."

"Do you think that's why the pirates kidnapped us? I thought they were going for ransom. That's what they told us, anyway."

"The pirates patrolling those waters are usually working for someone else. They could've been hired to stop you and then once they were successful decided to go rogue and trade you for ransom money instead."

She waved her arms out to her sides. "We're in the middle of New York City. Do you know how crazy that sounds?"

"As crazy as it sounds in the middle of some Scottish highland road or in some posh district of Copenhagen."

"Do you have people looking for Dahir?"

"We do, but there's also the possibility that Dahir is working with the other side."

She landed a fist on the granite. "Never. I tried to get him and his family out of Somalia. His life wasn't going to be worth much there after that rescue on the high seas. He'd become a target in Mogadishu even before Giles and Lars died."

"Tell me more about your feelings of being followed. Do you have any proof? Any evidence?" He watched her over the edge of his glass as he drained it.

Her instincts had been right about him following her, so she could be onto something. She might be a pampered rich girl, but she'd spent time in some of the most dangerous places in the world—and had survived.

"No hard evidence—a man on the subway who seemed to be following me, a persistent guy at a club one night, a jogger who kept turning up on the same trails in the park."

He studied her face with its high cheekbones, patrician nose and full lips and found it hard to believe she hadn't experienced persistent guys in clubs before. "These were all different men?"

"All different. I can't explain it. It's a general creep factor. I know you think because I come from a privileged background I don't have any street smarts, but

I've been in some rough areas around the world. We do have to keep our wits about us or wind up in hot water."

"I believe you. I looked you up online." He wouldn't tell her that he'd researched Nicole Hastings long before he'd gotten this unusual assignment. She might start feeling a general creep factor about *him*.

"Who sent you here? The Navy?"

"I'm reporting directly to my superior officer in the Navy, but it goes beyond that. I'm also reporting to someone from the intelligence community—someone named Ariel."

"Why would the intelligence community be interested in a couple of documentary filmmakers getting into trouble with some Somali pirates?"

"I doubt a bunch of ragtag pirates have the reach and connections to commit two murders in Europe and make them look like accidents."

"So, the CIA or the FBI or whoever thinks our situation is linked to something or someone else?"

"Could be."

She tapped a manicured fingernail on his glass. "Do you want more water?"

"No, thanks."

As she tipped a bit more in her own glass, she said, "What did you hope to find in my mail, anyway?"

"I'm not sure. I'm a sniper, not a spook. I was just checking out what I could."

"And what did you discover other than a request from Harvard?" She moved out of the kitchen with the grace of a gazelle and swept the mail from a table where she'd dropped it.

Hunching forward on his stool, he said, "Nothing. I

wasn't lying when I told you I didn't have a chance to look through it all."

She returned, shuffling through the large stack of envelopes and mailers. "Bills, junk, junk, bills, postcard from my mom, who's the only one I know who still sends them instead of texting pictures. More bills…"

Her face paled as she plucked an envelope from the fanned-out pieces of mail.

"What is it?"

"It's a letter from Lars—from beyond the grave."

Chapter Three

Nicole held the thin envelope between two fingers, fear pulsing through every fiber of her being, her mouth suddenly dry.

Slade launched from his stool and hovered over her shoulder. "How do you know it's from Lars? There's no return address, and it definitely wasn't sent from Denmark."

"I'd recognize his chicken scratch anywhere." She flicked the postmark with her fingernail. "New York, not Denmark."

"Was he in the city?"

"Not that I know of, but then, I haven't even been here a month."

"Are you going to open it or stare at it for a while?"

He was practically breathing down her neck, so she took a few steps to her left. She ripped into the envelope, and a single sheet of white paper fluttered to the counter.

As Slade reached for it, she snatched it up and squinted at it. "His handwriting always was atrocious."

"Do you want me to try?"

"It says—" she plastered the note against the granite and ran her finger beneath the squiggle of words "—'I instructed my friend to mail this letter to you if anything happens to me.'"

She gasped and covered her mouth. "He knew."

"Go on." Slade rapped his knuckle on the counter next to the paper, clearly impatient for her to continue.

She wanted to read this in private, shed tears in her own way. But Slade was here to help. He'd saved her once, from a ramshackle boat in the Gulf of Aden, and she'd trust him in a heartbeat to do it again.

She took a deep breath and started reading. "'It's the film, Nic. Somebody wants that film we shot in Somalia. I gave it to my friend in New York and told him where to hide it, and I'm putting out the word that the footage was damaged during the hijacking of our boat. Maybe they'll leave me alone. Maybe they'll leave us alone. If nothing happens and you never get this note, I'll put it down to paranoia and we'll retrieve that footage and make a hell of a documentary. If I die, don't look for it, and watch your back. Whatever happens, it was great working with you, Nic.'"

A spasm of pain crumpled her face, and one hot tear dripped from her eye, hitting the back of her hand and rolling off to create a splotch on the paper. "Oh, my God. He must've known someone was after him, too."

"Who's this friend?" With his middle finger, Slade slid Lars's note toward his side of the counter. He studied the words on the page as if they could tell him more than what she'd just read.

"He didn't mention the friend's name." She flipped the envelope back over and ran her thumb across the postmark again. "It was mailed two days ago, so his friend must've waited to send it, unless he just learned of Lars's death."

"Do you know Lars's friends in New York?"

"I met a few of them, but just casually at a dinner once and then at a party in SoHo."

"Was the party given by one of his friends?"

"I think it was, but this was a few years ago. These were people I didn't know, so they must've been his friends."

"We need to find this guy." He smacked the note on the counter and drilled his knuckle into the middle of it.

"Maybe we shouldn't." She threaded her fingers in front of her and then couldn't stop twisting them. "Maybe I should keep spreading the story that the footage was damaged and unusable."

"Because that story worked so well for Lars?"

"If they hear it from both me and Lars and they didn't find the film when they…killed Lars or Giles, maybe they'll believe it this time."

"If someone is looking for that footage, it must be important."

"Important?" She pressed the sweating glass against her cheek, hoping the cold moisture would bring her out of this nightmare. "It was footage of interviews with Somali women discussing education and property rights. I understand how that might mean something to the men in Mogadishu and the towns and villages where these women live, but I can't see those men traveling to Denmark or Scotland to carry out a hit to retrieve the footage."

"It must be something else, something one of the women said. Lars and Giles were murdered for a specific reason, not just because a few men were upset about the women's rights movement in Somalia."

She turned her back on Lars's note and put the bottled water back in the fridge. "I can't imagine what our interview subjects could've said that would get us in trouble—or how anyone would even know what they said."

"You conducted the interviews in private?"

"Of course we did. Those women were risking their lives talking to us."

"Who arranged the meetings?"

"Dahir. He was our translator as well as our facilitator. I tried to get him out." She rubbed the back of her hand across her tingling nose. "But the US government was uncooperative."

"The Navy has a hard time resettling people who help *us* out. I'm sure it's even more difficult for journalists to get their people out." He picked up the note and waved it at her. "We need to find out who sent this note for Lars and get him to turn over the film."

"I don't have any contact info for his friends here."

"What about that party? Do you remember where it was? Do you have any pictures? C'mon, people take pictures of their food. There must be something online. Social media sites?"

She snapped her fingers. "Lars was always filming at parties. It got pretty annoying, actually. He might've shared some video with me."

"That's a start."

"Follow me." She scooted past him out of the kitchen and crossed the living room to the small office she used when staying with Mom. Chanel woke up and trotted after them.

Leaning over the desk, Nicole shifted her mouse to wake up her computer and launched a social media site.

"How long ago was this party?" Slade crouched in front of the desk so the monitor was at his eye level.

"About two years ago, six months before we left for Somalia." She scrolled through the pictures on the left-hand side of her page, hoping Slade wasn't paying attention to all the pics of her and her exes—and she had a bunch. "Video, video."

"Wow, someone could follow your whole life on here. You should be careful."

The hair on the back of her neck quivered. Anyone would know she ran in Central Park, hung out with two of her best friends in Chelsea, visited a former professor at NYU. She'd opened up her life for any stranger to track her. It hadn't seemed to matter...before.

Her heart skipped a beat. "Here! This is it."

As Slade scooted in closer to the monitor, Nicole clicked on the video Lars had sent her of the party. She turned up the volume on her computer, and party sounds filtered from the speakers—voices, laughter, music, clinking glasses.

Slade poked at the screen. "That's you. Giles is behind you, right?"

She nodded and sniffled when she saw Giles's wife wrap her arms around him from behind. "That's his wife, Mila."

The camera shifted to three people crowded together on a love seat. "Do you know them? The man? Lars referred to his friend with a masculine pronoun, so we know it's a guy."

"He and the two women are Lars's friends. He's not the owner of the loft, though. That would be..." The camera swung wide, taking in two women and a man dancing and giggling with drinks in their hands. "This guy. Paul something. He's Danish, also."

"Paul something, Danish guy who lives in a loft in SoHo. We can start there."

She ripped a piece of paper from a pad and grabbed a pen. "Paul, Dane, SoHo."

"Shh." He covered her writing hand with his. "Can you go back? Someone's shouting out names."

She clicked and dragged back the status bar on the video and released. In a singsong voice with slightly accented English, a man called out. "Go, Trudy, go, Teresa, go, Lundy."

Closing her eyes, Nicole said, "That's Lars."

"I'm assuming those are the dancers. Is his name Paul or Lundy? Or is Lundy his last name?"

Her lids flew open. "It's Lund. It's Paul Lund. I remember now. He's an artist, a photographer."

Slade aimed the pen at her. "Write that down. What about the other guys? The guy on the sofa with the two women? The guy behind the bar?"

"I don't remember, but if we listen to the sound we might be able to pick up more names."

They kept so quiet, Nicole could hear Slade breathing beside her. She tilted her head to concentrate on the individual voices amid the chatter. She heard her own name several times, but that was natural.

Slade grabbed her wrist. "Davey. Did you hear that?"

She replayed the previous several seconds of the video and heard Lars's voice. "Davey, Davey, make it strong."

"You're right. That could be Dave or David. Lars always had a nickname for everyone, and I think he's talking to the guy pouring drinks."

"Okay, so we have Lars, Giles, Paul Lund and Davey." He took up the pen and scribbled the new name on the piece of paper. "There are two more men at the party—the black guy and the short one with the long hair. Do you remember them?"

"I don't remember their names. The white guy has an English accent. Can you hear him? That's not Giles." She played more of the video for him.

"Guy with English accent." Slade wrote it down. "And the other man?"

"The African-American could be an artist—sculptor, maybe. It was a very artsy bunch." She made a noise in the back of her throat when the video ended. "That's it."

"I think we went from nothing to something pretty fast, and it should be easy to locate Paul Lund."

"Then what?" She slumped in the chair and massaged the back of her neck.

"We'll find out what Lars did with that film. You know—" he'd been crouching beside her all this time and now he stood up, rolling his broad shoulders forward and back "—we keep calling this film or footage, but what physical form does it take?"

"I'm not sure. Lars used a digital camera, so he could've copied it to any storage device. It's not on-line, though, or he would've mentioned that."

"Then it's small enough to be hidden anywhere." He gestured to the computer. "Can you find Paul Lund now?"

She scooched to the edge of her chair and flexed her fingers. A few keystrokes later, Paul Lund's website filled the screen, displaying photos of nude people—in groups.

Slade whistled. "Interesting. That's not what you all did at the party, is it?"

She rolled her eyes at him. "How could I forget he took pictures of naked people? Maybe he was doing something different two years ago."

"Yeah, these are—unforgettable. Is there an address for a gallery or contact information?"

"It doesn't look like he's big enough for a whole gallery, but there's an email address and telephone number at the bottom of the page."

"Call him."

"Me? What should I say? I haven't seen him in two years."

"Start with the truth. Ask him if he heard about Lars and see if he'll talk to you."

As she reached for the cell phone she'd brought with her into the office, Slade tapped her forearm. "Put it on speaker so I can hear, too."

She entered the number in her phone and listened to it ring. She shrugged at Slade when Lund's voice mail picked up.

"You've reached Paul Lund. Please leave a message with your name, number and photograph number that interests you."

"Paul, this is Nicole Hastings. I'm a friend of Lars Rasmussen, and I wanted to talk to you about him. Please call me back as soon as possible."

She left her number and ended the call. "I hope he's in town."

Slade jerked a thumb at a picture of several people holding hands in a circle—sans clothing. "I don't think he needs to leave the city to find people willing to take their clothes off for art."

"I suppose not." She wrinkled her nose at the photo. "Should I contact you when he calls me back?"

"I'll wait."

She raised her eyebrows. "Here?"

"I'm staying at a hotel in Times Square. I'm not going all the way back there."

"Should we—I mean, do you want something to eat? It's after noon."

"I can just run out and get something."

Suddenly the thought of Slade Gallagher walking out that door and leaving her alone in this apartment gave her a jolt of terror. Someone had killed Giles, Lars and possibly Dahir. Was she next? Finding Lars's footage and turning it over to this Navy SEAL might be the only thing to save her life.

Unless…the guys who killed her friends found the film first. Would they leave her alone then? What about the women she'd interviewed? If the film got into the wrong hands, those women could be murdered—or worse. Whether or not the people after that footage wanted it to ID the women or not, their exposure would just be an added benefit. She owed it to the women who'd trusted her with their stories to retrieve Lars's film.

"How about it? Do you want me to get something for you, too?"

She glanced up at Slade, framed by the office door, Chanel wriggling in his arms. "We can eat here. My mom's housekeeper, Jenny, thinks it's her duty to keep the fridge stocked."

"You sure?" He rubbed Chanel behind the ear. The dog immediately stopped squirming and got the most blissful look on her face. Slade must have some magic hands.

Nicole blinked. "Of course, but I don't think Chanel's going to ever leave you alone."

"Not generally a little dog fan, but she's won me over."

"Looks like the feeling is mutual." Nicole took a step toward the door, but her phone stopped her. She looked at the display. "It's Paul."

She tapped the phone to put it on speaker and answered. "Hello?"

"Is this Nicole Hastings?" He had a more pronounced accent than Lars's, but not by much.

"Yes, Paul?"

"I got your message, and of course I'd heard about Lars. Damnedest thing. I had no idea he was suicidal. Did you? It wasn't that whole pirate thing you went through, was it?"

She raised one eyebrow at Slade. "Absolutely not. I'm finding his suicide hard to believe. Had you talked to him recently?"

"No, but I do have something for you."

"You do?" She placed a steadying hand over her heart. "What is it?"

"I'd rather show you. You're in the city?"

"Yes."

"Can you come by my studio this afternoon? It's at my loft, where I had the party. Do you remember it?"

"I do, but not the address."

Paul gave her the address of his loft studio, and they agreed to meet there in an hour.

When she ended the call, she cupped the phone in

her hands. "That was easy. He's just going to turn it over to me."

"Let's hope so, and then we have to figure out why it warranted the deaths of two, possibly three, people." He set Chanel on the floor, and she promptly flopped over on her side.

Nicole walked up to the dog and nudged her paw with the toe of her sneaker. "You hypnotized her."

"Yeah, we learn that in Navy SEAL training."

She widened her eyes, and then pursed her lips. "Liar. We still have time for a quick bite to eat."

"How far are you from SoHo?"

"It's about a half hour in a taxi." She plucked her neoprene running shirt from her chest. "I'm not changing. I never ran, anyway."

"The guy takes pictures of naked people. I don't think he's going to care what you're wearing."

He hadn't moved from the doorway, so she brushed past him and wished she hadn't. She had to admit to herself that she'd been attracted to Slade from the minute she'd seen him pass by the door of the infirmary on that ship. She hadn't told the guys at the time, but she'd had a feeling he'd been the SEAL sniper who'd rescued her.

They just would've laughed at her and accused her of falling for another adventure junkie. She'd had her share of mountain climbers, skydivers, big-wave surfers and even a Wall Street trader, but a Navy SEAL topped them all.

Once her pulse returned to normal, she called over her shoulder, "Sandwich?"

"Whatever's easy. We need to head out of here soon."

She slapped together a couple of sandwiches, and they finished them on the way to the lobby.

Leo jumped into action when he saw them. "Have a good one."

"We will." Nicole almost bounded to the taxi. She couldn't wait to get her hands on that film and turn it over to the Navy or whoever would ultimately take control of it. Maybe they'd even return it to her one day so she could make that film and honor Lars and Giles.

The heavy traffic delayed them ten minutes, but Paul was waiting for them at his loft.

After introducing Slade as a friend and then shaking his hand, Paul gave her a long hug. "I can't believe our Lars is gone."

"Did he say anything to you when he left you the note for me and the footage?" She extricated herself from Paul's bear hug.

He cocked his head to the side. "Footage? I just have the photos, Nicole."

Her gaze darted to Slade and back to Paul. "Photos?"

"Of course. I thought you'd want them." He crossed the large open room, his black-and-white photographs adorning the walls. He picked up a folder from a table and raised it in the air as he strolled back to her. "These."

She flipped open the folder and bit down hard on her lip as she stared at a black-and-white photo of her and Lars, heads together, deep in conversation.

"I took those the night of the party, before we all got crazy."

She shuffled through the remaining photos with a sharp pain piercing her heart. Hugging the pictures to her chest, she asked, "Was he in New York recently?"

"He was here a few months ago. Did you miss him, too?"

"I've been in the city for just about three weeks. Does that mean you didn't see him when he was here?"

"I didn't, and that makes me very sad, especially when I think I could've done something to help him."

Slade stepped back from a collection of photos he'd been studying on the wall. "Do you know why he was in New York? Did he see any of your other friends?"

"Funding for his next project, I think." Paul tugged on his earlobe, which had several piercings. "But he did visit Dave Pullman. You might remember him. He was at the party—dark curly hair, actor."

"Davey. He was pouring the drinks." A thrill ran up her spine, but she avoided looking at Slade to share her excitement. The less Paul knew about their mission, the better.

"Davey, yes. Lars and his nicknames."

"Do you have Dave's address and phone number?" As Paul raised his pale eyebrows at her, she stammered, "I—I have something I want to give to him, something I want to share. We didn't have a chance to go to Lars's funeral or a memorial for him, so it's important for his friends to remember him."

"Exactly why I wanted to give you those pictures." He held up one finger. "One minute."

He pivoted toward his desk, which must've doubled as his office, and scooped up his phone. He tapped it a few times and read off a phone number for Dave and an address on the Lower East Side. "I'm sure Dave will be happy to see you."

"Thank you so much for the pictures, Paul."

"Absolutely." He narrowed his eyes as he looked her up and down and then turned his gaze to Slade. "Would you two be interested in doing some modeling for me?"

They both answered "no" at the same time.

Five minutes later, they stood on the sidewalk in front of Paul's building. Nicole held out the folder of pictures to Slade. "Do you mind holding these while I call Dave? I don't want them spilling out."

"They're good pictures. The guy has talent."

"Not enough to entice you to pose for him?"

"Nope."

A smile tugged on her lips as she selected Dave's number from her contacts. She'd pay good money to see a nude black-and-white photo of Slade Gallagher.

The phone rang once on the other end and then rolled into a recording. She puckered her lips and puffed out a breath. "His number's no longer in service."

"Damn. I wonder if it has anything to do with Lars."

"We still have his address. Should we pay him a visit?"

"We're close, right?"

"We could walk, or it's a ten-minute taxi ride as long as we don't get snarled in traffic—and here's one now." She raised her hand at two oncoming taxis, and the second one swerved up to the curb.

Ten minutes later, the driver dumped them off at the end of Broome, where she told him to stop. "It's easier to walk down this street."

They found Dave's building, an old brick structure squeezed between a bakery and a taco shop. Nicole placed one foot on the first step and gripped the iron railing. "If he's not there, should we wait?"

"You can leave him a note. Maybe the bakery has some paper or a napkin to write on, but give it a try."

With Slade close behind her, she stepped up on the porch and reached for the bell. Before she could press it, the door swung open and a dark-haired man carrying a bicycle on his shoulder squeezed by them.

Slade reached past her to catch the door before it closed, but something about the man's hair had her jerking her head to the side.

He'd set the bike on the sidewalk, and his eyes met hers with a flicker of recognition.

"Dave? Davey?" She descended the step and moved beside him. "I'm Nicole…"

She didn't get a chance to finish, because Davey Pullman threw his bike at her and took off running down the street.

Chapter Four

Nicole stumbled backward and landed awkwardly on the bottom step at Slade's feet with a bike on top of her.

"Are you all right?" He crouched beside her, lifting the bike from her legs.

She flailed at his arms as he tried to help her up. "Go after him. That's Dave!"

"Are you sure you're okay?"

"It's a bike, Slade. Don't let Dave get away."

Slade jumped to his feet, shoved the folder of pictures into Nicole's arms and launched down the sidewalk after the man running in the direction of the Williamsburg Bridge. Could he run across the bridge?

Dave seemed to be slowing down and probably didn't realize he had company on his jog. Then he cranked his head over his shoulder, and his mouth dropped open. He swung back around and almost ran into the path of a taxi, whose driver laid on his horn.

Slade pumped his legs harder and caught up to Dave just as he started to enter a park. He didn't want to hurt the guy, but he *had* shoved Nicole to the ground with a bike. He had to pay for that.

Slade ground his back teeth and took a flying leap

at Dave. The smaller man's body folded beneath his as Slade smashed him face-first into the grass.

Panting, Slade rolled off him, keeping a knee pressed to Dave's midsection. "Why are you running? Nicole just wants to talk to you."

Dave grunted, and a few seconds later his eyes bulged from their sockets.

Slade eased up on the pressure he was applying to the man's stomach, but his knee beneath Dave's rib cage was not the reason for his bug eyes.

Nicole rolled up beside them on Dave's bike. She flicked the bell once before hopping off. "What is your problem?"

Dave finally found his voice. "I'm sorry I pushed you, but I don't want to talk to you. I don't want to be seen with you. I don't know anything."

Slade rested on his haunches next to Dave, still huffing and puffing on the ground. "Obviously you know something, or you wouldn't have taken off like that."

"And now we're talking very publicly when we could've been having a nice conversation at your place." Nicole waved her arms to take in the park. "Did Lars give you the Somalia footage or not?"

"I wouldn't take it from him. If he wanted to gallivant all over the world getting himself in trouble, that's his business, but I didn't want any part of it."

"Why did you think taking the film from him would be trouble for you?" Slade asked.

"Are you kidding?" Dave struggled to a sitting position and pulled a pack of cigarettes out of the front pocket of his pants. "Do you mind?"

Slade shrugged, and Nicole shook her head and said, "That's why you can't run very fast."

Dave shook out the crushed package and retrieved a book of matches from his other pocket. He lit a cigarette with a trembling hand. "Lars stopped by my place with a crazy story about someone being after him. He suspected it had something to do with the film he'd shot in Somalia, because someone had broken into a place he'd been staying with a woman in San Francisco and stolen some film he had there, but the Somalia stuff wasn't there."

"Why did he connect that break-in to Somalia?" Nicole swung her leg over the bike and propped it against a park bench.

"He'd just heard about Giles, and after the theft in San Francisco, he felt like he was being followed."

Slade glanced at Nicole. She'd had the same feelings.

"Did you see the film Lars was trying to give you?" Slade held his breath as Dave released another stream of smoke into the air between puckered lips.

"You mean the actual footage?"

"No. The physical thing—was it on a disc or what?"

"A little disc, like this." Dave held his thumb and index finger about two inches apart.

"Did you send his letter to me?"

Nicole had perched on the edge of the bench and clasped her hands between her knees. She had a bloody scrape on her right wrist from Dave's bike, and a flare of anger surfaced in Slade's chest. The guy was a coward in more ways than one.

Dave took a long drag from his cigarette and emitted words and smoke at the same time. "I wouldn't take any of it. He wanted me to hide the disc and send the letter to you if anything happened to him."

"Do you know who sent the letter for him? Because I got it today."

"I don't know, and I don't want to know. When I heard Lars offed himself, I was damned glad I refused to help him. Lars kill himself? You ever hear of anything more ludicrous?" Dave shook his head and crushed out his smoke. "They really were out to get him and that footage. If you're smart, you'll leave it alone."

"I can't. Someone's after me, too."

Dave's head jerked up, and he pushed to his feet. "What is it with you people? Why go looking for trouble when it finds you, anyway?"

"Well, now I'm in it, and this guy—" she aimed her finger at Slade "—is going to help me get out of it."

Was that what she thought? The pressure was really on, especially since this was an assignment way out of his comfort zone.

Slade rose to his feet and planted himself in front of Dave, in case he got any more ideas about taking off. "Who else did Lars see when he was in the city? Who else was here? We already know Paul Lund was out of town."

"Is that how you found me? Paul?"

"I was looking at video from that party at Paul's place almost two years ago. Were those all of Lars's New York friends? Are they still here? Were they here when Lars was in the city?"

"There are probably only two people from that party Lars would've contacted besides me—Andre Vincent and Trudy Waxman."

Nicole sprang to her feet and pulled her phone from the pocket of her sweatshirt. "Do you have their contact info?"

"I don't, but Andre's a sculptor. You should be able to find him, and Trudy's an actress. She's in some off-off-Broadway play right now. It's at the Gym at Judson, that church in Greenwich Village." Dave grabbed the handlebars of his bike and plucked out the folder Nicole had stashed in his basket and dropped it on the bench beside her. "Can I go now? That's all I know about it."

"Yeah, thanks." Nicole pocketed her phone. "I don't know why you had to run like that."

"Because I'm scared." Dave pushed his bike and put one foot on a pedal. Rolling forward, he turned and looked over his shoulder. "And if you were smart, you'd be scared, too."

As he rode off, Nicole plopped down on the bench again, rubbing her elbow. "Lars did a number on Dave. If he hadn't freaked him out so much, he would've been able to leave the film with him."

Slade crouched before her and took her hands. "You're injured. Does your elbow hurt, too?"

"A little." She rolled her wrist outward. "I didn't even notice that blood before."

"Let's get you back to your place and clean that up."

Tilting her head back, she cupped one hand over her eyes, shading them from the sun. "How'd you bring Dave down? Didn't anyone interfere?"

"I tackled him. There weren't that many people around. For all I know, they thought I was chasing down someone who'd lifted my wallet." He tugged a strand of her hair that had come loose from her ponytail. "And you riding in on that bike like the cavalry."

A big grin claimed her face, and he felt like a hundred suns had just come out. Nicole had those super-model good looks, but with a bloody smudge on her arm, her messy ponytail and all those gleaming white teeth, she looked like a happy-go-lucky girl next door—a really hot girl next door.

"That was pretty cool, wasn't it?" She launched herself from the bench, practically knocking him over. "Now we need to track down Andre and Trudy."

"We'll need a computer for that, and you still need to get that cut cleaned up."

They took another taxi back to the apartment, and Chanel proceeded to paw Slade's ankles. "Does this dog ever get out?"

"My mom has a dog walker." She wagged her finger at him. "Don't ask. She comes by every morning to feed and walk Chanel and then returns at dusk."

"That's not one of your duties when you stay here?"

"My mother doesn't trust me to walk Chanel. She doesn't trust me with a lot of things."

"Really? You seem pretty competent to me."

"For chasing down guys on bikes, but not domestic things."

He preferred women who could chase down guys on bikes to those who excelled at the domestic arts. Pointing to the door off the living room that led to her small office, he asked, "How about I look up Andre and Trudy while you wash and dress that scrape?"

"I'm going to take a shower and change. Is that okay?" Tucking the folder containing Lund's photographs beneath her arm, she crossed the room to the office. "I'll get you logged in. A sculptor and an actress—I told you Lars hung with an artsy crowd."

"So your mom doesn't trust you to walk the dog?"

She glanced at him over her shoulder. "Back to that?"

"I just can't imagine someone not trusting you to follow through. You seem incredibly capable."

"Capable in the wrong way." She bumped the office
door open with her hip. "According to Mom."

"Traveling to exotic and dangerous countries to expose important stories to the light of day isn't the right
way?"

She powered up her computer and entered a pass-
word. "Ah, my mother would rather have me here
heading up a multitude of charitable organizations she
founded with my father's money. It's not an unworthy
endeavor—just not me."

He pulled up a chair in front of the monitor coming
to life. They had more in common than he would've
thought. "I get that."

"Not many people do." She stepped back, tipping
her head at the computer. "It's all yours. I'm beginning
to think even if we find their phone numbers, we'd be
better off coming at these people with the element of
surprise."

"I think you're right." He tapped her arm above the
dried blood of the cut. "You take care of that, and I'll
find our friends."

"I won't be long." She swept out of the office with a
flick of her fingers.

He murmured, "Capable," at her back and then
turned his attention to the computer. It didn't take him
long to find Andre Vincent. The sculptor's work was
being featured in a series of modern art exhibits around
the city, with each artist rotating among the galleries.

Slade peeled a sticky note from a pad of them and
jotted down the name and address of the gallery where
Andre would be visiting tonight.

Trudy Waxman was almost as easy to locate. He looked up the Gym at Judson, which had a play listed on the calendar of events for tonight. When he clicked on the cast of characters, her name popped up.

Again, he reached for a sticky note and wrote down the name and address of the theater and the play times.

A gallery and a play—he hadn't crammed this much culture into one evening since he'd been back in San Francisco and his parents had dragged him to the opera and a fund-raiser with ballet dancers after. His eye twitched at the recollection.

"Any luck?" Nicole poked her head into the office.

She'd freed her hair from its ponytail, and the strands slid over one shoulder like a smooth ribbon of caramel.

"All kinds of luck." He gestured her into the room. "Found both of them."

She sauntered into the office and leaned over his shoulder to peer at the monitor, engulfing him in a fresh scent that reminded him of newly mowed lawns.

She snorted softly. "*Glinda Fox Gets High?* That's the name of the play?"

"That's it, and Trudy doesn't even play Glinda."

"I said Lars's friends were artists. I didn't say they were particularly good ones."

"Andre's stuff doesn't look half-bad, if you like lumps of stone with faces poking out of it."

"Ugh. Sounds hideous. Where do we find these lumpen treasures?"

He stuck one of the notes to his fingertip and waved it at her. "It just so happens that some of his work is going to be on exhibit at Satchel's Gallery in Chelsea, and the artist is going to be in attendance. It's part of some revolving show for artists."

"If we go there, are we going to have time to catch Glinda getting high?"

"According to my schedule—" he attached the second note to another finger and held them both up "—we can stop in at the gallery at seven o'clock and still have time to see the play at eight, depending on what we find out from Andre."

"Maybe after talking to Andre, we won't need to sit through the play." Nicole wrinkled her nose. "We don't really have to sit through the play, do we? We can just meet her after."

"Do you have anything better to do?" His gaze swept from her bare feet with painted toes to her glossy hair, noting along the way her jeans encasing her long legs, topped off with a plain black T-shirt. She looked stylish without even trying.

"Nope, but I'd like to eat some dinner before we check out that art show."

"I need to change, anyway." He tugged on the hem of his sweatshirt. "How about we head back to my hotel in Times Square, grab a bite somewhere near there and then go to Andre's show?"

"Works for me."

He walked the chair back from the desk. "Do you want to shut down your computer?"

"That's okay. It'll go to sleep and log me out in about ten minutes. Let me put on my shoes, and I'll be ready."

He followed her from the office and flicked off the light on their way out. She'd already brought a pair of shoes and a jacket downstairs and she slid her feet into a pair of animal-print high heels that put her almost at his height, with no self-consciousness at all.

Nicole reminded him a lot of the young, wealthy

women who populated his parents' circles in California—confident, self-assured and accustomed to their privilege—the type of woman he usually steered clear of.

But none of the rich girls he knew would step one foot in Somalia, or any other part of Africa, or Central America, or any of the other places Nicole had been to tell a story.

She slipped into the slim black blazer that skimmed the top of her hips and ducked beneath the strap of a small black purse that hung across her body.

"All set."

Leo was off duty, so the doorman with the second shift called a taxi for them, and Slade gave him the name of his hotel. When they got out of the taxi and made their way through the revolving door, Nicole turned to him.

"I'll just wait for you down here at the bar. Take your time."

"I won't be long." He strode toward the bank of elevators with disappointment stabbing his gut. Had he seemed too anxious to get her alone in his hotel room? He punched the button to call the car.

She had the right idea. They'd just met this morning—hardly enough time to be showering and changing in each other's presence. At her mother's place, a massive staircase and several rooms had been between them when Nicole had changed. He hadn't even heard the shower. Yeah, way too intimate too quickly.

Even though he *had* saved her life.

He raced through the shower and mimicked her outfit with dark jeans, a black T-shirt and black motorcycle boots. He grabbed a black leather jacket on his way out of the room.

When he spotted her in the lobby bar, she was chatting with the bartender over a glass of red wine. She had one of those personalities that got people talking—necessary in her line of work, completely unnecessary in his.

He started forward, navigating through the small tables, already beginning to fill up for happy hour. He perched on the stool next to hers and tapped her wineglass. "Do you want to finish that before we find dinner?"

"I could if you'll join me." She drew her brows over her nose in a V. "That is if you *can* join me. Are you on duty or something?"

"I'm not a cop." He nodded to the bartender, who rushed over. "I'll have what she's having."

She swirled the ruby liquid in her glass. "It's just the house merlot."

"Sounds good to me."

As she held her glass to her lips, she studied him over the rim. "What *is* your function? I've never heard of the US military operating stateside."

"Some do on occasion, but this is a special assignment. Off the radar, off the books."

"So, if one of the other snipers had shot the pirate who was holding me, would he be here instead of you? Is that how the Navy made the determination?"

"I'm not exactly sure. They called. I responded." The bartender had placed his glass of wine in front of him, and he clinked it against hers. "That's how the military works."

They finished their wine over casual chatter and then

walked a few blocks to a small bistro, where Nicole had a second glass of red.

At the end of dinner, she pinged her fingernail against her empty glass. "I hope I'm not going to be required to hop on a bike and chase someone down this time. I'm ready for a nap."

"Uh-oh. How are you ever going to stay awake for the play?"

"Wake me up when it's over."

They took another taxi to the gallery on West Twenty-Fourth Street, and Slade discovered this was Nicole's preferred method of transportation around the city. Her mother kept a car service on call, but Nicole had confided that she didn't like the ostentatiousness of it all, even though she seemed comfortable with most of the perks her father's wealth provided. He supposed she had to draw the line somewhere.

Fifteen minutes later, they sauntered into the gallery, a small space crammed with sculptures. Nicole saw Andre immediately and elbowed Slade in the ribs.

They feigned interest in some god-awful piece while Andre talked to a couple. When he was done, they wandered toward him until Nicole planted herself in front of him.

"Andre Vincent, right?"

"That's right." His smile dimmed a fraction as he looked into Nicole's eyes. "You're Lars's friend. The one he went to Somalia with to make that film."

"Did you hear about Lars?"

"I did, yeah. Shocking news."

"Did you see Lars when he was in the city?"

"I missed him, and now I'm sorry I did." His gaze shifted to Slade.

"This is my friend Slade."

They shook hands, and as far as Slade could tell, Andre wasn't lying about not seeing Lars. At least, he hadn't taken off in a sprint like Dave had.

Andre stroked his beard. "Was there something you wanted to ask me about Lars?"

"He left a note for me when he was in New York and gave it to someone to mail to me later." Nicole lifted her shoulders. "I was just trying to figure out who that was."

"You checked with Dave Pullman or that actress, Trudy? I don't remember her last name, but I think they saw him when he was in town."

"We checked with Dave, and we're on our way to see Trudy Waxman."

Andre snapped his fingers. "Waxman, that's it. Yeah, I'm sorry. That's crazy Lars would do that. No clue he was even depressed."

"Tell me about it." Nicole smudged a tear from the corner of her eye. "Thanks, Andre, and good luck with your show."

When Andre turned to greet a browser, Slade tapped Nicole's arm. "It's 7:40. Can we walk to the theater?"

"It's a little over a mile. If I weren't wearing these shoes, I'd say let's go for it."

"Taxi, it is."

Nicole gave a quick wave to Andre as they exited the gallery and then turned to Slade. "You believed him, didn't you? He seemed like he was telling the truth, but he could've been lying."

"That's a possibility, but he didn't seem nervous. If it doesn't pan out with Trudy, then someone's lying, or Lars has other friends you don't know."

"I hope Trudy's the one." She stepped into the street

and waved down a taxi as only a New Yorker could. A few blocks from their destination, she thrust some money into the front seat. "We'll get out here."

They hustled along the sidewalk to the theater, housed in an old church, and Slade bought two tickets. As they took their seats, he brushed his lips against Nicole's ear. "If it's awful, we can always grab a cup of coffee and wait outside for her."

She winked, and the gesture seemed intimate—or he was reading way too much into her every expression.

Thirty minutes later, they were still in their seats. The play wasn't bad, and Trudy lit up the stage every time she appeared on it. Nicole laughed in all the right places, nudging his arm as she did so, and he tried not to get too excited about it.

The sixty-minute running time didn't warrant an intermission, so at the end of the show, Slade jumped to his feet to stretch his legs. The rest of the audience joined him in a standing ovation, and the actors came out for a curtain call.

"Let's see if we can catch her in the back." Slade took Nicole's arm, and they squeezed past the people in their row and spilled onto the sidewalk with the others eager for some fresh air.

His hand inched down to hers as he led her around the back of the church. The church door opened onto a small quad, shared with another structure across the way. The actors were crossing from the church to this other building, and Slade and Nicole joined the stream of people.

Slade poked his head inside the room where the actors and their friends joked, jostled each other and passed around bottles of wine. He spotted Trudy sitting in a corner, taking off her makeup.

Gripping Nicole's shoulders, he turned her toward the actress. "She's over there. Wanna give it a try in here or wait until she's done?"

"By the looks of this bunch, we might be waiting a long time. Let's hit her up now."

Nicole squeezed past Slade into the room, and he followed as she wended her way through the crowd. She pulled up a chair next to Trudy and touched her shoulder. "Trudy?"

Trudy finished swiping a cotton ball across one eye and then met Nicole's gaze in the mirror. Trudy's red-lipsticked mouth formed an O, and she swung around in her seat. "You're Lars's friend Nicole. Did you get the letter?"

Nicole's eyes flashed toward Slade's face before turning back to Trudy. "I did. Thank you so much."

"How did you know it was me?" Trudy grabbed a glass of wine that someone handed to her and took a swig. "Lars wanted it to be anonymous."

"Process of elimination. I looked up Lars's New York friends, and your name surfaced."

Trudy wiped a bead of sweat from her brow and took another gulp of wine. "I suppose Lars should've anticipated that. I mean, you are a journalist, right?"

"In a sense."

"Do you want some wine?" Trudy fanned her face. "It's so hot in here."

Slade stuffed his hands in the pockets of his leather jacket. Trudy must be overheated from her performance, because the cool breeze from the open door had him chilled.

"No, thanks." As she glanced over her shoulder, Nicole dipped her head closer to Trudy's. "So, did Lars tell you where to hide the film, or did you hide it? Do you know where it is?"

Trudy bit her bottom lip, still red from her heavy lipstick. "He really didn't want me to tell you…or anyone. Something *did* happen to him, didn't it? I'm sure you don't believe he killed himself any more than I do."

"I don't believe it. That's why it's important to get that film and turn it over to someone." Nicole jerked her thumb at Slade. "This is the guy. The US government is now looking for Lars's film."

Trudy's eyes popped open as she stared at Slade. "You're kidding. I thought Lars was just paranoid, but you know, I'd do anything for that guy."

Sniffing, Trudy took another hit from her wine and almost knocked the glass over when she set it down on the cluttered vanity.

"Please, Trudy." Slade crouched down next to her bouncing knees. Her nerves must've been getting to her. "I don't think Lars knew the full importance of that film, only that someone was after it. We need to know where it is. We need to make sense of Lars's death."

"I understand. I have a key. It's…" Trudy trailed off with a jerky nod. She reached for her glass again with a trembling hand. "I feel…dizzy."

Maybe she should lay off the wine. Slade put a hand on her knee. "Tell us where the film is, Trudy."

With her breath now coming out in rapid puffs, Trudy put her hand to her throat. "I don't… I don't."

A spike of adrenaline rushed up Slade's spine. "What is it? What's wrong?"

Traces of spittle at the corner of Trudy's mouth marred her red lipstick. "I can't…"

Nicole dropped beside him as she tried to take Trudy's hands, now flailing at her sides. "Slade, what's wrong with her?"

"I don't know."

As Trudy gurgled, Nicole put her ear close to the agitated woman's mouth. "Trudy? What's wrong? What can we do?"

Slade shouted, "Someone get some water."

As Nicole staggered to her feet, Trudy arched her back and slipped to the floor, foam bubbling out of her mouth. She jerked like a fish on a line.

Nicole yelled. "Water! Someone bring some water. Trudy's sick."

Slade hovered over the convulsing woman and loosened the neckline of her blouse. He kicked the chair out of the way as her writhing head came perilously close to the leg.

Suddenly, her bucking body stilled and her eyes rolled to the back of her head. She'd slipped into unconsciousness.

Taking Trudy's limp wrist between his fingers, Slade pressed his ear against her chest.

Nicole had her phone in one hand as she grabbed a bottle of water with the other from a terrified bystander. She held the water out to Slade. "Will this help?"

Slade placed Trudy's arm across her midsection. "Nothing's going to help her now. She's dead."

Chapter Five

Nicole clutched her stomach and took a step back. Her head swiveled as she took in the room, people now pressing in on her to get a look at Trudy—dead on the floor.

The responsible party had to be someone in this room. Someone who didn't want Trudy telling them the location of the film. Someone who might have a clear shot at them now.

"We have to get out of here." She tugged at Slade's arm.

He pulled his sleeve over his hand and grabbed the stem of the wineglass, putting his nose to the rim. As he set it back down on the vanity, he called out, "Anyone call 911 yet?"

"I did." A woman still in her theatrical makeup held up her phone. "Is it the epilepsy?"

"I called." A man answered from the crush of people.

"I'm a doctor." A woman pushed through and dropped to Trudy's inert form. "Is she conscious?"

"I don't think so." Slade jimmied out of the circle that had formed around Trudy and nodded to Nicole.

She got it. He wouldn't want to be caught here. He might even be under strict orders to keep a low profile.

She stumbled from the circle herself, crouching and weaving her way through the jam of people as a siren wailed beyond the church's courtyard.

When she reached the door, Slade grabbed her arm and strode toward the church. The adrenaline flooding her system kept her legs pumping as she matched him step for step.

He steered her along the side of the church and out to the front, where the first emergency vehicle was pulling up to the curb. Hunching into his leather jacket, Slade veered to the right and away from the first responders.

Her heels clicked on the cement as she kept up with him, her fingers hooked in the back pocket of his jeans. They walked this way for about two blocks, silently, until Slade took a detour into an ice cream shop.

He pointed to a high table for two at the back of the shop, away from the window. "Let's sit."

Her feet didn't need a second invitation, and she perched on the edge of the chair, kicking off her shoes. "Trudy was murdered."

"Excuse me. Are you going to buy something?" The clerk behind the counter squinted and shoved his glasses up the bridge of his nose. "There's no table service."

"Hold that thought." Slade rapped his knuckles on the table in front of her, and he approached the counter. "Raspberry gelato, double scoop, two spoons."

He waited at the counter, back stiff, clutching some money in his fist, while the clerk scooped up the gelato. Slade exchanged the money for the dessert and stuffed the change in his front pocket.

When he returned to the table, he shoved the little cup of purplish-pink gelato in her direction.

She glanced down at it and saw the color of Trudy's cheeks instead. "How did they get to her?"

"It could've been the wine." He jabbed one of the spoons into the mound of gelato.

"I saw you smelling the glass. Did you notice anything?"

"Smelled like wine to me, but whatever she drank could've been colorless and odorless."

She put a hand over her mouth. "If it was the wine, then it was someone there, in the room. It had to be."

"Since nobody else dropped dead, I'm assuming someone targeted her glass—and saw us talking to her."

"Why would the people after the film want to kill her? They could've questioned her. No matter how loyal she was to Lars, Trudy would've given up the film to save her life."

He rubbed his knuckles against the sandy-blond scruff on his chin. "Next best thing to finding the film would be that it stays hidden and nobody else finds it. If someone happens to stumble across it, he or she wouldn't understand the significance of it. Hell, we might not understand the significance of it."

"That's if it stays hidden." She hunched across the small table, her nose almost touching his. "Trudy mentioned a key. Remember? She said she had a key."

Slade reached into the inside pocket of his jacket and withdrew a key chain, dangling it from his index finger.

Nicole's jaw dropped. "Is it hers? How did you get that?"

"In the confusion, when all eyes were on the doctor and I was sniffing the wineglass, I noticed Trudy's purse. I figured if she had any keys, they'd be in her bag, so I reached inside and snagged them."

Curling her fingers around the set of keys, Nicole asked, "Do you think the key she mentioned is one of these?"

"That's what I was hoping, but we have no idea what type of key Trudy was talking about. It could be a key to a safe-deposit box or a safe in her apartment, or a key to something we may never locate." Slade scraped a plastic spoon across the little mountain of gelato and shoved it in his mouth.

She dropped the key chain, which was the letter *T*, on the table with a clatter and spread out the five keys. She nudged the first one. "This looks like an apartment key, right?"

"Probably."

"But so does this." She tapped the second key on the ring. "This one looks like it would fit a padlock, and this one a bike lock."

"That one is some kind of locker key." He aimed his spoon at a short, stubby key with blue plastic on the top.

Pinching the key between two fingers, Nicole brought it close to her face and squinted at the raised writing on the plastic. "Just numbers, no location."

"Is there any place in the city that still has lockers? I know the airports and the train stations haven't had them for years."

"I took someone to the Statue of Liberty recently, and she had to put her backpack in a locker before going up, but I can't remember if those had keys or were electronic." Nicole ran the tip of her finger along the key's ridges and grooves. "How are we going to find out where this key belongs?"

"By using this key." Slade plucked one of the apartment keys from bunch and jiggled the ring in front of her face.

"We're going to break into Trudy's apartment?"

"It's not breaking in if we have a key."

"A key we stole."

"A key Trudy died protecting."

Nicole huffed out a breath and massaged her right temple with two fingers. "I'm exhausted."

"Have some." In the space between them, Slade held out a spoon piled high with purple gelato.

She opened her mouth like a baby bird, and he placed the plastic utensil against her tongue. She closed her lips around it and sucked the gelato into her mouth. As the tart, cold flavor invaded her taste buds, she squeezed her eyes shut.

When she opened her lids, her gaze met Slade's stare, his black pupils rimmed with the intense blue of his irises. "Are the police going to wonder about Trudy's keys? Are they going to wonder about the couple talking to her at the time of her collapse?"

"Probably. Did you know anyone there?"

"No."

"The scene was chaotic. I'm sure an autopsy will be ordered, since women Trudy's age don't typically fall into seizures and die, but the cops may not suspect foul play. And if they don't, they might not take that wineglass into evidence."

"I heard someone say something about epilepsy. Do you think this is just a coincidence?"

"No."

Nicole pushed the cup of gelato away, suddenly feeling sick to her stomach. "Who gave her the wine?"

"I didn't notice." He scooped up the keys and bobbled

them in his palm. "But we're going to find out where Trudy lived and do a thorough search of her place."

"What if she has a roommate?"

"We'll deal with that when we get to it, and we'd better do it soon. If the autopsy shows poison, the police will want to search her place, too."

Nicole pressed her palms against her temples. "This is too much for me to think about right now. I just want to go home, back to my mom's place."

"Is the building secure? Have there ever been any break-ins?"

Her heart did a double-time beat in her chest. "Not that I know of. Mom's never mentioned any. You don't think I'm safe there?"

"I broke in the back way, didn't I? Got to your mail. Nobody stopped me."

"Thanks for pointing that out." She folded her arms and dug her fingers into her biceps.

"I was sent here specifically to protect you, Nicole, and I plan to do that. I'm staying with you tonight at your mom's place."

A little thrill fluttered through her body that had as much to do with the thought of having this SEAL spending the night with her as it did being under his protection.

She smoothed her hands down the thighs of her jeans while she tried to paste a nonchalant expression on her face. The warmth that surged in her cheeks just told her she'd failed. She grabbed a spoon and shoved a glob of half-melted gelato in her mouth.

She talked around the sweet raspberry taste. "If you think it's necessary."

With the last word, a drop of gelato dribbled from the

corner of her mouth. As her tongue darted out to catch it, Slade's finger shot out to dab it from her lip and she wound up licking the tip of his finger.

They both said, "Sorry," at the same time.

She grabbed a napkin from the dispenser. "Just goes to show you how tired I am."

"Then let's get out of here." He lifted the cup by the rim between two fingers. "Do you want any more of this?"

"No." She'd probably end up wearing it down the front of her T-shirt.

He dumped the cup in the trash, and they snagged a taxi a half block away.

When they got to the apartment on the Upper East Side, Slade seemed to vibrate with electricity. His body tensed up and his head swiveled from side to side. The hand on her back became insistent as he guided her past the doorman and into the lobby of the building.

He jerked his head toward one corner of the lobby. "Camera there. Does anyone get past the doorman?"

"Not if they don't live here or aren't with someone who does. The doormen know all of the residents."

Slade nodded as if ticking off items on an internal checklist. As they entered the elevator, he tilted back his head. "Cameras in here, too."

"Feel better now?"

"Makes it more secure, but not impenetrable—nothing is."

"You're just full of good news tonight."

When they stepped inside the apartment, Chanel greeted them by spinning around and dancing on her hind legs.

Slade picked her up. "Does she need to go out?"

"Livvy, the dog walker, was already here, and believe it or not, my mother trained Chanel to use a litter box. It's in the laundry room. She'll be good until tomorrow morning." She pointed at the ceiling. "There are a few rooms up there. You can take your pick."

He shrugged out of his leather jacket and dropped it over the back of the sofa. "I'm going to bunk down here. I'd rather be close to the front door than tucked away in some bedroom with the door shut."

Nicole eyed her mother's white brocade couch, threaded with gold, and shrugged. Mom let Chanel sleep on it, why not a six-foot-two Navy SEAL protecting her daughter?

"I'll get you a blanket and a pillow. There's a half bathroom down here, and I'll find a toothbrush and some toothpaste for you. Anything else?"

"Soap and a towel in there?"

"Yeah. Be right back." She took the stairs two at a time and threw open a cupboard in the hallway. She pulled a blanket from the bottom shelf and ducked into one of the bedrooms to drag a pillow from the bed.

She made a stop at the bathroom connected to her bedroom and found a new toothbrush, still in its packaging. She balanced it on top of the folded blanket and pillow as she carefully descended the staircase.

Slade glanced up from scratching Chanel behind the ear and patted the sofa cushion beside him. "Am I going to have to share my bed with her?"

"I'm afraid so." *Lucky girl.*

She dumped the blanket and pillow next to him, retaining the toothbrush in her hand. She waved it in the air. "Brand-new."

"Thanks. I'm sure Chanel and I will manage."

"Oops, I forgot the toothpaste." She bent forward to place the toothbrush on the coffee table, but it ended up on the floor as her hand jerked. "Where did that gun come from?"

"My hotel room. I had it in my jacket pocket." He traced a finger along the handle. "A little smaller than I'm used to, but it'll do."

"I didn't realize you had a gun with you."

"How else am I supposed to protect you? Does it bother you?"

"I've seen plenty of guns—big ones—up close and personal on my travels. Our translators, including Dahir, used to carry weapons. As long as it's not pointing at me, I can handle it."

"Do you want me to get the toothpaste? Just tell me where it is. You don't need to go running up and down the stairs for me."

"It's the least I can do for you and your…gun." She spun around and called over her shoulder as she jogged up the stairs, "Do you need anything else?"

"We're fine."

She took a used tube of toothpaste from her mother's bathroom and paused to study her flushed face and glittering eyes in the mirror. She was accustomed to a certain level of danger when she went on assignments. Now that danger had followed her home. Did she have to look so…thrilled about it? Her mother was probably right about her. She'd never settle down.

She dismissed the woman in the mirror and glided back down the stairs.

Slade had gotten rid of Chanel, along with his boots and socks. With one bare foot resting on the opposite knee, he was checking his phone.

"Here's the toothpaste."

"Thanks, Nicole." He held up his phone. "Looks like the news about an off-off-Broadway actress dying after a performance is out."

"Do you think they would've killed her if we hadn't contacted her?"

"Yes, and don't think we led them to her, either. If that wine was poisoned, it was spiked before we got there. They were either determined to get the location of the film out of her, or wanted to make sure that she wouldn't pass the info along to someone else."

The events of the day seemed to hit Nicole all at once, and her shoulders sagged beneath the weight of all the recent deaths. "I'm calling it a day. Hope you sleep well, but not too well. I wouldn't want you to miss someone trying to break into the place."

He saluted. "Chanel and I are on the job."

She turned a dubious eye on the little dog, who'd returned to Slade's side, curled into a fluffy ball next to his gun. Her mom would have a fit if she could see her precious pup now.

"'Night, Slade."

"Good night," he called out, his voice muffled as he shook out the blanket.

Nicole plodded up the stairs and got ready for bed in slow motion, exhaustion seeping into every muscle of her body.

As she crawled between the sheets, her phone, which was charging on her nightstand, buzzed. She reached over and swiped her finger across the display to wake it up and then entered her pass code. A text from an unknown sender popped up, and she read it aloud.

"'Heard about Trudy. I'm outta here.'"

Must be Dave. She didn't blame him.

She plugged her phone back in and burrowed into her pillow.

She might be out of here, too, if she didn't have a hot Navy SEAL on guard in her living room.

Chapter Six

The following morning, Nicole woke up to find that the hot Navy SEAL could also make coffee. She trailed downstairs, yawning and inhaling the scent of freshly brewed java.

He raised a cup of the stuff in her direction as she wedged a shoulder against the arched entrance to the kitchen. "Just in time."

"You know your way around a kitchen."

"I know my way around a coffeepot, although the gadgets on this one could rival the control panel of a Blackhawk helicopter."

"Is that coffee black? Because I like mine with lots of soy milk."

"Soy milk?" He shook his head as he opened the fridge door. "How do you manage to get by in some of those primitive locales you frequent without soy?"

"When in Rome." She shrugged. "I can make do when I have to. I'm really not high maintenance, despite my current surroundings."

"I already figured that out." He placed the coffee cup and a carton of vanilla soy on the granite island in the middle of the kitchen. "You wouldn't have lasted two minutes in some of the countries you visited if you were high maintenance."

She pulled up a stool and parked herself at the island. Pouring the soy into the coffee, she watched it fan out in gentle circles until the black liquid turned toffee. She inhaled the sweet vanilla as she took a careful sip.

"I can manage a basic breakfast, too, if you have some eggs."

"I don't usually eat breakfast unless I go out, but help yourself. I'm sure Jenny stocked eggs in the fridge." She warmed her hands on the mug. "What's the plan today? Are we going to search Trudy's place?"

"Once we find out where it is. Do you think Dave knows her address?"

"Uh, yeah, about Dave." She hooked her bare feet around the legs of the stool. "He sent me a text last night. I guess he heard the news about Trudy, and I don't think we're going to get another crack at him."

"Can I see the text? How do you know it's from him?"

She hunched her shoulders to her ears as an insidious trickle of fear dripped down her spine. "Just the context of the message. He said he'd heard about Trudy's death and he was out of here."

"I'm going to start my eggs." He pulled open the fridge door and continued talking with his head stuffed inside. "And you can run up and get your phone."

"Aye, aye, captain." She unwound her legs from the stool and shuffled across the cool tile. Slade pretended to be all easygoing, but he was really quite bossy.

She took the stairs two at a time as if she were on a mission. She swiped the phone from its charger on her nightstand and studied the text message on her way downstairs to make sure she hadn't missed some sinister subtext.

She stood at Slade's shoulder as he cracked an egg with one hand into a bowl. She held the phone in front of his face. "This is it. Pretty straightforward...don't you think?"

He squinted, moving his lips as if trying to decipher some ancient code. "I suppose. Wouldn't make much sense for anyone else to send a message like that."

"You mean like Trudy's killers?" She yanked back the phone and tossed it onto the counter.

"We can't rule out the possibility that they might try to reach out to you one way or another."

"That's why you're here, isn't it? In case they try to reach out to me?"

"That's right."

She could live with that. Rubbing her chin, she asked, "How'd you sleep last night?"

"Chanel and I slept great." He dumped the egg mixture into a skillet of sizzling butter.

"Did she sleep with you on the sofa?"

"All night."

"Sorry about that. At least you're not allergic." Nicole twisted her head over her shoulder. "Where is the little rascal?"

"Back on the sofa. Where else? Does she need to go out this morning?"

"She does. I usually take her out before Livvy gets here for the morning walk."

"Do you feed her in the morning?" He scuffed the eggs off the bottom of pan with a plastic spatula into fluffy mounds.

"Livvy does that after the walk."

He lifted one eyebrow. "I thought you were staying here to take care of the dog while your mom was gone."

"Not really." She picked up the fork on the counter and jabbed a clump of scrambled eggs. "If I weren't here, my mom would be boarding Chanel, but that doesn't mean she'd completely dismiss the dog sitter in favor of me. I told you before, Mom doesn't trust me with that sort of thing."

He shoved the plate of eggs toward her and she shook her head and held out the fork to him.

"Any reason in particular? Did your mother come home one time and find Chanel's fur tangled? Paws dirty? Teeth unbrushed?"

She laughed and took a swig of coffee. "Mom just knows I'm busy, and come to think of it, if we're going to be chasing around the city looking for that film footage, I might just have Livvy take Chanel with her. I hate leaving the dog home alone all day."

"Is she much of a watchdog?" He loaded up his fork with eggs. "I mean, she didn't even curl her lip at me."

"She doesn't have a vicious bone in her body, and I really have to take her out now." She whistled. "Chanel!"

The little dog came careening around the corner of the kitchen and slid across the tiles, stopping only when she hit Slade's ankles.

"She's ready, but I'll tell you what." Slade waved his fork in the air. "Why don't you get dressed, and I'll take Chanel outside."

She sucked in the side of her cheek. "You're worried about me going outside on my own?"

"You said it yourself, Chanel's no watchdog. It'll give me a chance to sort out the neighborhood."

"In case you haven't figured it out already, this is a very good neighborhood."

"No doubt, but I want to suss out the lay of the land, take a look at the building. When I was watching you the other night, it was dark outside. I didn't get a sense if someone would be able to scale the walls or reach your windows from the outside."

"That would be nearly impossible. We're on the tenth floor."

"Nothing's impossible. Someone got to Trudy."

Nicole threw a quick glance over her shoulder as if expecting someone to come charging through the front door. "The leash is hanging on a hook inside the closet in the foyer."

"Does she have a preferred route?"

"There's a small square with a patch of grass about half a block down. You don't have to go all the way to Central Park. Livvy will take her there later."

"Maybe you can start making some calls to Paul Lund or Dave, or maybe not Dave, and see if you can get Trudy's address, or do a computer search."

"Okay, I'll get on that. You don't have to take Chanel far."

"Don't worry. I won't be long."

Did he think she was scared to be on her own in her mom's apartment in broad daylight? "I just meant, she's a small dog, small legs. It doesn't take much to exercise her."

"I'll remember that."

She left Slade eating his eggs, still dressed in all black from the night before—the disastrous night before. Would the people looking for that footage really have gotten to Trudy if they hadn't led them to her?

Once in her bedroom, Nicole opened her walk-in closet and leaned against the doorjamb. "What do you wear to a break-in?"

Of course, as Slade had pointed out, they had Trudy's keys. Would the police be there? Had Trudy's death been categorized as a murder? What else? Twentysomething women didn't just drop dead after theatrical performances...unless they were ill.

Nicole showered quickly, deciding on a pair of boyfriend-cut jeans, a loose T-shirt and running shoes—in case they needed to make a quick getaway.

Slade hadn't returned from walking the dog, so Nicole headed to the office and fired up her computer. She did a search for Trudy Waxman and came across a small news item about her death at the theater. The article didn't mention murder.

She spun her phone toward her on the desk and sent a text to Paul Lund. Dave Pullman would probably refuse to answer even if he did have Trudy's address.

When she heard the key scrape in the lock, she jumped to her feet and hung behind the office door until she saw Slade emerge from the foyer with Chanel at his heels. She let out a small, measured breath.

"How'd it go?"

"We met a chocolate Lab, a pug and a mutt." He swooped up Chanel in his arms and unclipped her leash. "She seemed most taken with the mutt. Loves those bad boys, I guess."

Starting forward, Nicole brushed away the prickles of heat from her cheeks. Slade Gallagher couldn't be referring to himself. He was no bad boy, with his surfer good looks and easy acceptance of all her mother's high-end accoutrements.

"That mutt is Charlie, and they're already good friends. Did Charlie's owner, Emma, wonder what you were doing with Chanel?"

"I told her I was your friend and had offered to walk Chanel around the neighborhood."

"Great. I'm going to have some explaining to do when my mom comes home. Emma is just about the nosiest person on the block."

"I'm sure you'll think of something." He opened the closet door and slipped the leash over the hook. "Did you have any luck with Trudy's address?"

"Couldn't find anything online, but I also texted Paul Lund. No answer yet." She sank to an ottoman and crossed her legs beneath her. "There was an item online about Trudy, but there was nothing about murder."

"It'll take the coroner's office a few weeks to get a toxicology report if there's no apparent cause of death."

"If the NYPD doesn't suspect foul play, will the police even go to her apartment?"

"I'm not sure. If the police don't suspect murder, they probably won't search Trudy's place, but they may talk to anyone who lives there with her."

"And if she does have roommates? How are we going to get around them to search the place?"

"Let's find her place first. If there are any roommates there, we'll deal with them. You knew Trudy, sort of, or at least you knew Lars. If we get caught, we can use that as an excuse."

It took Paul Lund another hour to text her back, but when he did it was good news.

"Bingo." Nicole held up her phone to Slade, stretched out on the floor, playing with Chanel. That dog was going to miss Slade when he returned to being a SEAL, and Chanel wasn't the only one.

Slade turned his head to the side, one furry paw planted on his cheek. "He sent the address?"

"Her place is in Brooklyn."

"Did he mention anything else?"

"No. He doesn't know she's dead."

"Makes you wonder how Dave found out so quickly. Unless you were searching for Trudy's name, her death didn't exactly make prime-time news."

She snapped her fingers. "You answered your own question. Once Dave knew we were looking for Andre and Trudy, he was probably expecting something bad to happen to them—and he didn't have to wait long."

"How long does it take to get to Brooklyn and how are we getting there?"

"We can take the train. It won't take too long, less than an hour." She tapped her phone. "I know this neighborhood, full of film school hipsters, and unless Trudy had better gigs than that off-off-Broadway play last night, I can guarantee you she has roommates."

"Unless she has rich parents."

She studied Slade as he tossed Chanel's plush toy across the room for signs of sarcasm or snarkiness, but his strong, honest face didn't show signs of either. He puzzled her, and she wanted to find out more about him personally, but how did one ask one's bodyguard about the private details of his life?

He liked dogs—that much she knew—and they liked him. Who wouldn't?

Flicking some dog hair from the front of her T-shirt, she shrugged. "Do we go over now or should we wait?"

"Let's go, since we don't know what we're going to find there."

The bell at the front door made them both twitch and sent Chanel into a tizzy.

"That has to be Livvy. Leo knows to let her up." Nicole scooted off the ottoman and then hesitated at the front door as Slade hovered behind her, his warm breath on the back of her neck. Licking her lips, she hooked the chain and inched open the door.

"It's just me." Livvy stepped back from the crack in the door and spread her arms.

Nicole swung open the door. "Right on time. Chanel's going to be starving. She had a busy morning."

Livvy stepped into the room and inclined her head when she saw Slade. Her light blue eyes did a quick assessment of the man in front of her, and she must've liked what she saw. She dimpled and held out her long fingers. "Hello, there. I'm Livvy, the dog sitter."

"Slade, the out-of-town friend." He took Livvy's hand and returned the smile, not looking lethal at all.

"I think those are the only kinds of friends Nicole has—out-of-town ones." Livvy swept up Chanel and met her nose to nose. "Hello, gorgeous."

"We already let her out for a quick walk this morning."

"Okay, I'll feed her and take her out for a longer walk to the park."

Nicole opened the door and poked her head in the hallway. "No other charges today?"

"Not today. Chanel has me all to herself." Livvy shook the little dog gently.

"You should see it when Livvy's walking four or five dogs at once—a true art." Nicole took a few steps backward and grabbed her purse from the coffee table. "We were just on our way out."

Livvy leaned forward, allowing the dog to scramble from her arms. "Before you go out, can I ask a favor?"

"Of course."

"It's colder than when I set out this morning. Can I borrow a jacket for my walk?"

"You can wear that blazer draped over the chair, or I have an NYU hoodie in the coat closet in the foyer."

"Thanks, I'll take the hoodie. That blazer looks— expensive." Livvy wiggled her fingers in the air. "Have fun."

When they got to the elevator, Slade turned to her. "Does she make a living as a dog sitter?"

"I know what my mom pays her, so I can believe it. She has a lot of high-end clients."

"I need a job when I retire from the Navy. Maybe I should look into dog sitting."

In the elevator car, she bumped his shoulder with her own. "You'd be great, and all the society matrons would love you."

"Ah, society matrons."

She pounced on his words. "Sounds like you know the breed."

"Very well."

The doors opened onto the lobby and she lost her chance to ask what he meant as Leo greeted them with a wave. "Did you see Livvy? I sent her up."

"She's all set. She'll be taking Chanel for a walk in about thirty minutes."

Leo held open the door. "Taxi?"

"Actually—" Nicole pivoted on her toes, changing direction "—we'll go out the back way. Mail come?"

"It did."

"Then I'll pick it up on the way out. Thanks, Leo."

"Have a good one."

She led Slade back to the mailboxes, even though he knew exactly where they were. She opened hers and peeked inside, holding her breath.

"You look worried. Anything unexpected?"

She flicked through the envelopes and ads. "Nothing. I'm going to leave it here."

They slipped outside into the alley between her mother's building and another high-rise. The wind whipped through the space and she zipped up her jacket. "Livvy wasn't kidding. It's chilly out here."

"I need to stop by my hotel again on the way and change clothes. I did have a shower at your place, but I could use a clean shirt."

"We can make a stop."

"You can wait in the lobby again…or come on up this time."

Forty minutes later, she wished she'd chosen the lobby as Slade peeled off his black T-shirt and tossed it on the bed.

She averted her gaze from his solid muscles by squinting at her phone. The guy was just too good to be true, and too hard to resist. He probably didn't feel the same connection to her she did to him. He'd saved her life on that boat in the Gulf of Aden, but he'd probably rescued a lot of people. While that moment had been indelibly impressed upon her mind, it was all in a day's work for him.

He crouched in front of a suitcase in the corner of the room, his back and shoulders flaring up from the waistband of his black jeans. Nicole swallowed and wandered to the window.

"Nice view." Times Square below barely registered on her brain.

Slade rose to his feet and turned around, a blue T-shirt clutched in one hand. "Yeah, it's great. That view is also how I know the military is not funding this little operation."

"Not the Navy?" She crossed her arms. "Who, then?"

"Some organization deep in the intelligence community. My superior officer won't even tell me, but I was specifically requested for this assignment. One of my team members was put on a similar assignment last month."

"Are they related?"

He pulled the T-shirt over his head, thank God, and then skimmed his palm over the top of his short sandy-blond hair. "Someone must think so."

"Do you?"

"There's a guy—" he ran a knuckle across the scruff on his chin "—and I'm only telling you this because you're involved and have been involved in matters in the Middle East. He started as a sniper and got on our radar during the conflict in Afghanistan, but he's branched out and may be running his own organization. We think he might've been involved in your kidnapping and in these follow-up killings."

"For what reason?" The gears of her mind had already started whirring. This would make a hell of a story.

"A broader terror organization. He'd been planning an attack in Boston last month, and someone we rescued from Pakistan a few years ago was targeted because he unwittingly had information about the plan."

"The attack at the symposium held at the JFK Library?"

"That's the one."

She pressed one hand against the glass of the window, feeling dizzy. "What would he have to do with a story about the women's movement in Somalia?"

"We don't have a clue—right now. Hoping Lars's footage can clarify that."

"Then we'd better get moving."

Slade sat on the edge of the bed and pulled off one motorcycle boot. "I'm changing shoes."

She kicked out her sneakered foot. "In case we have to make a run for it?"

"Are you sure you don't want to wait here? You'd be safe."

"I thought I was your ticket to Trudy's apartment. At least I had met her once or twice before. I doubt some woman is going to trust you, especially after her roommate just dropped dead."

"That's right, but if you don't want to go you don't have to go." He tied his Converse and stamped his feet on the carpet as he stood up.

"Oh, I want to go."

He reached into the closet and pulled a gray sweatshirt from a hanger, the other hangers clacking in protest.

"You could be living in the lap of luxury and safety on the Upper East Side, attending charity balls and golf tournaments."

She tilted her head to one side. "You sound like you know that world well. Why?"

"I'm from it."

During their forty-minute trip to Brooklyn, Nicole grilled Slade about his background, which wasn't all that different from her own—except his upbringing had played out against the backdrop of a wealthy beach community in Orange County, California.

"So who's your father going to get to take over his business since you've opted out?"

"His business, his problem."

The set of his jaw indicated that his father had tried to make it Slade's problem, too.

"But still, your parents must be incredibly proud of what you do, who you are."

"Would you say your mother is proud of your chosen field?"

"Oh, that?" She waved her hand. "No, but I don't run around saving people's lives."

"Really?" He stretched out his legs and tapped his feet together. "'Cause I've seen your films, and you come pretty damned close to doing just that with your exposés."

A little glow warmed a spot in her heart. "Thanks, but it doesn't come close to what you do, and my mom just thinks I'm crazy."

"Same."

The train swayed, and her shoulder bumped his. He didn't move away and neither did she. She pressed against him and felt more than his solid presence in her life right now. She felt a connection, a kindred spirit.

She'd dated plenty of wealthy guys, and they'd always sided with her mother. She'd also dated guys who were dead broke, and most of them had a hard time figuring her out. Slade got it—got her.

After the train arrived at the station in Brooklyn, they emerged onto a busy sidewalk. "Are you up for a walk? There's no subway deeper into Greenpoint."

"Let's walk. I need to stretch my legs."

Fifteen minutes later, as they turned onto Trudy's street, Slade said, "At least there are no cop cars out front."

"So, either they already came and went, or they aren't even considering homicide."

Slade took her arm at the bottom of the steps. "You got this?"

"If there's a roommate, I'm going to tell her that Trudy had something of Lars's to give me, and I'm there to pick it up."

Slade tried the front door of the building, but it didn't budge.

"The key's probably on Trudy's key chain."

"But if there's a roommate, she's gonna wonder why we didn't just buzz." He pressed the button next to Trudy's apartment number.

The speaker crackled to life. "Yes?"

Slade mouthed an expletive while Nicole leaned into the speaker. "I'm looking for Trudy Waxman."

An audible gasp whooshed through the speaker. "A-are you a friend?"

"A friend of a friend—Lars Rasmussen."

"Lars, yes." The woman sniffed. "I'm sorry, I have some bad news...why don't you come up?"

The door buzzed and clicked, and Slade pushed it open. "Ready?"

"I guess so, but how are we going to search the place with a roommate hanging around?"

"We're going to have to get in when the roommate's

gone. In a way, it makes it easier. We know what we're dealing with instead of being surprised in the act."

They trudged up the three flights of stairs and knocked on the door of number 311.

A woman with a red-tipped nose cracked open the door. Her eyes widened when she spotted Slade hovering behind Nicole. "C'mon in."

Nicole figured she'd get right to the point. "What's the bad news?"

"Trudy passed away last night after a performance."

Nicole clapped a hand over her mouth as Slade squeezed her shoulder. "How?"

"Not sure yet, but it looks like it was her epilepsy."

"Epilepsy?" Nicole's mouth dropped open—for real this time. So she had heard right last night. "I didn't know she had epilepsy."

"Well, you weren't really her friend, were you? What's your name?"

"Nicole Hastings." She and Slade believed it would be best to stick to the truth, since Trudy might have mentioned her.

"That's right. You worked with Lars. I'm Marley."

Slade asked, "Is that the official cause of death?"

Marley's gaze darted to Slade.

"I'm sorry." Nicole tugged on the sleeve of Slade's sweatshirt. "This is my friend Steve."

Marley shook Slade's hand. "I don't know if it's official or not, but the cops came by here last night when one of Trudy's cast mates gave him our address. He told me she'd had a seizure and had passed before the EMTs even got there."

"That's horrible. I'm so sorry." Nicole touched the

other woman's shoulder. "Now I feel sort of stupid being here."

"Why did you come?" Marley dabbed a shredded tissue to her nose.

"Trudy told me that Lars had given her something for me."

"Oh." Marley opened her arms to encompass the cluttered room. "What was it?"

"That's the thing." Nicole lifted one shoulder. "I don't know. Trudy didn't tell me."

"That's...strange." Marley bit her lip. "If I come across anything, I'll let you know. Trudy's sister is coming out in a few weeks to collect her things, and I'll let her know, too."

"Thanks, I appreciate it." Nicole took a half turn around the room. Did Trudy have her own room here? "Nice place. How many bedrooms?"

"We have two bedrooms and one bathroom. I'm going to have to find another roommate, but I can't even think about that right now." Marley's eyes welled with tears.

"I'm so sorry." Nicole patted Marley's arm. "We'll get out of your way."

"That's okay. A bunch of us are going out later to celebrate her life." Marley cocked her head to the side. "That's weird, isn't it?"

"What?" Nicole's heart skipped a beat. Was Marley suspicious about the epilepsy story?

"I mean, Trudy told me about Lars...about his suicide, and now she's dead, too."

"Both too young."

"Well, I can understand why you'd want something from Lars. I'll let you know if I find something."

Nicole gave Marley her cell phone number, and they said their goodbyes.

Slade waited until they hit the sidewalk before speaking. "We're going to wait until Marley goes out, and then we're going back in."

"Did you see that place? It's crammed with stuff. We'll never find it—whatever *it* is."

Slade tugged on a lock of her hair. "I didn't think you'd give up so quickly."

"I'm not giving up." A spark of heat flared in her chest. "I'm all for doing a search."

"That's what I want to hear." He pointed to a coffee place across the street. "Let's hang out over there, keep an eye on Marley's building and make our move."

They got their coffee and settled at a table by the window with a clear view of the apartment.

Nicole popped the lid from her cup and slurped the vanilla-scented foam from her latte. "How did Trudy's killers know she had epilepsy?"

"Good question. Maybe they broke into her place earlier, searched through her stuff and found her medication. They formulated a plan from that. I should've known it wouldn't be straight poison that killed Trudy. None of these deaths looks like murder."

"And who would know to connect them except me?" She took another sip of coffee and glanced over her shoulder at the sandwiches in the refrigerated case. "How long do you think we'll be waiting?"

"Who knows? We couldn't ask her what time the friends were getting together without sounding too suspicious. Marley already thought it was strange that you didn't know what Trudy had for you."

"You're right." She dug into her purse for her phone.

Might as well check some emails. They could be here until nighttime. "Wow, looks like I've missed a bunch of calls."

"I think you have time to return them. Like you said, we could be here for a while."

"They're all from Livvy. I hope Chanel's okay. If anything happened to that dog on my watch, my mom would disinherit me." She touched her phone to return Livvy's call.

Livvy didn't waste any time. "Nicole, where have you been? I got hit by a car and it was hit-and-run—the bastards."

"Oh, my God. Are you all right?"

"I'm at the hospital now, waiting for X-rays. I may have broken my foot or my ankle. All I know is I can't walk on it and it hurts like hell. Don't worry about Chanel. She escaped unscathed. I can't say the same about your sweatshirt, though. That thing's trashed."

A chill zigzagged down Nicole's spine. "That's right. You borrowed my sweatshirt."

"It has a rip and some oil stains on it now, sorry. Now I'm really glad I didn't wear that blazer. My partner, Andi, picked up Chanel and took her back to our place. I hope that's okay."

"That's fine. D-did you see the car that hit you?"

"Came out of nowhere. I would've been dead if Chanel hadn't seen another dog, making me cross the street faster."

"Do you need anything?"

"Andi's taking care of everything. Just give her a call when you're ready to get Chanel. We have two other dogs at our place now, so we can handle her."

When Nicole got off the phone with Livvy, Slade was staring at her, eyebrows raised.

"Livvy got hit by a car, walking my mom's dog and wearing my sweatshirt."

Slade nodded once. "It's your turn now."

Chapter Seven

Hearing him say aloud what she'd already acknowledged to herself sent a new river of chills cascading through her body. "Livvy said the car came at her out of nowhere. All she saw was a dark blur."

"They must've been waiting for you outside and you got lucky when we decided to go out the back way. Livvy is tall and thin like you. Wearing your sweatshirt—" he snapped his fingers "—she was a dead ringer for you."

"Really bad choice of words." She hugged herself, sort of wishing Slade's arms were holding her instead of her own flimsy limbs.

"I take it Livvy is okay, since you were having a conversation with her."

"Better than Trudy." Nicole swirled her lukewarm coffee. "She may have broken her foot or ankle."

"Chanel?"

"Probably saved Livvy's life by chasing after another dog. Pulled her away from receiving the brunt of the car's force. Livvy's partner and roommate took Chanel home with her."

Slade drummed his fingers on the table. "The people after the footage are still trying to make these deaths appear like accidents or suicide, but they must realize you're onto them now if they know you went to see Trudy."

"I guess they don't care what I think, but they probably don't want the police crawling all over these incidents." She hunched forward on the table. "Do you think they know you're here? That the CIA, or whoever you're representing, is in the loop?"

"Hard to tell. If someone was watching us at the theater, he spotted us together." His blue eyes narrowed. "She's leaving."

Nicole jerked her head up and watched as Marley took off down the street. "Wherever they're getting together for this wake must be close, because it looks like she's heading in the opposite direction of the station."

"Then we'll have plenty of time to do our search."

When Marley rounded the corner, Slade pushed back from the table. "Let's go."

They crossed the street and let themselves in the front door of the building with Trudy's key. They paused on the stairs and put on the gloves Slade had insisted they bring. A second key worked for the door to the apartment, and Slade clicked it behind them and slid the lock across the top.

When Nicole raised her brows at him, he shrugged. "Better to have Marley trying to figure out how her door got locked from the inside than having her walk in on us tossing her place."

"Let's start with Trudy's bedroom." Nicole made a beeline for the short hallway off the living room and turned into the bedroom on the right-hand side, a stark contrast to the rest of the apartment. "Ah, this is much better."

"Well, we know who the messy one is. It'll be easier to search in here, too."

Nicole took a turn around the neatly ordered room with its stacks of fabric-covered boxes and shelves lined with books and accented with framed photos.

"I'm going to start looking in here." Slade grabbed the knob of the closet door and folded the door back. He held up the stubby key. "A box or safe for this."

Feeling like a voyeur, Nicole eased open the nightstand drawer.

She scanned the contents of the drawer, her gaze tripping over a few condoms, a small bottle of massage oil, some matches and a dog-eared paperback—a pulp fiction Western from the '40s. The title of the book blurred through the tears in her eyes. That book had belonged to Lars.

Sniffling, she picked up the paperback and thumbed through it. Lars had loved the old American West, and it seemed as if Trudy had loved Lars.

She ran a hand across the cover and placed it back in the drawer. "Find anything yet?"

"Nothing. She doesn't have a safe in the closet. You?"

Nicole closed the nightstand drawer. "No."

She wandered to the bookshelves and studied the titles with her head tilted to the side. Lots of plays. Trudy had obviously taken her craft seriously.

Nicole took a seat on the padded stool in front of the vanity, very similar to the one Trudy had been sitting at the night she died. She poked through the makeup and brushes and then hunched forward to study the photos wedged in the mirror's frame.

She caught her breath. "She has a selfie of her and Lars."

Sneezing, Slade backed out of the closet. "Recent?"

She plucked the photo from the mirror. "According to the time stamp, from his last visit here."

"That's strange." Slade hovered over her shoulder at the vanity. "Who prints out selfies? Most people leave them on their phones."

"Trudy obviously had a thing for photographs." She waved at the framed pictures on the shelves.

"Where was it taken?"

"Not sure." She brought the picture to her nose. "Looks like a fast food place or something. See the sign behind them?"

"Hot dogs." Slade poked the picture with his finger. "No, corn dogs. That's an R and an N."

"Corn dogs? I don't know many places in the city that sell corn dogs."

He flicked the picture with his finger. "Who says they're in the city? Look at the sky to the right of the corn dog place. Do you see any other buildings behind them?"

She niggled her bottom lip between her teeth. "Corn dogs. The last time I ate a corn dog was when I took my out-of-town friend and her daughter to Coney Island."

"Could that be Coney Island?"

"Could be, which would help, wouldn't it?" Nicole slipped the photo in her pocket. "It's probably important to figure out every place they went while Lars was here."

"Would help a lot." Slade leaned in closer, his hand brushing her shoulder. "Any more pictures of Lars?"

"Not here—a few group shots on the shelf, all older."

"I don't see much else in here, do you? Let's check out the bathroom."

With shoulders colliding, they crowded the entrance to the small bathroom, where chaos reigned supreme.

Nicole shook her head. "I honestly don't see how Trudy put up with such a slob. Marley's going to have a hard time finding another roommate."

Slade squeezed past her and tugged open the medicine cabinet. "Do you think this is how Trudy's killers found out about her epilepsy?"

"Maybe." She joined him at the sink and nudged a few prescription bottles with the tip of her finger. "If the police ever do get around to investigating her death as a crime, hopefully they'll find some evidence here."

"In the meantime, we haven't found much except a picture possibly taken at Coney Island. It doesn't look like she kept Lars's film, whatever its form, here in her apartment."

"Unless it's somewhere in that mess." Nicole wedged her hands on her hips and tipped her head toward the living room.

"I don't think Trudy would leave something that important in this jumble of stuff, especially if the stuff belonged to her roommate."

"Probably not. Do you think it would be too obvious to ask Marley if she was here when Lars visited and where Trudy took him?"

"She might think it's weird, but what of it? Marley's not trying to hide anything. Give her another try. You can make up some reason—maybe just trying to figure out what he left you."

"I'll give her a call. Now, let's get out here." She eyed the creeping shadows in the room and shivered. "I don't like being in someone else's space."

"You'd make a lousy thief." Slade unlocked the in-

side deadbolt and then closed and locked the door behind them—just as they'd found it.

She trudged down the three flights of stairs ahead
of Slade, since the staircase was too narrow for them
to walk side by side. She tripped once, clutching the
banister.

"Whoa!" He touched her waist. "Careful."

A smile curved her mouth. When Slade Gallagher
had your back—literally—it was like having a guardian angel flapping his wings around you. Except Slade's
wings were a pair of muscled arms.

They stepped onto the sidewalk as the sky dimmed
around them.

"You must be starving, because I am and I had some
breakfast. Do you want to pick up Chanel and check
on Livvy?"

"Speaking of Livvy, I wonder if the idiots figured
out yet that they targeted the wrong person."

"Even if they haven't figured it out, the driver must
have realized by now that the accident didn't result in
a fatality. He'd be watching the news for sure."

"I must be the only one left standing between them
and that film." Nicole pulled off her gloves and shoved
them into her purse. "Scary thought."

"Nicole? That you?"

At the sound of Marley's voice behind them, Slade
stiffened beside Nicole and took her arm, squeezing it
in warning. He didn't have to warn her. She'd play it
cool, even though she felt anything but.

Nicole pasted a smile on her face and turned around,
almost tripping over her own feet when she saw a man
next to Marley. Good thing her guardian angel still had
possession of her arm. "Marley."

"Did you forget something?" Marley stumbled and her own guardian angel grabbed her around the waist.

"No, no." Nicole tilted back her head. "Are we back on your block? We just stayed in the neighborhood and then grabbed a late lunch."

"Well, I drank a late lunch." Marley's laugh ended on a hiccup and a sob.

The man's arm moved to Marley's shoulders. "Sorry, she is a little upset. You understand."

The man's slight accent matched his formal phrasing. "Of course, yes. I'm sorry. I'm Nicole and this is S-Steve."

She'd almost forgotten Slade's made-up name.

"Hello, I'm Conrad."

"Nicole knew Trudy, too. Wasn't she the best, Nicole? Wasn't she the best roommate ever?"

"Yeah, she was." Slade pinched Nicole's arm, and she cleared her throat. "You know, I thought of something after I left your place, Marley. Where did Trudy take Lars when he was visiting?"

"Shh." Marley put two fingers to her lips, smearing her lipstick across her mouth. "Conrad was going out with Trudy."

"Oh." Nicole put up her hands. "Lars was Trudy's friend. She probably mentioned him to you."

"We had just started dating each other, nothing exclusive." Conrad shrugged. "I am going to help Marley home. She drank much in a short time. Please excuse us."

"Take care, Marley."

Marley's head dropped to the side, resting against Conrad's arm. "'Night."

Slade's hand pressed against the small of Nicole's

back as he propelled her down the street. "It's a good thing Marley was drunk. She probably won't even remember meeting us in front of her building."

"Probably not, unless Herr Conrad tells her, but like you said, I don't really care if she's suspicious of my motives. I already told her that Trudy was going to give me something from Lars. She can think what she wants. At least Conrad didn't seem too upset about Trudy hanging out with Lars."

"The way he was touching Marley, I think Conrad has already moved on." Slade finally slowed his pace as they rounded the next corner. "I wish we really *had* been eating lunch. I'm hungry."

"I think there's a block of trendy restaurants and bars around here—probably where Marley got her drink on." Nicole pulled out her phone. "I'll look it up."

Fifteen minutes later, they were sitting inside an Italian restaurant with a bottle of red wine between them.

Nicole took a sip from her glass and closed her eyes as the warmth from the wine spread through her chest. "I'm going to give Livvy a call. Maybe the police found out something about the car that hit her."

"Try to get some info on the car or driver." Slade held up a piece of buttery garlic bread from the basket the waiter had just dropped at the table. "Don't mind me. I'm going to devour this."

Rolling her eyes, Nicole placed the call to Livvy.

"Hi, Nicole. I'm still alive."

"Don't even joke about it. What's the verdict?"

"Broken foot. How's that for a dog walker?"

"I'm so sorry. For a little extra money, do you and Andi want to keep Chanel there? I'm sure my mom would be fine with it, and I'm…" She glanced at Slade wolfing down his second piece of garlic bread. "Kind of busy."

"That would be great, if you're sure Mimi won't mind."

"Believe me, my mom trusts you with Chanel much more than she does me. Send Andi over to pick up Chanel's food and toys, and I'll have a check for you."

"Thanks, Nicole."

Between bites, Slade nudged the toe of her shoe with his own.

"Livvy, did you remember anything more about the car or the driver?"

"Just a dark blur, and I didn't see the driver at all."

"Did anyone else? Were there any witnesses?"

"One guy said he saw the car speed up coming around the corner, but he didn't get a make or model. Said it was a man driving, though." She coughed. "I told the cops all this."

"I'm just curious. Have Andi come by tomorrow for Chanel's stuff and tell her to give me a call first."

"Will do. Thanks for checking on me."

Nicole ended the call and took another sip of wine—she needed it. "Hit-and-run, no witnesses."

"Not surprising." Slade shoved the bread basket her way. "Have some before I inhale the rest."

She picked up a piece of garlic bread and ripped it in half. "If they were trying to kill me by running me over, they must not be interested in recovering the footage."

"Maybe they already know what's on it and just want to stop anyone else from seeing it."

"How do they know Lars didn't copy and send the footage to multiple people?"

"They don't." Slade wiped his greasy fingers on a

napkin and then swirled his wine before taking a sip. "But whatever outcome they fear from having that film go public or having it fall into the hands of the wrong people obviously hasn't occurred yet. They know nobody has made any significant sense of what Lars filmed—including Lars."

"So it can't just be the interview subjects speaking out on behalf of women's rights. If that were the case, they'd want that film so they could punish those women." She slumped in her chair and stuffed some bread in her mouth. "I don't get it."

"Give your brain a rest and eat." Slade gestured to the waiter, who came scurrying back to their table.

They both ordered the lasagna and a salad to share, and Nicole hadn't realized how hungry she was until later when she dug into the food.

As she twined her fork around a strand of cheese, she said, "I'm going to have to come back here. The food's great."

"Maybe it's just your hunger that makes it seem special."

Or maybe it was the company. She dabbed some tomato sauce from the corner of her mouth. "You've practically licked your plate, and you're trying to tell me you didn't enjoy it?"

"I didn't say I didn't like it." He pressed his thumb against her chin. "I liked everything about this meal."

Her cheeks flushed. "Do I have marinara sauce all over my face?"

"No."

She parted her lips on a quick breath, waiting for his explanation of why he'd touched her chin.

His crooked smile told her he didn't plan to give her one. "More wine?"

"Two glasses with food is my limit. No food, one glass."

"And what's your limit for some faceless stalker out gunning for you? I think you have a good excuse to imbibe."

"Since he's still out there gunning for me, I should've limited myself to water. In fact, I'm going to have a cappuccino."

"I guess Marley doesn't have the same rules as you do. Maybe you can hit her up tomorrow when she's sober and ask her if she knows where Trudy and Lars went."

"I'd better give her plenty of time to get past her hangover, and we may have already nailed down one place, if that corn dog stand matches up to the one in Coney Island."

"We can check it out when we get back to your place tonight, but if they did go there, it's probably significant. Who goes to an amusement park when you feel your life is in danger?" Slade pushed away his own half-full wineglass. "You know what? I'm gonna miss Chanel."

Nicole snorted. "Liar."

"I'm totally serious." His eyebrows formed a V over his nose. "I've always had dogs, but my current lifestyle doesn't allow pets."

"Your current lifestyle doesn't allow a lot of things. Wife?" She held her breath. She couldn't believe she hadn't asked him this question before. What if she'd been salivating over another woman's husband?

"No wife, but some guys manage. We do go home between deployments."

She thanked the waiter for her coffee and picked up the thread of the conversation. "Must be tough on their wives."

"The ones I know are some of the strongest women I've ever met. They make it possible for those guys to do their jobs."

His blue eyes kindled with admiration. Slade Gallagher seemed to appreciate strong women.

Her phone buzzed in her pocket, and she pulled it out. "It's Marley. Maybe she thought of something. Hi, Marley."

A man responded in accented English. "Sorry, this is not Marley. I met you when I walked her home."

"Conrad, right?"

Slade glanced up from studying the check.

"That is correct."

"Is Marley okay?"

"She is fine, just…snockered." He paused for a few seconds. "I think I know what Trudy's friend Lars left for you."

"You do?" She kicked Slade under the table and turned on her phone's speaker, keeping the volume low.

"Yes, I have something and can give it to you tonight, if you like."

Slade hunched forward, his head cocked toward the phone on the table between them.

"What is it?"

"It is in a padded envelope. Do you want me to open it?"

"No, please. I'll come and get it. You're still at Marley's?" He had to be if he was using her cell phone.

"I left her sleeping and do not want to disturb her,

but I'm still in the area. Are you still in Brooklyn, or did you go back to Manhattan?"

"I—I'm still here. We decided to have dinner before going home." She frowned at Slade. "Why do you still have her phone if you left her place?"

"I am returning to her place. You understand."

"Completely." She smirked at Slade. He'd been right about Conrad moving on from Trudy. "I can meet you."

"That is perfect. I'm at a bar on Union, and there is a small park across the street. Can we meet there?"

Slade tapped her hand and lifted his shoulders with his hands out.

She nodded. "Why there and not the bar?"

"Trudy told me something about this package. I want to give it to you in private."

"Okay. What time?"

"Thirty minutes by the playground on the corner of the park."

As soon as she ended the call, Slade said, "That was strange. Why would Trudy give the package to him?"

"Maybe she didn't. Maybe she told him about it, and when he met me tonight he decided to get it from her place and hand it over to me."

"You should've told him I was coming along."

"I'm sure he knows that." She tapped the check on the table. "Let's take care of this and get over there. I'll have just enough time to finish my cappuccino. Maybe this is our lucky night."

"I don't trust the guy. Why wouldn't he just meet us in the bar?"

"Remember Dave? He didn't want to be seen with us, either."

"Yeah, but Dave had already talked to Lars. This

guy Conrad probably never met Lars and doesn't have a clue about what's going on, and how did he know you live in Manhattan?"

"Marley could've mentioned it. Besides, he was dating Trudy. She probably told him about Lars's strange request. Conrad ran into me tonight and figured he'd hand over the package."

"Or maybe once he put a *snockered* Marley to bed, he thought he'd try his luck with you."

"And he just happens to know about Lars and the package?" She rolled her eyes. "This is our chance, Slade. Let's take it."

"All right, but I'll be right by your side."

"I'm counting on it." In fact, she wouldn't have it any other way.

Twenty minutes later, they strolled up to the park with the empty playground on the corner.

Slade faced the well-lit bar across the street. "I feel like marching in there and telling him to hand over the package. This is ridiculous."

"And scare him off?" She shoved her hands in the pockets of her jacket and kicked at some bark in the playground. "Let's just wait for him."

The chains on the swings creaked in the wind, and Nicole hugged her jacket around her. She'd rather be in that bar than out here, too.

Slade started whistling, and she turned toward him to ask the name of the song. She jerked back, her eyes widening. "What is that red light on your forehead?"

"Red light on my...get down!"

Then her easygoing SEAL lost all his senses as he lunged at her and tackled her to the ground.

Chapter Eight

Slade heard the bullet whiz over his head as he took Nicole down.

Her knee gouged his thigh as he landed on top of her, and she grunted softly. He'd probably knocked the wind out of her.

His lips close to her ear, he whispered, "Stay down. That red light you saw on my forehead was a laser marking the spot for a bullet."

She gasped beneath him and then choked. "Where did it come from? Are they still out there?"

"Let's get over to the slide, but stay down." He'd pulled his weapon from his pocket and clutched it in his hand, finger on the trigger.

Nicole must've done this before because she assumed the position and army crawled through the bark to the base of the slide.

Slade stayed behind her, his gaze scanning the tops of the trees. When they reached the slide, he rolled over and studied the skyline. He nudged Nicole's shoulder and pointed to a three-story building next to the bar. "I think he's up there. To get that bead on my forehead, he had to have some height. Unless he's in the trees."

Nicole twisted her head over her shoulder to take in

the trees behind him. "I'd feel more comfortable know-ing where he was before I make a move."

"We don't have to make a move yet. It'll be interest-ing to see if Gunther shows up."

"It's Conrad, and if you're thinking what I'm think-ing, he's not going to make an appearance."

A scuffle of leaves had Slade grabbing Nicole's calf and squeezing. "Shh."

The wind picked up his hushed whisper and rustled the branches of the trees with it. If Conrad wasn't the shooter, he could be on his way to deflect suspicion—or to make sure his man had hit the intended targets.

As they huddled together against the cold plastic of the slide, Nicole's breath came out in short spurts, tick-ling the back of his neck.

His muscles ached with the tension, and his eyes burned in their sockets as he peered into the darkness, his gaze darting from the swings stirring in the breeze to the shadows cast by the jungle gym.

He eased out one long breath between clenched teeth.

"We're going to get out of here—on our bellies. I don't want you standing up until we reach the sidewalk, and you're staying on my left. We don't want to give this sniper any opportunity."

"Got it. Wouldn't want to make it easy for him."

"Head down, face in the bark, let's move."

A split second later, Nicole flattened her body against the scattered pieces of bark and scooted out from their hiding place. He kept to her left from where he figured the first shot had been fired. He hoped it was the last shot.

He sealed his lips against the dry bark as it scratched his chin and the side of his jaw. They couldn't give the shooter one glimpse of their faces, which would give him his bull's-eye. The sniper's scope probably had night vision, but Slade knew too well the difficulty of hitting a dark target level with the ground.

He bumped Nicole's shoulder. "You're doing great, just a few more feet until the sidewalk. We're rolling into the gutter and hunching behind that car."

"Can't wait."

Slade's hands skimmed the rough cement of the sidewalk as he extended his body into a human log and launched himself at the gutter.

Nicole hit first with a thud.

"Are you okay?"

"I rolled faster than I thought I would. I guess that happens when you're fueled with fear and cappuccino."

Slade grabbed the bumper of the car and pulled himself up to his knees. He put an arm around Nicole's shoulders as she crouched beside him. "We're going to cross the street, hover in that doorway and wait for the next taxi. Are you ready?"

"What I'd like to do is go into that bar and find Conrad."

"Not a great idea."

"Do you think he's in there waiting for some kind of signal?"

"I could give him a signal…or two, but I doubt he's in the bar, and we don't need to expose ourselves any more tonight." He grabbed her hand and they ran across the street, doubled over at the waist.

A taxi came out of nowhere and honked at them, and Slade pounded on the hood to stop it since they might not find another.

The driver's scowl melted away when he realized

they wanted a ride. He took them to the train station, and ten minutes later they collapsed into a couple of seats as the train lurched into motion.

Nicole's eyelashes dropped for about a minute and then she was studying him with that curious spark in her green eyes. "Conrad hit up Trudy after she met with Lars, probably fished for info about Lars and then killed her when he found out we were in contact with her. Does that about sum it up?"

"I don't think she was killed just because we contacted her, and you forgot the part where he tried to have us killed, too."

She smacked her forehead with the heel of her hand. "Silly me."

He gave voice to one more concern. "I hope Trudy's roommate is going to be safe."

"Oh, God." Nicole plowed her hands through her hair, loosening stray bits of bark. "I'd call her, but Conrad has her phone."

Slade dragged his own phone from his jacket pocket. "I can place an anonymous call to the police to do a well check at Marley's place. I can say we saw a man carrying her into the building, which is pretty close to the truth. At least that might get the police over there and scare off Conrad if he has any plans of returning."

"Could you do that? I'd feel better and not like we completely abandoned her."

"We can't check on Marley ourselves. We could be walking right into an ambush." He held up the phone. "I'll make the call."

Nicole listened intently as he spoke to the police and grabbed his arm when he ended the call. "What was that all about?"

"Seems we got a little lucky, if you want to call it that. There may be a serial rapist in the area, and the police are going to check it out right away."

"That's terrible, even though it's a win for Marley. Could this night get any worse?"

A muscle jumped in Slade's jaw as he turned his head to the side. "I think it just did."

Her knee bumped his as she jerked her head in his direction. She squinted into the glass partition to the next car. "What do you see?"

"A man moving down the center aisle in the next car. He's hunching forward like he doesn't want to be seen."

"Then he's successful, because I don't see anything except a woman reading and a man with big headphones on."

Slade sat up straighter, craning his neck and lifting his chin. "I swear I saw him. He must be slouched in a seat."

Nicole slouched herself, sticking her legs in front of her. "I don't want to see him, either. I'm exhausted."

Licking his lips, Slade glanced to his left, where a couple had their heads together over a cell phone, looking at pictures. Beyond them, a single man and two young women took up a few seats between them and the next car.

"I think we should move." Slade lurched to his feet and grabbed her hand.

"If he comes after us, we're going to run out of train."

"Not if we move fast enough. We'll get to the station in Manhattan before he gets to us."

She tilted her head to the side to look past his body into the next car. "I still don't…"

Her words died on her lips as a head with a dark

cap popped up and back down. She gasped. "Did you see that?"

"I did. I'm thinking we were followed. Get moving to the next car and stay in front of me."

The man in their car glanced at them with half-hearted interest as they shuffled down the length of the train car.

When they reached the end of the car, Slade gave the door a shove and they stumbled into the next car. This one contained a few more people than the previous one, but nobody seemed to care about a couple bursting into their space.

Slade twisted his head over his shoulder and said, "He's on the move."

Nicole stumbled as she reached for a seatback to steady herself. The train curved to the right and the rails squealed.

"Keep going." Slade propelled her forward with a hand on the small of her back.

Nicole was panting now and slammed two hands against the next connecting door. It burst open.

The faces in the next car stood out sharply as Slade's gaze darted from person to person. He just wanted to put as much space as possible between Nicole and the impending doom tracking them through the train.

Of course, that guy would have to get through him to get to her, and he'd never allow that.

As they crashed into the next car, Nicole said, "Only one more car before we're trapped."

"He'll be trapped, too. I just don't want things to get messy on the train."

"Messy?" Her eyes widened as her gaze dropped to the bulge of his hand in his pocket. He wouldn't hesitate to use his weapon in this public place to protect her—after all, that's what he did. The guy following them through the train wouldn't hesitate to use his, either.

They hustled into the last car just as an announcement came over the loudspeaker that the next stop was in Manhattan.

Nicole turned and lined up her spine against a silver pole, wedging her feet against the floor of the car. She could slide down that thing in a second if she had to. Would the attacker come in with guns blazing?

Slade made a half turn and squeezed Nicole's arm. "Get ready to hit the deck."

Nodding, she squared her shoulders and tensed her body. He knew he could count on her to follow his direction.

As he started to move back toward the previous car, she grabbed on to his belt loop. "You're going the wrong way, aren't you?"

"I'm going to be his welcoming committee." Slade reached the door connecting the last car to the previous one and hopped onto the seat to the left of it.

This action finally got the attention of the handful of people in the car.

Slade raised his voice. "There's a man with a gun. Everybody get down."

Not everyone in the car listened, so Nicole nudged the leg of the woman sitting across from her. "He's serious."

Another woman screamed, and as the train slowed to a stop, their pursuer shoved open the final set of doors.

But Slade was ready for him.

Chapter Nine

The man raised his weapon. Slade swung from the bars. He hit the guy dead center with both feet. The man flew backward, his gun spinning from his hand. He crashed against some empty seats.

People in both cars tumbled out of the train onto the platform, a shrill voice raised, calling for the police.

The man sprawled half on the seat, his knees on the floor, but it didn't stop him from reaching for his weapon. Slade got there first, stomping on the man's wrist with his foot.

He snatched up the gun and then got in the man's pale face and growled, "If this wasn't a public place, you'd be dead. Next time."

Slade slipped back into the last car where Nicole was still waiting for him. He took her arm just as two police officers boarded the train.

"Did you see a man with a gun?"

"I didn't see a gun, but there was a fight back there." Slade jerked his thumb over his shoulder and guided Nicole from the car before any more questions could come up.

Once they got onto the platform, they both picked up the pace, maneuvering through the crowds.

"Is he...was he..."

"The bastard's still alive. I can't leave a dead man in the middle of a train, but I have his weapon and maybe we can get some prints. He wasn't wearing gloves."

"Will the police arrest him?"

"On what charge? He has no gun, unless he has a spare on him, and he'll just claim someone attacked him on the train and will refuse to pursue the matter. The other side has even less reason to get mixed up with local law enforcement than I do."

When they got to street level, Nicole grabbed on to a lamppost, her body sagging against it.

Slade curled an arm around her waist, and her slight frame trembled against him. "I'm sorry, Nicole. We need to get out of here. I don't know how badly I hurt him. He could come after us again."

She blinked her eyes a few times and tossed her hair over her shoulder. "I know. I'm okay. I'll snag us a taxi."

And she did just that. He expected her to collapse in the backseat, lean against him, but she pinned her shoulders against the seat of the taxi and cleared her throat.

"They're going to take any opportunity they can to kill me, aren't they?"

"Looks like they don't want you getting your hands on the film—whether or not you know what to do with it."

"They have to figure my current companion—" she jabbed his arm with her index finger "—is more than some guy on the street. That has to have them doubly desperate."

"I guess Trudy never did tell Conrad what Lars gave her. He doesn't know what he's looking for."

"But we do."

She outlined the bulge in the pocket of his jeans and for a quick minute he thought she was making a move on him, but she was just tracing the outline of Trudy's key chain. "And as soon as I get home and back to my computer, I'm going to do a little research on the lockers at Coney Island."

Slade patted his jacket pocket. "And I'm going to find out where I need to take this gun to get fingerprinted. Maybe we can narrow down the group that's after this film if we can start ID'ing some of its members. We have Conrad, the owner of this gun and the sniper who was taking potshots at us."

"Potshots? That seemed like more than a potshot to me."

He snorted. "Amateur."

"So, we could be dealing with three different people here in New York, or maybe someone's doing double duty."

"I don't believe Conrad was the sniper. Conrad had to be available in case we sauntered into that bar instead of meeting him at the park. They could've even used him to track us down in the park so the sniper could get off his shots."

"Do you think the man chasing us through the train was the sniper?"

"No. He got after us too quickly. That sniper was probably still in position waiting for another opportunity when we jumped into the taxi. So, yeah, we could be looking at three different people."

"They're sparing no expense or manpower—whoever *they* are." She wrapped her arms around her lithe body and shivered. "If you hadn't shown up when you did, I'd be a goner by now. There's no way I would've known how to handle this onslaught."

"I don't know." He smoothed his hand down her arm. "You're pretty savvy in the field. It's clear you've had practice at this."

"I've been in some gnarly situations, but these people just keep coming at me from all directions." She covered her eyes with one hand. "I'm not sure how much more I can handle."

"You don't have to handle it alone, Nicole." He patted her knee. "I'm right here."

The taxi squealed to a stop in front of her mother's building. She shoved some crumpled bills at the driver in the front seat and said, "Time to get to work."

Slade's senses were on high alert from the curb to the elevator, but once inside the car, he wedged a shoulder against the mirrored wall and released a long breath. Back to work.

Toby, the nighttime doorman, had assured them on the way in that nothing unusual had happened at the building and no strangers had been sniffing around. But Slade still approached Nicole's apartment as if he expected to find armed assailants hiding behind the drapes. He flicked back the drapes with the barrel of his gun under Nicole's watchful eye.

"Are you going to check out the entire place before we get down to business?"

"Just a quick surveillance. Any more news from Livvy?"

"Just a text that Chanel is doing fine."

"Nothing from Marley, I suppose…or Conrad?"

"He's probably trashed the phone by now. He won't be going back to Marley now that we're onto him, but we need to find a way to contact her to warn her about Conrad."

"We'll get to her. Don't worry."

He searched the place more carefully than he'd let on to Nicole, and only then did he unclench his jaw and relax his muscles.

He must've communicated his tension to her, because she hadn't moved from her post by the corner of the kitchen, arms and legs crossed, since he started his survey.

He nodded to her. "All clear. Do you wanna break out the computer?"

"I wanna break out a bottle of wine. You up for that?"

"Absolutely. I'm glad you changed your mind because we deserve it." He cocked his head at her as she pulled that bottle of white from the fridge. "You know, I don't think I ever thanked you for saving my life tonight."

"I saved your life?" She twisted the cork out of the bottle with a small pop. "All I remember is you swinging through the train car like Tarzan."

"At the park. You saw that red dot on my forehead."

"Yeah, I was such an idiot, it didn't occur to me what that was." She poured the golden liquid into two glasses and then tipped a little more into each.

"You noticed it, which is more than most people would." He took the glass from her hand, the tips of his fingers brushing across her knuckles. Her skin felt smooth and soft and ignited a longing in his chest that he hadn't felt in years.

Her lips parted, and her lashes dipped once as if in acknowledgment of his silent yearning. Then she flashed her pearly whites and gulped back some wine, breaking the spell.

"Then you're welcome, but I owed you big-time for taking down that pirate. A small token of my gratitude."

He took a swig of the expensive sauvignon blanc, the fruity taste flaring in his mouth before he swallowed. "Why'd you spit on him?"

"What?"

"The pirate. I watched you through my scope after I took him down, and you spit on his body."

"Did I?" Her laugh gurgled in the back of her throat. "What a barbarian I am. I suppose it was instinct. I was so mad that we'd been captured. So terrified. So relieved. When that many emotions are running through your mind all at the same time, I guess your animal instincts take over. You must've thought I was a crazy woman."

"I thought it was pretty kick-ass."

A small smile curved her lips. "We still have some work to do. Where are you taking that gun?"

"I'm going to send an email from my phone right now." He pointed across the great room. "Office?"

"Yeah." She wrapped her fingers around the neck of the wine bottle. "I'm taking this along."

As he followed her into the office, he said, "I miss Chanel. It's too quiet around here without her."

"That little puff of fur turned into a real hero, didn't she? She practically saved Livvy."

"That was when the people after you were still trying to make their hits look like accidents. The sniper tonight and the guy on the train indicate a level of frustration that just turned dangerous."

She sat down in front of the computer and woke it up

with a flick of the mouse. "I think Giles, Lars and Trudy already found it dangerous—lethal, in fact."

"Of course. That's not what I meant." He brought up the secure email on his phone and sent a message to Ariel about the gun he'd taken from the man on the train.

Nicole had been busy clicking away on her computer and now leaned back in her chair. "This is interesting."

He crossed to the desk in two long strides and ducked his head over Nicole's shoulder to peer at the monitor with its display of colorful pictures. "What's this?"

"It's Coney Island, home of corn dog stands."

"Did you find the place that was in Trudy's picture?"

"Not yet, but look at this."

He leaned in closer, and despite diving into the dirt at the playground and rolling around the floor of a train, Nicole still smelled like fresh flowers.

She tapped the screen at his hesitation. "Lockers. Coney Island has lockers, the type you originally had pegged for Trudy's key."

"Good sleuthing. Seems pretty risky for Lars to leave something as important as that film in an amusement park locker, though."

"Risky but unexpected. Anyone might guess a safe-deposit box or safe under the bed, but a locker at the beach?" She raised her arms over her head in a stretch, interlocking her fingers. "I can't think of anywhere else close where that picture could've been taken. Of course, they could've gone to other places while Lars was out here and just didn't take any pics."

"Yeah, but Lars's visit wasn't a vacation. He came through New York specifically to hand off the film to you and in your absence gave it to Trudy instead. I doubt Trudy took him to all the tourist spots."

"It's too bad I wasn't here."

"I don't know about that. I wasn't here, either, and you didn't have the same level of suspicion then. You would've been an easy target." His hands moved to her shoulders in a protective move.

"I'm glad you're here." She tapped his knuckles with her fingertips.

His hold on her shoulders turned into a caress, and she seemed to melt beneath his touch. Dropping to his knees next to her chair, he wedged a finger beneath her chin and turned her head toward him.

He ran the pad of his thumb across her bottom lip, waiting for some sign that this wasn't the stupidest idea on the planet.

She sighed, her breath tickling his thumb, and her eyelashes fluttered.

He took that as two signs. Angling his mouth over hers, he touched his lips to her lips. The wine he'd just consumed tasted better this way.

Nicole closed her eyes and twined her arms around his neck, pulling him into her special realm where everything seemed more intense—the taste of the wine, her sweet scent, the pillowy softness of her lips, the music of her sighs.

He deepened the kiss, his tongue probing for hers, toying with it in a sensuous dance that ignited a flame in his belly. The thudding of his heart drowned out the voices in his head that had been urging caution from the minute he'd laid eyes on this woman through his scope.

With her arms still coiled around his neck and her lips pressed against his, he slid one hand down her back and the other beneath her thighs and pulled her into his arms. From his knees, he rose to his feet with a tight hold on this long-limbed beauty.

He didn't even have any idea where her bedroom was in the vast area upstairs, but he'd be happy to take her anywhere.

Slade moved from the office with the precious bundle in his arms and made for the stairs.

Nicole had broken their kiss when he'd lifted her from the chair in the office. Now she cupped his face in her hands. "You do not have to carry me upstairs."

Looking into her green eyes, he narrowed his gaze. "Because you don't want this?"

"Oh, I want whatever this is, but you don't have to lug me up the staircase to get it."

He chuckled. Yep, like no other high-maintenance society girl he'd ever met.

"No lugging required. You're as light as a feather."

"That may be, but I just survived a sniper's bullet and an attack on the train. I'm not going to risk tumbling down the stairs, even if I do end up on top of a hot Navy SEAL."

"You don't have to take a fall down the stairs to wind up on top of this Navy SEAL."

He winked at her as he set her down on the bottom step of the winding staircase.

Just as she took his hand and he felt like his head might explode, the jangling ring of a telephone jarred his senses.

"What the hell is that?"

"It's called a telephone. It's my mom's landline, which she refuses to give up."

"It's gotta be close to midnight. Who's calling her

at this hour?" Even as he asked the question, a whisper of apprehension made the hair on the back of his neck stand at attention.

"The phone has an answering machine, so whoever it is can leave a message." She tugged on his shirtsleeve.

As he planted a foot on the next step, the person on the other end of the phone did start leaving a message—one they could hear.

A man's accented voice rushed over the line. "Nicole. It's Dahir. We need to talk. It's urgent—life or death."

Chapter Ten

She jerked away from the promise of Slade's warm touch and stumbled off the bottom step. She pounced on the phone in the kitchen, Dahir's voice acting like a magnet.

"Dahir? Dahir? It's Nicole."

Her translator grunted in surprise. "Nicole? You're there? I didn't know you'd be at this number."

She could've asked him why he'd called her mother's place, but he was probably just hitting up all her numbers. "Well, I am here, and I'm so happy to hear from you. You're well? Safe?"

"I am. I am. You heard about the others? Giles? Lars?"

Slade touched her arm, and she punched a button to put the phone on speaker. "Of course I heard. Giles's death was a tragedy, but when Lars supposedly committed suicide, I knew something wasn't right. Where are you?"

"I'm here in New York. That's why I cannot believe in my...luck that you are here, too."

"How did you get here? I've been trying to track you down forever."

"After the kidnapping, I had to hide out. It wasn't safe for me—or my family."

"I'm so sorry, but how did you manage to get to New York? Did the US government help you after all?" She glanced at Slade, hunched over the counter, but he shrugged.

"I can't really say, Nicole. I'm here now, and I must meet with you."

"Do you know why Giles and Lars were killed?"

Slade tugged on a lock of her hair and put a finger over his lips.

She drew her brows over her nose. He didn't trust Dahir?

"I have a good idea why they were killed. That's why I need to talk to you."

Slade tapped the telephone receiver.

"Can you just tell me now over the phone?"

"I can't, Nicole. I have to give you something in person."

Her heart jumped. "Lars's film? Do you have Lars's footage of the interviews we did with the women?"

"I can't tell you over the phone. It has to be in person. I'll tell you everything tomorrow night."

"Tomorrow night? Why not earlier? I'll meet you anywhere."

"I can't make it until nighttime. There are…things I need to do first, and please don't talk to anyone else about this or do anything else to find the film. It's not what you think."

Dahir's voice had gotten louder, his accent thicker.

"Are you okay, Dahir?"

"I'm fine." His voice cracked. "It's my family who's in danger. Please just do as I ask you."

"I will. I will."

Slade nudged her foot with the toe of his shoe and she waved him off.

"I'm staying with a friend in Harlem. There's a club not far from his place. It's dark, crowded, noisy. We'll meet there."

He gave her the name of the club and told her to be there at eleven o'clock.

"Nicole?"

"Yes."

"Come by yourself."

"I'll see you then, Dahir. Be careful."

"You, too."

When she ended the call, Slade exploded. "You are *not* meeting that guy at eleven o'clock at night in some club by yourself."

"It's Dahir. I trust him."

"Trust nobody, and even if he's on the up-and-up, how do you know he hasn't been followed? He might lead whoever killed Giles, Lars and Trudy right to you."

"I think it's a chance we have to take. Maybe he has the film. Maybe Lars left a copy with him."

"I'm coming with you." He held up his hands as she opened her mouth. "I'll stay out of sight, but if you think I'm letting you walk into some lion's den by yourself, you're smoking something."

"I'm not smoking anything, and I'm counting on your being there. In fact, I'm not making a move without you, but I think we should put our trip to Coney Island tomorrow on hold."

"Why should we?"

"You heard Dahir."

Slade rolled his eyes. "I heard a bunch of gibberish that didn't make much sense."

"He said it's not what I think and warned me against taking any more steps to find the film. His family's lives may depend on that, and I'm not going to be responsible for anyone else getting hurt." She drummed her fingers on the counter. "You know what? The amusement park at Coney Island isn't even open tomorrow, anyway. It's Friday, and until the summer, Luna Park is open on the weekends only so we have to wait."

"Well, that's that, I guess. Okay, we'll see what Dahir has. He may just want help from you. Maybe he's here illegally, because I sure as hell know we didn't bring him over."

"I'll give him that help if that's what it is. Dahir put his life on the line for us every time he translated for those women and told their stories for them."

"All right. I'll probably get an email back regarding the gun and where to take it for fingerprinting. I can work on that tomorrow while we wait for this meeting. I'm also going to head over to that club and scope it out beforehand."

She stifled a yawn. The moment between them had passed. She didn't know what she was thinking, anyway. She'd been carried away by the gentleness of his touch. She couldn't get involved with another adventurer, no matter how good his kisses felt.

"I, uh, left the wine in the office. I'm going to grab that and put it away…unless you want more."

He watched her beneath heavy-lidded eyes, the tension of his previous expectations melting from his face. "I don't need any more…wine. Are you turning in for the night?"

"I am, Slade. I'm just so tired. It all hit me after Dahir's call. I'm sorry…"

He put two fingers to her lips. "Don't apologize. I'll get the wine and put it away. You get some sleep."

She replaced the phone in its cradle and turned, pausing on a half step. She could have him in her bed, making love to her, holding her. And then what? When this was all over, regardless of the outcome, he'd be halfway across the world protecting someone else, putting his life on the line for someone else—and she'd be waiting for a call. She couldn't lose anyone else, and Slade Gallagher already meant more to her than he should.

Huffing out a breath, she turned toward the staircase. "Good night, Slade."

"Good night, Nicole."

THE NEXT MORNING, Slade beat her to the punch again and did a good job filling her mother's kitchen with his shirtless presence as he made coffee.

Was he trying to make her regret her decision last night? As the muscles in his back bunched and flexed while he reached for the coffee mugs, she wiped a little drool from the corner of her mouth and regretted it mightily.

He swung around, the fingers of one hand hooked in the handles of both mugs, looking like some hunky maid service. "Coffee?"

"Yes, please." She sat at the granite island and sank her chin into the palm of her hand. "You look…chipper."

She'd expected him to be morose and sullen over his missed opportunity last night—just as she was.

"I slept well, despite missing Chanel, and woke up to an encouraging email."

"About the gun?"

"Yeah, I'm supposed to bring it to the FBI office here in Manhattan."

"Am I allowed to tag along?" She pointed to the fridge as he placed her coffee in front of her. "Soy, please."

"Yeah, of course. I want you tagging along. It's just safer, for now."

"I'm hoping Dahir will hand over the footage tonight. Once you guys have it and turn it over to the CIA, I should be out of the loop, right? There's no reason for this terrorist cell to target me anymore, unless they go in for revenge." She bit her lip as she swirled a stream of soy milk into her coffee. "They're not in that business, are they?"

"We don't exactly know who *they* are. It may not even be a terrorist group." He drummed his fingers on the counter. "That's why it's important to get the prints from this gun today."

"Are they expecting you?"

"In a few hours."

"I'm going to call and check on Livvy before we get going. Did you see anything in the news about an altercation on the train last night?"

"No, but then that wasn't big enough to make it to the local morning news. I'm sure our friend didn't give the NYPD much information."

"I'll take a shower and get dressed. I suppose we'll have to stop off at your hotel again so you can get a change of clothes." She grabbed her coffee mug and slid from the bar stool. "You know, if you're going to make a habit of spending the night here, you might as well just pack a bag."

He opened his mouth to respond, but she twirled

around and headed for the stairs. Was she sending him mixed messages? She usually didn't play coy. If she wanted a man, she let him know in no uncertain terms—and she wanted Slade Gallagher.

Forty minutes later she came back downstairs wearing a long cotton skirt and a denim jacket. A visit to the FBI office should be nice and sedate. At least, she wasn't planning on crawling through a playground on her belly or dashing through a moving train. Although with Slade by her side, either one of those was a distinct possibility.

Still parked in the kitchen, Slade glanced up from his phone as she wedged her hip against the center island. "Are we still on schedule for taking in the gun?"

"An Agent Mills is going to meet us."

"How much does he know about our...your assignment?"

His mouth quirked. "Just enough to run the prints through the Department of Justice and Interpol databases, if necessary."

"I hope identifying this guy sheds some light on the motivation behind getting this footage."

"Yeah, I'm beginning to believe more and more that your kidnapping by those pirates is also linked to all of this. That was their first attempt at stopping this film from getting anywhere, but those Somali pirates were freelancers and had their own ideas about what they wanted from your capture."

"Then the SEALs probably saved this group the inconvenience of taking out the pirates themselves."

"Possibly." He'd eaten some eggs for breakfast and put his dishes in the sink.

"You can leave those. Jenny will be over today to

clean the place." She felt a warm tinge in her cheeks at the way Slade's mouth tightened. "Honestly, Jenny likes to have something to do when she comes over."

He ran the water in the sink over the dishes. "I'm not judging."

"You kind of had that—" she stretched her lips into a straight line "—disgusted look."

"I'm sorry. It just sort of reminded me of…things."

"I know. I know. High-society, high-maintenance divas." She waved her hands in the air. "Would it make you feel better if I told you my mom was a Vegas show-girl when she met Dad?"

"Really?" His eyebrows jumped to his hairline.

"She was, so while she definitely enjoys the money Dad left her, she never forgets where she came from and our housekeeper, Jenny, adores her. The two of them spend more time gossiping about celebrities than in any kind of lady of the manor–maidservant relationship."

"Is that why your mother is so accepting of what you do and the men you date?"

Nicole snorted. "Accepting, maybe, but she thinks I'm crazy. She worked long, hard hours as a young woman and doesn't understand why anyone would want to work if they didn't have to. And the men I date? What do you know about them?"

"Not much." He lifted his shoulders. "I know about the guy who died on Everest—sorry."

"Yeah, crazy son of a bitch." She rubbed the end of her tingling nose. "Are you ready?"

"Let's do it."

They took a taxi to Slade's hotel and she tried to wait in the hotel lobby again, but Slade wouldn't hear of it. "Let's just be on the safe side. I won't be long."

This time he spared her the visuals of his perfect body, although she could still hear the shower over the TV and her imagination probably got her hotter than the real thing.

Then he burst from the bathroom in a T-shirt and jeans and she shook her head. Nothing about Slade was hotter than the real thing.

"You okay out here?"

"Just fine." She sat up straighter in the chair and lowered the volume of the TV. "I did take a sparkling water from the minibar, if that's okay. I'll pay you for it."

"I'll itemize it on my expense report." He pulled a plaid shirt over his T-shirt. "I don't think I need a jacket today."

"That's why I'm wearing this." She swished her skirt around her knees. "I think spring is on the way."

He pulled on his boots and stamped his feet. "Okay, let's find out who was chasing us last night."

Handling the weapon carefully, he placed it inside a manila envelope. Then they grabbed a taxi to the federal building.

Agent Justus Mills didn't keep them waiting long. Nicole grinned to herself—had he fulfilled the prophecy of his first name?

He shook hands with Slade and then her, raising his dark eyebrows to his bald pate. He must've been well versed in discretion, since he didn't say a peep about her presence even though she could tell he was dying to.

"I've got a room in the lab set up." Mills jerked his head toward a long hallway. "Last door on the left."

Slade and Mills walked side by side and Nicole followed them, taking quick glances right and left into the sterile, boxlike rooms they passed. What did the FBI use these for, prisoner interrogation? She really had no clue how the FBI worked. She just hoped they could give them some answers.

Mills stopped in front of a larger door than all the rest on the corridor and swiped a badge at the card reader on the wall outside. A green light beeped and the door clicked.

"This way." Mills pushed open the door and held it ajar as she and Slade scooted past him.

Now *this* looked like the FBI of her imagination. Computer servers clicked and whirred in the chilly room and intense people stared at their monitors, searching for clues in the lines of text that scrolled across their screens.

Mills led them to a room off the main lab and snapped the door shut behind him, as if to make the point that what went on out there wasn't what was going on in here.

Mills spread his fingers and pressed all ten fingertips on the table, which already contained items for lifting the prints. "You have the weapon?"

"I had to check it in when we came into the building, but you must've cleared that ahead of time, because they gave it back to me once I got through the metal detector."

"It was all cleared beforehand." Mills jerked two thumbs up at the ceiling. "Someone at a very high level is guiding this operation."

"I don't even know who that is." Slade pulled a hand-kerchief out of his front pocket and reached into the envelope. "I unloaded it and have tried to handle it without putting my own prints on it, but my prints are readily available if you need to check them."

"Yes, your prints have already been pulled, so they can be ruled out." Mills hunched forward and inspected the weapon Slade had placed on the table. "Nice piece. If we don't find a match here, we send the prints to Interpol. We can do domestic while you wait, but Interpol will take a few days—unless your people put a rush on it. I get the feeling it's that important."

"It is. Are you going to dust in here?"

"Yep. Dust, lift and transfer to the cards while you watch. Those are the orders I have."

"Do you mind if I sit down?" Nicole placed her hand on the back of one of the uncomfortable-looking chairs.

Mills answered, "Be my guest. The actual procedure won't take long."

She watched while Mills did the honors and Slade peppered him with questions.

"You have the capability to do the domestic match here with the computers at DOJ?"

"Right here while you wait. You can go down to the cafeteria and get some weak coffee, if you want. Your temporary badges will get you in there."

"How long will the fingerprints take?"

"Thirty minutes, maybe more, maybe less. I have your cell phone number. I'll text you whether or not we get a hit. If not, I won't hold you up, and we'll send the prints on to Interpol."

Fifteen minutes later with the fingerprinting process completed, Mills picked up the gun by the barrel. "I do have orders to keep the weapon, though."

"I know that. I got the same orders."

Nicole pushed back from the table. "Does that cafeteria have food as well as weak coffee? I could use some lunch."

"Take the elevator to the basement and you'll see the signs, or just follow the smell of grilled cheese."

"Grilled cheese?" Nicole smacked her lips. "Now that's a serious cafeteria."

Slade shook Mills's hand. "Thanks, man. I'll wait to hear from you. If it's going to Interpol, you'll let me know when those results come back?"

"I'll let you know and I'll let my superior here know. She and I are the only ones who are aware this is going down, so it must be top secret."

"Like you said, pretty high-level stuff."

Mills blew out a breath and on a rush of words, asked, "Is it true you're a Navy SEAL sniper?"

"SEALs don't operate stateside. You know that, Mills."

Ten minutes later, Nicole stood at the lunch counter, inhaling grilled cheese. "Mills wasn't kidding."

"We don't have to stay in the building. There's a whole city block out there dotted with restaurants. Those prints aren't going anywhere."

Nicole put her hands on her hips. "What? And miss out on grilled cheese sandwiches?"

She proceeded to order one with a soda while Slade opted for the weak coffee.

He paid for their food at the register while she filled up her cup with diet soda, and they wandered to a free table in the corner. Signs around the room warned of unauthorized personnel.

Nicole sized up the room beneath her lashes. "I suppose the spooks aren't supposed to talk business in here."

"This is the FBI, not the CIA."

She picked up one half of her sandwich. "The FBI doesn't have spooks?"

"Agents, but I'm sure they're not supposed to discuss business any more than the *spooks* are."

"Or Navy SEAL snipers on secret, illegal missions."

"Illegal?" He sipped his black coffee and grimaced.

"Oh, c'mon. You know it, I know it and Mills knows it. The only ones who don't seem to know it are the guys—and the girls—who gave you this assignment."

"Oh, they know it, all right, but they think it's worth the risk of some political fallout or embarrassment."

"They can always claim national security. Isn't that what the government always does?"

"Have your years as a documentary filmmaker turned you into a conspiracy theorist?"

"I've seen my share of government conspiracies." She bit into the sandwich, her teeth crunching through the toasted bread and meeting the melted cheese inside. "Mmm, this is good."

"Just like Mom used to make?"

"Ha!" She dusted the crumbs from her fingertips onto the plate. "I just got through telling you Mom was a Vegas showgirl and then a trophy wife. She didn't do grilled cheese…or lunch, for that matter. Yours?"

"Not my mom, but Rosalinda did. She was our housekeeper and made sure I had a pretty standard childhood."

She leveled a finger at him, noticed some melted cheese on the tip and sucked it off. "That's the difference between me and you, Slade. I didn't want the normal childhood. You spent too much time feeling guilty about your family's wealth."

He threw his head back and guffawed at the ceiling. "Thanks for the psychoanalysis."

"You're welcome. Anytime." She took another bite of her sandwich and held the other half out to him. "Try it, rich boy."

Slade took a big bite that demolished almost half of the half. As he wiped his mouth with a napkin, he held up one finger. "That's my phone."

He swiped a finger across the display and sucked in a breath. "They have a match."

Chapter Eleven

Slade's heart beat double time as he and Nicole returned to the lab. Agent Mills met them at the door and let them inside without a word.

Staring at the back of Mills's shiny, shaved head as he followed him into the lab, Slade asked, "So, he's domestic?"

"Sort of." He ushered them into the room where he'd lifted the prints and snapped the door behind them. He tapped a manila folder on the table. "It's all in there."

Slade flipped open the folder and looked into the eyes of the man he'd kicked in the gut last night. "Yep, this is the guy."

"Who is he?" Nicole sidled next to him, pressing her shoulder against his, her breath coming in short spurts.

"Marcus Friedrich. He's German, or at least he was before he became a US citizen as a teenager." Slade ran his finger along the sheet of paper, skimming through Friedrich's life.

"German, just like Conrad, even though that's probably not Conrad's real name. What is this, a German terrorist cell?"

"Technically, Marcus is American. He moved here

with his parents when he was six years old and got citizenship ten years later."

Mills cleared his throat. "Friedrich has a record—nothing big, but the fact that he was a weapons specialist in the US Army complicates things."

A white-hot flash of anger zapped Slade's body. "Someone who served in the armed forces is involved in terrorist activity? That's always the worst."

"He was dishonorably discharged, if that makes a difference." Mills cleared his throat. "Terrorist activity?"

Slade scratched his head. If Mills hadn't figured that out by now, he probably shouldn't be a special agent for the FBI. He was most likely fishing for more intel. "We don't know at this point, Mills. I'm just guessing."

"Are you supposed to go after this guy now? Call the NYPD? Call us?" Mills flicked the edge of the folder with his blunt fingers. "He has an address in New York, out in Queens."

"I'm sure I'll have my orders once I report this." Slade thrust out a hand. "Thanks, Mills. I'll take it from here."

"And I'll report back to my superior just to close the loop. Glad to help out the… US Navy."

They turned in their badges when they checked out of the building, and Slade took a deep breath when they hit the sidewalk. "We now have one name in this network. That's gotta help."

"Agent Mills seems to think Marcus is just a petty criminal."

"A petty criminal who's a weapons specialist and who chased us through a train to stop us from finding Lars's footage. He's more than a petty criminal."

"Wouldn't the FBI know that?"

"The FBI was charged with running those prints, nothing more. The agency isn't going to be looking for the same connections as the covert ops group running this show."

"So, the brain behind your assignment isn't just the CIA." Nicole waved at a taxi barreling down the street.

"Nope, but I'm not in the loop. I was sent here to protect you and gather some info."

"I'd say you're doing a lot more than gathering some info. I think once I meet Dahir tonight, we're going to blow this wide-open for this covert ops group—and they don't even have to get their hands dirty."

They stopped talking when they slid into the back-seat of the cab on the way to Nicole's place.

Slade dropped Friedrich's folder in his lap. "Are you going to get your NYU sweatshirt back from Livvy?"

"I think it's a goner." She raised an eyebrow at him. "Why, are you trying to find an excuse to visit Chanel?"

"Well, there's that, but I wouldn't mind asking Livvy a few questions." He pressed a palm against the folder. "We have a picture to show her. I'm just wondering how many guys we have out here working on this."

"I'm wondering the same thing, and they must've been set up for a while here if Trudy started dating one of them."

"Friedrich even has a place here."

"Are you going to track him down?"

"If that's what the folks upstairs want me to do. I'm going to file a report and touch base when I get back to your place, but I need to pick up my laptop first." He leaned forward, tapping on the Plexiglas separating the front seat from the back and gave the driver the new directions to Times Square.

"Laptop, shirts, toothbrush." She drummed her fingers on his thigh. "You need to pack a bag with some essentials and bring it to my mom's. Why fight it?"

He shrugged at her light tone, but she was the one fighting it—this attraction between them. Maybe it wasn't the best idea to bed the woman you were trying to protect, but he didn't want to miss his chance with her. If they didn't take this…connection between them to the next level, she might be gone from his life for good once he finished this crazy assignment.

He left Nicole waiting in the taxi while he ran up to his hotel room to grab his laptop. He shoved a few things in a small bag while he was at it. Might as well take Nicole up on her offer.

He tossed the bag on the seat between them. "Toothbrush."

By the time they got back to her mother's place, Nicole had called to check on Livvy and casually mentioned they might drop by to visit her and bring more of Chanel's toys.

Slade held the door open for Nicole as she finished the call. "She's okay with it?"

"Of course, and you can ask Livvy anything. She might think it's strange if you're questioning her about a picture, but I'm sure you can think of something."

"I don't want to impersonate a police officer, but I'll figure out something." He punched the elevator button, and when the doors opened on the floor, Slade's five senses went into overdrive.

The building seemed secure enough, but these guys were pros and there was a team of them operating to bring down Nicole. His blood pumped hot through his veins whenever he thought about the danger to Nicole's life. Maybe this high-level team of spooks should just get her out of the city and to some super-secure location, but he had a sickening suspicion that they wanted her right here to draw out this particular terror cell.

She shoved open the front door. "Do you want to check under the beds?"

"It's that obvious, huh?"

"Your face gets—" she stroked her chin "—sharp and your eyes narrow like a cat's. Your nostrils flare."

"Wow. Who knew?" He gave the downstairs a once-over anyway before setting up his laptop in the living room. "I'm going to write up some notes and send them off. Then we'll find Friedrich's address and if we're really lucky, we'll find Friedrich."

"You're not going to wait for orders to track him down?"

He shrugged. "They put me on this assignment, so I'm going to make the call."

"What'll you do with Friedrich if you find him?"

"What I couldn't do on that train—question him, and then send him somewhere else where the interrogation methods aren't quite so friendly."

"While you're doing your notes, I'm going to catch up on some emails and a little of Mom's business. You'd be surprised how much work it is to be a society doyenne—or maybe you wouldn't."

"I don't know. The way you talk about your mom makes it sound so much more interesting than what my mom does." He patted his computer. "Don't you use a laptop?"

"Just for my work when I'm in the field. I prefer the desktop in the office for the mundane tasks."

She brought him a glass of water and carried her own toward the office. Before she disappeared through the door, she called over her shoulder, "Have fun."

Slade sent the findings on Marcus Friedrich to his contact email for Ariel and received a simple acknowledgment. He knew the covert ops agency on the other end of that email address would be turning Friedrich's life and especially his contacts upside down, but he'd have to take the initiative on this end to locate the man. He was supposed to be the muscle in this operation—the hit man, if necessary.

And if that was necessary to protect Nicole, he was all in.

When he clicked Send on the last email of the day, he stretched and downed the rest of his water. He hadn't heard one squeak out of Nicole from the office, so he put his laptop aside and strode to the office door.

She'd abandoned the desk and chair for the sofa in the corner, where she lay curled up, one arm hanging off the edge.

He crept up to the sofa and crouched next to it, studying Nicole's beautiful face, her long lashes curved on her cheek. With the lively animation smoothed out from her face, she almost looked like a different woman, someone he didn't know.

Nicole's vitality would always be a part of her appearance, the way her green eyes lit up with curiosity, the laugh lines that crinkled at the corners of her eyes, the expressive mouth that could quirk into a smile as easily as it could purse with annoyance.

Something new had crept into her face, as well—

dark shadows beneath her eyes. Fatigue, worry, fear had all left their mark. He should just tuck her in right now and investigate Friedrich's home in Queens by himself. She'd be out late meeting with Dahir tonight, and she needed the sleep.

If only he could clone himself and leave his duplicate here with her, armed and ready to protect her. He could call on Leo downstairs to keep an eye on her.

He tugged on the throw blanket hanging across the back of the sofa and shook it out. As he placed it over her legs, she stirred, tucking one hand beneath her cheek.

Unfolding the blanket, he pulled it up to her chin and then stopped when he became aware of a pair of green eyes watching him. "Did I wake you?"

"Don't worry. It wasn't a deep sleep. I think the events of last night—and the night before, and was there a night before that?—finally caught up with me and hit me over the head like a somnolent sledgehammer, if you can imagine that."

"Mmm, not quite."

She squirmed up to a sitting position. "Were you going to sneak out on me?"

"I hadn't decided yet. It might be dangerous showing up at Friedrich's house."

"If he really lives there." She kicked off the blanket. "It also might be dangerous right here."

"I know. That's why I asked about a safe house for you in the report I just wrote."

"What?" She bolted upright, her eyes fully open. "A safe house? Is that like witness protection or something? I can't leave here. I'm supposed to be looking after my mother's place."

"Really? Your mom can't pay someone to do what you're doing? You're not even taking care of Chanel anymore."

"I have stuff to do, a life. My editor is working on my most recent film, and I have to be available for questions, decisions."

"And how are you going to be available for that if you're dead?"

The light faded from her eyes, and she slumped against the arm of the sofa.

Slade's gut wrenched as he watched the fire die—and he was the one who'd doused it. He grabbed her shoulders. "Someone's after you—*you*. They don't care about the film right now. They just want to make sure you don't get your hands on it. They've made that pretty clear. I don't want you getting hit by a car, shot in a park or assaulted on the train—and I can't be here forever."

Her body jerked under his grip. "What does that mean? Are you leaving? Is the shadow agency pulling you off this assignment?"

"Not yet, but that's a distinct scenario if we don't find Lars's footage, or even if we do and can't make sense of it. A Navy SEAL can't be on permanent assignment in New York City—even if I want to be." He stroked the side of her neck with his fingers.

Nicole fell into his arms, where he'd wanted her all along, and buried her face against his chest.

He threaded his fingers through the tangles in her hair as he pressed his lips against her temple. "I'm sorry. I don't want to scare you."

"Yes, you do," she murmured against his shirt. "And you should. I need to be very afraid. What did your superiors say about this safe house for me?"

Massaging the back of her neck, he said, "They haven't responded yet. They haven't responded to much of anything I've sent them."

"I get it." She pulled away from him, her eyes meeting his, almost nose to nose. "They need me, don't they?"

"What do you mean?" He shifted his gaze to a point just above her left ear.

Her delicate nostrils flared. "I thought you were into straight talk, Slade. The powers that be, Ariel, the ones pulling the strings need me here in Manhattan, searching for that film to draw out the bad guys."

"That thought did occur to me."

"Bastards."

"They did send me out here to watch over you."

"Oh, really?" She broke away from him, swinging her legs over the edge of the sofa and nearly knocking him over. "Then why were you sneaking around my mailbox? If you were sent to look out for me, why not just approach me? I think they wanted you to watch me, all right—watch while someone tried to kill me, allowing you to move in and nab the guy after the fact and pump him for info."

Slade didn't have much of a comeback, because the same thing had occurred to him—only he'd never have allowed that to happen. He shrugged and rose to his feet. "It didn't play out that way, did it?"

"That's because whoever chose you for the assignment obviously didn't have a clue about your personality. You don't play waiting games."

"I was chosen because I saved you once, but none of my sniper teammates would've bought into that plan— which makes me believe the people at the top aren't military." He caught her hand and squeezed it. "Their original intentions don't mean I can't force them to find a safe house for you."

"I just might take you up on that offer, but right now I'm going to get ready to storm a not-so-safe house in Queens with my partner."

After changing her skirt for a pair of dark jeans and low-heeled boots, Nicole joined him in the kitchen, where he raised a banana at her.

"Hope you don't mind. I should've had one of those grilled cheese sandwiches at the FBI cafeteria."

"Help yourself. We can get some dinner after we check out Friedrich's house and before we meet Dahir. We're just a couple of social butterflies."

"I wouldn't call these social engagements."

"Two days ago I wouldn't have, but now?" She shrugged. "It's all I got."

They took her mother's car service to Queens, since Nicole had sworn off trains for the time being, but Slade had the driver drop them off several blocks away from the address in Friedrich's criminal file.

Friedrich knew Slade had taken his weapon, knew he hadn't been wearing gloves and probably knew they'd made him from his fingerprints. Slade didn't expect the guy to be at home cooking dinner. He didn't know what to expect.

Old homes with peaked roofs and faded wood siding lined the streets in this area. An empty lot with a chain-link fence around overgrown weeds interrupted the line of houses.

If a terrorist cell was funding Friedrich's stay in New York, it hadn't gone all out for him. The run-down neighborhood had Slade checking his pocket for his gun.

"Wait." Nicole grabbed his sleeve. "Do we have a plan? The guy tried to shoot us down in a train. What's to stop him from taking potshots at us from his window as we approach the house?"

"We're not walking up to the front door and knocking. We'll approach from the side or the back, guns drawn."

"Gun—only one of us has one. What happens if a cop happens to cruise by while we're peeping in the windows with a gun out?"

"Then I use my get-out-of-jail-free card. The brass won't be happy, but they're not going to leave me hanging in the wind."

"You sure about that?" Nicole gave the chain-link fence a rattle and then continued down the sidewalk.

A block later, Slade stepped off the curb. "Let's cross the street here and do a little reconnaissance."

A few small businesses broke up the unrelenting stretch of battered residences, and Slade turned toward the first shop window and pretended to study the wares. Instead he was studying Friedrich's house in the window's reflection.

Nicole breathed heavily beside him as she discovered a newfound interest in locks and keys. "See anything?"

"Small front yard with a dumpster out front at the curb, so I don't know what that's all about. It looks like there's a path that leads to the side of the house and maybe the back. Houses aren't too close together, and the one on the right looks boarded up and abandoned."

"So, we veer to the right."

"Exactly."

"I don't see any cars out front."

"That doesn't mean anything. Are you ready, or do you want to go into this locksmith shop and wait for me while I have a look around?"

"I'll come with you. I've come this far."

"Do as I tell you and hit the deck when I say so."

"Don't I always?"

"As a matter of fact, you do."

They backtracked down the sidewalk and then crossed the street again, approaching the house from the side. They traipsed across the lawn of the abandoned house and then followed the dried grass and weed-strewn path along the side of Friedrich's latest address.

"Gloves?" He pulled his own out of his pocket and tugged them over his hands.

Slade peered into the first window they came to, the skewed and broken blinds giving him a glimpse into an empty bedroom.

He whispered, "Looks like whoever was living here might have moved out already. He may have left a while ago."

As he sidled along the brown siding to the next window, Nicole hooked her finger in his belt loop. He cupped his hand over his eyes to look into the frosted glass of the next window. "This has to be the bathroom, and I can't see anything."

He put a hand out behind him to stop Nicole while he reached the corner of the house that led to the back. He eased around that corner and squinted at yet another dumpster. Maybe they'd tossed out a bunch of trash before they moved.

The dumpster squatted on a cracked cement patio

next to a rusted-out barbecue. A sliding glass door led from the house to the patio.

He crept along the back wall with Nicole breathing down his neck. He rested his hand on his weapon inside his pocket. He didn't need any surprises coming out of that sliding door, but he'd be ready for them if they did.

Pointing to the sliding door, he said, "Look at that."

She poked her head around his shoulder. "The glass is broken."

"It looks like someone already tried to break in here."

"Not a surprise in this neighborhood." She poked his waist. "That makes it easy for us, right?"

"A little too easy."

He placed a gloved hand against the glass door and inched his fingers closer to the gaping hole. "I could reach right in here and open the door."

"Then let's do it. Maybe they didn't leave anything behind, but perhaps you can pick up more clues to their identity. The house can be dusted for prints."

Slade sawed his bottom lip with his teeth. The air felt heavy and still, and he felt like he should hold his breath for something.

"They wouldn't leave any clues like that."

Nicole stepped around him and faced the door. "Let's find out." She gripped the door handle. "You reach in there and unlock it, and I'll yank it open."

Slade placed his gloved hands against the door again, running them across the glass. He stuck one hand through the hole in the door.

As Nicole leaned back to slide open the door, the setting sun behind them glinted off the window, highlighting a silver strand running across the bottom of the door.

Nicole tugged once before Slade's adrenaline kicked in. "Stop! Get back! Get back!"

He hooked an arm around Nicole's chest and threw her body behind the dumpster on the patio.

Then the explosion behind him rocked his world.

Chapter Twelve

The ringing in her ears wouldn't stop. Between half-open eyes, she followed a billowing scrap of material on fire, floating through the air. She hoped it wouldn't land on her.

She tried to suck in a breath of air, but her lungs wouldn't expand. The air settled on her tongue instead, a dark, acrid taste filling her mouth.

She squirmed beneath the heavy, solid object on top of her but couldn't move. Had the house fallen on her, just like it had on the little pig in his flimsy wood construction?

The implacable object on top of her shifted. It spoke. It touched her face. She couldn't hear a word Slade was saying, but she didn't care. He was with her and he was safe.

Orange flames danced behind his head, illuminating his sandy-blond hair and giving it all kinds of highlights, making him look like an angel with a glowing halo.

Slade rolled off her body and hauled her to her feet. The fire from the burning house scorched the side of her face, and she turned it toward Slade's chest.

He half dragged, half carried her into the empty lot next door, over the fence downed by the blast.

Finally, she gulped in lungfuls of fresh air, or at least air that didn't have soot and particles floating in it. She glanced over her shoulder at the house consumed in flames, her gaze then darting to a cluster of people in the street.

Someone called out. "Are you okay over there?"

"We're fine. Call 911," Slade shouted back.

He hustled her through the empty lot, holding her steady as she stumbled through weeds and trash. When he got her to the sidewalk, he grabbed her shoulders and spun her toward him.

"Are you hurt, burned? How's your hearing?"

"I can hear your voice now, although my ears are ringing. I'm fine." She looked down at her jeans, which seemed to have little burn spots in them, and brushed some dirt from her skinned palms. She should've put on those gloves when Slade told her to. "I think."

Curling an arm around her waist, he said, "Thank God. Can you get on your phone and call the car service? Have him pick us up at that fast food place across the street from where he dropped us off."

"Are you hurt?" She reached up and cupped his jaw. "Your beautiful golden eyelashes are singed."

"I'm okay, and the eyelashes will grow back. Let's get the hell out of here." He grabbed her hand and strode down the sidewalk, away from the burning house and the gathering crowd—and the sirens wailing in the distance.

"How did we survive that blast, Slade?"

"I noticed the trip wire seconds before it was triggered and managed to get us behind that dumpster. A trash can saved us."

She squeezed his hand. "*You* saved us."

When they got to the corner, she pulled out her cell phone and called her mother's car service. "Give it about fifteen minutes and pick us up across the street from where you dropped us off. We'll be waiting on the side-walk for you."

Five minutes later, they reached the fast food restaurant and Slade touched her cheek. "Go wash up a little. I'll do the same and then I'll get us something to drink. How do your lungs feel?"

She scooped in a deep breath, which caused a slight burning sensation in her lungs. "Feels like I just smoked three packs of cigarettes, but it's not that bad."

They parted ways in the short hallway containing the restrooms, and Nicole shoved through the door. She walked to the sinks and gripped the edge of the counter as she stared into the mirror.

Black smudges marred her cheeks and her hair looked as if someone had taken a crazy hair dryer to it. Burn marks dotted her jacket, and the heels of her boots were misshapen and partially melted away.

Her body jerked as adrenaline spiked through her veins. She'd almost died in a bomb blast. She had an urge to run. Her gaze darted from mirror to mirror to mirror and the blood rushed to her head so fast she reeled with dizziness.

The nausea punched her gut, and she staggered to the first stall and threw up in the toilet. She retched a few more times and felt better for it.

Back at the sink, she said to her reflection, "If you can't run, get sick."

She filled her palm with soap from the dispenser and lathered up her hands. She washed her face and rinsed out her mouth. Then she wet down a paper towel and brushed it over the burn spots on her clothes—now she just looked trendy instead of like an escapee from a burning building.

A woman charged into the bathroom with a baby hooked to her hip and barely gave Nicole a glance. The mom busied herself with the diaper-changing station, and Nicole finished her high-end toilette by running her fingers through her tangled hair.

She left the bathroom in better shape than she'd entered it and even managed a smile when she saw Slade by the soft drink dispenser.

He held up a cup. "Didn't know what you wanted."

"For some reason, pink lemonade sounds about right."

"You look better." He quirked an eyebrow at her. "You're gonna have to trash those jeans, though."

"Oh, I don't know." She ran a hand across her thigh, the denim of her jeans dotted with holes. "I think they look pretty fashionable."

"If you say so." He tipped his drink toward a plastic table by the window. "Let's sit down before we both collapse."

She filled her cup and grabbed a couple of napkins before joining Slade at the table. She sucked up pink lemonade, although her taste buds still seemed tainted with some chemical taste. She sloshed the drink around in her mouth.

"They were expecting us in a big way."

She nodded. "A big bang way."

"They lured us with the broken window on the sliding door, making sure we entered through the back."

"Anyone could've gone through that door. Kids. Transients in the area. The owner of the house." She rattled the ice in her cup. "They just don't care who they hurt."

"That's for sure. They would've been just as happy to nail a bunch of FBI agents as the two of us."

"Why wasn't it a bunch of FBI agents, Slade? Couldn't your unit or command force have made that happen?"

"Eventually. It would've taken the FBI a day or two at least to get the authority to descend on that house. As far as they could tell, there was no imminent danger. Friedrich is just a small-time crook who hadn't done anything lately."

"Except go after a few people on a train."

"That's off the FBI's radar. If more than just a few people at the agency knew about this operation, they could make a stink to shut it down. We have to be careful. We're stepping all over their territory."

"I hope Dahir has the goods tonight and we can put a stop to this." She folded her hands around her cup. "I've faced danger before and that kidnapping by the Somali pirates was no picnic, but this seems…more serious. I never really believed the pirates were going to kill us. They were in it for the big payoff."

"Probably." He pointed out the window. "I think that's our car. Are you sure you're up for a meeting with Dahir tonight? It could be more of the same."

"Exploding buildings? I doubt that. I told you, Dahir is loyal."

Besides, my own personal SEAL has my back.

LATER THAT EVENING after a dinner of takeout pizza and Caesar salad, Nicole stretched out on the couch and watched the flickering images on the TV of the FDNY putting out the flames on a burning house in the Jamaica area of Queens.

She snorted as the reporter said that the cause of the blaze was still under investigation but authorities suspected arson. "Ya think?"

"The firefighters had to know from the get-go that the fire was caused by an explosive device. They're being careful about the info they're releasing. I wonder why." Slade tossed a crumpled napkin into an empty pizza box.

"What did your superiors have to say about it?" She nibbled on a piece of crust. "Did anyone ever respond to your report?"

"Nope. It's not that kind of assignment. In fact, it's not like any kind of assignment I've ever been on."

"Seems like the kind of assignment where they hang you out to dry."

"Don't worry about me." He squeezed her calf. "You're sure you want to go out and meet Dahir?"

"Of course. He may give us everything we need."

"Then we'd better get going. I want to have some time to scope out the place before he gets there—or before anyone else does."

"My guess is that nobody even knows he's here. He must've traveled on forged documents if your people don't even have a record of him entering the country. I'm sure he's here on the sly."

"We'll see, won't we?" He wagged a finger over her stretched-out form. "You're not going to a club in that getup, are you?"

"These?" She plucked at her baggy sweatpants that she wore *only* at home, usually in private and never in front of anyone. She was getting too comfortable with Slade. "Give me fifteen minutes to change and slap on some makeup."

She slid from the couch, hiding her grimace from Slade. If she was sore now from that dive behind the dumpster, tomorrow she was going to need a whole lot of something to ease the pain.

Upstairs, she stripped out of her comfy sweats and shimmied into a pair of black leather pants. Maybe she'd gotten a little *too* comfortable in Slade's presence—not that she wanted to seduce him. Not that she *had* to seduce him. He'd been hers for the plucking last night before Dahir called, but she'd sworn off men with dangerous passions—and Slade's commitment to his SEAL team and his desire to protect his country at all costs *were* his passions.

She pulled on a lacy white camisole and buttoned a white silk blouse over it. A pair of high-heeled black booties completed her ensemble.

Now she just needed to put on some makeup, including some eyebrow pencil to fill in the brows that had been singed in the blast—wasn't that what every woman did before a night out in Manhattan?

After making up her face, she twirled her hair into a low, loose chignon. If she was going down tonight, she'd look stylish on the descent.

She sashayed down the staircase and had the satisfaction of seeing Slade's mouth hang open for a brief second. He recovered quickly.

"You look...nice." He smacked his chest, covered by

a black cotton T-shirt. "It's a good thing we're not going in together or I'd be seriously outclassed."

"The only fashion accessory you need is your big gun."

He patted the pocket of his jacket. "Got that."

"Taxi or car?"

"Let's take the car again. It's safer when I'm packing heat."

"It's also safer for a quick, discreet getaway."

"I thought you trusted Dahir?" He rolled his shoulders and winced.

"Are you in pain?"

"Nothing a couple of ibuprofen can't mask. You?"

"Oh, yeah." She stepped off the last step, brushing past him. "I'll call the car service."

A half hour later, the car stopped one block away from the club. Slade leaned forward and addressed the driver. "Ms. Hastings is waiting in the car for now. You can idle here or take a few trips around the block."

"I'll wait here for as long as I can, sir. If I'm not here when you come back, wait by the corner of that building and I'll pick you up or drop off Ms. Hastings—whatever you want."

"Thanks, Pierre." Slade liked this driver. He hadn't said one word or raised an eyebrow when he'd picked them up in Queens, slightly worse for wear than when he'd dropped them off and with sirens wailing in the distance.

Slade gave Nicole a quick, hard kiss on the mouth and a wink. "I'll do a recon and be right back."

He stepped out of the town car and jogged across the street, dodging a few taxis. He spotted the blue awning of the club up ahead and cut over a block early.

All these places had to have side or back entrances to meet fire regulations.

He slipped into an alley and maneuvered around a few dumpsters. The dark blue building that housed The Blues Joint stood out from the rest, and Slade approached the back entrance.

He tried the door handle, but it didn't budge. He pounded on the metal door with his fist.

A minute later it cracked open and an eyeball traveled the length of his body and back again. "The entrance is around the front—and there's a cover charge."

"I'd be happy to pay the cover charge, but I'm wondering if I can come in this way and look around for a place to position myself."

The door opened wider and a substantial-looking African-American man stared him down. "Position yourself for what?"

"I have a client coming in here later and I don't want to be in the way. You understand?"

"No." The man folded his arms, resting them on his massive belly. "What kind of client?"

"I'm a bodyguard. My client's a top model." He shrugged. "You know, probably delusions of grandeur. Nobody would notice her anyway, but she's borrowing some pretty expensive jewelry tonight and I'm supposed to watch over her. I don't want to create a scene. You feel me?"

The man puffed out his cheeks for a few seconds.

"I mean, the broad's willing to pay for it." Slade pulled a wad of bills from his pocket and slipped it into the other man's hand. "I'm Nick."

"Eli." The cash disappeared as Eli dipped his head. "Yeah, sure."

The door widened and Slade squeezed past Eli, who hadn't exactly given him a wide berth. Slade hesitated at the top of a staircase. "Where does this lead?"

"That goes down to the club. This level has a small dining area around the front. We don't allow food downstairs, but some patrons come early for the show, have a meal and head down to hear the music."

"Can you see the club from the stairs?"

Eli leveled one finger in the direction of the staircase. "Help yourself."

Slade ducked beneath the low ceiling and jogged down the stairs. At the first landing, he got a full view of the club, already half-full with the band tuning their instruments on the stage. Was Dahir already here?

He scanned the patrons, but didn't see anyone resembling Dahir. The meeting was in another forty-five minutes, and Slade planned to camp out right here to watch Nicole.

He went back up the stairs and met Eli at the top. "The main entrance leads right to the club, right?"

"Yeah, that's street level in the front."

"Are many more diners going to head this way?"

"A few."

Slade took another couple of bills from his pocket. "Okay if I station myself on the landing? I think I already paid the cover charge, and if there's a drink minimum, I'll order a coffee."

Eli stuffed the money in the front pocket of his black shirt. "I think this takes care of the drinks, too. But if there's any trouble in here? I never saw you or spoke to you, and I have no idea how you got in here. You feel *me*?"

"Absolutely." Slade retreated to a pantry off the kitchen and called Nicole.

"Where are you?"

"I'm in the club, in the kitchen. I have the perfect lookout perch to watch you. I don't think Dahir is here yet, but if he's here when you arrive and he's sitting too close to the stage, ask if you can move toward the front of the club, closer to the door. I don't have a clear view of the tables ringing the stage."

"Okay, I can do that. You're not coming back to the car?"

"No, I'm good here. Oh, and you're some top model who's wearing some expensive jewelry."

"What?"

"I had to concoct some story to get in here. You're a real diva who thinks she deserves protection."

Nicole laughed her bubbling laugh, born of years of private schools, financial security and confidence. He'd heard it a million times on the lips of the girls he was expected to date, but Nicole's confidence came from living in the real world. Her self-assuredness came from a belief in her work. In short, she was nothing like the girls he'd grown up with.

"I can play that role to a T, rich boy, but you should've warned me. I could've piled on some of my mom's jewelry to really get into character."

"That's okay. There's only one guy we need to convince, and I'm pretty sure I already did that with a wad of cash."

"Okay, so what do I do for the next half hour?"

"Have Pierre take you on a sightseeing tour around Harlem. Whatever you do, have him drop you off in front of the club at eleven o'clock and go straight inside."

"Gotcha. I'm actually looking forward to seeing Dahir. I haven't seen him since we all left that Navy boat after our rescue."

"I hope it's the reunion you expect—and not something else."

Nicole cleared her throat. "Should we have some sort of signal in case things start heading south?"

"You're getting good at this espionage stuff. Get a drink, make sure it has a straw, and if you need help, stick the straw in your mouth and flick it with your finger. That's not something you'd do naturally, but it wouldn't seem odd if someone did do that."

"Really? Shoving a straw in your mouth and flicking it around isn't odd?"

"You have a better idea, Ms. Bond?"

"My hair's up. If I sense something hinky, I'll let my hair down."

"What if it falls down by accident?"

"It's not going to do that. Trust me."

"I do trust you, Nicole Hastings, and I'll be watching you in about a half an hour." He ended the call and stayed put in the corner of the pantry.

The band had started playing and their smooth jazz tones floated up the staircase, luring more diners from the restaurant. About twenty minutes later, Slade eased out of his position and crept downstairs.

Hearing a heavy footfall behind him, Slade spun around and Eli almost took him out with a stool.

"Whoa, my man. I was just bringing you something to sit on."

"Sorry, thanks. I'll take it." He gripped one leg of the stool and continued down the last few steps. He tucked the stool in the corner of the landing and straddled it.

Eli had joined him on the landing. "You need anything else?"

"I'm good." Slade pointed across the room at another landing. "What's over there?"

"Bathrooms, accessible from another staircase near the stage." Eli poked his shoulder. "Is that your girl?"

Slade glanced down at Nicole floating through the room, her loose white blouse billowing behind her. He held his breath as she continued toward the stage, finally stopping at a table in the corner but still within his line of sight. He eased out a breath.

"Yep, that's her."

"I could tell. She's definitely supermodel material."

"Yeah, she is."

"I'll leave you to it, man." Eli snapped his fingers and pointed at him. "Remember, if anything goes down, I don't know you."

"Never saw you before in my life."

Eli hauled his considerable girth downstairs to the club.

Slade shifted his gaze to Nicole, and his heart stuttered when a man joined her at the table. If he had his rifle and scope, he could zero on him and get a better look.

Nicole jumped up from her seat and threw her arms around the man, who was half a head shorter than she was.

Slade rolled his shoulders. Had to be Dahir.

The translator glanced over his shoulder once and took a seat, facing the front door. The man wasn't taking any chances.

Nicole and Dahir hunched toward each other, presumably to catch each other's words over the wail of a trumpet. Slade's heart thumped in time with the syncopated rhythm of the drums as he watched Nicole and Dahir through narrowed eyes.

Just get the goods and get out.

Dahir had pulled out his phone, and Slade responded by flicking the safety from his gun and dragging it out of his pocket.

With their heads together, Nicole and Dahir studied the phone. Maybe he was showing her the footage and explaining its significance. Then they could get out of here.

Slade licked his dry lips, feeling more like he was on a sniper detail in Iraq than sitting in a jazz club in Harlem. The hair on the back of his neck refused to stop quivering. His jaw refused to unlock.

Two drinks magically appeared on the small table between Nicole and Dahir, and all his senses ratcheted up another notch. Had he missed the waiter taking their order?

Maybe Nicole had ordered something when she first walked in the door.

Slade kept an eye on the bun on the back of Nicole's head—still in place as she smiled and nodded over the phone. She wouldn't be so happy if Dahir were showing her that footage. She must be looking at pictures, but she needed to get down to business.

And then something changed.

As Nicole reached for her glass, there was a sharp movement from across the table and it crashed to the floor. The noise and activity drew a few glances from the other patrons nearby, but the band seemed to drown out the sound for most of the other customers.

As Nicole bent forward to pick up the shards of glass,

Dahir shot up from his seat and tilted his head back to take in the landing across the way.

With a rush of adrenaline, Slade jerked his head toward the other staircase by the bathrooms. The barrel of a weapon glinted in the lights.

Slade hopped up from the stool, swinging his gun toward the threat across the room, but he was too late.

A flash of light lit up the landing as the man fired into the club below—and the fight was on.

Chapter Thirteen

As Nicole started to sit up, she heard a thwack above her. She knew the sound—she'd heard it around the world. She slid from her chair and dropped beneath the small cocktail table.

A split second later, Dahir fell to the floor next to her, copious amounts of blood leaking from a bullet hole in his forehead.

A few people screamed, but the music continued, the band unaware of the drama unfolding in the club, their dissonant chords matching the confusion raging through Nicole's brain.

Slade couldn't be responsible for Dahir's death. She hadn't signaled anything, had been aware of nothing amiss as Dahir shared pictures of his family back in Somalia.

If not Slade, then some other shooter—someone hostile.

Dahir's blood continued to soak the club's dark blue carpet and slowly more and more patrons understood just why the man at her table had dropped like a rock.

Chaos erupted all at once as a collective realization hit. And then something else hit—the back of the chair where she'd just been sitting splintered into pieces as another bullet made contact.

She flattened herself on the floor and started crawling toward the front door. A few people stepped on her during the stampede for the exit, but others joined her in a slithering journey to safety.

A crack and a thud behind her, toward the stage, didn't slow her path, but someone yelled, "He's been hit. The shooter's been hit."

The shooter? Which one? Slade was up there, too. Had he been hit?

Nicole couldn't breathe for the second time that day, but this time fear instead of smoke clogged her lungs. She scrabbled against the carpet, turning herself around to head back toward the stage.

She reached forward with one hand and hit a shoe. Seconds later, Slade was on the floor next to her, nose to nose.

"You're going the wrong way. Stay down and keep moving for the exit. I got him, but I don't know if there's anyone else in here gunning for you."

They shimmied on the carpet next to each other until they reached the door. Slade pulled her outside and she drank in the evening air with big gulps.

This time they got away before they even heard a hint of sirens, running down the sidewalk with a crowd of other people escaping the mayhem in the club.

After traveling a city block, gasping for breath at the fast pace Slade set, Nicole pulled on his arm. "Should I call for the car now?"

He glanced at her hand on his sleeve and sucked in a breath. "You're bleeding. You're hurt."

Turning her hand over, she inspected the cut on her fingers. "It's from the broken glass that Dahir knocked over."

"Right before the shot that killed him."

"I think I know what happened." She curled her fingers over the blood smudged on her hand. "Dahir brought those drinks to the table with him, and before I could even take a sip of mine, he knocked it over."

"What are you saying? Do you think there was something in the drink?"

"I'm not sure, but he was nervous even when he was showing me pictures of his family." She retrieved her phone. "I'm calling for the car."

Pierre must've been close, because less than ten minutes later, the black town car cruised up to the curb. They both piled in and Nicole slumped in the seat, her head tilted back.

A few hot tears coursed down her face and she dashed them away. They had an agreement to keep mum in front of Pierre and any other driver, although he must have his suspicions. She didn't need to involve anyone else in the train wreck of her life. Anyone within two feet of her was entering some sort of death zone.

Silently, they made it back to her mother's place, and as soon as she double locked the door behind them, she let loose. "Dahir saved me, Slade."

"Maybe, but why did he lure you to that club in the first place? It's obvious the second bullet had your name on it. The shooter's mistake was killing Dahir first. I guess he figured you'd pop up and he could take care of you next."

She marched to the kitchen and perched on the edge

of a stool at the island. "His mistake was not realizing there was another sniper in that club. You're sure you got him?"

"I almost shot him before he nailed Dahir. I saw him, or rather his weapon, when Dahir looked up in his direction after knocking over that drink. I got my shot off right after he killed Dahir and got off his second shot. Thank God you were still on the floor."

"That proves it."

"Proves what?" He joined her at the counter and tapped the back of her injured hand. "Let me clean that up for you."

She stretched out her palm for him as he ran a paper towel beneath the faucet and squirted some soap on it.

"Once Dahir knocked over my drink, he knew he'd signed his death warrant."

"Then why'd he come all this way to find you and do their bidding? What's clear is that this was a setup, orchestrated by the people after you and using Dahir to get to you." He dabbed at the dried blood on her hand and swiped the paper towel over the cut, which had bled out of proportion to its size.

"I can't explain that. Maybe he had a change of heart once we saw each other again. He was showing me pictures of his family back in Somalia." She bolted forward and grabbed Slade's wrist. "His family. That's how they got to him."

"Do you think they're threatening his family?" He slipped out of her grasp, dumped the bloody paper towel in the trash and grabbed a dry one. He pressed it to her cut.

"I know they're threatening his family." She snapped

her fingers several times in a row. "One of the things he said to me was that he hoped I could protect or do something for his family if anything happened to him."

"So, the group used his family to get him to lure you out."

"Can you help them, Slade? Please. We owe him this."

"Do we? While I understand his motivation, he put your life in danger. He should've contacted us *before* he set you up."

"Really?" She crumpled the paper towel in her fist and jerked back from him. "I told you I tried to help him before with no success whatsoever, thanks to you guys."

"Us guys?" He held up his hands. "Don't blame me."

"I'm gonna blame you now if you can't do something for his family. He saved my life. I'm sure of that."

"I'll get on it. Or at least I'll relay the information to the people who can actually do something about it." He pulled up a stool and sat beside her.

"I'm sorry." She rubbed her knuckles across the soft denim covering his thigh. "I didn't mean to blame you. I'm just so devastated by Dahir's murder. That means everyone who was on that boat in the Gulf of Aden is dead—except me."

He covered her hand with his. "We're going to keep it that way. Did he tell you anything about the footage, what was on it?"

"We didn't even get that far. He just said that I probably knew why we were meeting."

"Maybe he didn't even know why that film is so important." Slade closed his eyes and pinched the bridge of his nose. "This brings us back to the key and the search for that locker. It's the best lead we've had yet and I allowed myself to get distracted by other issues that resulted in nothing."

"We couldn't have searched for the locker anyway with Luna Park being closed, and it's not like I could've ignored a meeting with Dahir."

"No, but I had a strong suspicion it was a trap, and I shouldn't have let you go through with it. I could've met with him instead."

"You're not trying to blame yourself for what happened, are you?" She touched his face. "Dahir would never have gone for that…and neither would your superiors. They need me to bring these people out of the woodwork, and we both know it."

Slade captured her uninjured hand, threading his fingers through hers. "That was never my plan. I hope you know that."

She pressed her palm against his. "I do, and I even understand the perspective of the people running the show."

"How did such a pampered girl like you—" he drew her hand toward him and kissed her wrist "—get so tough? I saw it on that pirate boat and I see it over and over again here."

Leaning forward, she rested her forehead against his. "I'm not that tough, Slade. Just like on that pirate boat, I have you as my backup. You give me strength."

He cupped her face, his fingers toying with her earlobe. "And you make this assignment worthwhile."

Worthwhile. The word echoed in her head and struck a chord in her heart. That was the difference between Slade and all the other thrill seekers in her past.

Slade took his risks for a purpose. He worked for a greater good beyond that of his own ego.

She turned her face toward the hand cupping her jaw and pressed a kiss on his palm, roughened by the work he did protecting others…protecting her.

Their eyes met, and along with the usual electricity that flashed between them, there was a hint of understanding, of acceptance.

She wasn't the spoiled rich girl type he'd come to loathe, and he wasn't the irresponsible risk taker who put himself above everything else, above her.

Slade would never put his needs above hers.

Tipping forward on two legs of his stool, he brushed a thumb across her lips and then kissed her mouth.

She nodded toward the floor. "You're going to fall off that thing."

"Then let's take this to solid ground." The stool fell back as he rose to his feet. He cinched her waist with both hands and pulled her up and against him in a gentle embrace. "I'm not carrying you this time. You come of your own free will…or not at all."

He released her and turned his back on her but before he even got out of the kitchen, she ran up behind him and wrapped her arms around his waist, resting her head against his strong back—a back that carried the weight of the world, the protection of innocent people everywhere, of her.

Without turning around, he squared his shoulders and said, "When this is over, I go back to doing what I do."

"I wouldn't have it any other way. You're a warrior."

She hugged him tighter, hugged him as if her life depended on it.

He turned in her arms and brushed the hair from her face. He kissed her temple, her cheekbone, her ear, her chin. "Then you're my warrior princess, Nicole Hastings."

How they ended up on the floor in front of the fireplace, naked and breathless, their limbs entwined and tangled, she couldn't exactly remember. She only knew nothing had ever felt so right.

After another long kiss in a mind-swirling number of long kisses, Nicole straddled Slade, running her hands along the hard planes and ridges of his body. "Are all SEALs built like you?"

"Absolutely not. I'm a prime specimen." He stroked her thigh, his rough hands abrading her skin. "And I hope you just take my word for it and that ends your curiosity about any other SEAL you might encounter."

She leaned forward, brushing the tips of her breasts along his chest. "I have no curiosity about any other man... SEAL or otherwise."

He cupped her bottom with both hands, kneading her flesh, urging her forward until her face hovered above his. Slade's tongue tickled her earlobe and then he bared his teeth against her collarbone.

She gave a little shiver at the contrast between soft and hard. Although Slade's body didn't seem to have one soft spot on it, except for his lips, he had a surprisingly tender touch. Those lips pressed against her throat as if measuring her erratic pulse.

His hands slid up her back. "Are you cold?"

"No—excited." She bent her head and tickled his chest with the ends of her hair.

"Me, too."

As she wriggled against his hard erection, she gave him her best wicked grin. "I can tell."

He closed his eyes, catching his breath. "That feels so…good, which is a really weak word for what I'm experiencing right now."

She shifted her body to the side, not wanting this to end too soon, and trailed her fingernails across his chest. Now it was his turn to shiver.

"Are *you* cold?"

"I'm so hot I'm surprised I don't have steam coming out of my ears."

"Who says?" She flicked his earlobe with her tongue, and he chuckled.

He pulled her down next to him and pressed the length of his body against hers, their flesh meeting along every line. His breath was hot and heavy on her cheek.

The adrenaline and heightened sense of awareness that had been flashing through her body ever since the shooting at the club hadn't subsided. Every touch from Slade set fire to her skin and engendered a hunger deep in her soul that she couldn't seem to satisfy, no matter how many times she explored his body or indulged in his kisses.

"I want more of you." She slid down his body, burying her head between his thighs, taking him into her mouth.

He bucked against her, and his fingers dug into her

scalp. "You could've warned me. My head just about exploded."

She replaced her mouth with her hand, stroking the tight flesh that she'd moistened with her tongue. "Is that a double entendre?"

"Why are you asking me questions now, in French, no less? Just keep doing whatever it is you were doing down there."

"Aye, aye, Captain." She dabbled the tip of her tongue along the insides of his thighs—didn't want his head exploding too fast—and then closed her lips around his girth once again.

Slade shuddered and moaned, teasing her hair into a tangled mess with his fingers. When she started getting creative, he clamped his hands on her shoulders.

"We're finishing this another way."

She worked her way up his body with kisses until she met his mouth. She whispered against his lips, "I'm all yours."

And at this particular moment, she meant it.

Flipping her onto her back, he answered gruffly, "And I've been all yours from the minute I saw you through my scope."

She braced for the onslaught of this hard-as-nails man, but he turned tender on her again by kissing her eyelids and smoothing one large hand over her breast, his fingertips toying with her nipple.

She clawed at his backside, desperate for him to be inside her, desperate for him to slake her need.

He prodded her, opening her slowly, filling her up. Her passion rose swiftly as he claimed her inch by inch, until her head thrashed from side to side with the wanting of him.

Driving into her to the very hilt, he growled, "Is this what you want?"

Did he expect her to form words? Actual thoughts? All she could do was wrap her legs around his hips and go along for the ride—and what a ride it was.

As hard as he'd been in her mouth, she'd expected him to reach his climax almost immediately…but the man had tricks and he exulted in using them on her, bringing her to heights of desire only to leave her at the precipice, almost weeping with frustration.

Then he stopped fooling around and got down to business. He scooped his hands beneath her derriere, tilting her hips upward. He must've been paying attention to her responses because when he took her this way, the fluttering in her belly threatened to overcome her.

The rhythm of their bodies as they connected and then pulled apart put her into a trance, and she couldn't think anymore. Her nerve endings throbbed and pulsed, and all the muscles in her body tensed once before her orgasm roared through her.

She thought it would never end, and then Slade had his own release, and the pounding of his flesh against hers made her toes curl and her body turn to jelly. She tried to clamp herself around him, tried to increase his pleasure, but she felt boneless and weightless.

All the teasing, all the buildup, all the waiting had resulted in a climax that had drained her of all reason.

He kissed her mouth before he rolled to his side next to her, closing his eyes.

She panted beside him, waiting for the trembling

of her limbs to subside. He'd just taken her someplace she'd never even imagined—and she wanted to go back there again and again.

She smoothed her hand along his damp shoulder and followed her touch with a kiss. "Is it just me, or was that mind-blowing sex?"

"I was thinking the same thing, wondering, does she have sex like this all the time? Like a freight train blasting over you at a hundred miles an hour. Like some spell where all you can do is feel and every sense is in overdrive."

"Took the words right out of my mouth." She tried to pinch his waist, which was next to impossible as he didn't seem to have an ounce of fat on him. "You're not lying to me, are you?"

"Look at me." He poked a finger against his flat belly. "I'm a mess—in the best possible way, but I'm drained."

She touched her tongue to his salty nipple. "You don't look like a mess to me. In fact, I want a keepsake of this moment."

He raised his eyebrows. "What do you have in mind?"

"Just one little picture…or two." She crawled from their makeshift bed on the floor toward her purse on the chair. "I swear my phone will never be hacked. Your picture will never wind up online."

"What kind of pictures are we talking about here?" He scrunched up a pillow behind his head and punched it a few times to watch her progress.

"Let's just go with it." She grabbed the strap of her purse and yanked it from the chair. It fell open on the floor, scattering its contents. Spying her phone in the jumble, she grabbed it. As she picked it up, she scooped up a cocktail napkin at the same time.

"What's this doing in my purse?" She held it up between two fingers like a white flag.

Slade squinted in her direction. "It's from The Blues Joint."

Then she saw the writing on the back of the napkin, along with a spot of blood. Her heart pounding, she smoothed the napkin against her knee. "Slade, Dahir left me a note before he died."

Chapter Fourteen

Slade shot up, scrambling to join Nicole next to the contents of her purse. "Does the note say where the film is?"

"Ah, no." She pinched the napkin by its corners and turned it toward him, swinging it in front of his face. "It's a bunch of numbers—fifteen, twenty-three, nineteen."

He poked the napkin with his finger. "What the hell does that mean? A combination?"

"We already have a key. We don't need a combination, too."

"A time? Three twenty-three, maybe?"

"You're seriously asking me? I don't have a clue, Slade—or rather, I only have a clue." She waved the napkin. "This one."

"We need to find some lockers at Coney Island tomorrow. There just might be a combination lock as well. It's our best chance of finding the film. Once we get it, we're going to have to figure out what we have quickly. The film itself isn't going to do us any good if we don't know the significance of what's on it."

"And the CIA or this Ariel person is going to have to act fast on the info, because if we have the film and don't know the importance of what we're holding, this terrorist cell is still going to try to get it back before we can figure it out and take action. Right?"

"You're right." He creased one corner of the cocktail napkin. "Hang on to this. Dahir went through a lot of trouble to write this down for you. It has to mean something."

Nicole covered her white face with one shaky hand. "Here I am having sex on the same night my friend and coworker is murdered. I feel…"

"Hey." He wedged a knuckle beneath her chin and tilted up her head. "That's what happens sometimes after the heat of the fight. We're riding high, the adrenaline is pumping. We need an outlet, a release. Your feelings were natural, and they don't mean Dahir or his death means less to you."

"I'm spent. I can barely lift a finger." She raised her hand to test out her theory.

"It's all hitting you now. You're coming down from the rush." He dragged the blanket from the floor and draped it over Nicole's shoulders. "It's my fault. I knew what you were probably experiencing and I shouldn't have taken advantage of your state. It's almost like taking advantage of someone when they're drunk."

Her head snapped up. "Stop. I knew what I was doing. I don't want you to think I regret what happened between us, because I don't. It's just that…I think I need to feel sad now. I mean, I *am* sad."

"Like I said." He cinched the blanket beneath her chin. "You're coming down hard—and I'm going to be right next to you when you hit the bottom."

Her eyes filled with tears, and she leaned her forehead against his chest.

"Let's get to bed." He stroked her hair and kissed the top of her head. Then he pushed to his feet and put the napkin with Dahir's cryptic message on the counter, wedging it beneath the telephone. "Do you want your phone charging down here or in your room?"

She sniffed. "I'll take it up."

While she shoved items back into her purse, Slade tossed the pillow back on the couch, not sorry he wouldn't be spending another night there.

He pulled on his boxers and bunched up the rest of his clothes under one arm.

Nicole hadn't been kidding. Her slow movements indicated lethargy, and as she crouched down to gather her own scattered clothing, she nearly fell over.

"Whoa." He caught her. "Let me get those for you and lock up down here. You get up to bed and don't worry about anything."

As she plodded upstairs, clutching her clothes to her chest, he checked the doors and windows and hit the lights. Nicole had let the blanket slip from her shoulders, so he folded that up and placed it on his former bed.

Then he washed a few dishes in the sink and filled up a glass with water. By the time he got to Nicole's bedroom, she'd burrowed under the covers, leaving the light on in the connecting bathroom.

He brushed his teeth and splashed some water on his face and then crawled between the sheets next to Nicole.

He spooned her naked body against his, kissing the side of her neck.

She sighed. "I really don't regret making love with you, Slade, because that's what we did, isn't it? We made love, and it made me feel whole and safe and alive."

"We made love, Nicole."

And God help him, he meant it.

THE NEXT MORNING, Slade wrapped his arms around Nicole as he'd done all night, and then realized he had a cool pillow instead of a hot woman in his embrace.

He opened one eye, peering at the light coming through a gap in the drapes. Nicole didn't have an alarm clock in here and he'd left his cell phone downstairs, but that light at the window meant he'd slept through a good portion of the morning.

He rolled out of the bed and stretched. A light floral scent wafted from the bathroom. Nicole had managed to shower and get dressed and he'd slept through it all. What a bodyguard.

A sliver of fear pricked the back of his neck, just like it did whenever Nicole was out of his line of vision. He jogged downstairs, calling her name.

Poking her head out of the kitchen, she said, "What's all the racket?"

His pulse returned to normal. "You're up early."

"I couldn't sleep. You were right when you said the events of last night would hit me, they did—like a sledgehammer." She pointed to the TV. "There was a story on the shooting. It's all very vague. They haven't identified the gunman yet."

"Our FBI contact will move in on that one, and hopefully we can ID another member of this cell."

Nicole had made coffee, and the smell perked up his senses. His head still felt groggy, almost as if he'd taken that drink meant for Nicole last night. But he didn't need to take anything—Nicole Hastings was his drug of choice, and he didn't think he could ever OD on her.

She poured him a cup of coffee, her head tilted to one side. "You okay?"

"A little groggy. I feel stupid that I slept through everything this morning when I'm supposed to be protecting you. Usually, I'm a light sleeper."

"I guess that's the danger of mixing business and pleasure." She buried her head in the fridge.

He narrowed his eyes as he took a sip of coffee. Was she back to regretting their hookup? No, she'd been right last night. That was no hookup. Maybe she was regretting the depth of feeling on both sides. She'd hinted her next man was going to be the buttoned-down type.

He'd vowed never to get involved with a rich society woman, but after meeting Nicole, he'd learned not to generalize. Maybe she needed to give him a chance, too.

She popped out of the fridge holding an egg in each hand. "Do you want some breakfast before we check out those lockers?"

"Yeah, but do you mind if we go out to eat? I'm getting sick of my scrambled eggs."

"I'm sorry, I'm not much of a breakfast person."

"You weren't exactly expecting guests, either." He picked up his coffee cup and sat down on the sofa in front of his laptop, charging on the coffee table. "I'm going to check my messages and see if Ariel got back to me on Dahir's family and the ID of the shooter last night."

"I'll give Livvy a call and check on Mom's dog."

Slade powered up his computer. "Ask her if the cops have a lead on the driver or car, especially since we haven't had a chance to talk to her yet."

"I think we've been a little busy."

He launched his secure email, and a flurry of messages scrolled by. His gut knotted as he clicked on the first email from Ariel.

It was short and not so sweet, like most of her communications. Dahir's family missing.

Slade glanced over the top of his laptop at Nicole perched on a stool chatting with Livvy on the phone. She didn't need to know this information right now, even though it might make her feel slightly better that Dahir hadn't betrayed her. Dahir *had* been trying to protect his family—but she'd figured that out all on her own.

This terrorist cell was powerful and far-reaching enough to have operatives in New York and still be able to kidnap a family in Somalia.

Vlad—his sniper team's nemesis in Afghanistan—could he have developed a network like this? Slade double clicked on the next email, which contained slightly better news.

Nicole had ended her call to Livvy and was watching him with her eyebrows raised. "Well?"

"The FBI ID'd the shooter from last night—Phillipe Moreau."

"A Frenchman?"

"An elite sniper, a gun for hire."

"No allegiance to a particular group or country?"

"Not that we know of." Rubbing his chin, he squinted at the picture of Moreau that Ariel had attached to the email. "That could've changed. And that exploding house yesterday?"

"Yeah?"

"Bomb-making factory—the whole house. That's what Marcus Friedrich was doing there, so it wasn't a big step for him to rig that door with an explosive."

She cupped her face with both hands. "Oh, my God, right out there in Queens? Who knows how many other attacks they've been planning?"

"Their operation seems like a well-oiled machine to me. That's why this footage puzzles me. What could be so important that they'd put other projects on hold to get this film?"

"Hopefully, we're on the verge of discovering that." Nicole hunched forward slightly and he held his breath. She asked the dreaded question. "Dahir's family? Any news on them?"

"Not yet." He skimmed through the remaining emails and closed down his laptop. "I'm going to shower and change—and we don't even have to drop by my hotel."

"Then we'll feed you and take a trip to Coney Island."

"Can we take the car service out there? I think that's the safest way to go—no more shooters on trains, and let's get Pierre again since we know him."

"It's fine. I think I mentioned my mom has that service on retainer, so she's charged for it whether we use it or not."

"Ah, money."

She shook a finger at him. "Don't tell me you don't have something similar, rich boy."

"In California we don't have car services. We just have cars—and lots of 'em."

"At your place, we'd just survey the garage and eenie-meenie-miney-moe between the Lambo, the Ferrari and the Maybach."

"The Porsche—don't forget the Porsche." Slade stashed his laptop beneath the coffee table and bounded up from the sofa. "Give me fifteen minutes."

He dashed upstairs and past the bed with its rumpled bedclothes to the cavernous bathroom. He took a quick shower, trying not to think of the night he'd spent with Nicole.

In the harsh light of day with a man's family missing, he had to put his feelings about Nicole on the back burner. That's exactly how it felt, deep in his soul, simmering on a back burner, still warm, still stirring his blood.

He decreased the water temperature in the shower and finished rinsing off in a lukewarm spray. He got dressed in record time, just in case Nicole got any bright ideas about barging in on him—because he had no willpower to resist her.

When he made it downstairs, Nicole was on the phone again, and she waved at him as she continued talking. "Chanel is fine, Mom. She sort of saved Livvy's life. She's a hero."

Nicole rolled her eyes at him. "I just thought Livvy could use the extra income right now since she can't exactly walk dogs. Chanel will be fine over there. I'll bring her back home after…in a little while."

Nicole listened to her mother for a very long time, all the while making faces. "Love you, too, Mom. Have a great time and don't worry about a thing. Everything's under control."

She ended the call with a sigh. "That woman could talk your ear off."

"Everything's under control? That couldn't be farther from the truth."

Nicole lifted her shoulders. "What she doesn't know can't hurt her."

Amen to that.

Nicole slid into the backseat of the town car and Slade followed her, nodding to Pierre as he held the door open.

When the car lurched away from the curb, Slade turned to her. "It's not very warm out. Do you think there will be many people there?"

"Not as crowded as summertime, obviously, but there are arcades and shows and other things to do there besides go to the beach."

Slade bobbled the key in the palm of his hand. "I have a good feeling about this—we have proof that Lars and Trudy went to Coney Island, and Trudy mentioned a key before she died, and this is definitely no ordinary key."

"Yeah, but we don't even know if Coney Island has these kinds of lockers, and if it does, how long will it take us to try every locker?"

"Don't be so pessimistic. You said it yourself. It won't be that crowded, so maybe not many people using the lockers this time of year. I'm sure there will be plenty of lockers with their keys intact, and we can bypass those."

She tilted her head at him. "You *are* feeling confident. I like it."

After crawling through traffic in Manhattan, the car moved faster once they hit Brooklyn. It was still almost an hour before Pierre rolled through the parking lot of the beachside amusement park.

Slade tapped on the darkly tinted glass that separated driver from passenger, and the partition magically slid open. "Pierre, can you pick us up here? I'm not sure how long we'll be, but Nicole will text you when we're ready in case you want to leave and come back."

"I'll probably stay here, sir, although it's been a while since I had a corn dog."

Nicole laughed. "We'll get you one."

As Pierre made a move to get out of the car, Slade stopped him. "We can manage. You don't have to keep hopping in and out of the car to open the door for us."

Nicole jabbed him in the back as he exited the car, but he ignored her. She'd never felt guilty about her family's wealth because her parents had managed to do so much good with it. Maybe Slade's parents weren't as generous with their money.

She could probably get a better sense of them and what made Slade tick once she met them. She tripped, the toe of her sneaker catching the edge of the curb. *If* she ever met them.

Slade caught her arm. "Careful."

Inhaling a deep breath of salty air, she said, "This way."

They bought tickets for the amusement park, since it was the only way to get inside, and wandered around the entrance area looking for lockers, without any luck.

Wedging her hands on her hips, Nicole said, "We should've just asked when we bought the tickets."

"I didn't think we'd have to. I thought they'd be right up front with the bathrooms and the stroller rentals."

"Men never ask about anything important." She marched back to the ticket counter and grabbed the first attendant she saw. "Excuse me, do you have lockers here? You know, maybe for a purse?"

"Sorry, no lockers here."

Her shoulders slumped and she made a half turn before the attendant called after her. "But Luna Park next door has lockers."

Her head snapped up. "We don't have to pay to get in there, do we?"

"No, just for the individual rides."

"Thanks." She grabbed Slade's arm and dragged him toward the front of the park. "Renewed hope."

They wandered into Luna Park, which had signs all around announcing its opening for the season.

Slade uttered an expletive and grabbed her arm. "Nicole, this is their opening weekend."

"I know. We lucked out."

"No, we didn't." He shook his head. "If Luna Park wasn't open last month, how would Lars and Trudy have been able to get a locker here?"

"Oh." She bit her lip but refused to lose hope. "Maybe they didn't have to get inside to get a locker. Let's ask first this time."

She approached a park worker who was sweeping up popcorn. "Excuse me. Where are the lockers?"

"Back by the ticket kiosk." He jerked a thumb over his shoulder.

Nicole shook off Slade's hold and skipped ahead. When she reached the kiosk, she tripped to a stop and spit out the same expletive Slade had chosen earlier.

He almost bumped into her and then whistled when he surveyed the rows of blue lockers facing them—electronic lockers, not a keyhole in sight.

The woman at the ticket counter poked her head forward. "If you want to rent a locker, you need to buy a card and the card works on the lockers."

Nicole swore under her breath again, and the ticket seller raised her eyebrows.

"No keys?" Slade pulled Trudy's key from his pocket. "Like this?"

The woman squinted her eyes. "No. All our lockers are electronic now."

Dead end.

Blowing out a breath, Slade pocketed the key and took Nicole's hand. "Maybe we should check out those lockers at the Statue of Liberty you mentioned."

"There are some old-style lockers by the beach."

Nicole glanced up at the kid still pushing his broom at imaginary dirt and poked Slade.

He showed him Trudy's key. "You mean like this? With a key?"

"Yeah. There are a couple of rows of them, right beneath the boardwalk. You stick in some quarters and you can pull out the key. I think they're going to be destroyed, but they're still there."

"Thanks."

They exchanged one look and then rushed from Luna Park as if they'd just been on the tilt-o-whirl and were going to lose their lunch.

Slade asked, "Which way to the boardwalk?"

"Follow me. I know what area he's talking about."

They skirted Luna Park, and she pointed down some wooden steps that led to the sand. "Down there."

When they reached the bottom, there was a slab of cement tucked beneath the boardwalk and two rows of faded blue metal lockers gaping at them.

Slade put out a hand for a high five and she smacked his palm. "This is it, and there can't be too many possibilities, since it looks like only a few are in use."

Nicole swooped in on the first bank of lockers, her sneakers scuffing the sand beneath her feet. "And someone did most of the work for us already by leaving the doors ajar."

Walking down the first row, she called out when she

saw a closed and locked locker. Slade followed her, trying the key on each.

She tapped a locker in the middle of the second row. "Here's another one."

Slade stepped in front of her, slipped the key in and turned the lock with a click. "Bingo."

Leaning her chin on his arm, she asked, "Is it in there?"

"Yep." Slade dragged out a padded oblong goldenrod envelope and ripped off the top. He puckered it open and peeked inside, then showed it to her. "It's a mini computer disc."

"Oh, my God. We found it." Nicole twirled on her toes on the sandy cement. "It's over."

"Just about." Slade folded over the top of the envelope and stuffed it in the inside pocket of his jacket. "Get on the phone and text Pierre and let's get out of here."

Nicole sent Pierre a text and then jogged up the wooden stairs with a lighter step than on the way down. They passed in front of the entrance to Luna Park, and she sniffed the air as a distinct deep-fried odor wafted on the breeze. "Pierre's corn dog."

She veered toward the entrance, digging in her pocket for her ticket stub. "I can't find my ticket, and we didn't get our hands stamped."

Slade held up his own ticket stub. "I'll get it. Wait here."

She leaned against the front gate, watching Slade as he strode to the same corn dog stand that was in Trudy's picture. What a stroke of luck it had been finding that picture.

The long black car pulled up to the curb where the

buses usually parked, and she waved to Pierre. She couldn't see him through those tinted windows, but he could see her.

She glanced over her shoulder at Slade waiting in line and pointed toward the car, which he probably couldn't see. He'd figure it out when he left the park and saw the town car.

She walked to the waiting car and slid into the back-seat. She tapped on the divider window to let Pierre know his corn dog was on the way.

The car lurched forward and squealed away from the curb. The violence of the motion threw Nicole back against the seat. Didn't he realize Slade wasn't in the car, and what was the big hurry, anyway?

She pounded on the glass with her fist and shouted, "Pierre, stop. We left Slade behind."

The partition glided open and someone pointed a gun at her through the space, and then a face followed.

"We left Slade behind? That's even better."

Chapter Fifteen

Where the hell was Nicole going? She usually followed orders without question. What had she been pointing at?

"Can you hurry it up a little?"

The pimply-faced kid pushed his paper cap back on his head. "You wanted three, right?"

"Just give me one." He jabbed his finger at the corn dog wrapped in foil on the tray next to the deep fryer.

The guy handed it to him, and Slade snatched it and swung away from the window.

"Sir, you already paid for three."

"Keep the change."

With his heart hammering, Slade jogged out of the park. Nicole was no longer standing by the gate. She was gone.

He forced himself to breathe. Maybe she'd walked to the designated meeting place with Pierre ahead of him. She should've waited. They weren't out of the woods yet.

With a quickening pace to match his quickening pulse, Slade turned the corner toward the main parking area and swallowed. No car. No Nicole.

He dropped the corn dog into a trash can and made a beeline for the meeting place. Where had Pierre gone?

Could security have waved off the car and Pierre made a circle around the parking lot with Nicole in the backseat?

He peered over the sea of cars in the parking lot and caught his breath when he saw a black town car hauling ass through the exit. That couldn't be their car. That couldn't be Pierre. The driver had checked out. Slade wouldn't have allowed Nicole in the car with just any driver.

A scattering of people stared at him as they made their way toward the amusement parks. He must look as frantic as he felt.

As he stuffed his hand in his pocket to retrieve his phone, he heard a low moan. He froze. He cocked his head to one side and heard it again.

He stepped off the curb, following the sound around the back end of a bus. His gut lurched when he saw Pierre's bloodied and battered form leaning against the back tire of the bus.

Slade crouched beside the driver, whose face had been beaten and whose hands clutched at his midsection, where blood oozed through his fingers.

"My God, what happened?" Slade punched in 911 on his cell.

"Sorry. I got out of the car for a smoke. They snuck up on me, punched me a few times and knifed me in the gut." He coughed and gurgled, and a trickle of blood leaked from the corner of his mouth.

A woman behind Slade yelped. "Is he okay?"

"I'm on with 911 now." Slade gave instructions to the 911 operator as he pulled off his jacket and then ripped off his shirt. He nudged Pierre's hands away from his wound and pressed his shirt against it to try to stop the bleeding. "EMTs should be on the way soon. Hang in there, man."

"Nicole?"

"Gone. I think they got her." Slade pressed harder against Pierre's stomach with both hands. "I'm assuming they took the car."

Pierre gasped and nodded.

A few more people gathered behind Slade, tossing questions at him that he had no intention of answering unless one of them was a doctor.

A siren keened in the distance, and Slade cranked his head over his shoulder to the onlookers. "Make sure the emergency personnel know where to go. Wave them over here to the bus."

Several people murmured behind him, but they all sounded on board.

Pierre's eyelids fluttered. "Nicole."

"It's okay, Pierre. I'll find her." He *had* to find her.

"P-pocket."

Slade leaned close to Pierre's mouth. "What?"

"Right. Jacket. Pocket."

Slade jammed his hand into the pocket of Pierre's ripped black suit jacket, his fingers colliding with a hard, square object. He yanked it out. "What is it?"

The ambulance screeched to a halt behind him and the EMTs jumped out and rushed toward them, dispersing the crowd.

"What happened to him?"

Slade cleared his throat, curling his fingers around the object from Pierre's pocket. "Someone beat him up and knifed him. Bad wound in his stomach."

Pierre's eyes opened again, and he grabbed Slade's sleeve. "Right jacket pocket."

Again, Slade ducked his head as the EMTs tried to shove him to the side. "I have it, Pierre. What is it?"

Pierre's bloody lips stretched across his teeth in a macabre smile. "GPS for the car."

Slade fell back, allowing the EMTs to get to work on Pierre. He put his jacket back on over his bare torso, feeling for the mini disc in the inner pocket, and dragged himself to a bench around the corner. He didn't need to talk to the police right now.

Cupping the GPS in his bloodstained hands, he studied it.

Pierre, or the car service, must have it linked to a tracking device on the car. He turned it over in his hand and noticed the USB port. He needed to access a computer—fast. Who knew how long Nicole's abductors would stay in that car?

Where the hell could he get to a computer out here? He didn't have time to go all the way back to the Upper East Side.

He pulled out his phone and searched for the nearest library and got a hit a few miles away. Damn. He needed a car. His gaze shifted across the blanket of cars in the parking lot.

He didn't like the idea of ruining someone's day at Coney Island, but he didn't have a second to waste, and he couldn't hang around here anymore for the cops to question him about the attack on Pierre.

Hunching into his jacket, he ducked behind a car and weaved his way through the lot, keeping an eye out for a likely vehicle to hot-wire. Not only would he not be talking to the police, he'd be stealing a car beneath their noses. So much for his low profile.

Fifteen minutes later he was wheeling out of the

parking lot in a late-model sedan and heading to the nearest library.

On the way, he tried Nicole's number, but as he expected, not even her voice mail picked up. Most likely her captors had disabled her phone so it couldn't be pinged.

When Slade reached the library, he parked the stolen car in plain sight—no sense in trying to hide it, but the police wouldn't be looking for a stolen car at the library, anyway. He parked himself in front of a public computer and connected the GPS.

The application for accessing the car's data was straightforward, and Slade's heart skipped a beat when he saw the car still moving in an eastward direction. Then it skipped another beat when he realized they could be heading to the airport.

He wasn't doing any good following the car's—and Nicole's—progress on a computer screen. He had to get this GPS tracking data on his phone so he could follow them in his new car.

He entered an SOS communication on his phone to the number for tech support he'd been given earlier. After several back-and-forth messages and entries on the computer and his phone, the folks in tech were able to download the GPS data he needed.

He sent another terse missive to Ariel to let her know he had the film but was on his way to rescue Nicole. If Ariel believed his mission was over now that he had Lars's footage in his hands, she didn't know the Navy SEAL sniper team.

The computer cranked and whirred as he cleared all his history from it, or at least as much as he knew how. Tapping his phone, he activated the GPS as he exited the library and hopped into the car. He'd left out the part about the stolen vehicle in his email to Ariel, but he'd make sure somehow it was returned to that Coney Island parking lot and its rightful owners.

Starting off with a lead foot as he followed the magic yellow dot on his display, he soon eased up. The last thing he needed was to get pulled over and arrested for stealing a car. Nicole needed him, and he was going to deliver.

The car moved closer and closer to JFK, and with every inch, Slade's stomach dipped. They couldn't very well haul a kicking and screaming woman onto a commercial flight—and he had no doubt Nicole would be kicking and screaming—but what if they had a private plane stashed at the airport? What if they planned to take Nicole away? What if they'd already knocked her out? Sedated her? Killed her?

He slammed his hands against the steering wheel. *No!* They needed her to get the film from him. They must know by now she didn't have the disc on her. They'd use her to get the film from him—*then* they'd kill her...and him, too.

Suddenly, the yellow dot on the display stopped moving in an area near the airport—validating Slade's darkest fear. He continued heading in the direction of the town car, the stationary yellow indicator acting like a beacon of hope for him. Even though it had stopped moving, it was all he had—all he had left of Nicole.

Slade drove for another forty-five minutes, panic rising in his gut as he kept one eye on the unmoving target. The GPS led him to a parking structure about a half mile out from the airport, and he glided down the second level until he spotted the black town car with the tinted windows.

He didn't expect them to be sitting there waiting for him, but he drew his weapon anyway and approached the car silently from the side, gun at the ready.

Releasing a long breath, he tried the door while peering in the window. At least they'd had the courtesy to lock up.

He broke the window with the butt of his gun and quickly disabled the alarm system. He brushed the glass from the driver's seat before sliding in and shutting the door behind him.

Placing his hands on the steering wheel, he inhaled Nicole's lingering scent in the car. Then he shook his head. Daydreaming about Nicole was not going to save her.

He started searching the car—the seats, the floor, the glove compartment. Then he tried his luck in the backseat. Nicole's scent was even stronger here, and in a strange way it gave him hope. Bending forward, he inspected the floor and saw the corner of a white piece of paper peeking out from the floor mat.

He freed it and shook out a dirty envelope, but it was so much more than that. Nicole had jotted down a few quick notes. She'd been able to tell him about the two men who'd abducted her—Conrad, Trudy's ex, and a stranger with a French accent.

French? The gunman in the club who'd killed Dahir was French.

So, Nicole had left a few clues. How had she known he'd find the car? Had she known about the GPS or did she just have some ridiculously misplaced faith in his superpowers because he'd saved her once before?

That rescue operation had been child's play compared to this. He was no spook, but he'd have to pretend to be one. Just as he was working out a plan to try to track their movements, his cell phone rang.

He glanced at his cell, which showed Nicole's number on the display. He didn't have to track them after all. They'd reached out to him.

He answered. "Yeah?"

Conrad's voice, his German accent more pronounced, greeted him. "Hello, *Steve*, although we all know you're really Slade Gallagher. Do you have the disc?"

"Do you have Nicole?"

"You know we do."

"Safe? I want to speak with her."

"Fair enough, but just know my associate has a gun pointed at her head in case she tries something funny."

Hot anger pounded behind Slade's eyes, and he squeezed them closed for a second. "Put her on."

Nicole's voice, sounding firmer than Conrad's, came on the line. "I'm sorry, Slade. I should've waited for you at the gate. I got into the car, and this scumbag pulled a gun on me. At least you have the film footage. Take it wherever it can be analyzed and don't worry…"

She grunted and Slade gripped his phone so hard it cut into the sides of his hand. "Don't touch her."

"She tried funny business. You're not going to listen to her, are you, Navy SEAL hero? You bring us the disc and we'll hand her over to you."

Yeah, right.

"Where are you?"

"I suppose we don't have to tell you that if you bring anyone with you, she's dead on the spot. No questions.

We hear a siren, a helicopter, a boat, see anyone other than you approaching...*fftt*."

The noise Gunther made sounded like a silencer, whether he meant it or not, but Slade got the idea. Slade wasn't sure he'd trust the chain of command to rescue Nicole, anyway. They'd want the disc first and foremost.

"I'll come alone. Where are you?"

"Where are *you*? Still at Coney Island?"

Slade's mind whirred into action. "No. I'm back in Manhattan."

"Then it should take you a while to get here."

That's what Slade was hoping he'd think. Conrad had no reason to believe otherwise.

"Where's here? Where do you want me to go?"

Conrad whispered something Slade couldn't catch and then spoke up. "We're in a little seaside town about halfway between the airport and Montauk. Since it's going to take you a long time to get out here, let's set up this little meeting for later tonight. We have a few things to arrange first, anyway."

So did he.

"Give me the time and the location."

Conrad reeled off the directions, and Slade scribbled them down on the envelope Nicole had used to describe her captors.

"We'll have Nicole on the beach in front of the house at ten o'clock. We'll be able to see your arrival from land, air or sea, and if you do anything other than approach us with your hands up, Nicole is dead. If you try to show up before the appointed time, Nicole is dead. If we see any suspicious activity on the beach in the hours before our meeting time, Nicole is dead. Got it?"

"Got it." Slade ended the call and immediately placed another.

He'd bring Conrad the disc, all right, but he had no intention of giving it to him in some phony exchange for Nicole.

He'd see him dead first.

Chapter Sixteen

Nicole shifted on the uncomfortable chair, her arms tied behind her back. She'd tried to escape once after they'd given her some food and had gotten a kick to the small of her back for her efforts.

She didn't want Slade to give up that disc. Too many people had died trying to protect it. If she had to be the next in line, so be it.

Her gaze darted between the two of them, speaking German, their faces devoid of emotion, and she swallowed hard. Yes, they would really kill her.

She surveyed the front room of the small seaside cottage that had to be worth a couple of mil. They must've rented it…or maybe they'd just broken in.

How would they have known about the trip to Coney Island? They probably followed them or somehow gotten their travel information from the car company. Maybe they'd scouted out this location earlier or just figured it was a deserted enough spot to carry out the exchange.

Slade would have to be a fool to think these two men would simply allow him to give them the disc and saunter off with her into the sunset—and Slade was no fool.

Knitting her eyebrows, she glanced out the window

at the Frenchman strolling in front of the house, back and forth, back and forth. He wasn't taking any chances of a surprise attack.

What could Slade do at this point? If he came in shooting, Conrad and his buddy would kill her. And with Frenchie out there on patrol, Slade, and whoever he might bring with him, had no opportunity to take them by surprise.

There were boats docked at a small pier several yards down the beach, but there was no way Slade could come in on a boat without being noticed.

She chewed on her bottom lip. She'd heard the meeting time was ten o'clock, and it had to be close to that now—and she was still sitting here.

She eyed Conrad and cleared her throat. "How did you kill Trudy?"

Conrad looked up from his phone and glanced over his shoulder at Frenchie making one of his endless rounds. She'd already figured out pretty quickly that the Frenchman discouraged any communication with her, and the majority of his exchanges with Conrad were in German, which she didn't understand. He wanted to keep her in the dark.

But Conrad liked to talk. He liked to brag, and if she was going down tonight, she at least wanted to know what it was all for.

He shrugged. "Trudy had epilepsy."

"Which you used somehow to cause her death and make it look like her condition was at fault."

"It wasn't hard, really. I replaced her medication with…something else. I was going for the dramatic. I thought she'd collapse in the middle of the play, which needed something to liven it up." He rolled his eyes. "You saw it. Dreadful."

Nicole gritted her teeth. "And the woman walking my dog?"

"Sloppy, I agree. I'm actually glad that turned out the way it did, since she wasn't you anyway, and I do like dogs."

"It's just the two of you? Where are the rest of your buddies?" She strained against the rope binding her wrists. There had to be a way she could help Slade so that they both didn't die.

"Buddies?"

"There's you, the sniper in the park outside the bar and the man who followed us on the train—Marcus Friedrich—the one who rigged that house in Queens with the explosives." She tossed her head back to get the hair out of her face. "Marcus was ID'd from the prints on his gun. Not too bright, is he?"

"That's why he excused himself from this operation."

"So, that man—" she tipped her chin at the window "—is the sniper from the park?"

Conrad narrowed his eyes as if trying to figure out where her line of questioning was leading. He pressed his lips together, probably figuring his French friend was right—better to keep mum about the details of their operation.

"The shooter in The Blues Joint was French, too, but he's dead. How'd you get Dahir to cooperate with you and lure me out? His family?"

"Dahir Musse's family is gone."

Nicole blinked, feeling the blood drain from her face.

Conrad grinned and then studied his fingernails. "My turn. What's your SEAL doing operating in the

States? Isn't that illegal or something? Maybe I should report him."

He seemed to think this was hilarious, since he giggled for several seconds.

She dragged in a deep breath to clear the shock of the news about Dahir's family.

Conrad could be lying about that, and he wasn't too bright, either, since he'd just revealed it was just the two of them and Slade wouldn't have to deal with a third party. Not that it did a whole lot of good, since the two here had a clear view of all approaches to the cottage and a gun to her head whenever they needed it, and of course, Slade didn't know how many he'd have to handle.

And he *could* handle them—she had faith in the rich boy.

A knock on the front door had her jumping out of her skin, and then the Frenchman called out, "It's time. Bring her out. No chances. Do you understand?"

Conrad snorted lightly. "*Oui, ja,* yes."

He picked up his gun from the table and pointed it at her. "Get up very slowly. I don't have to tell you. At this point, any move you make out of the ordinary will result in your death. Do you understand?"

"*Oui, ja,* yes."

Smirking, he waved at her with the barrel of his gun.

Licking her lips, she rose to her feet, her gaze pinned to the window and the darkness beyond. Slade was out there somewhere, and she hoped he had a hell of a plan.

SLADE SURFACED AND hauled his weapons bag onto the boat, keeping out of view of the beach just about a half a mile away. As he peeled off his wet suit, his friend and team member Josh Elliot broke the surface of the water and joined him.

"You for sure know there are just two of them?" Josh unzipped his own weapons bag and yanked out his .300 Win Mag.

Cradling the M107, his weapon of choice, Slade said, "Two grabbed her. They might've picked up more along the way or met someone at that house, but I don't know. I guess we'll find out soon enough."

Josh slid his scope in place. "Isn't this exactly how you met this woman? She's the one who was on that boat when we took down those four pirates, right?"

"I wouldn't say we exactly met at that time—only through my finder."

"It's a helluva way to pick up women, bro."

They worked in silence, breathing heavily as they assembled their sniper rifles—or maybe that was just *his* breathing. He'd never been more nervous before an operation.

He'd never been in love with a rescue subject before, either.

As soon as he'd learned how much time he'd have to prepare, he knew what he had to do to rescue Nicole. That spy stuff wasn't his strong suit, but this? *Second nature, baby.*

He'd made a few calls, arranged to have some weapons delivered and managed to locate one of his team members, Josh Elliot, who happened to be in the States preparing for a trip to South America for some reason he wouldn't reveal to Slade.

Studying a map of the area and the coastline revealed exactly what he needed to do to get close to the house without being seen. The terrorists' first mistake was doing the exchange on the beach.

He got it. They'd figured the beach would be deserted at night, a reasonable place to hold a woman at gunpoint. They'd also reasoned that on the beach, in the open, Slade wouldn't be able to sneak up on them, bringing other people with him.

Guess they forgot about the *sea* part in SEAL, because they had to know who he was by now.

Josh grunted as he positioned his weapon. "The powers that be think it's Vlad we're dealing with, don't they?"

"I may have heard his name once or twice."

"You know what that means, don't you? He's luring each one of us out, one by one. You know about Foley's run-in with Vlad's operatives in Boston, don't you?"

"Yep." He slid a sideways glance at Josh. "Are you up next?"

Josh rolled his shoulders. "Bring it on."

Slade grinned at his good luck in finding Josh stateside. Josh was one tough SOB, all about justice—his own brand.

Josh clicked his tongue. "Looky, looky. They're waiting for you."

Slade shifted forward, aiming his weapon at the beach—two men, just as Nicole had indicated—and Nicole. This was how he remembered first seeing her—strong, fearless, standing tall with a gun at her head.

"I'll take the guy who has Nicole. You can have the other guy."

"Of course you'll take the guy who has Nicole—*hero*."

And just like last time, Nicole shifted away from

her captor. Could she sense his presence? "You ready, Josh? They're going to start getting antsy in about one minute."

"No time like the present, dude."

Slade tightened his finger on the trigger and did the honors. "Five, four, three, two..."

The terrorists on the beach dropped. Never knew what hit 'em.

This time Nicole didn't spit on the body at her feet. She turned her face to the ocean and raised two thumbs.

Chapter Seventeen

Hours later, with the light of day making its first appearance, Nicole hovered over the back of the sofa where Slade sat, hunched over his laptop.

"Here we go." Slade tapped the keyboard. "I don't think I've ever anticipated a movie more than this one."

"Does Ariel know you're having a peek at the footage before sending it off?"

"Yeah, she wants me to—and I'm going to send it off to them right now, anyway. They can have a copy while we look at this one." He took her hand and kissed the inside of her wrist. "Conrad and Frenchie are gone and Marcus Friedrich may be on the run, but there are others to take their place. The sooner we figure out the significance of this film, the better."

She came around from the back of the sofa and sat beside him, her shoulder meeting his.

Slade double clicked the video file, and as the film came to life on the monitor, Nicole covered her mouth with one hand.

"Look, it's all of us." She jabbed her finger at the image on the screen. "Me, Giles and Dahir."

She was giving instructions to Lars, who was laughing and cutting up, while Giles was making goofy faces. Now they were all gone, including Dahir's family. A sob bubbled in her throat, and Slade put his arm around her, pulling her even closer.

The footage switched from the four of them joking around to Lars testing his focus on her practicing interview questions to Giles and Dahir in a deep discussion. Then the interviews started.

Tears blurred her vision as she watched the brave interview subjects talk about their lives and their hopes and dreams and the courageous acts they were taking to make those hopes and dreams come true. She sniffed. "I hope one day I can tell their stories."

"This is incredible stuff." Slade squeezed the back of her neck. "You did some amazing work here."

They continued to watch the film. Lars had already done quite a bit of work on it, merging all the different shoots into one. The story, with Nicole's narration, took them from village to village, from town to town, including shots of the war-torn countryside and their trips in the ramshackle Jeep with Giles at the wheel and Dahir getting them out of some tight spots. Too bad he hadn't been able to get himself out of the tightest spot.

"I don't see it." Slade ran a hand through his short sandy-blond hair. "Unless this well-oiled terrorist organization, which was responsible for two deaths overseas and two more here, wanted to stop these women from speaking out, I just don't understand their frantic need to stop this footage from going live."

"There was that woman's husband who walked in on us. Go back to that."

"Where was it?"

"I scribbled it down on this sticky note." She plucked a pink note from the edge of the laptop screen and read the time aloud. "It's at forty-three, thirty-two, fifty-one."

Slade's hand froze above the keyboard. "What did you say?"

She waved the note stuck to her finger. "Forty-three, thirty-two, fifty-one."

He snapped his fingers. "The note. Dahir's note in the club. Where is it?"

"By the telephone. Do you want it?"

"Please."

She crossed the room to the kitchen and grabbed the note, still smudged with Dahir's blood. When she glanced at the numbers, she squealed. "It's a time stamp of the footage."

"Exactly. Read off those numbers."

As she bolted back to the sofa, she recited, "Fifteen, twenty-three, nineteen."

She parked herself next to Slade again as he dragged the indicator back to the fifteen-minute mark.

Pointing at the screen, she said, "This is where we talked to that woman outside in that noisy area near the town of Badhadhe."

"Can you switch up the focus, away from her and more to the background?"

"Of course, but we have to go outside of the film Lars created and to the individual footage. Pause this and get to the other files."

Slade followed her instructions and soon they were looking at the raw footage of that interview.

Hunching in closer, Slade said, "Watch that road in the background. There's a truck going through that gate. Another truck. Look at the men at the entrance."

Her gaze shifted to two men talking across the road from the interview. One looked directly into the camera and pointed. The other turned around.

Slade froze the frame and jabbed his finger at one of

the men. "Nicole, he's a known terrorist. That gate and the road across the street from this woman's home leads to a terrorist training camp. *That's* what they didn't want us to see. *That's* why they ordered pirates to kidnap you and your crew—to kill you and destroy your film. But the pirates had their own ideas, and the film got away from the terrorist group running that camp—and now it's in our hands."

She broke down then, covered her face with both hands and cried like a baby.

LATER THAT MORNING, Slade got the word that a drone strike had lain waste to the terrorist training ground on the outskirts of Badhadhe.

When he got the news, Nicole poured two glasses of wine and brought one to Slade, standing at the window and gazing into the street below. "The homes near that training camp weren't hit, were they? Those people we talked to...?"

"Spared. The training camp was far inside that initial entry gate." He clinked his glass with hers and said, "Vlad got the message loud and clear."

"The CIA is sure this Vlad guy is behind the training camp and the effort to find the footage?" *And all the other death and destruction that followed.*

"I received a report from Ariel, along with the news of the drone strike. All of the operatives—Conrad, whose real name was William Brandt, the French sniper, the other Frenchman and Marcus Friedrich—can all be linked to Vlad."

"But you don't know Vlad's real name or even his nationality, do you?"

"No, but he's coming in hard. His terrorist cells are international, and we don't know his endgame...yet. My team has sparred with Vlad before. We just nicknamed him Vlad because he favors a Russian sniper rifle."

"You've sparred with him before, and he seems to know all of you."

"He knows we were the ones who rescued your crew from the pirates."

"And then he tried to take each one of us down. Do you believe that was all about the film or all about you?"

Slade swirled the wine in his glass. "Oh, he wanted that film, all right. Look what happened when we got our hands on it. But the fact that it was our rescue? He's taking a certain pleasure in that."

Nicole shivered and took a gulp of wine. Hopefully this was over for Slade, but what about his teammates?

She nudged his arm as he took a sip of his wine. "Too bad your friend Josh had to leave so quickly. He was pretty hot in that intense, mean-streets kinda way—obviously not a rich California boy."

"Definitely not." He tugged on a strand of her hair. "I thought you were giving up on the adventurous sort."

She gazed at him over the rim of her wineglass. "Never."

The look in his blue eyes made her heart skip several beats, but she had other news to share. "Oh, I called the hospital where Pierre is staying. He's out of the woods. He's going to be okay."

"Thank God. And Livvy?"

"Healing nicely and enjoying Chanel's company."

"Good, because she's going to have Chanel's company for a while when you join your mother in Italy."

She set her wineglass down on the windowsill and grabbed the front of Slade's shirt. "I thought you detested frivolous society girls with front-row seats at the fashion shows."

He placed his glass next to hers and rested his hands

on her hips. "When that society girl is also a kick-ass filmmaker who can change the world, I can excuse a little haute couture."

He kissed her long and hard just to make his point. "And what about you? I thought you were ready to settle down with an accountant whose only risk was drinking a chardonnay with a steak."

"When that risk taker also happens to be saving the world, one life, one bullet at a time, I can grit my teeth and bear it." She smoothed her hands over his face. "As long as he comes back to me."

"Where else would I go? I love you, Nicole Hastings. You're in my blood and have been ever since I saw you on that pirate boat in the Gulf of Aden."

"I love you, too, rich boy."

"Does that mean you'll wait for me? I have at least one more tour, maybe two."

"What else would a snooty society girl have to do?" She tugged on the hem of his T-shirt. "Now, follow me. We have two days together before you have to go back to saving the world."

He swept her up in his arms effortlessly and nuzzled her neck as he carried her up the stairs. "The world can wait."

* * * * *

*Look for more books in Carol Ericson's
gripping series*
RED, WHITE AND BUILT
later in 2017.

*You'll find them wherever
Mills & Boon Intrigue books are sold!*

MILLS & BOON®

INTRIGUE
Romantic Suspense

A SEDUCTIVE COMBINATION OF DANGER AND DESIRE

---

sneak peek at next month's titles...

In stores from 18th May 2017:

Hot Zone – Elle James *and*
Son of the Sheikh – Ryshia Kennie
Cavanaugh Standoff – Marie Ferrarella *and*
Murder in Black Canyon – Cindi Myers
The Warrior's Way – Jenna Kernan *and*
Bodyguard with a Badge – Elizabeth Heiter

Romantic Suspense

Cold Case Colton – Addison Fox
Killer Cowboy – Carla Cassidy

Just can't wait?
Buy our books online before they hit the shops!
www.millsandboon.co.uk

Also available as eBooks.

MILLS & BOON®

are delighted to support
World Book Night

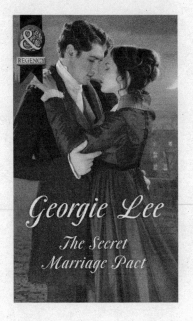

Georgie Lee

The Secret Marriage Pact